BRUCE

Mem

SIMON & SCHUSTER

SIMON & SCHUSTER
Rockefeller Center
1230 Avenue of the Americas
New York, NY 10020

SIMON & SCHUSTER and colophon are registered trademarks
of Simon & Schuster, Inc.

For information regarding special discounts for bulk purchases,
please contact Simon & Schuster Special Sales at 1-800-456-6798
or business@simonandschuster.com

Designed by Karolina Harris

Manufactured in the United States of America

10 9 8 7 6 5 4 3 2 1

Library of Congress Cataloging-in-Publication Data

Wagner, Bruce, 1954–
   Memorial : a novel / Bruce Wagner.
      p.   cm.
   1. Family—Fiction.   2. Self-realization—Fiction.   3. Tsunamis—South Asia—Fiction.
4. Hurricane Katrina, 2005—Fiction.   I. Title.

PS3573.A3693M46   2006
813'.54—dc22   2006044397

ISBN-13: 978-0-7432-7235-3
ISBN-10:   0-7432-7235-8

WAGNER

orial

New York   London   Toronto   Sydney

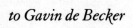

to Gavin de Becker

Margaret, are you grieving
Over Goldengrove unleaving?
Leaves, like the things of man, you
With your fresh thoughts care for, can you?
Ah! as the heart grows older
It will come to such sights colder
By and by, nor spare a sigh
Though worlds of wanwood leafmeal lie;
And yet you will weep and know why.
Now no matter, child, the name:
Sorrow's springs are the same.
Nor mouth had, no nor mind, expressed
What heart heard of, ghost guessed:
It is the blight man was born for,
It is Margaret you mourn for.

—*Gerard Manley Hopkins*

Passage to India!
Lo, soul! Seest thou not God's purpose from the first?
The earth to be spann'd, connected by net-work,
The people to become brothers and sisters,
The races, neighbors, to marry and be given in marriage,
The oceans to be cross'd, the distant brought near,
The lands to be welded together.

(A worship new, I sing;
You captains, voyagers, explorers, yours!
You engineers! You architects, machinists, yours!
You, not for trade or transportation only,
But in God's name, and for thy sake, O soul.)

—*Walt Whitman*

Memorial

JOAN

37now but thinks of herself as 40, to soften the coming blow. "Then," the litany goes, "I'll be 50—a woman in her 50s." "Then I'll be 63." "Then 70. Then 76, 77." "Then I will be 81—83." She doesn't go so far as to muse upon a future place of residence or quality of caretakers, shuddering when she passes assisted living homes, *extended care America,* thinking of her mom, but is certain of one thing, that she will be alone: all the while feeling those ages to be just round the corner, come in a blink, knowing intellectually re the fleetingness of time that there were many celebrated men and women, avatars, essayists, and intellects who could back her subjective notions with hard text or admirably glib spiritual pronouncement. Easy to evoke, even during mundane daytime chores, those philosophical flights of grad school days gone by, wild and romantically jagged cerebral nights. Stanford semiotics, string theory and such, rhapsodically sprayed like Halloween gunk on the trees and bushes of verbiage, space and time—collapse of reason and rationale like so many symphonies pounded to the size of the head of a pin, *Gödel, Escher, Bach,* so be it. Wasn't that the dream of this life?

She'd been having a specific dream-within-the-dream for over a year now, as if her mind, that great computer, were searching for a lost j-peg: the Perfect Memorial file. In a nocturnal reverie she called the Castle of Perseverance, details of the catastrophe were vague and illegible, as 10-minute-old skywriting on a still summer's day or the half-erased chalkmarks of simple equations upon green slate. Joan floated there too, billowy charcoal housecoat open like the commodious wings of that tree-flying squirrel she saw on a Discovery Channel doc, or a whimsical matron's smock in a children's book, and she could always just about make out the smokily verdant terrain below. The locus of the Event—"mound zero" is what one of her wittier lover-confidants called it—for which, in nondreaming life, her firm, ARK, had been hired to commemorate, the REM/Rem locus, as it turned out, was neither domestic nor international but hovered somewhere above, in a cottonball Canadian Christo-wrapped airspace 5 full skycrapers above. Sometimes a super-structure the firm had bid for and lost—there were a number of them, more than Barbet wanted to count—but one in particular, in China, seemed persistently to shanghai her nightworld, grafting failed CG skinsketch onto gauzy somnambulist con-structions. In the dream, millions were to be memorialized, when the truth is ARK (10 years ago aptly, chicly named) had been hired by a billionaire whose brother and sister-in-law died near Chen-nai in the Christmas tsunami. The monument in Napa was to represent just the 2 of them, swept into a full-moon lake of man-groves, left hanging in trees like ornaments, though of course the design would have to be something beyond, as if representing all swampy, swami'd souls, because while the Northern Califor-nia tribute was to sit on 400 obscenely private acres, it would be-come a well-known thing, famously endowed, famously elegiac. It had already been written about in the architectural trade and popular press, as if there was a difference between them anymore, and, if secured, would inevitably lead to other commissions. *No doubt.*

The jewel box site and predictably pending dumbass dustup over elitist venue mandated things be done just right. While Joan slept, ghosts of the battered, float-bloated dead wafted and moaned, debris-spun like dirty shredded cardboard Niagaran barrels, the hundreds of thousands never to be seen again devi-ously commingled with intransigent Katrina-killed old folks in attics (again she thought of Mother), wet silvery heads jammed into memorabilia-choked roofs with their rictus mouths, Pontchartrain floaters and bloaters and jokey FEMA hieroglyphs on sodden walls of Sumatran mud and Gentilly lace. Upon awak-ening, Joan became uneasy, as if somehow her ARK's desire and egoistic need to win said competition was unclean. It was the kind of dream, scrim of hallucinatory blowback, that sent her out for mocha latte in a daze, bypassing the stainless steel Impressa, wondering with embarrassment when she gave the barista her order if she'd actually forgotten to brush her teeth.

II.

RAY

Ray lives in City of Industry with his roommate, Ghulpa, and fluffy terrier mix Friar. Friar's full name is Friar Tuck. Ray sometimes calls him Nip/Tuck (after Ghulpa's favorite show) or just the Friar.

Near midnight they came busting down the door, a whole crew of LAPD and sheriffs, to cuff the crusty 76 year old diabetic. They threw in a stun gun that started a small carpet fire. He had a heart attack. Ghulpa hollered and the Friar got shot in the hip when one of the officers' pistols went off. All a mistake *con brio,* police had the wrong address, admitted as much, and there was Ray, Raymond Rausch with his yellow ribbons for the soldiers in the front window, on his stomach like a roped calf and shocked at how calm he'd remained through the home invasion calamity. Even the paramedics took note.

He befouled himself but limned the story sans trousershit for weeks to whoever would listen, how cool and collected he was, mostly he told the writer from the *Times* who was working up one of those nakedly Pulitzer-aspiring series about wrong-door break-ins, and recounted for the ACLU folks as well. Kept saying the whole time he was only worried for his doggie. All gave kindly props and thankfully never learned about the pants crapola, conversationally trying to relate Ray's bravado to the vague idea formulated that he was some kind of war vet, but the amicable old Republican said no, never been in a war, though not for tryin, born a cool customer, not one to be ruffled by a well-intentioned batter-ram entry. He'd seen enough *Dallas SWATs* and *Law & Orders* to know that snitches weren't the most reliable folks on the planet.

Ghulpa usually chimed in during interlocution, subtly sardonic, that Ray was too busy having "a hot attack" to get worked up, true enough, small infarct as it turned out, not much damage incurred. But that was Ghulpa. She liked taking the wind from his sails. She was from Calcutta and nothing rattled her, for real. Plus she was modest, happy her musty-smelling old man inexorably steered journalistic attentions to dear shot-up Nip/Tuck. It wouldn't have been right for him to be mouthy about how he had been on the futon, spooning his Indian galfriend at commencement of the doorshatter, small fire, pistolshot, dog yelp, and painseizured beshitting. (To bed boast wasn't Ray's way.) They weren't intimate like that but still she was grateful, and he was proud how wet-hen feisty she got at the cops for busting in. He wasn't even sure she was legal but BG put herself out there, got in everyone's face, Ray never saw that side of her before (not really), not in spades anyway as they say. They'd only been together 11 months, longest ride he'd hitched in 30 years, since Marjorie, never thought of her as wife material for chrissake done with all that. So proud of BG, cataract'd eye twinkled when she spoke with such righteousness to the *Times* or ACLU or whomever; Ghulpa's accent danced, lit, and lilted around strings of rational invective, articulate as hell and logical in that adjunctive bobbleheaded Hindu way. *Might have to make an honest woman of her yet.*

Lawyers circled everywhere since what Ray called the Mishap. (BG called it the Tragedy. He called her BG for Big Gulp.) All manner of folk held forth about the city settling with Ray for unholy amounts; listening to them, pantshit was a *good* thing—the docs must have ratted—adding a few zeroes to the actuarial tally of infarct infractions. *Plus* the shot dog. Even the police chief was upset about that and rang to express himself personally. But Ray didn't *feel* like suing, anyone, any*how*. He liked cops, always had, was a *Cold Case File* fanatic. Didn't want to shake nobody down. Not his style. Shit happens, ain't that right (pantshit anyway), and it was a shock more *didn't*. Sure the money'd help, always did, but he wasn't wild about the way that felt. In his taxonomized, infarcted heart. That's just how he was built, even though Ray Rausch didn't have a pension. Had about $22,000 socked away— what was left from the 60 he'd got when he sold his share in the shop—and Social Security after Medicare deductions was about 780 a month. Rent 565, without utilities, went up about $35 a year but he got by. The city gave seniors a break on gas and electric. Hell, breakfast at Denny's was $3.40 and he couldn't even finish what was on his plate, thank God the merry old Friar liked pancakes and wet toast. Paying for Rx was a little tough (Kaiser was $50 a month but seeing the medicos still cost money and there wasn't any dental coverage). That's why he never did anything about his dentures and skipped the blood pressure pills, the Zetia and Lipitor most of the time (the only med he can't do without is his Lunesta), and even the one that made him pee less, until Big Gulp got on him about it. (She kept promising to "hook" him up with a Canadian pharmacy, and blushingly joked about "scoring" Viagra off the Internet. Like her cousins, she was computer savvy.) She was a good woman and seemed to have a little nest egg, those cousins in Artesia saw she never went begging. BG pitched in with the rent and the groceries; he didn't like that too much, *I'm old school,* but she got mad if Ray didn't let her contribute. Helluva gal. So: if the city or someone wanted to drop 20 or 30 thou on him, fine, wouldn't turn it down. They'd play poker at Morongo, he'd show his old lady how the *real* Injuns do it, Native American style. He always had pretty good luck at the tables but it was a long time since he'd been. Oh it would be *great* fun to "pick the pockets" of those turquoise-jeweled reservation drunks, brown trash he called them, Geronimos with Jet Skis, ponytails, and Lexus SUVs. If the City of Industry wanted to give him a little stake to play 21, well, happy days.

The legal beagles (Ray's quaint sobriquet) said he could get millions but it *still* didn't set right, not his idea of the American Dream—that would be someone else's. Why on Earth should he loot the City of Industry? (He always called it that, like the song: *I'm the train they call the City of New Orleans.*) The stalwartly named senior-friendly municipality had a program to replace old kitchen appliances and once even fixed a broken window in the rent-controlled dining room: why would he want to gouge them? As long as he had tight pussy, loose shoes, and a warm place to shit he'd be fine. *At least I got the shoes and the shitter. Heh heh.* Long as they paid Friar Tuck's medical bills—which were gonna be *hefty*—and there was enough to buy the Gulper a dress or 2, long as he had his trusty Circuit City Trinitron to watch *Cold Cases* and old *Twilight Zones*, he'd be just fine. Hated the whole notion of needy sadsack dementia trainees. Like the woman downstairs who took the bus to the airport on Sundays, to watch the planes. Called it her "holiday."

No, he didn't need that. Raymond Rausch could look after himself and his own. Skip the fantasies.

III.

CHESTER

LOCATION scout, turned 41 in May. A Taurus who drives a Taurus. 283,000 miles on them both.

Wants to be a producer, all he needs is a stake, like the men who put together a mill for the *Saw* movies. Did it all on their own and now they're gazillionaires except for the guy who dropped dead out of the blue, 42 years old, the one who cooked up the whole torture idea in the *1st* place, telling the *Times* in a big write-up the week before he croaked that it felt like he'd "won the lottery"—he won all right. That was hubris for you, karma, whatever the *My Name Is Earl* guy would call it. Sometimes a person should keep certain thoughts to himself.

Chester scours this longitudinal utilitarian Thomas Bros. dream with wondrous, hazelnut eyes, a city divided into sunshot grids, seeing things no one else could, can, did, ever would, a gypsy-seer that way, a wizardly douser. But LA, like everything else, was being digitized, devoured, and decoded, memorialized like some newfangled karma/chimera/camera chameleon, converted to numbers by a new breed of men yielding images for film and television the way high-tech farmers got the most from crops, square by square mile. Chess couldn't quite keep up—like an old silents star trying to get a grip on the talkies. Out of breath on Sunset Blvd. Scouting used to be an art, now hardly needing the human touch let alone eye which afterall had been and still was Chester's strength, what he was actually semiknown and respected for, his uniquely vintage prepostmodern unstereotyped timeless gaze, a quirkily monopolychromatic horizontal 6th sense. The vets of the game, middling aestheticians who went by their gut, still call (enough were around because of the union, guys like Chess who, before graduating to location managers, used to take those same incremental ankle-swiveling panoramic shots, painstakingly pasted into manila folders at the end of each exhausted day, flatfooted but effective Hockney montages), compensating him richly enough for the trouble, sometimes $800 a day on the proverbial Big Feature, but more often half that now. Commercials and videos his daily or weekly or sometimes monthly bread. Chess was younger than most of the managers and 20 years older than the new breed of digitizers, a generation more like paparazzi than scouts. Depending on luck and size of production, he could still draw down enough to go to Jar or the Porterhouse Bistro or whatever new steakhouse with a lady on his arm, like a proper man. Though lately indies and MTV paid pisspoor and every time he turns around he sinks 2 grand into the car, doesn't even take it on desert or Angeles Crest scouts anymore for fear of breaking down and dying out there, so, on top of everything, he is renting cars and praying that someone steals the Taurus from his garage like they've done twice before in the last 10 years.

To keep his health insurance he is forced to pay dues, and finally, miracle of miracles, even get a digital camera (the amiable location managers laughing when they heard that one), sweating while he figures out how to scan images into the old Mac that Maurie gave him. Learning how to do this shit is pure, unadulterated hell. No one even looks at those beautiful manila Fotomat dioramas anymore. They're stacked in his closet like archival antiquities.

His best friend is Maurie Levin, a scripter who does procedurals and episodics. Maurie sold a spec a hundred years ago to *Walker, Texas Ranger*. Maurie knew Brad Grey back in the day. Maurie has a ton of ideas for reality shows. Maurie has a hippie girlfriend called Laxmi, pronounced *Lakshmi,* supposedly the name of an Indian goddess, and she's always talking about karma and that's why Chester's always talking about it (he has a crush). Maurie's one of those locomotively funny Jews who gets shitloads of pussy. Maurie says he likes em young but if they're older you better be sure they're "certified preowned." They haven't spoken for a few weeks when Maurie calls to say that A&E is going to shoot a reality pilot he created and he needs "that eye of yours" to find a location for the presentation reel. That's what he calls it: a presentation reel. (Maurie says it's *low-budge*.) They are paying $650 with the promise of multiple days—not bad, especially as Chess is currently rent-challenged, living in West Hollywood in a converted garage. His landlord is Don Knotts's daughter. Maurie says he needs to find a hospital for the shoot. Easy. Off the top of his head, Chess knows a bunch. Hospitals in LA are always going under and every single one is for rent, even those half occupied by religious groups or Meals on Wheels–type foundations, homeless dot-org whatnots. There was a finite number and it was just a matter of getting the shoot dates, then making a few calls.

Over coffee, Chester asks about the show. Maurie says it's a *"Desperate Housewives/General Hospital* thingie, but *real,"* whatever *that* means. Chess doesn't watch network, only *The Shield* reruns, Larry King, and occasionally Letterman if he happens to be up. Which isn't too often. The 2 buddies always yammer about making a movie from Maurie's scripts, Chess producing. Chester had a few scripts at home in "the Herlihy Archives" and occasionally broke them out to refresh himself on plots and characters over inferior coke and a few Coronas, scratching his head at who the fuck he might approach for financing. Maybe Brad Grey. Or the Bing guy. Or that guy Cuban who did *Good Night, and Good Luck.* He'd settle back, do a few lines, and read awhile then catch himself laughing. Maurie was actually a pretty funny guy, all Jews were funny, it was in their genes, he had to admit the guy knew story structure, the Jews were fuckin funny *and* knew story structure, but most of the time whatever genre Maurie was working in was slightly impenetrable. At least to Chess. Chess knew that wasn't his strongsuit, wasn't supposed to be, his job was to find the money, like the *Saw* guys. The hard part was, and this was Chess's problem not Maurie's, that you couldn't really sum them up in a couple of sentences which is what the money people always wanted. Chess had to work on that. That's where the beer and the blow came in.

They talk about the old scripts, Chess reminding him of some of the bits, but Maurie is psyched on this A&E thing. Chess asks what other locations they need and Maurie says a hospital is the priority. If they find the hospital, they can "dress" some of the rooms, and pretty much have everything covered.

IV.

MARJORIE

MARJ Herlihy resides in Beverlywood, off Robertson. Until Hamilton passed, a few months back, she'd been married 27 years—her 2nd husband. They'd lived well even though Tremayne Clothiers always seemed on iffy financial grounds. (When his partner died 8 years ago, she told Ham to re-name it Herlihy Clothing, or *Herlihy-Tremayne,* but he said that would only confuse the buyers. He finally agreed but never got around to it.)

After the fatal heart attack, she was surprised to learn a secret: long ago, Ham had bought a policy called "term life." By paying a premium, her husband's trust was insured for $2,000,000, all of which became hers. Marj wasn't sure what the genesis of this idea was—she'd never even heard of "term life"—maybe he'd had a premonition. At death, he had already owned the policy 14 years and it wasn't cheap, something like $7,000 per annum, but it wasn't exorbitant either (considering the unhappily fateful re-turns), except for the fact that had he outlived the 20 year contract none of the payments were refundable; he had probably kept it from her because she would never have sanctioned such an arrangement. She might have called it wasteful. Now that he was gone, every time Marj turned around she seemed to be listening to an ad for term life on the radio or reading about it in the paper. By the time she paid off the house and various debts, there was over a million left.

She had loved Ham dearly but not the way she loved Raymond, her 1st. Hamilton was a bland, steady rock, fit and handsome, a golfer and compulsive tennis player. He was sociable and liked to tell people he "brought Marj out," meaning out of her shell, be-cause she tended to turn inward. Adopting her kids had been *his* idea, and made him such a bigger man in Marj's eyes. The chil-

dren loved him too but never warmed up to being Herlihys instead of Rausches; they never exactly understood, it was as if they
had been forced to wear cloaks which kept them warm but didn't
fit. Schoolmates teased them about suddenly having different sur-
names.

When Chess and Joan came to the wake, it was the 1st she'd
seen of them since Christmas. They didn't show much emotion.
Marj wasn't proud of the fact she hadn't spent much time with her
kids—it felt like having strangers in the house. On bad days, she
blamed herself for being the type of mother who'd been so determined not to meddle that she'd done irreparable damage all
around; on good days, she blamed Raymond. The divorce had
come so early and the family had been deeply fractured; never a
good thing but sometimes there is perseverance and triumph. It
was their lot never to recover, not even with name changes and the
syrup of Hamilton's mayoral good cheer. No one knew where Ray
had gone and the kids didn't seem too interested in finding out.
(Probably for the best.) They got along with Ham, which was easy
because of his sunny, silken handyman's disposition. Still, there
was always a disconnect. As time passed, Chess and Joan went
their own ways, and the rare occasions they did come over they
were on smiley autopilot, as if to trigger early release from visitors' jail. They didn't divulge much about their lives; neither Marj
nor her husband had ever been invited to any of the places her son
and daughter lived. She wouldn't admit it, not even to Ham, but
that pained her. He must have known.

She was close with her neighbor. Cora was nearly the same age,
and a widow too, though it seemed like her kids and grandkids
were always dropping by. She subtly lorded her familial bounty
over Marj but the old woman never let on that she knew what
Cora was up to. Besides, the neighbor helped more than hurt and
was wonderful after Hamilton died. Cora's little Pahrump
squealed and strangle-yipped all the time but when her Ham
passed on, she relocated the spaniel to a different wing of the
house so he wouldn't grate on Marj's nerves—a small act, yes, but
one of great kindness. Long ago, the old woman told herself that

people did what they could; that was an ingrained sentiment of her father's. (She still had the needlepointed PATIENCE heirloom pillow Joan and Chess used to throw around when they were kids.) Overall, she felt blessed to have Cora next door. Steady, haughty Cora, loyal and royal in her own way, and vigilant.

Life after Hamilton Herlihy was strange because it was oddly the same as when he was alive, only now he was absent. Marj tried to express this conundrum to her daughter but Joan was so busy (for which Mom was grateful) that she listened as distracted loved ones do or anyone really who's obliged to indulge someone trying to make sense out of the death of a partner or pet or relationship, glossing over whatever is said, skating away then skating back, concealing one's distraction, and that was all right, Marj knew she was guilty of doing the very same thing herself. She never spoke to her son about how she felt; Chess had too many turbulent feelings of his own, and troubles as well. At least, that's what she surmised. She was actually bemused when he came to the memorial and even more surprised he didn't ask for money. Though she was starting to get a feeling in her bones, like she got before it rained, that he would soon call to ask, now that the mourning period, in his mind anyway, was officially ending.

Marj kept buying lottery tickets, never missing a day, not even when Ham was buried. Who knew? It might bring luck. The good and the bad always had a habit of coming one's way when least expected (to paraphrase her father). She busied herself by vi-sualizing the article in the *Times,* category: human interest, Cali-fornia section, *Gift From Beyond—Widow Wins $93,000,000.* It reminded her of that saintly couple who picked the right numbers a few years back, a husband and wife who raised money to bury newborns thrown into Dumpsters. O, the Lord worked in myste-rious ways! Rich folks won the lottery and so did the poor and ag-grieved. (The rich always fared better.) Goodness, she had just read an article about a couple with criminal pasts who won the Super Lotto and within a year, both were dead.

One thing Marj didn't share with her daughter, Cora, or *any-one,* was a wild-eyed, magical idea that had grown inside her over the last few weeks with an ineluctable pull: Widow Herlihy had made up her mind to go to India and revisit the hotel Dad brought her to when she was a girl—the very best time of her life, a time she was convinced had made her the person she was today, suffusing her disposition, her entire existence, with a kind of diurnal poetry and peasant's optimism, a time that allowed her to suffer all life's vicissitudes, coloring her day-by-day mood with the lingering incense of nonsectarian spiritual hopefulness.

In the winter of her life, Marjorie Herlihy would travel to Bombay and check into the very suite that father and daughter once shared at the Taj Mahal Palace, a stone's throw from the Majestic Gate of India.

V.

JOAN

S HE was at ARK, in Venice, looking at the Rizzoli book: *Zaha Hadid.*

A dangerous object, 4 volumes of squiggly drawings and vaunted nonsense, each one a different size, slipcased into the special berths of a sharp-edged, thick, plastic, bloodred mothership. When architects and book designers met, it was a supercalifragilistic hagiographic clusterfuck. The collaborators reveled in making a fine arts tomb: a vanity memorial enshrining the master builder who'd become an ostentatiously overdesigned object himself, essayists and typographers working with pharaonic zeal, the book a sacred extension of the guru's body, a highfalutin Pritzkerama requiring the dignified, calibrated, meticulous touch of latex'd surgeons in an amphitheater (patients aestheticized upon a table). But Joan thought this one just looked cheap, inside and out: vomitous tracts discretely *en brève,* with requisite untidily tidy references to Hegel, "excavations," and other opaquely Boolean folderol embroidering endless built and virtually built projects of dubious digital coherence contained within. The print resolution was shoddy. Were they so Olympian they thought no one'd give a shit?

There was only *one thing* she liked in the entire unappetizing enterprise: the ski jump at Innsbruck. No, not true; there was something else. As far as she could tell (she hadn't skimmed everything, nor would she), there wasn't a photo of Hadid. Maybe this was simply the pomposity of inverted egotism. How had this woman gotten so famous, anyway? She was even curating, no, "guest designing," the content of *literary magazines.* (Dopey sci-fi computer renderings at the head of each short story that would have looked more at home on *Wired* subscription blow-ins.) Perhaps a paucity of female architects had dictated her arc—Joan's

ARK swallowed by Zaha the whale—or the mere miracle that she'd managed, with grace and alacrity, to remove herself from King Koolhaas's shadow—a Grand Chess Master's trick, Joan had to admit . . . or her dramatic looks, the Baghdad-born thing, feminist warrior-ship masthead, unclassifiable geodesic goddess in a woman-killing theocracy, the sheer *improbability* of it, plus unkempt *Fat Actress* kohl-smeared gypsy-soprano factor that made her rock-star notable. Of course none of Joan's acid observations interfered with the awareness she wanted to *be* Zaha; wanted books written on her own work, international forums centered around her own ideas, phantom or realized, wanted her very own (Mary!) band of Lilliputians to clamber on the papal bull of her *mons* zero. But she (Joan) was still relatively young. That kind of momentum took time. *Oh God—*

If she won the Freiberg Memorial, Ms Herlihy resolved to be happily, gloriously nichified, for a few years at least, like the early Maya Lin. Lin cut her teeth on a few mems before moving on to that wonderfully minimalist library in Tennessee, private homes, sculptures, the whole 9 yards; she was probably already designing tea and coffee sets for Alessi, just like *El Zorro,* though it was unlikely the Target audience could possibly be interested in ZH's cold, arcane "liquid metal piazza" or the "Z Island" Corian kitchen with verbena scent dispensers (commissioned by Ernestomeda) or the 80,000 dollar "Aqua" polyurethane resin silicone-gel-topped table she'd done for that *Wallpaper* kid's pretentious Established & Sons (Barbet told her the "kid" was married to Stella McCartney) *or* the chandelier she created for Sawaya & Moroni and displayed at the Milan furniture fair. Next would come ZH chairs, ZH linen, ZH sunglasses . . . *how about ZH dildoes? ZH superabsorbent adult diapers? ZH Fentanyl pain patches?* But so what. Even Gehry had done a Wyborowa bottle. Now he was working for Tiffany.

OK. It was clunky, but she liked elements of Hadid's Cincinnati museum though didn't agree with whoever had said that *it was the most important American building to be completed since the end of the Cold War,* or with the surreally profligate comparisons to *Malevich, Lissitzky, Balanchine, Duchamp, Sant'Elia, Breuer,* and *Saarinen.* Maybe she *did* agree. Maybe comparison = rip-off = genius. Maybe Joan was too precious. Preciosity = Death.

One good memorial and you could write your ticket. You could rev up those museum extensions like Ratso Renzo; you could *do the Hadid* and knock off an Ordrupgaard. But Maya Lin was an *artist* as well, as like so many of them, a multimedia superstar, and, cum Meier, was represented by Gagosian. Naturally, Lin had a book out—*de rigueur*—with a close-up of her hand holding a smooth stone on the cover. ("I think with my hands," she says in the text.) *I think with my cunt,* thought Joan. *That's my problem.* The ARKitect hadn't focused on sculpture or paintings or anything other than buildings that had remained unborn. As she got older, she thought it myopic, an error in judgment that caused latenight stress and remorse, an oversight born of self-loathing and petulant sloth, to have been so singularly fixated on having things *built* (that's why architects were architects, she kept telling herself, though she never planned to be one "on paper" only), part of her thought if she'd have been able to just *let go,* the sheaves of renderings would have built themselves, harvest come home. Another delusion, no doubt. She knew she'd been grandiose, and didn't have much to show for it. She had committed that most American of sins: failed to move laterally.

Now the Napa commission would save her.

JOAN was introduced to Lew Freiberg by Pradeep, the Indian consul general she had an affair with a few years back. (He of "Mound Zero.") The occasion was a party in Brentwood. A genteel gathering: the screenwriter Melissa Mathison, the architect Steven Ehrlich, the gardener Nancy Jones, the actress Phoebe Cates, the editor of *Tricycle,* the editor of the Jewish magazine *Tikkun,* a puckish travel writer named Pico (like the boulevard), a surgeon from Médecins Sans Frontières. The cappuccino klatch was ostensibly about raising money for victims of the Tsunami. There were a lot of professional Buddhists on hand, whose smug

West Side affluence always set Joan's teeth on edge. They *loved* to hear themselves talk, *loved* going on about meditation decathlons, death and impermanence (and how amazing the caterers were), when the truth was they'd be the 1st to snitch off friends when their hour with God—or the torturer—came.

Lew Freiberg was unlike the others. He was abrasively charismatic, cocky, a skeptic without being cynical. Head slightly bowed, eyes looking up at the blissed-out power-minglers through longish lashes, he seemed to judge everyone with his heart. Lew lost his brother to the Big Wave. Pradeep had known the Freiberg clan a long time, and the dead ones, Samuel and Esther (Samuel's wife), as well. The family had a longstanding interest, not to mention an attendant antiquities collection, in all things Indian. The assorted holding companies were stitched together by around $7,000,000,000, the tiniest portion of which Lew wanted to spend creating a memorial to the couple on his drowned brother's 400 acre property in Napa, land that would remain in trust *in perpetua*.

At the end of the evening, Lew asked Joan if she wanted to visit the site.

VI

RAY

Nip had been transferred to West LA for surgery. (The lawyer handling Ray's case was handling the Friar's too.) The old man was still in the CCU and Big Gulp said she was going to raise holy hell the minute she got a bill for a single thing, and that meant either Ray's or the dog's medical care.

So far, so good.

Ray had his own DVD in there. Big Gulp brought him ribald American comedies, old *Twilight Zone*s, and her collection of *Nip/Tucks*. There was a *Forensic Files* marathon in progress on Court TV but the facility didn't have the cable thing together so he defaulted to his Rod Serling favorites.

A few of the classic half-hours actually took place in hospitals and that tickled him. One was about a woman who had a recurring dream each night of sleepwalking past the nurses' station to the elevator. She always went straight down to the morgue. In the basement, somebody with a joker's smile appeared at the steel doors and said, "Room for one more." Big Gulp pretended the shows were silly but Ray could see they scared the bejesus out of her. Another episode, a famous one, was about a disfigured gal going one more round with the plastic surgeons. No one ever said what was wrong with her, just that she was born looking a certain way. What intrigued Ray was how the whole thing took place sometime in the future, where being ugly was an offense punishable by excommunication and forced segregation. He wasn't a sci-fi buff but the old man liked how artfully it was shot: you never saw anyone's face, neither the woman's nor her doctors'. Damn innovative. At the end, they reveal that the surgery has completely failed, but when they finally unbandage the gal's face you can see she's a real beauty—it's the *doctors* who are monsters. That one always sent Big Gulp running for the door with a shudder. (He couldn't quite figure her; those *Nip/Tuck* shows weren't a walk in the park in the gore department.) The funny thing was that Ray remembered watching that episode with his ex-wife, and how Marj had burst into tears; at 1st he thought she was faking. (When he saw the crying was for real, he thought it terribly sweet.) Ghulpa was a little tougher. The only thing that could make her yelp like that would be the sight of one of those Bengal tigers she was always going on about.

Another of Ray's favorites starred a very young Robert Redford. An elderly woman's apartment building was slated for demolition. She was the last tenant left but refused to move. Redford played a cop who gets shot nearby and is asking for help. At 1st, she stands at the door, paranoid, thinking he's "Mr Death." But Redford is injured, and so fresh-faced—Jesus, he must have been in his early 20s—that she finally lets him in. A bond develops. He's the 1st person who really listens to her, and the 1st company she's had in maybe years.

They tried to revive *The Twilight Zone* a few times since the Golden Age but never got it right. Maybe it was something about being filmed in black and white or the extinct theatrical craft of actors like Agnes Moorehead and Burgess Meredith. The old man thought the writing was superb. Rod Serling was one of those special characters—Ray loved that he smoked on camera, just like Ed Murrow, and even Johnny Carson—a real creator of mood and dialogue. That era, *Playhouse 90* and Paddy Chayevsky and those General Electric shows, was gone forever. He tried watching *Curb Your Enthusiasm* and *Deadwood* but they left him cold. Either the comedy couldn't hold a candle to Skelton, Burns, and Berle, or the "Western"'s language was so vulgar he forbade the sometimes curious Big Gulp to tune in. (Though he did enjoy *Rescue Me*.) Even the big network commercials were obscene. One of them showed a handsome older couple dancing. It said "Second Marriage"—and turned out to be an ad for adult diapers. She could watch that crap with the cousins. Not in his house.

He only kept the cable for his *Cold Case Files*.

VII.

CHESTER

SOMEONE called from the LA *Times*—the "My Favorite Weekend" feature.

Each Thursday showcased a half-celebrity nitwit expounding on how they typically wiled away their Friday through Sunday. The lady on the phone said they wanted to do something different, and focus on an Industry person who was "below the line," kind of like those promos for the *Times* in movie theaters that show animators or key grips or bestboys in their habitats. She'd been given Chester's name by a location manager of a Hyundai commercial he had scouted, and especially sparked to the idea that Chess was a guy who made his living knowing Los Angeles inside and out. He certainly knew where the Lautners, Lloyd Wrights, and Googie coffeeshops were buried. She wanted to email some questions and follow up with a phone interview.

Fine with me. Fine and dandy.

The funny thing is he'd just been goofing on "My Favorite Weekend" with Maurie. He fished it out of the Herlihy Archives: the days-old column spotlit Fran Drescher, the sinus-challenged former TV star who had suffered through a home-invasion rape and uterine cancer. Chess wondered if they were related, in a cause and effect kind of way.

The headline read NOW JUST FRIDAY NIGHTS ARE FEVERED.

> Some of my most fun times are when I go out with a posse of my girlfriends and paint the town rouge.... Alicia Keys was fabulous. We got to go backstage and meet her, and we saw Tom Cruise too, and pretty soon the people in his posse were introducing themselves to the people in our posse—it was so much fun.

"I want my Mapo! I want my rape-o!" said Maurie, over the phone.

"That's harsh," said Chess, with a laugh.

"Yeah, well, life's a bitch and then you get posse-fucked." Then he sang, *"Hold me closer, tiny cancer."*

Maurie said they should get together and talk about his A&E "dillio." He wanted to know if any progress had been made with locations. Chess said he was still looking but Queen of Angels seemed promising. Then Maurie mentioned an empty clinic in Alhambra where a friend just shot a Fiery Furnaces video. Chess scribbled down a phone number and said he'd check it out. They made plans to have dinner at Chameau, a Moroccan dive on Fairfax that had migrated from Silver Lake. Maurie's girlfriend, Laxmi, would join them. Chess really had a hard-on for her. He was a sucker for strawberry-blond Manson creepy-crawlers—freckle fields and tiny tits, intrepid, sociopathic girls-next-door with Sweet 'N Low hankerings for all things mystical.

Roll-up for the mystery tour—

On the way to the restaurant, Chess wondered if he should ask Ma for money. She must be doing all right. He'd only talked to her once since the funeral. That was dumb. Might be awkward—though she'd probably be happy to hear from him. Of course she would. Maybe he'd just put in a call without asking for bread, tough it out awhile longer, get the check from the A&E gig, then rock on over to Beverlywood. That would probably be better form. How much should he hit her up for? The most he ever got in one lump was 5 grand. (Asking Joan would be out of the question.) She never pressed but he was always careful to pay off debts to Marj. He wanted her to know he was good for it in case he ever got in a really tight spot, that he wasn't a deadbeat. Maurie always said it was best to appear prosperous when asking for hand-outs (even a guy like not-too-long-ago-beleaguered Trump sued some journalist who wrote a book saying he was only worth a couple hundred mill) and maybe Chess would do a little posturing before he popped the question. Cash out A&E and buy a new suit. Rent a Jag or an Escalade for a few hundy, just for the day, then drive on

by. Tell Mom he was in the middle of producing his old friend
Maurie Levin's new script and needed something to tide him over
between bank drafts. Tell her there was some temporary international monetary snafu, it was a Canadian/UK/German coproduc-
tion and the Krauts were being crabby, whatever. The Canucks
were being canny. The Brits were being Britney. He'd ask Mom to
dinner at Ruth's Chris or Mastro's in Beverly Hills. Spago, wherever. Or maybe they'd go Indian; she was a freak for India, from
when they were kids.

Chess began to have warm feelings about Marj but couldn't
separate them from the fantasy of unsolicited largesse. He imagined her giving 10 times what he planned to ask for, the act of
spontaneous generosity opening a new era of intimacy between
mother and son. There was no reason to feel guilt; he wasn't going
to leave her hurting. It was the opposite. He would give her the
collateral of his heart, knowing it would make her feel better to
help her son. Chess knew she'd been left cash and property, and
had jewelry as well—old-style brooches and pins, earrings, whatever. She had to be sitting pretty. Hamilton was an ace provider.
He didn't know if the house was paid off. Wasn't his place to ask.
He wondered, fleetingly, if you could find out that sort of thing
online.

About a mile from Chameau, he began to parse in his head the
"My Favorite Weekend" questionnaire the chick had faxed over,
thinking he'd use tonight as a typical evening out with friends at
an exotic local fave. (He'd have to "take its pulse"; sometimes
these boîtes died a sudden death.) He needed to come up with
something special for Sunday brunch; Sunday brunch was the
"My Favorite Weekend" cum shot. He never went out for breakfast but it'd be nice to say he was a regular at JAR's or Casa del Mar
(Inn of the Seventh Ray, Father's Office, City Bakery, and the
chink places in Monrovia were played out—MFW had already
covered them) and that before brunch it was a "ritual" to take his
girlfriend—he was *definitely* going to have a fictional girlfriend—
to the Echo Park/Palisades/Hermosa Beach farmers' market for
fresh flowers, dried fruit, star anise, whatever. That kind of gay

horseshit. Maybe throw in poor old Trader Vic's before they tore it down. But since he was a location scout—that was the angle— they'd probably want him in diverse parts of the city instead of the usual Santa Monica, Malibu, or East Side haunts. He could go to Memphis (Jane's Room), or Ford's Filling Station, or 'Sup Nigga, or the hungry cat, or the Bucket (Eagle Rock hamburger joint), or some Jap joint (for yoshoku). *Fine and dandy.* It'd probably be better if he went to a chocolatier in Altadena or the coffeeshop at the Long Beach airport or maybe bought his fake old lady a customized scent at that place on Abbott Kinney. Then he thought he should do his homework because he might have read about the perfume place in a "My Favorite Weekend." (Got the idea, subliminally.) Maybe it wasn't even there anymore. He could probably go online and find out which My Favorite Weekenders frequented wherever. He didn't necessarily want to bother the chick about it but could feel her out when they had their follow-up phone interview.

VIII

MARJORIE

THE Super Lotto was now at $78,000,000.

She went to Riki's, on Robertson. It used to be called "You Are My King Liquors," but when the owners sold, Riki not very effectively covered the sign with his name. He was always promising customers that one day when he had the time, he would "do it right."

When she bought her tickets, Marj always wore the lucky lapel pins Ham had given her on their 20th: malachite peas in gold pods and a green jeweled parrot with blue enameled feathers dropping down. They were designed by Jean Schlumberger in the 50s and sold at Tiffany's. Ham got them at auction. (Her husband had a wonderful eye. One year, he surprised her with a vintage sapphire bracelet by Seaman Schepps. He collected vintage pictures of society ladies in Charles James and Madame Grès that he hung in the apparel offices downtown.) She filled out the lottery form as usual, picking her children's birthdates and Hamilton's too. She used to spend $3 but since Ham's death, she was spending 5.

Riki was from Bombay—she could never help but think of "Rikki-Tikki-Tavi," the Kipling story Father read to her at bedtime. He didn't speak much but boy, could he smile, greeting each customer as if they were an old friend (many were). Riki had a son in high school who occasionally helped out. The young man had the same kind, winning disposition, and perfect manners, to boot. Marjorie often felt she should engage them in conversation—afterall, she'd *been* to Bombay as a girl, for almost a month with her *own* dad—but the words never came. That was all right; it was enough to feel their warm familiarity. Just being in the shop made her feel like a culture buff, a woman of the world. Besides, she didn't remember much about the city, mostly recalling the grand hotel they had stayed in, the Taj Mahal Palace—to make any further claims would have been a shallow and possibly embarrassing assertion. It would have devastated her to be thought of as "the ugly American." (Not that they had those sorts of judgments in them, though one never knew.) One thing she did ask was if a person was supposed to say "Bombay" or "Mumbai." The city names had changed, which seemed to happen periodically, all over the world. The son unleashed that winning transgenerational smile and said, "Bombay. If you are the cool people, you call it Bombay."

As Marj rounded the corner toward home, she saw Cora watering the lawn and the neighbor waved her over for a coffee. Cora said her son Stein bought her a machine that made "perfect cappuccinos." She stage-whispered that it cost $3,000 and Marj literally gasped when she heard the figure.

One of the pipes did the foam part and the old woman let Cora enjoy herself. Cora loved talking about money. She knew Hamilton had left Marj "comfortable" and was always fishing for a number. Marj knew Stein was richer than Croesus and showered his mother with gifts the way wealthy children do to substitute for quality time. Then she chastised herself, remembering she had neither gifts nor visits from those she had brought into the world. She treasured her daughter's drop-ins, few and far between as they were; at least Joan was honest, and didn't try to buy her off. Joan had a life. She'd have hated if her daughter sent costly care packages as a charade. Marj's lips pursed again in quiet reprimand, cringing at her judgments. Pahrump, the King Charles, limped into the kitchen, and Cora scooped him up in her arms. Pahrump cried out.

"Why is he limping?"

"They think it's something degenerative—don't they, Pahrump?"

She planted kisses on the foppish dog's snout.

"Poor, poor thing."

"Well," said Cora, fussing over him. "Not *too* poor. You have a

3,000 dollar cappuccino machine, don't you, sweetheart? That's a limited edition, did you know that, Rump? You can make Mama a cappuccino, can't you. We can teach you how to make Mama a cappuccino, wouldn't that be fun?"

Cora asked if she'd thought about traveling.

The old woman blinked and said, "Yes." She hadn't planned on confiding to anyone just yet but it seemed as if Cora had been doing a little mind reading.

"We should take a cruise, Marjorie—once Pahrump gets a teeny bit better. 2 lonely gals. We could get lucky!"

They laughed. Cora pursued the topic and Marj realized she was serious. The neighbor began talking about cruises to Mexico or the Caribbean. She'd read an article. Men were employed by ships to dance with the widows—that was a comfort because Cora said she didn't like the idea of being a wallflower.

"If youz gwannah pays your moneh," said Cora, in a creaky imitation of Marj knew not what, "youz gottuh gets yo moneh's worth."

Marj surprised herself by suddenly saying, "I've been thinking of going to India."

"India! But why?"

"I was there as a girl."

"But it's so dirty!"

"Oh, I don't remember that. I just remember how beautiful it was."

"Well, I know Stein does *lots* of business with them. The Indians. They outsource. *Very* good at that. But it is *not* the United States! He's been there a few times and, Marjorie, you *cannot imagine* what he describes. The *filth*. The homeless. The *smells*. Did you know the hospitals charge the mothers to see their babies?"

"What do you mean?"

"The mothers have their babies, then the nurses or *whatever* they are, *snatch* them away—and the new moms have to pay *rupees* to have them brought back. You have to bribe someone to hold your newborn!"

"I cannot believe . . ."

"Oh, I *assure* you, I read it in the *Times*! In Bangalore. It's extortion! $12 for a boy, 7 for a girl! One of the mothers-in-law had to pawn her earrings! And they throw *acid* on the Untouchables. If you're not of a certain caste, you either have to clean waste from the toilets *without gloves*—the *toilets,* if you can *call* them that—and if the elite think you're not doing your job correctly, they throw acid on you! I saw pictures of a *horribly* disfigured man in the *National Geographic* when I went for my epidural. And the elephants! The elephants come out of the jungle and *snatch* the peasants, and tear them to pieces! Oh no no *no,* Marjorie, I do not think *India* would be a suitable place for Pahrump. *You* don't want to be snatched by some big ol elephant, do you, Rumpelstilskin?"

Marj felt slightly uncomfortable having shared her dream only to be called a fool. She knew she was being oversensitive, and Cora didn't mean anything by it. The 2 women spoke of their husbands awhile, then agreed to see a movie later in the week at the Westside Pavilion. Cora walked her out and Pahrump limped after but paused inside the doorway as if before an invisible gate. (Usually he bounded into the frontyard.)

The car Stein bought his mother gleamed in the driveway. He'd traded in the Mercedes when his father died and leased a new Audi through his company. Cora put an eye on Marjorie's Imperial and said, "When you gonna get rid of that old thing?"

Marj shrugged.

"Sweetheart, get an *Audi.* I know you've got a pile of money sitting there—Ham would have wanted you to be *safe.* You need *side airbags.* The Audi drives like a *dream.* It warns you if anything gets *near* the rear bumper. Parallel parking is a *dream.* And there's a *camera*—I don't know how to use it yet!—so you can actually see a *small child* behind you. Do you know how many people back over small children each year? Stein calls it 'auto versus small child.'"

Pahrump barked.

"All right, baby," she said, turning toward him. "Mama's coming. I guess you want another cappuccino, huh?"

Cora went back in without saying goodbye.

Mⁱᵃʳʲ reclined on the La-Z-Boy. She thought about what she'd do if she won the Super Lotto Plus. She would provide for her children of course and maybe buy a place on some land—no 2nd floor so she wouldn't have to climb stairs. She'd had it with stairs. She started to think she would pay off the house before realizing she *had* paid it off, with term life, that in fact she had a nice savings, and no worries. She'd already *won* the lottery, so to speak, and was grateful. She'd had a good life, and a good husband, and her children were healthy and seemed happy, as far as she knew. She was footloose and debt-free and in reasonably good physical shape herself. A bit lonely but who knew? Might be something to that cruise idea afterall. (The thought made her blush.) Then she pushed all that nonsense from her head, supplanting it with her dream of India. There was a train she'd read about called the Deccan Odyssey that was supposed to rival the Orient Express. You could go on it for a week—its starting point was Bombay. There was an onboard spa and hot showers and dining cars and manservants and all day long you could visit temples or wade in the Arabian Sea. The other night she had been watching *A Passage to India* on television, when there it was, a sign in the train station: THE DECCAN QUEEN. It nearly made her neck hairs stand on end.

She smiled at the sculpture of the Indian elephant goddess that graced the mantelpiece along with a picture of Ham, photos of Joan and Chester as young children, and a silver Jesus. There *was* bounty in her life—and new beginnings.

IX

JOAN

S HE lay in bed watching Larry King. That was a guilty pleasure. Why should she watch Larry King?

It was probably something her mother enjoyed. What
would Zaha think? She doubted if *El Zorro* ever watched TV. ZH
assuredly watched outlandishly cutting-edge films only available
in PAL. Her best friends no doubt were the moviemakers
Haneke and Kusturica, or Barney & Björk, and Joan imagined
she'd cultivated Hedi Slimane to make dandruff-proof caftans for
the whole psychotically pretentious claque. Or maybe she was a
buddy of that hack Indian director, the Maya Angelou/Penny
Marshall of Orissa who was married to the scholar everyone ludi-
crously compared to Edward Said. *Edward S'Hadid.* To be sure,
ZH would soon be directing something à la *The Cremaster Cycle.*
*The Clitoris Cycle. The Cycling Clitoris. The Recycled Arclitect. Ar-
clitoridectomy.*

But maybe I'm wrong . . .

Could be that ZH was just a homie, an early aficionado of *The
Office,* a *Spamalot* freak, mobbed up with Eddie Izzard, Billie
Connelly, Sacha Cohen, and Eric Idle. A *Spinal Tapp*er.

Fattie.

Fat fatiscent Fatimite.

Hogwart.

Digitally rendered museum-addition ski-jumped Iraqi cunt.

Larry King was a salacious, cartoony comfort—all Beavis and
Butt-Head sharp bones, wisecracks, and chicken soup. Joan knew
why she had a soft spot for him: she'd projected onto him the dad
she never knew. Occasionally, she caught herself thinking:
Wouldn't it be bizarre if Larry King turned out to be my father?

Lately though he was getting a mite ghoulish; maybe it was age.
She had saved a bunch of his shows on TiVo and was finally scroll-

ing through them. The 1st she lit on was about a pretty blonde whose face got mauled by a cougar. Joan deleted it after about 20 seconds. The next one featured Dr Phil's sister-in-law. She'd been driving along when someone threw a can of sulfuric acid from an overpass; it broke the windshield and dripped on her. They showed pictures from the hospital, her face all burnt. Dr Phil's wife's *sister!* Totally surreal! The 3rd *Larry* was about a black woman down in Texas whose boyfriend killed her mom then turned around and shot her face off. The ex was swathed in bandages—all you could see was one eye. Joan almost laughed out loud: Larry really had a *Phantom of the Opera* thing goin on! But the 4th show really creeped her out. Some white chick got murdered in the Village and Larry was hosting the boyfriend and the victim's mother. He whipped through the interview by rote, bored and antsy, you could almost see his wheels turning *(Why the fuck are they on? I should've booked Tammi Menendez again),* holding back like a borscht bowl vampire—his guests nothing but long necks awaiting the fang—before rushing in, a white cell plasma TV Weegee in suspenders. Joan thought it so *weird* that people agreed to go on talkers just because someone they loved had been murdered or brutally taken from them. Even Susan Saint James! Monologuing about her little boy (angel with de-iced wings), and how she couldn't bear to touch his clothes! Pornographic *sharefests* were the New Dignity.

She deleted the *Larry*s and switched to the 24 hour Health Channel. It was right at the beginning of one of those *Medical Incredible*s, a segment about a woman in her early 30s with a one-in-a-million reaction to a common antibiotic. Within 12 hours of taking a bitsy pill, she'd "sloughed" 100% of her skin. As Mom and friends spoke on voiceover, there were shots of her in a medically induced coma, patented cellophane-like sheets of bioengineered dermis made from shark cartilage and cow tendons stapled to her body as a protective sheath. Joan couldn't believe what she was seeing; she felt like Liv Ullmann in *Persona,* cowering in front of the psych ward TV watching a monk set himself on fire. Toward the end of the hour, her doctor said that around

Christmas there was a ray of hope—a tiny patch of skin began to "recolonize." The woman made her dramatic camera debut at the end. She was kind of Goth, kind of Echo Parky, a little overweight but eerily luminous, as if lit by a Tim Burton lantern she'd swallowed. She visited the ICU, hugging everyone who had taken care of her. She told the camera that her skin was now like a baby's, tissue thin, and she had to walk under a parasol for the next few years when out in the sun. The doctors said she wouldn't begin to wrinkle until she was in her late 60s, and that was when Joan lost it.

How exquisite.

She cried and cried and cried.

X.

RAY

HE left the hospital.

Ray's lawyer sent a Town Car. The old man was nonplussed, but Big Gulp ate it up from the backseat. She looked lovely. She wore a turquoise sari, hair in dark plaits. BG had a goofy, toothy grin; if the city wound up giving him a little money, maybe he'd have em straightened.

THEY met barely a year ago on the Santa Monica pier. Early morning, chilly weekday. He'd gone there to fish just like he used to decades ago, when his marriage was in trouble. She stood on the far end, staring off. He thought she was a jumper. He struck up a conversation—he was so old, he figured that would be the only reason she'd talk because she looked shy and skittish by nature. (It took months before she showed her ballbusting side.) They spoke of fish. She used to sell it, she said, at market in Calcutta. He couldn't make the words out very well. Thick accent; low, furtive tones. Something about mustard seeds and how she'd worked as a nanny. How she wound up doing the same thing for the "CG"—the Indians liked their acronyms—the consul general in San Francisco. It was tortuous but he finally understood: she took care of some kind of ambassador's kids. Ran away. Didn't explain further. Ray (at 1st she thought his name was Raj) asked if she was a "wanted woman" but he didn't think she got the joke, which probably wasn't so funny and was even maybe true, and that she might have misinterpreted his comment as lurid. She said she had to go and he told her he'd be there the next day, same time. He hadn't planned on saying it, nor the subsequent possibility of her reappearing, and as the words came out he suddenly half dreaded the thought of getting up early and driving all the way from Industry (where he'd just moved after pulling up stakes in Mar Vista) for nothing. But lo and behold, she showed up 25 hours later, wearing the same clothes as before. She looked hungry. "I don't feel like fishing," he said. "Let's get some breakfast." After some of that trademark headbobbling and balking, she finally agreed.

When they got to the car she became hesitant. She saw the Friar and was afraid. Ray said the dog was fine and opened the door to let him pee, introducing Ghulpa as he wagged his tail and ignored her, and she patted his head, all the time with that nervous, tooth-packed grin. He put the dog back and suggested they walk to McDonald's. (He was going to take her to Norm's but that was 7 blocks away and Mickey D's was just around the corner.) They had thin coffee and McBreakfasts and didn't say much because he wanted her to feel at ease. Not that there was a whole lot to chat about. It was mostly subterranean.

He learned that she'd never married. Ghulpa looked around 42 but as Ray got older he had become a poor judge of age, especially a lady's. He told her he married only once, a lifetime ago, with 2 kids he no longer knew. That puzzled her; how could that happen? He shook his head, saying he didn't think he'd been "ready" to have a family. (It sounded cavalier though he didn't mean it to.) He added that his wife was a "ballbuster" then thought, Now why did I say that? Ghulpa didn't know the phrase and he laughed, relieved. He would choose his words more carefully now because he wanted to court her, not as a sexual being, but as a man in the September of his years who wanted a companion, a female companion, *this* female companion, dropped before him like a swarthy outmoded mermaid, without the baggage of a culture that he had exhausted and had exhausted him in return.

"I do regret not knowing them. The children."

Now something in *her* seemed relieved; that he'd taken her question seriously, and considered it, like a serious man. Ray saw how sorrow wasn't foreign to her and drew comfort from her demeanor during his confessions. They both exhaled.

"I wonder about that every day—wonder how I let that . . . But you get to be my age and there's a lot of water under the bridge you can't quite explain." He wondered if she knew what he meant. He'd muffed it anyway. "I guess as time goes by and you get closer to your Maker, you become all right with it. You don't have much choice. You try to forgive and be forgiven. *Jesus, I sound like a fundamentalist.* You pray for that. To live and let live. You try to let go of things too." The platitudes somehow felt right. *Longitudes and platitudes.* "You feel pretty bad but with time you become all right with it, and all right with God. At least you hope you do."

Ghulpa smiled, lips closed over buckteeth to disarming coy effect, because she saw the 2 of them were alike—in some ways.

"How old are you?"

"A man never tells."

"60?"

"Well now I wish!"

His heart fairly fluttered, and that *had* been a while.

"58?"

Ray's eyes twinkled at the sweet con. There was an innocence about her that was inviolate.

"You're good, Ghulpa. You're *very* good. And you're a helluva nice lady."

Pleased as punch, he was.

WHEN the Town Car pulled up to the apartment complex, the ancient landlord stood there holding a bouquet of 7-Eleven–bought flowers, because she liked the tenant in 203B, and knew that soon the City of Industry would be giving him booty with which he might be generous.

XI

CHESTER

CHESTER and Laxmi were on their way to the empty clinic to meet with the landlord about renting it for the shoot. Maurie was the one who suggested she keep his friend company, and Chess was glad. He was out-of-control attracted to her and had the feeling Maurie knew it. Chess thought, *Maybe he's being kind or maybe he's just perving.*

Laxmi was around 27. Her hippie parents were divorced and her dad lived in Pune. He was a failed Jewish poet who'd hung with Ginsberg during the latter's early 60s Benares sojourns; a pretty boy, almost a generation younger than the Beat Buddha, and Laxmi said that she was never able to confirm if "they'd gotten it on." He headed a big company now, the usual software collective—he was "way ahead of the outsourcing curve," she said—having lived in India on and off for 40 years. Even though he was a successful businessman, he was a "renunciate, in his own way." Chess asked what that meant and she said her father was a *sanyasi,* that he meditated and that Ganesh was "his personal adviser." (It all sounded seriously fucked up, but Chess was entranced. He knew about Ganesh from storybooks Mom used to read from but Laxmi made the elephant-headed god sound like some mobster-guru.) Laxmi's father was rich but never gave her money, instead offering to pay her way any time she wanted to come to Pune, something she planned to take him up on one day. She said her name had been given her because Laxmi was the goddess of good fortune. "Meaning, *money.* Dad is a Jew to his teeth." She said she would rather have been named Padma (her supposed middlename), which meant *lotus,* and asked Chess if he'd ever read something called the Lotus Sutra. He shook his head. " 'Suppose there was a wealthy man,' " she began to quote, " 'who had a magnificent house. This house was old, and ram-

shackle as well. The halls, though vast, were in precarious, perilous condition . . . ' "

She fell silent, unable to recall what once she had so fiercely,
and without comprehension, committed to memory.

W HEN they got to Alhambra, it was dusk. Maurie's car was
at the end of the cul-de-sac. A handwritten sign on a piece
of cardboard stuck to the front door said GO AROUND BACK. Laxmi
and Chess strolled to the alley entrance. Rusty barrels overflowing
with medical detritus swarmed with flies.

"I don't know where the guy is," called Maurie, from inside.

Chess and Laxmi stepped into the ruined building.

"What time was he supposed to be here?"

"About now."

"Shit, it's really trashed," said Chess, looking around. "What
were they shooting, a satanic ritual training video? Too small,
anyway. It *stinks*. What was this, an animal hospital?"

"Yeah. Supposedly the guy went nuts or something."

"Huh?"

"As in 'apeshit.' "

"What guy?"

"A veterinarian. Caught his wife with someone he worked
with and, like, killed her, then killed the kid. Bashed their heads
in with a fucking ball-peen hammer."

"Oh my God," said Laxmi. "I think we should split."

"Are you serious?" asked Chester.

Maurie nodded. "I don't think they ever found the guy."

Chester shrugged, like he wasn't in the mood for any of
Maurie's campfire bullshit. "It's too small," he said. "Plus it's
righteously fucked up. It's a health hazard."

"Let's go see the other rooms. I mean, we're *here*. I was in traffic
for 2 goddam hours."

"This is like a horror film," said Chess. "This is like *Saw.* "

They laughed uneasily.

It grew darker as they went farther into the honeycomb of

shambled rooms, each saturated in bad odors—like someone had set animal fat on fire. Laxmi said maybe it wasn't safe and to be careful not to touch anything. There were dirty syringes and rolls of stained cotton gauze underfoot. Chester said how crazy it was that someone was showing the place as a location before it had been cleaned—he wondered aloud if what they were seeing were props or not, but then Maurie said the clinic had been scouted but never actually used. *Whuh?* Chess was acting more macho than usual because of Laxmi. Maurie made a few lame jokes then shouted, "Look at this!"

A dead dog had been nailed to a door, like a wolfish Christ.

Laxmi screamed and began to run then screamed again as she plowed into the arms of a gaunt, grizzled, wild-haired man in a bloody green surgical gown. He had a big gun. He asked why they were "trespassing" and when Chess began to explain, Maurie quickly motioned to let him do the talking. They *weren't* trespassing, said Maurie, they were scouting locations for a TV show, and had an appointment to meet someone. The man kept saying they were trespassing and Maurie started shaking and said he was sorry if there was a misunderstanding and they'd leave right away. If he "would let us." The guy suddenly asked if Maurie had slept with his wife. No, said Maurie, of *course* not, I don't even *know* your wife—but Chess could tell that his friend's panicked posturing came out snarkier than Maurie would have liked. Then he began to insist that Maurie "looked just like the dude" who slept with his wife and "molested" his children. Maurie laughed nervously, trying to deflect as his eyes futilely darted for an exit strategy.

The man opened fire and Maurie's chest lit up in red blotches as he reeled backward. Laxmi screamed, running to Chess, who stood protectively between her and the meth'd up maniac.

"Shit motherfucker, you shot my friend!"

"Oh my God!" said Laxmi. "He's going to kill us!"

"You raped my wife, didn't you?" said the gap-toothed killer, his wrath now turned upon Chester, who couldn't process what was happening.

"I don't know what you're *talkin* about, man!"

"Just like that dog I nailed to the door! That dog touched my little *girl* too—see what I did to it? That dog was a *lurcher*. Ever heard of a *lurcher?* Them is *gypsy dogs.* They're bred for stealth, stamina, and speed. 2 can bring down a deer. Know what the farmers do if they catch em? Cut their tails off. Cain't walk without their tails!"

"I don't fucking know what you're—oh Jesus oh God oh shit oh Jesus . . ."

"You *mo*-lested my little girl! How ya think that feels, dude? As a dad? Are you a dad?"

"No, man . . ."

"You ain't a *dad,* you a *fag.* That's why I had to *kill* her—that's why I had to kill em both! Cause I couldn't let em walk the earth with that shame on em. Couldn't let em live, without protectin em from *ridicule.* You are *one sick madre, dude!* Did you enjoy it? Did you enjoy it when you were with my wife and little girl?"

"Man, stop! Just fucking stop! I don't know your wife, and neither does my friend! And you fucking killed him!"

"Ah'm gonna nail you to the wall, bitch! Cause you a goddam child molestin faggot *lurcher*—"

Maurie groaned. "Help me. Help me . . ."

He began to twitch grotesquely, as if in seizure. Chess kneeled beside his friend.

"He's still alive! We gotta call 911, man! Just get the fuck away and let me call 911! We'll say it was an accident, just run the fuck away and let us get help!"

The madman fixed him with that bizarre *Deliverance* hillbilly grin.

"You cain't help him *now.* Step aside! I'm gonna do the girl the way you done my wife!"

Laxmi let out a bloodcurdling bellowshriek.

"*You. Keep. Away!*" said Chess, standing ramrod straight. "Keep away from her!" The goddess of good fortune clung to his waist from behind as the madman moved closer. "I said stand down! Stand the fuck away! *I'll* stay—but let her go! You let her go!"

He ogled the couple, lasciviously stroking his chin. He slowly raised the gun. "Are you freaked out?"

Chess braced himself to be shot.

"I *said: Are you freaked out?*"

"Yes!" said the traumatized warrior, lips trembling in shock and fear. "Now just let her—"

"Well, you *shouldn't* be. Cause you're on *Friday Night Frights!*"

Chess was cornered. He tensed, gave out a deafening war cry, then bolted backward with superhuman strength into a wall of glass bricks. But the wall did not give. His pants were soaked in urine.

A bunch of men suddenly poured into the room; Chess thought they were the police. Everything was in slo-mo. *Why did I move back instead of forward? I was trying to make a hole for us to escape. Why hasn't he shot*—one of the men had a camera on his shoulder—they were all dressed in civilian clothes. Were they undercover? What was happening?

The madman threw down the gun and gleefully shouted. "The TV show! *Friday Night Frights!*"

Now he spoke without the twang. He was an actor.

Maurie stood up, melodramatically dusting himself off as the camera recorded his miraculous recovery. Laxmi, who bolted when Chess smashed into the wall, reentered, looking baleful and faintly agonized. She tried to smile at the probing lens.

"Are you OK?" she said to Chess, maternally.

Chess stutter-strobed his head like a dog just out of water, as if to throw off everything that had happened.

"See?" said Maurie, pointing to the red ragged splotches on his polo shirt. "They're squibs! Like *The Wild Bunch! Bonnie and Clyde! Pulp Fiction!*"

"It's a TV show, man," said someone in civvies. He carried a clipboard and had a small black box attached to his belt. They were all wired for sound.

"Friday Night Frights."

"Whoa," said Chess, wincing a smile. He still couldn't put it together but the name sounded familiar: *Friday Night Frights.* It was a joke, though—he knew that much. He turned to Maurie. "You piece of shit."

All laughed heartily.

Everything was being filmed.

"Your friend set you up!" said the clipboard man.

"C'mere," said Maurie. "Gimme a hug."

The 2 friends embraced and a relieved Laxmi joined them as the crew laughed and hooted and patted Chess on the back like he was way cool for having aced a reality show rite of passage.

XII.

MARJORIE

PAHRUMP had his diagnosis: leukemia.

The awful thing was that Marj had just read in the paper about a pet hospice in San Francisco. A woman there specialized in putting the animals down. She let them lick peanut butter or cream cheese from one hand, if that was the kind of food they liked, while giving them a fatal injection with the other.

She sat with her neighbor as she cried. Cora said she was going to spend whatever it took to get "my baby" healthy again. Pahrump didn't *seem* so bad; Marj asked if she was going to get a 2nd opinion. Cora said she had the best doctors "on the West Coast" so why would she?

"The worst thing is, Mr P just got accepted to day care. Heads 'n' Tails, on LaCienega, by San Vicente—it's *very* hard to get into. That's where Reese Witherspoon keeps her dogs. The poor thing went through the *most* rigorous peer review. Marj, it's worse than preschool! And he *sailed through.* Everyone loved him! *Reese's* dogs loved him. They said he was 'gifted'—didn't they, Mr P? But now . . ."

The neighbor quickly composed herself then buzzed around the kitchen making dinner "for my Rump."

She showed Marj the bottle of custom canine water that she poured in the doggie bowl. Pahrump was finicky about his H_2O and always a little dehydrated, but now Cora gave him a special kind that came all the way from a river at the bottom of a glacier in Washington.

"Mount Rainier—Jerry and I were there once, in a custom RV. Can you imagine me camping? Have you ever drunk mountain water, Marj?" She looked down at a somewhat forlorn Mr P, who eagerly awaited his supper nonetheless. "No chlorine or fluoride, which are tough on the kidneys." She said Pahrump's rank breath seemed to have "improved." He'd been putting on weight—this was months before the diagnosis—so she had him on a strict diet. Now she regretted it. Well, that was going to end *today*. From now on, she'd have Stein FedEx "grub" from New York. A place called the Barkery. "And a shop called Pawsitively Gourmet, isn't that adorable?" Cora said the food was actually made for human consumption, so she and Pahrump could have dinner together. There were desserts like truffles and "pupcakes" (from the "pawtisserie"), almond butter waffle cones topped with carob, and oatmeal biscuits in the shape of fire hydrants. She couldn't resist pulling her neighbor into the bathroom and showing off Mr P's array of beauty products: tea tree oil shampoo, nail polish from Paul Mitchell, Earthbath Mediterranean Magic, and a misty spritz for his coat that was "kind of like eyeshadow." Some of the products were *very* important because they stopped P from itching; Lord Rump had been known to scratch himself raw. Once a week, Stein sent over a mobile pet spa that gave her baby a hot oil treatment with Bulgarian lavender and African sage soil. As she spoke, she occasionally broke into quickly suppressed tears. Why had this befallen her little prince? Why? Marj touched her neighbor's arm and said there were some questions that could never be answered. But she had a feeling that Pahrump would be "just fine."

THE old woman went home and sat in front of the TV. She was in the middle of reading a slim book about Jesus' visit to India as a young man. A lot of people questioned if he ever really made that historical trip to Orissa but Marj didn't doubt it in her heart. Jesus reputedly gave sermons and traveled as the Buddha did amongst people of various castes, and learned the art of healing in the holy city of Benares. She had seen pictures of Benares and it reminded her of Venice. It was supposed to be a city of death but seemed so alive.

Marjorie thought more and more about her own journey. She

would have to start planning soon. At night she sat in bed and steeped herself in delicious memories of the Taj Mahal Palace, her conjurings enhanced by a trove of clipped and yellowing pages from *Look* magazine. The colonial wedding cake of a hostelry, filled with marble halls, dark incense-laden recesses, and a seemingly limitless army of servants clad in shiny boots, turbans, and maroon or blinding white linen, was in a most enviable section of that dense, aromatic, splendiferously beleaguered city: just behind the legendary Gate of India, a tiny Arc de Triomphe perched like a launching pad for genies on the Sea of Oman. (Both hotel and Gate were at the very beginning of David Lean's glorious film as well, just before Judy Davis and Dame Peggy board the Deccan Queen.) There was an island her father took her to by motorized dinghy—the Elephanta Caves—you could actually see the water-bound site from their hotel room, and, remembering, Marjorie's eyes teared up at the exoticism of it.

She would soon be there!

The most phenomenally eccentric thing about the Taj was the chestnut she insisted her father recite (after a draught of Kipling) each night before bed. It seems the English architect who designed the palace went home during its construction; upon returning from London his eyes told him the workmen had built the hotel the wrong way round—its facade faced the water and its back, the city! Mortified by the error, he drowned himself in the bay. Whenever Dad told that story she trilled with glee and he tickled her and said that his Marjorie Morningstar was a bonafide scoundrel and a scamp too. How she adored him! She could smell him still.

She would use the same agency that handled the holiday trips she took with Ham to Italy and Alaska; her husband had never favored a "passage to India." Trudy always got the best deals. Marj didn't know if India was a specialty but the Travel Gals were generally pretty well versed, and where there's a will (Ham's), there's a way, *No pun intended*. She laughed aloud at her little joke then lazily drew a finger over the page of the atlas from Bombay to Bangalore to Madras to Calcutta to Benares to Agra to Delhi to

Jodhpur and back to her precious Bombay, the trail always like a gloriously twisted wedding ring of 22 karat gold.

EVERY few days, she visited her Wells Fargo home branch and the teller wrote down Marj's balance. She'd never had that kind of money in her life. She thought of calling Joan and talking to her about the trip though she didn't like to bother her busy daughter. Still, she knew that her youngest shared a love for the subcontinent as well. It was "genetic." Straight through her teens, she adored the Indian saris and statues Marj brought home from shops and flea markets; she read to her little girl about Ganesha, remover of obstacles; they made pilgrimages to the zoo to marvel over the elephants. (She was entranced when told of the Elephanta Caves, where Mama had visited with Joan's grandfather.) The pale, pretty child drew pictures of the Taj Mahal—not the hotel but the *real* Taj Mahal—and even then showed an extraordinary talent for detail and perspective. Marj was so proud: proportions always so beautifully done, with fastidious decorations, crosshatchings, and subtle hints of pastel evoked with a stubby pencil and crude crayons. Even as she grew older, Joan asked if they could one day visit the memorial in Agra, and while Marj didn't say it, she knew Hamilton wouldn't look kindly on mother and daughter traveling alone, and that he'd never consent to join them. Maybe *now* Joan might want to come, for at least part of the trip. The old woman decided not to make any proposals. She would mention her plans to visit Bombay, and leave the rest to Joanie. She wasn't going to bend anyone's arm—that wasn't any fun.

Besides, Marj felt perfectly fine "flying solo."

XIII.

JOAN

JOAN kept seeing Thom Mayne at Peet's, on Montana. She and Barbet were already taking meetings with Lew Freiberg about the Mem. Lew was in the middle of buying a house in Bel-Air. (He was in the middle of buying houses everywhere.) He was staying at Shutters, which he kept saying he couldn't stand. Thom Mayne was ridiculously tall, cranky-looking, and gorgeous, and Barbet hated him more than ever since he'd won the Pritzker.

One morning before they met with Lew, Barbet triumphantly brought in a page he'd torn from the "My Favorite Weekend" section of the *Times*. The headline: ALWAYS ON THE GO, EVEN WHEN HE'S AT HOME. Barbet read out loud, punctuating each of Mayne's sentences with great, insane flourishes.

When I get home, I just want simplicity, stability, and routine. Just walking our dog, Isis, going to get a cup of coffee, and looking for heirloom tomatoes at the Santa Monica Farmers Market. 8:30 on a Saturday night will usually find us at *Table* in Venice, a new restaurant opened by David Wolfe of *2424 Pico* fame. The place is funky and laid back, very 70s Venice . . . Surfer son Cooper often accompanies us as he's an adventurous eater and loves David's cooking. I had real severe back problems about 10 years ago . . . so my wife, Blythe, got me going to yoga . . . My back problems have gone away. But I'm not at all into yoga as a spiritual thing.

"Who the fuck is he *kidding?*" said Barbet. "His dog *Isis* and his Adventurous Eater Surfer *Son*—oh, *he fancies David Wolfe's* cuisine!—whoever the fuck *that* is, '*of 2424 Pico fame*'—how fucking adventurous! How fucking *adventitious* . . ."

"Adventitious? What is 'adventitious'?"

He ignored her query. "And that bit about the yoga—God forbid we think *Mr Morphosis* has a spiritual side! Mr Polymorphosis Perverse! What a sanctimonious prick-monster."

"Oh come on, Barbet, you'd *love* to be telling the LA *Times* about your 'favorite weekend.' "

"Right! Saturdays: browsing for Milton's *Paradise Regained* at Dutton's Brentwood, then brunch at Axe, Percocet at Horton & Converse, Pilates with Demi at the little gym on Nemo, LP hunting for Lord Buckley and Stan Freberg at Amoeba, a jaunt to Maxfield's to pick up that groovy little Rick Owens leather coat and the 20,000 dollar vintage Hermès strap-on I've had my eye on. At night? Sirk at the Aero and a salad on Montana—Locanda Portofino! But *Sundays,* I would *sorely* enjoy watching you shove said froggy dildo up Thom Mayne's growling, hairy ass."

"I wish."

S HE'D been working with Barbet for 7 years, sharing the same bed intermittently for 5. After lust burned off, an unspoken agreement to see other people. He was still her confidant—maybe surrogate sib was more accurate—and no one made her laugh like he did. (Typical Barbet joke: "What did the SS guard say when the Jewish girl asked why Dr Mengele only experimented on her twin? 'He's just not that into you.' " Another: "Baraka is the new black.") He knew she had an ongoing dalliance with Pradeep, the CG, which had incidentally worked to ARK's advantage: to whit, the Freiberg Mem. It was business, so he was careful not to make any jokes about that relationship, nor inquiries—even the usual friendly insinuations were *verboten*. For that, she was glad.

They still fucked but things had definitely cooled since the (augural) coming of Lew Freiberg. Barbet was cagey; her affairs rarely dampened his ardor (the effect being predictably the opposite), but now the subtext was they had hooked the Big Fish and her partner didn't dare befoul the waters. Joan needed to take care on her end as well—she didn't like that pimped out feeling. Anyhow, she wasn't at all sure what to do about the formidable Mr F

and his low-flame fornicatory advances. The whole thing was in-
candescently taboo for a multitude of reasons. Billionaires *were*
different from you and me. She was finished with Barbet—that
way—at least for now. The last time she stayed over, Joan caught
him, back toward her, douching in the shower after a shit. She
stayed hidden as he washed his ass from the faucet with the same
bar of soap she scrubbed her face with in the morning after shav-
ing her legs. Payback: to sleep with this man out of incestuous
convenience then cover her skin with the microbial cologne of his
excrement to greet the new day.

At 50, Lew Freiberg had been married 4 times and was
currently separated from his last, an aspiring children's book
writer. Soon after they met at the Ehrlichs', he told Joan she was
his "type"—pronounced with a kind of convivial semitic brazen-
ness. He was always flirty and suggestive during Memorial design
meetings; he would wait till Barbet went to the balcony for a
smoke before tossing a crude bouquet of innuendo. She could
handle it. In fact, it felt *great* to be desired by someone so inconceivably rich. As a girl, she had always wanted to be abducted by
pirates.

ARK was far from being a frontrunner in the Mem competition. (Barbet liked to call them "the ark horse.") There was Gehry,
who Freiberg originally met through the Newhouses, though
Barbet didn't think Frank was all that serious about it. Frank
didn't seem to be all that serious about anything. There
was talk of something being created by Andy Goldsworthy—
the artist seemed a shoo-in to decorate the grounds of the main
Mem—he of the Holocaust garden recently installed on the roof
of a museum in Battery Park City; or maybe an outdoor installation by Tony Cragg. The usual rumors of Herzog & de Meuron
(Lew liked the "Sydney Blue eucalyptus" they'd used at the De
Young), or Jean Nouvel; the farther-out hints and whiffs of con-
tenders such as sand sculptor Jim Denevan, David Hertz, Santa
Monica's Predock/Frane, Toshiko Mori, and England's David
Adjaye—of course OMA was in there too (Barbet called it
"melanoma"), the agency of *Special K,* Auntie Rem, Barbet's old

mentor and perennial adversary. Joan knew it had been a fluke that ARK was in the regatta, and her seaweed sex, the body heat between herself and patron, was the kelpy glue that kept the firm in play. She didn't care. She was too old and it was too late. She just wanted the job. Needed it. It was defining, and would define her.

She made a date with Lew to get together before he went back up north, but this time without Barbet.

XIV.

RAY

How did it happen? The relationship hadn't been sexual. A few days after he got home from the hospital, she got on top and guided him in. He wasn't even sure he could do that anymore; a long time since he'd even felt himself hard.

Throughout, she kept herself covered with a white muslin blouse he had bought her in Artesia's "Little India." That's where her cousins owned a shop, and where she was living when they 1st met, a week after going on the lam. Before, when in LA, she had a room adjoining the consul's suite at a hotel in West Hollywood called the Wyndham Bel Age. Sometimes the CG would stay on a few days after his wife and children returned to San Francisco. In that case, Ghulpa joined her cousins at the house in Artesia. They'd cook and catch up and go to a concert in Cerritos.

When Ray finally met the extended family, everyone smiled with closed lips and bobbling heads. The thing the old man liked was that no one had to do any explaining, nothing was compulsory, he didn't have to say who he was or why he was so old or what he did for a living or what he and Big Gulp were up to. Didn't have to announce his intentions. No one was judgmental, just friendly. BG and the cousins spoke Bengali. Sometimes it was pretty obvious the ladies were talking about him but it seemed they wanted Ray to know it, all very coquettish and warm, lots of sweet laughter, and he soaked it in. He'd been away from women way too long. Hell, he wasn't a bad-looking geezer and occasionally got the feeling they were extolling his physical virtues, not his decrepitude—could be a cultural thing. (He allowed he may have gotten that one wrong.) Now suddenly they were sleeping together, a for-real shackjob, a very adult arrangement, and he knew Ghulpa was too old to conceal it through pride; and old enough to share with the cousins whatever details she wished out of the same emotion. He didn't know much from Indians but the onus on women of a certain age without a partner seemed universal. For all he knew, the ladies were sitting around asking Big Gulp when she thought the old fart would pop the question. Maybe he was remiss but he couldn't fathom getting hitched. He'd always been extra gentlemanly with her because that part of his life had already peeled off, like shadows do if you walk quickly at dusk. He couldn't know her expectations. He would cross that bridge when she led him there.

Straddling him, grunting, her sweat-beaded bindi like a tear in the 3rd eye, Ray Rausch wondered if his brush with death had made Ghulpa affectionate this way; accelerating the process, so to speak. He could smell the Cadbury on her breath but they didn't kiss that much during the act, more with lips than tongues. (Indian gals sure loved their Cadburys.) He remembered that 1st day on the pier, he had wondered about her, if she was a loose woman, because her purse gaped and he caught a glimpse of a toiletry bag, zipper half-open as well, stocked with toothbrush, toothpaste, and tampons. Later, he realized most Indian ladies carried that sort of thing—and loved their sweets. Big Gulp always talked about having "floss on bamboo sticks" back in Calcutta. It took him a heck of a while to realize she meant cotton candy.

That was how it happened: dark, fathomless, Ghulpa's almond eyes whitening in their sockets toward the end as he felt himself seize inside her while she clawed his gray-haired chest, threadbare patches from where bandages and EKG suction "thingies" (BG's favorite word) had been roughly ripped away. He had the fleeting thought he might have another heart attack—die in the saddle—but there was no pain, only surprise, and then he felt the dig of her nails, *that* was what hurt, finally grabbing her tiny hands so she'd lighten up just a little. That's when *she* seized, slowly arching her head, which ever so slowly came back down to bobblesmile its naughtily sated sumptuously wayward Cadbury grin. *Everything old is new again.*

Ghulpa went to the powder room and after a minute returned with a hot cloth. She wiped him down then covered her man up in the thin Target comforter just like swaddling a baby. She disappeared again and he lay there dreamy as a girl. When she came back, BG turned on his television, kissed his cheek, and went to the kitchen to cook. He felt mannish, restful, and comfortable in full measure.

Tomorrow they would visit Nip/Tuck at the animal hospital on Sepulveda. It was a long haul. *The fellow in the paper was right, they ought to build monorails in LA, not subways. Subways are for cold climates. Wouldn't it be a hoot to hop a monorail and see the Friar? Chess and Joanie loved the ones at Disneyland. He'd heard there were monorails in Vegas now.* He mightily missed that dog. The Friar was gonna get himself a hero's welcome, for sure—their lawyer had suggested piñatas and party hats. It was the 1st damn thing Ray and the man could agree on.

The smell of spices wafted in and he heard Big Gulp singing.

XV.

CHESTER

"I DON'T understand you, man," said Maurie. "Why wouldn't you agree to sign the form?"

"Because I look like an *asshole*. Do you think I want the world to watch me pissing my pants?"

"You can't even *see* that. It's too dark."

"Fuck off, Maurie."

"Did you tell them you hurt your back?"

There was something accusatory in his tone that Chester didn't like.

"Yeah, I told them I hurt my back. Cause I *did*. It's cut up from the glass and I've got a weird pain."

"You *always* have a weird pain. Just take your Vicodin like a good little boy."

"I can't believe you did that, man. I might have to get a fucking epidural. My mother's *dead husband* used to get epidurals and he was in his *fucking 70s."*

"Then see a *chiropractor*. Shit, *Laxmi'*ll give you a *massage,* she's got a *certificate*. Stop being such a baby! Look, we each got a little bread for our trouble. How bad can it be?"

Friday Night Frights gave them 15-hundred apiece. Maurie brought over a tape for him to watch, and the producers had been calling, eager for Chess to sign a waiver. They backed off when he said he'd injured himself. (Don Knotts's daughter had already provided the number of her acupuncturist.) He wondered if he needed an X-ray. Maybe he should just go to an ER. Someone from the legal department of *FNF* had phoned as well, trying to make nice. The cunt said she could maybe "find" 25-hundred dollars if he'd agree to absolve them of responsibility. Chess had been in enough fender-benders to know better. Did they think he was stupid? It was tricky and bogus, and tweaked his mood.

"What about your *Manson girlfriend?*" said Chess.

He wouldn't say it directly but felt grossly betrayed by Laxmi's participation in the stunt. Blindsided and humiliated. All of his fantasies had been shot down—her involvement was a major hard-off.

"It was a *joke,* Chess, OK? You're the only one who doesn't seem to *get* it. Plus, you got *paid.* Aren't you the guy who's always bitching about not making rent? You still owe me 7-fifty, if you haven't forgotten."

"So now you want your 7-fifty?"

"*No,* man. I'm just saying: I did it cause I thought it would help—*everybody.* OK? Things are a little tight with me right now too, OK? I thought it'd help us *both.*"

"I always pay my debts, Maurie. Haven't I always paid back anything I've ever borrowed?"

"You've been really great about that," said Maurie, in earnest. He seemed almost contrite. "And that's not even the fucking point. Why are we talking about $750? You're a *friend,* and would do the same for me. I don't give a shit about that 7-fifty, OK? OK? We've been through a lot together. We're gonna make a *movie* one day. OK? All right? We'll make our *Saw* or our whatever. I just think you're being a little prideful here, Chess. You said they offered you 25-hundred. Why don't you just take it?"

"Because I don't want to look like a schmuck. I don't want this shit on cable *or* the Internet."

"Maybe they'll give it to you *anyway.* To make it go away. It's a wash. They probably have a *fund* for that shit."

"If they have a fund, they should give me 5."

"Then ask for 5. But don't get *greedy* or you'll wind up with zip. You know, I'm *thinkin* about it, and I'm not even sure everyone agrees to be on . . . but you'd be *nuts* not to. It's a *goof*—a goof that could put you 5 grand ahead. It's not like you're on *Dateline,* showing your *schvanz* to a tweener! It's a hip show. People download it on their iPods."

"*Great.*"

"You're being *way* too serious about all this, Chester."

"What did Laxmi get paid?"

"500."

He shook his head disconsolately.

"Hey man, I'm sorry you whacked your back. OK? I don't think you're gonna wind up in a wheelchair, I really don't. It's all, like, *no big deal.* It's only a big deal if you *make* it one."

He told Chess to take an Ativan and chill. He left the tape, along with a DVD compilation of past *Friday Night Frights.*

C HESS watched a few oldies but goodies. The host was some faded TV star he couldn't place. 1st he walked the audience through what they were about to see, to minimize viewer confusion—the *FNF* skateboarder demographic had total ADD. At the beginning of each segment, the camera freeze-framed on "Perp" (sometimes with an "Accomplice." That would be Laxmi) and "Vic." The Perps gave short interviews directly to camera saying why they thought it'd be fun to fuck with whatever friend they'd set up. People were thrown into incredibly well-choreographed, unnerving situations, which initially seemed absurd or unlikely to the home viewer but distressingly convincing to the Vic. Most of the stunt scenarios were drawn from the *Texas Chainsaw/Alien* canon—the effectively familiar date movie genre. Common themes were plague or radioactive outbreaks, creepy *Village of the Damned* kids with telekinetic powers, Big Foot/UFO shenanigans, and the like. The deranged serial killer motif was a fave. Chess hated to admit it but he became engrossed; from a purely psychological perspective it was amazing to watch how people reacted to life-threatening situations. He sat through 5 full half hours, astonished that none of the Vics—*none of them*—ran, not even when it seemed certain they were going to be slaughtered. Some froze in their tracks like the actors in *Blair Witch,* voices becoming eerily basso as they pleaded not to be hurt; others were manic and jokey, like the bespectacled nerds who get impaled in splatter films. A couple of them grew quietly grim and nonreactive, as if watching a movie in their heads, waiting for the part when they got killed. In one show, a Vic was about to be set on fire with a blowtorch by a disfigured Freddy Krueger type. Chester was blown away when the kid—who, earlier in the segment, before the shit hit the fan, revealed he had "taken the calling"—actually shouted, "Go ahead! Do it! Light me up! Cause I'm a Christian, and I'm goin to Heaven!" (Chess thought, *That boy could really clean up on the evangelical circuit. All he'd have to do was run the clip at the Crystal Cathedral.*) Another thing he noted was how young everyone was, which explained why, when the Vics realized they'd been had—"Are you freaked out? Well, you *shouldn't* be—you're on *Friday Night Frights!*"—they were so quick to forgive after reflexive disbelief and rain of bleeped expletives. When teens got spooked or shamed (kind of where they lived anyway), they were resilient by nature and physical constitution, not to mention super-reactive to peer pressure. A teenager's ego ultimately demanded he show himself to be a good sport or risk further abuse—there was no way his friends would allow him *not* to sign the release. Also, kids were less likely to have fucking heart attacks. That's why Chess couldn't understand why they went with a guy who'd hit 40. Must have been a programming aberration. He guessed they were trying something new but it sure as hell didn't fly. The producers had to be kicking themselves; whoever hatched the bright idea was probably on his way to being terminated.

He looked at his own segment over and over, a hastily edited approximation of what would air. They had deliberately left out the part where Maurie said what a hoot it would be to fuck over his bosom buddy. (Also, the tape was unsweetened as yet by cheesy musical "stings.") There he was, walking through the empty clinic, a cocky Judas (wasn't Judas the New Saint?). . . . Chester's bit about the satanic ritual training video, and how the place looked like something out of *Saw*. . . . Laxmi's stage-yelp at the crucified taxidermist's dog. When the hollow-eyed, stringy-haired psycho appeared, he looked ridiculous, the acting campy beyond belief; Chess was shocked he hadn't snapped to the put-on from the get-go. (*But why the fuck would I?*) Laxmi *did* seem gen-

uinely distressed, gaze flitting between "the maniac" and Chester
. . . he wondered if right then she was maybe having 2nd thoughts
about the prank. *That cunt. That stone pony stunt cunt.* His heart
sped up as the clip came to a close.

He put the tape on slo-mo, to see if he could catch the stain of
urine on his trousers. Maurie was right—it wasn't there, at least
not at this resolution. They'd probably find a way to insert it digitally. If George Lucas could make whole movies of shit that didn't
even exist then some Geek Squader surely could figure out how to
make it clear to the world that Chester Herlihy had peed himself.

XVI.

MARJORIE

S HE went to Riki's for more lottery tickets but it was closed.
A news van was there. A tall white pole spiraled from its
roof. A woman was interviewing people gathered outside.
The storefront was plastered with flowers and handwritten notes.
Marj asked someone what happened and a man said Riki had
been shot last night. She started to faint; he lowered her to the
sidewalk. The lady with the microphone came over. She kneeled
beside Marj for an impromptu interview but a neighborhood girl
shooed at her.

"Get away!" said the girl in anguish and disgust, blocking the
cameraman's view. "She's old! Get *out* of here!"

The lady backed off with a phony, apologetic smile.

Marj thanked the girl, who then helped her up. She asked if
there was anyone to call and Marj said no, she'd be fine, she just
had the wind knocked out of her. The man who said Riki had
been shot came over and that was when Marj saw the girl had
been crying. The girl said she couldn't believe someone would
have killed such a good man, that he was her friend, if the killer
had only asked, Riki would have given him money or food or
whatever he needed. The man said he'd only been to the store
twice but when he heard on the news what happened, he came
right over. He said he was a poet and had gotten into a long, "eru-
dite" conversation with Riki about Indian writers. He'd spent
about an hour in the shop reading his own poems to the shop-
keeper in between customers. He had already written some stan-
zas *in memoriam*. He pointed to the scribbles, a piece of paper
wedged into the metal accordion fencing now surrounding the
store's facade. Votive candles burned weakly beneath yellow
CRIME SCENE bunting.

As she slowly walked home, Marj thought about the sudden

widow and the beautiful son. She wondered if they were hidden away in the store's recesses or at the police station or at home. Maybe they were already doing a *puja*—she thought that was the word—a ceremony of mourning. *Indians are so close-knit.* She wondered how much of the family lived in Bombay and hoped they had lots of friends in the local Indian community who would comfort them. But how could anyone be comforted after something like that? It made her sick and she felt herself become faint again; she was almost home.

It was hard enough when Ham passed; still, that was natural, a natural death. She decided to offer them monetary help as soon as they resurfaced. Marj didn't think they would be offended, and just now, didn't care. It was what her heart told her to do. She could track them down through the police then thought it simpler to offer condolences when they came back to close shop. Though maybe they *wouldn't* close; maybe they would persevere. Indian people were used to adversity. She truly hoped they'd stay on. The neighborhood wouldn't be the same without them. Perhaps it was selfish of her. And that young girl—so sweet, and so touching! Riki had that kind of impact on the world. It broke her heart.

Cora was outside with Pahrump.

"Terrible!" she said. She had watched a news report about the murder. "Did you hear?"

"Yes! I was just there—I went to buy a ticket."

"Was he black?"

For a moment, Marj was confused.

"I'm sure it was a black. *Stinky, smelly animals.*"

Pahrump darted this way and that, giving no indication he was ill. Cora leaned down and grabbed him.

"Did you see the collar? Steinie gave it to me. Don't ask how it works but Steinie says that if Pahrump *dares* leave the yard—and you *wouldn't,* would you, Rump?—a message pops up on his cellphone. You *know* how my son is with technical things . . . where he got the ability, I'm not sure. It certainly wasn't his father, no no, it wasn't *Jerry.* Jerry was a Samsonite, like the Unabomber!" She stroked behind the dog's ears. "And *if,* God forbid, Pahrump should ever run away, Stein could use his phone to find him, just like one of those things they put on a car. A hijack or a low-jack or a whatever." She laughed. "Stein says if I ever left him in the car—which *will* never happen—Marjorie, can you imagine me forgetting about my Rumper? Leaving him in a hot, stuffy car? Well, if ever I get Old Timer's disease, the collar would call Steinie's cellphone and let him know my Pahrump was *hot under the collar.* Don't ask! I'm afraid Steinie is going to put one on *me!*"

Marj wobbled toward the house.

"Let's go see a movie!" Cora called after her. "Let's see what's at the Pavilion."

The old woman had turned away from her neighbor and was focused on getting to the front door.

"My poor Pahrump—he starts treatment tomorrow. Poor baby! You're going to be a brave little soldier, aren't you, Rumpus? You know why we named him Pahrump, Marjorie? Did I ever tell you? When Jerry and I bought him, it was Christmastime. And Jerry always loved the 'Drummer Boy' song. That's why we call him that: *Pah rum-pum-pum-pum.* Me and my drum. *And* because he's got a tiny supermodel rump—don't you, Rumpelstiltskin!"

Marj made a beeline for the La-Z-Boy. Her blouse was soaked in perspiration and after a minute or so, she was fast asleep.

XVII.

JOAN

I N bed with Pradeep at the Wyndham Bel Age—talking about Lew Freiberg.

Watching Larry King. The topic: migraines.

A few experts were on, plus a passel of longtime sufferers, including Larry's *wife* (the old Jew had *chutzpah*), and actress-turned-director Lee Grant.

"Did you see Lee Grant's face?" said Joan, nonplussed.

"I tried not to look."

"Did you see it was *out of focus?*"

"Not really."

"Oh my God, Pradeep, look! You have to! It's like that Woody Allen film! Pradeep, you have to *look.*"

She forced him. Larry King's wife was on the left, in clear focus. Lee Grant was on the right—a blur.

"They have a gel on the lens!" she shrieked.

"The woman's in New York. Maybe it's a technical thingie."

"That is *insane.* I am telling you they have something on the lens—or in front of it. She would *have* to have requested that. *It's the most bizarre thing I have ever seen.*"

"So what?" he said, ever the diplomat. "Why make a fuss? Warren Beatty does it. Whenever he gets photographed, he brings his own lighting people. What's the problem?"

"It's *so sad.*"

"Zaha Hadid had it on Charlie Rose."

"Oh, bullshit."

For a moment, he got her attention.

"I know you have a *thingie* about Zaha."

She turned the channel in antic disgust.

✳ ✳ ✳

THEY had originally met at some welcome-to-the-neighborhood fete for Frank Gehry. Pradeep made frequent trips to LA; when his wife wasn't visiting her parents in Delhi, she preferred to remain in the Bay Area with their 2 young children. There was an instant attraction between them which Joan thought weird, from her end anyway. He had Bollywood good looks, or at least that was her idea, because she'd never seen a Bollywood film. Not really her type.

The party was at Dennis Hopper's metal house in Venice. There were a lot of artists there (Hopper considered himself one of them)—both Eds: Moses and Ruscha; Robert Williams and John Baldessari. In profile, Ruscha's wife, Danna, looked like an empress on a Roman coin. Bono and Kirsten Dunst and the 2 Germans, Wenders and Herzog, and even a Caltech Nobelist. Joan just felt stupid. She was starstruck and her usual engine of contempt had been flooded—she stalled out and got drunk. Funnily, she found herself as attracted to Gehry as she was to Pradeep, and spent half the night with an eye on both. Barbet wanted to introduce her to Frank but Joan was too filled with self-loathing. What was the point? Gehry was gemütlich and gnomishly, gnostically bewitching, a wizard-changeling sitting on a bus bench at Fairfax and Beverly—a wolf in gefilte fish clothing. He was like a creature out of Bellow, I. B. Singer, or whatnot. He showed off a watch he designed, with his name etched on the back, and an aggressive starlet asked if she could wear it awhile. He graciously acceded. An hour or so later, with Jack Benny timing, he said, "So, can I have my watch back?" The tough little gamine didn't look like she wanted to part with it just yet and that's when Gehry gallantly said, "You can have it."

The rest of the evening, attended by his gorgeous young son, he told everyone, in that nearly imperceptible voice, how the famous gal had stolen his watch, words modulated like a deadpan imp, he got a great kick out of it, which made it all right. Still, Gehry was hard to read. He could look right through you and that scared her. He jetted around the planet kibitzing like a cosmic potentate, and Joan noticed how his face could darken into impenetrability as

easily as becoming mawkish at the mention of a recent visit to his
old Canadian grade school where they sang to him the national
anthem. Once, cheating on Larry King, she watched pre-heart attack Charlie Rose. (Letterman was the pioneer. Months later, Joan
saw Rose on *Larry* the very night before Larry guested on *Rose*—
it was like swapping spit. The whole near-death thing disgusted
her. Charlie Rose was about as near death as Karl Rove was to en-
listing. Cardio-Charlie was telling Larry—they shared the same
Manhattan surgeon—how he was in Syria having shortness of
breath and how he got their doctor on the line and their doctor
said you better get your butt to the City of Light and Charlie of
course happened to have an apartment in Paris, and happened to
know Bernard-Henri Lévy, and Bernard-Henri Lévy happened
to know a cardiologist willing to see him at 7:30 Friday night, and
the cardiologist happened to know the best mitral valve man in
the world who happened to be out of the country but happened to
return on Monday to give Charlie the once-over. When Larry
asked how the trip back to the States was after his recovery, Charlie said fine, a friend from New York sent a jet, and there was a
doctor onboard. Joan kept thinking, *what if you're some poor
schmuck with 4 kids and a fatass wife in tow on some National Lam-
poon European Vacation and you're having chest pains and shortness
of breath? What if you're not motherfucking pigvalve man-about-
town Charlie Rose?*) His guests were Gehry, Renzo Piano, and
that relic Ada Louise Huxtable. Piano was like an Italian Thom
Mayne, a bad actor playing an arrogant duke (his dukes were always up); Huxtable, a doyenne courtesan, mummified madame
out of *120 Days of Sodom,* some Edith Head–wardrobed *Fountain-
head* buzzard. Charlie Rose was an incorrigible architect buff and
wanted the whole world to know it. (He'd even done a whole
hour with David Childs, who looked and talked like a cousin of
BTK. CR said, "David, I've had the 'signature' architects on this
show—you know who they are. But here's what the world says
about David Childs: 1) You're the guy who gets the building built;
2) You get along remarkably with your clients and patrons. . . ."
Joan hung on her chair, waiting for number 3: *You are a bloodless*

bureaucrat without talent or vision—but the unctuous host never delivered.) Rose looked like a ghoul with a hairpiece, a cross-dresser doing roadshow *Guys and Dolls;* those idiotic gesticulations of faux passion and creepily orchestrated adolescent enthusiasms made Joan cringe. (Other times, he'd morph into a rouged-up 2-bit Casanova.) The frank Piano player got the architects to shoot the usual no-brainer shit, the Bilbao Effect, all that deadly dialectic about museums servicing art or museums as art-in-themselves, Rose and Huxtable with their heads so far up the celebrated men's asses—Charlie and the Chocolate Factory!—you could practically see their scalps crowning in Frank and Renzo's mouths. Renzo had *his* head up Frank's ass (the ultimate museum add-on) all the while pretending he wasn't a man to suck up to anyone but G-d—how it nauseated her! Piano actually said, "I am a craftsman—I do work with my own hands, so I never take on too much. Yes, we have 100 people in the office, but . . ."

Gehry was the only one who got away untainted—that was the true Bilbao Effect, in action!

Sex with Pradeep had a quality of innocence, something lacking in her connection to Barbet. The counsel was all feeling; with Barbet, she was always being hustled or hustling. That was exciting too, though not in the long run.

"Tell me what you know about Lew," she said after room service came. She tore into her veal as he spoke.

"An unusual man."

"Is he dangerous?"

"He would have to be. A bit. No?"

"Did he beat up his wives?"

"Not that I know of!"

"How close was he to his brother?"

"Very."

"What exactly were they doing in India? The brother and wife?"

"Bumming around, in their *fashion*. On the way to Sri Lanka.

The Maldives. They weren't the Phi Phi-Phuket sort. They'd have been better off if they'd wound *up* in the Maldives during the Wave. They found them both in a tree, you know—a sundari. The water pushed them up. It was a 'spirit' tree, with a beautiful yellow sash around the trunk. I have a digital photo."

"What is that? A spirit tree."

"It's special. It's 'recognized' by the villagers. The monks leave offerings for it, you know, food and water. This tree took the Freibergs in its arms, so to speak. They just hung there. Esther was still wearing her jewels. No one would go near them; they did not retrieve the bodies. It's actually quite beautiful. *In its fashion.*"

"What happened?"

"Relief workers finally got them down. There were elephants all around, clearing debris. Even the elephants stopped what they were doing to gather there! Around the spirit tree. Amazing. I was told this story by a very straight-arrow guy who works for Guerdon, so no one made it up. It is not an *urban legend.* Did you know Lew wanted to cut the tree down and bring it to Napa to re-plant? I think he wanted it for the Memorial. The government hasn't allowed it (so far!) because those kind of trees are nearly extinct. He asked me to intervene—I made a few inquiries, but they won't. They never will. Which is good for *you,* my Miss Joan, because if they'd allowed it, poof! There goes your Mem. But maybe Mr Koolhaas, with his *delinquent Dutch charm,* will convince them yet!"

XVIII

RAY

BIG Gulp drove Ray to the West Side to see the Friar. It took almost 2 hours through late-afternoon traffic. Ray kept talking about monorails.

He tired easily and didn't like to admit that he wasn't up to driving yet. It was a big car, a Monte Carlo that pulled a bit to the right. BG said he should get something new if the city gave him money but Ray was sentimentally attached. He'd give it a bath and a major tune-up, put on some new radials, patch up the upholstery. No need to trade her in.

Ghulpa looked fine in her royal-blue sari. They parked and she walked him to the entrance. His woman was kind and solicitous. He was proud to have her on his arm.

The hospital was like nothing he'd ever seen. The animals were called "patients" and waiting rooms were segregated for cats and dogs. The facility had an ER yet also treated cancers and genetic conditions. While Ray and Ghulpa waited, someone brought in a sick parrot; a few minutes later came a rabbit in its death throes. He wanted to laugh, but these were the folks who saved his dog's life.

The plant manager gave them a VIP tour (Nip/Tuck's shooting had garnered lots of press) of the pristine radiology suite, CT scanners and ultrasound, the ICU, incubators with nebulizers, blood and plasma banks. A dozen fully accredited surgeons were on call 24 hours a day. The manager said he had just come from tending a snake with pneumonia. Ray, dumbfounded and impressed, said, "Well, now I've heard everything."

Friar Tuck wasn't well enough to be brought out to a visiting room, so Ray said, "Let's bring the mountain to Mohammed." He was in a cage and squealed and shook when he saw his master. The old man's eyes moistened at the reunion. BG stood back with a toothy, lip-sheathed smile. Ray talked to him through the wire, saying "Don't you worry. You'll be home in no time." The doctor said "Friar" was doing real well but Ray winced at the long rail-road-track-stitched scar where he had been shaved. They'd put a titanium pin in his hip, and Ray joked he might want to come in for one of those himself. The doctor played along and said he'd do just as good a job as they would at Cedars or UCLA. Ghulpa brought sandesh wrapped in aluminum foil, Nip/Tuck's favorite. The medical men said that would be OK and the dog took a nibble, almost out of politeness, before spitting most of it out. Then he puked and one of the aides took over and told them not to worry, that it was the taste and smell that "set him off," and there were lots of things he would need to get "acclimatized" to.

The ACLU attorney met them at the appointed time. He gave the dog a friendly, cursory wave—just another client who stood to benefit from pending litigation. Before they left, standing in the lobby, the lawyer asked the plant manager to "ballpark" what the hospitalization was going to cost, "in toto." Ray goofed on him. "Now, there he goes—are you talking about Toto again from *The Wizard of Oz?* Cause *that* is one expensive pooch." The manager was hesitant to commit to a hard figure but said "probably in the neighborhood of 15,000." The Friar would have to go to rehab after being discharged—hopefully someplace close to Industry—for aquatic therapy. All at additional cost.

They followed Mr ACLU to Spago. Big Gulp had trouble keeping up with the silver Mercedes, whose driver yapped away on his cellphone instead of keeping tabs on her in his rearview. Ray slept and snored.

The beautiful Asian hostess greeted counsel like an old acquaintance. She sat them in the bright and leafy garden. The old man thought it an awfully fancy place for an ACLU fellow—weren't they supposed to be defenders of the poor? He wondered who was footing the bill. They were being treated like they'd won the lottery and Ray wasn't sure he liked that. After a glass of red, he loosened up and enjoyed the moment. Ghulpa excused herself and the lawyer began to speak of a case—"another break-in"—that had come to his attention. A man was bludgeoning and killing old women, then "having his way" with the bodies, after death. The police interrogated him and asked how the sex was, "on a scale of one to 10." The murderer said, "A 14. Your eyes would have rolled back in your head." Ray wondered why he was telling him this, as if it somehow related to his own case. Mr ACLU was probably going to represent that monster. Hadn't been read his Miranda's, or whatnot. Luckily, Big Gulp returned before any further history could be provided; the lawyer nodded gravely, summarizing a tacit gentleman's agreement that she would not be brought up to speed on the details of their mantalk. Instead, he embroidered, saying everyone had a destiny that couldn't be changed. He directed his words at Ghulpa, because of her Indian provenance. "Karma," he added. Implicit in the remark was that it was those old women's destiny to be slaughtered and raped, it was the old man's destiny to have his door broke down and his dog shot, and the *lawyer's* destiny to collect untold shitloads of $$$ for the inconvenience. *He's a slick, lowlife shyster but it's too late to change horses. Who has the strength. Anyhow, Big Gulp seems to approve, and right now she's running the show.*

He said his work for the ACLU was "mostly pro bono." Ghulpa didn't know what that meant but this time didn't ask. His main practice was libel and defamation and he taught at Loyola one night a week. Ray wanted to make sure the lawyer was aware that he hadn't yet agreed to sue the police. He said that he was. And he knew Ray liked cops. He told the couple "the action" wasn't personal, everyone made mistakes, he wasn't an enemy of the men in blue, on the contrary, he was a big supporter *(Who does he think he's kidding?)* but in this case a lawsuit could very well make another wrong-door break-in less likely to happen. He made it sound like suing the police was Ray's civic duty. The next time, there might be kids in there, he said. *Children* could get killed. It was all about forcing cops to be more "fastidious" with their intelligence. Ray wasn't the 1st person to have his door busted in by mistake. It happened mostly to inner-city families— to moms and babies—and was often "racial." Again, he looked toward Ghulpa. The police (in this case, "the LAPD, with an assist from the Sheriff's Department, Industry Station") needed to be held accountable. With an increasing sense that the Indian wore the pants and was on the money trail, he was careful to remain inclusive as he spoke, head oscillating between the 2 like a space heater. The attorney clearly couldn't have cared less about the details of their living arrangement but intuition told him that the woman in the sari would be his best advocate.

B Y the time they got home, it was 9 o'clock. Ray said he was "toast." Ghulpa made sure he took his vitamins and medication; he'd inadvertently skipped the afternoon dose. She fed him dal soup and tea with basil and cloves, then "pressed" his feet. A cultural thing. Boy, it felt good. She rubbed cinnamon oil on his calluses and gave him powdered seed of bastard teak with gooseberry juice. *It will make you young again.*

The landlord knocked, apologizing for the lateness of the hour. A man in a suit had stopped by earlier with a note; she didn't feel safe leaving it at their door. BG grabbed the envelope and smiled, waving the woman away. After the landlord left, she accused her of intercepting a private "communiqué." She held it to the light to see if it had been "tampered with." Watching her, he smiled. "That's a busy body," said Ghulpa, carefully separating the words.

Ray settled into the easy chair and opened the handwritten letter. It was from Detective Lake, who said he was "at the scene" shortly after the "incident" occurred. He was sorry for everything that happened, and he'd dropped by the hospital a few times to visit, but Ray was with his doctor or asleep, and he "didn't want to disturb you any more than we already have." A business card with a gold shield was stapled to the watermarked stationery—classy. He wrote that Ray should call any of the numbers if he wanted to talk, including the cell (he'd used a pen to add his home phone). The old man thought it a kind gesture; nothing suggested ulterior motive. Strictly *mano a mano.* The detective added that he was a dog lover, and even asked after the Friar.

"If there's anything I can do for you," he reiterated, "please don't hesitate to call."

XIX.

CHESTER

THE chiropractor said he might very well have nerve damage and referred him to an orthopedist. Which freaked him out because he'd never had pain like this, pain that migrated and stabbed, pulsed and tingled, and didn't relent. It actually kept him up at night—*definitely* not a good sign. Plus he was narco-constipated.

The entire culture was geared toward intractable pain: every magazine, every paper and electronic news show featured chronicles of incurable, idiopathic, undiagnosable agony. There was a lot Chess was suddenly learning about, and none of it was wonderful: like how a body in constant anguish somehow rewired itself neurologically, *becoming addicted to the pain itself,* which made the cycle nearly impossible to break. The field of pain management had become sexy, like software in the early 90s. Tekkies and pharmacologists were all over it—the eroticized iPain index was riding high. *Pain*tients were being treated with off-label potpourris of antidepressants, antipsychos, and antiseizure meds, which alchemized to fake out the nervous system, convincing it that everything was copacetic. Now here he was, one of the gang. *The gang that couldn't shit straight.* That's how fucked up *his* karma was.

For now, Chess was in Hydrocodone World—the muscle relaxants and anti-inflammatories didn't really count. It was Vicodin Nation: you could download Vike (swoosh!) RAPsodies to your Nano or have the dope FedEx'd with Vi@gr☺ and V@1ium from weirdass gray zone Internet pharmacies impossible to call back—impenetrably virtual. Flip on the tube and watch real-life addicts score Vs off dying cancer dads on *Intervention,* or firemen boosting Vs on *Rescue Me,* or a chick who feeds her habit by multiple pharmacy/doctor-shopping for *V*s on DVDs of *Six Feet Under.* It bled from cable to network: a cancelled NBC meller fea-

tured a pill-popping priest *(Episcopal—Vicodin, 500 mg),* and Fox
had an Emmy juggernaut about a cranky, genius MD *(Brit playing American—Vicodin ES, 750 mg),* each with backstories justify-
ing their reasons to indulge. Like you needed one. It was enough
that the key grips, writers, producers, and directors were users,
making 10s of millions, buzzed out of their skulls! Well, maybe
the grips weren't making millions but they sure were fuckin
happy. Just like the good old coke days. Only now it was legal.

Chronic pain was a *serious* mindfuck. Chess had panic attacks
during the day and broke sweat, claustrophobic in his own body.
It'd been less than 2 weeks but already he understood why people
killed themselves—nowhere to run, nowhere to hide. Weed
didn't even help (maybe a little) and that spooked him because
he'd always heard that maryjane killed pain, that's what the old-
time lymphoma *Brigadoon* hospice brigade was into. It made
sense that people turned to magnets and biofeedback and guided-
imagery and all manner of fool's gold voodootoxins but he definitely didn't want to die like Coretta Scott King in some beachy
New Age Tijuana hellhole. Chester Scott King! He watched a
segment on *60 Minutes* about a lawyer—an attorney!—in New
Jersey, an affable dude who'd undergone futile back surgery. The
guy wound up moving to Florida and was so wigged about keeping an emergency stash that he took extraordinary measures (who
wouldn't?) but the Feds accused him of hoarding pills with counterfeit subscriptions—and gave him 20 years for trafficking!
Where's Limbaugh's lawyer when you need him! He refused to
plea bargain because it would have been tantamount to a criminal
confession *plus* it'd be harder for him to get meds on the street.
The motherfucker was already in a *wheelchair,* aside from *addi-
tionally* being diagnosed with MS! The irony was that upon incarceration the state had been forced to provide the martyred, hapless
junkie with a morphine patch. At least now he was chill, though
Chess wondered why the street docs hadn't done that in the *1st*
place. (The report didn't touch on that.) The new prisoner could
not *believe* he had been taken away from his family; his old lady
couldn't even bear to tell their kids that Daddy'd been jailed. *60*

Minutes interviewed one of the men who locked him up and it was so scarily obvious the guy didn't have a *clue*—he seriously thought that the fucker was dealing! He said there was no way a person could be taking 25 painkillers a day, and Chess knew that was *total bullshit*. The more he thought about it, the more pissed he became at his "friend." He was in a hallucinatorture tailspin, all because of Maurice the Jew's fucked up little stunt.

A lawyer phoned who'd heard about his case. Chess didn't ask but figured someone on *FNF* had tipped the guy in exchange for a kickback. (Pretty much how the world worked.) The timing was good because he'd been thinking about getting some advice—giving Marj a jingle to find out who handled his stepdad's legal shit (he didn't want to bother Karen Knotts again)—so that was fine and dandy. Actually *better,* because when he called his mom he didn't want to be coming from a needy place. Didn't want her to worry. Just keep it simple and ask for bread. Though maybe now he wouldn't have to. Maybe he wouldn't but would anyway.

Chess was surprised when the caller said he had successfully represented "other folks" who'd been cavalierly mistreated (translation: grievously injured) by the unsolicited intrusion of reality shows. "I ain't talking *American Idol* either." He said they were "lower than the lowest tabloids," and nobody ever had to have PSS therapy or surgery because of something written about them on Page Six. At least not that he knew of. It hadn't occurred to Chess that an army of maimed, humiliated "contestants" was out there but when he listened to the guy, of course it made total sense. The litigator ran down some of the cases: the guy who was told by bogus airport security that he'd have to lie on the conveyor and pass through the tube along with his briefcase and computer (he got whacked by something inside); the honeymooners in Vegas who checked into their room only to discover a "dead prostitute" in the bathtub. "The newlyweds didn't think it was so funny. Nor did I." He went on to insinuate that these people were lavishly compensated for their physical and emotional stress, "made whole, and more so," and for the 1st time since the Night of the Living Pantwet, Chess began to feel better.

They made an appointment for brunch. (Another "My Favorite Weekend" opportunity, and the meal would be *gratis*.) He told Chess to make sure he saved medical receipts and that he ended *any contact whatsoever* with the producers of *Friday Night Frights*. Henceforward, he should refer *all calls* to his representative—if, of course, Chess agreed to the offer, which he did on the spot. That pleased the lawyer, who then asked if the production company had "compensated" him for being on the show. Chess said yes but he hadn't cashed the check. "That was smart," he said. "*Very* smart. Keep it in the drawer for now. My mama always told me to keep it in my drawers!" Adding, "We're going to be scribbling some zeroes on that 15. A whole *lot* of em."

THE doorbell rang, and Chess was surprised to see it was Laxmi. She looked pale and distraught, avoiding his eyes. He invited her in. There was a haze of smoke. She asked if she "could have some." They finished the roach and he rolled a fresh joint.

She was braless. She wore all kinds of layers and carried a bumpy, red rubber mat. Her nipples popped the fabric like pebbles, and she had post-yoga breath, like a dog's. She watched him limp to the couch before bursting into tears.

"I am *so sorry,* Chester. I *so* didn't think it was going to be like that! I never even *saw* that show before! I thought it was going to be *totally innocuous*. I am not even *speaking* to Maurie, I am *so upset.*" She started to cry again and he passed the reefer.

It was nice that she came over. Kind of brave. He never understood the allure Maurie held—maybe she was just dumb. Laxmi reminded him of that actress Heather Graham; he wondered if Heather Graham was dumb. He boiled water for green tea.

She settled down a bit then nervously said she had something for him. Laxmi pulled out 5 hundred-dollar bills, the amount she admitted to having been paid for being an Accomplice on *FNF.* He was tempted to take it but was mindful of what the attorney said, which made it easier for Chess to turn her down and even look gallant. The offer touched him though. She was pretty much a mess and he could relate. He sat on the couch and reassured her that he was OK. He downplayed the physical trauma side.

They smoked the weed and got mellow. It felt comfortable and right. About half an hour went by. Not much talking. A light breeze through the window. Suddenly she grinned ear-to-ear, like a kid with a fidgety secret; he thought it was one of those passing dope-flash insights but Laxmi said she had something *else* for him—"and this time, you're not going to say no." She reached into her bag to retrieve a silk pouch she had made herself. Chess uncinched the drawstring; a filigreed ivory elephant lay inside. Laxmi said it was Ganesha and she really wanted him to have it because that's what *he* was, a protector, he'd protected her in that obscenely ludicrous moment. Standing between her and the moronic actor, Chess had remained vigilant, with full intent to guard her against all harm. She was really "hit hard" by that—Chester's paternal instincts—and it tripled her guilt over being involved. He turned the sculpted animal over in his hand, inspecting it with a *Chesshire* smile. He thanked her. Laxmi asked about his back. She said that she didn't live so far away; she could help with errands or take him to the doctor if he needed.

She left. There had been some awkwardness (for him) because he thought there was maybe a sex vibe going on, but if that were true neither was up for it just yet. *Fine and dandy.* There were lots of "layers"—still, it was *very* cool. Like the lawyer's call, it gave him something to look forward to, to feel better about. Endorphins or pheromones or whatever had kicked in and for the moment he was cum-drunk and pain-free.

Chester held the elephant in his hand. It was nicked here and there but intricately painted and carved. It looked old, and made him trip on his mother and the trinkets she used to keep around the house. Maybe Laxmi's dad had given it to her and she was passing it on, or maybe it was something she just wanted to get rid of. That would still be OK. The bottom line was she didn't have much money, and any kind of gift would have meaning. *Give it to me.* Laxmi was the goddess of good vibes and good fortune, Ganesha the "remover of obstacles." The whole thing was yummy. All was forgiven. *All apologies.*

He began to laugh at his crushy high school machinations, his paranoia and frisky wheel-spinning, and the laugh soon became a full-on hacking pothead jag.

XX.

MARJORIE

SHE went to the Travel Gals but Trudy was on holiday. Nigel said he could help. Marj told him she was interested in visiting Bombay and he got out the brochures.

Nigel was young and energetic, and "totally obsessed" with India. He said Mumbai—that's what he called it—was "very cool but insane" and there were *so many* other places to consider: the holy city Varanasi (formerly Benares; he said they burned corpses there "24/7, except for the *kiddies,* who for some reason get *wrapped,* not burned," before backing off, admitting that the 35-hundred year old mecca was probably an "extreme destination" for someone Marj's age. But the old woman remembered it was where Jesus had taught. Bodh Gayā ("Hello, Dalai!"), Kerala (*"fabulous* ayurvedic spas"), and the Konkan coast, pearl-shopping in Hyderabad ("It's like their Silicon Valley"), the *"superdeluxe* spas and 6-star hotels" of Jaipur, and of course, Agra, jewel of the Taj Mahal. ("Oh my God! They've opened it at *night* now, whenever the moon's out. You *have* to go at night. That was *so smart* of them.") He was literally all over the map. Goa was a Portuguese beach town with beautiful churches but "it skews a bit toward the ravers. Lots of crazy Israelis, and *tons* of Indians! But *super* friendly." Nigel said it was he and his "husband's" favorite place. She brought up Calcutta, which he said was "dirty beyond words" and a place to avoid "unless you're into *rasgulla* and Mother Teresa." If she *was,* he would *definitely* recommend the Grand (where Nigel and his spouse had bivouacked). Calcutta had an incredible zoo as well, "if animals are your thing. But careful! People still get eaten by tigers!" He laughed. "Actually, though, Calcutta—it has another name now but I am *so burnt out* on the musical name chairs; it's like 'cold cuts' or 'Katherine Kuhlman' or *whatever*—Calcutta actually is supposed to have an *amazing* kind of intellectual/bohemian/café scene. We just didn't have the greatest time there because Demetrius got sick."

He asked if she wanted anything to drink because one of the kids was making a Starbucks run. Nigel put in his order, adding that Calcutta also had a very cool movie studio.

Do you want to go to Bangalore? Then he sang the question, substituting Bangalore for San José. *Or Hampi? Are you into Buddhism?* If she was, she *had* to visit Bodh Gayā, birth- or deathplace of Buddha ("I always forget which"). "My husband bribed a guard so we could sleep under the bodhi tree—that's where Buddha got enlightened. Ask me how cold it was! Ask me if there were a million mosquitoes and mutant locusts that tried to wriggle through our netting like little circus strongmen, and I'll enlighten you! Let's scratch Bodh Gayā off the Marjorie wishlist! But Dharamsala! That's where the Dalai Lama lives when he isn't doing his World Tour Thing. You might even have a Richard Gere moment. Dharamsala is the anti-*Chicago!*" She didn't know half what he was talking about but found him a delight nevertheless. Then, thumbing more intensely through the literature piled in front of him, Nigel said that Rajasthan was *awesome,* and there were *amazing* medieval deserts, fortresses, and elephants galore. The hotels were "10-star castles in the sand like the Rambagh Palace and, there's, like, a *ton* of Oberois."

The girl finally came with his latte and Nigel grew serious.

"I don't know if you heard about this, Marjorie, but it might be something that interests you. It was even on *60 Minutes.* You know, the *hospitals* in India are really giving *American* facilities a run for their money. Demetrius and I—we got married last year in Maui—watched a whole thing on TV. There's one in Chennai—*excuse me,* it's now *Madras*—called the Apollo, like the theater in Harlem? It is *amazing!* We are talking a 7-star hotel. It is *so* not depressing, like hospitals in the States? Where no one even knows you're a patient and you can like totally *expire* while waiting for someone to help you go to the bathroom! Or the nurse is one of those death-angel serial killers! In *Bangkok,* when you go to the ER, they meet you at the car. Even if you just have the *flu.* They *sit* with you while you fill out the *forms.* They have signs that say, 'If You've Been Waiting More Than 15 Minutes, Please Let Us Know.' America should be *ashamed*. Marjorie, do you *know* how many people die from *bugs* they pick up in hospitals? The statistics are *so frightening*. They're 'superbugs'—antibiotics won't even *kill* them anymore. (I *so* think the drug companies are behind it. My husband's a rep, and *he* said they've probably already developed the killer antibiotic but they're going to let tons of people *crash and burn* before they unleash it. Just like the oil business: supply and demand. Forget your Redux, Seroquel, and Vioxx blues: superbugkillaz gonna drive a bull market! That's what Demetrius says!) The *Indian* healthcare system, from this report they had with Mike Wallace, is *so much better* and *cleaner*. I mean, all the doctors are trained in America but go back because they want to help their country. Isn't that *so* great? Helping your country! What a concept! They do *quintuple bypasses*. They do *facelifts*. Oh my God, Elaine Young just died—the Beverly Hills realtor with the botched cheek implants? She had *46* operations, and her plastic surgeon killed himself! She finally grew a tumor where the silicon had migrated, she looked like Babydoll from hell! And everything costs like a 10th of what it costs here! I mean, I *so* can't wait for Michael Moore to *rip* the healthcare system in this country! (Demetrius said that's his next target.) Michael Moore should go to India for a gastric bypass while he's at it! Did you see how much weight Peter Jackson lost? I wonder if he'll put it back on. They always do. But Demetrius said Michael Moore is going to make a movie about how fucked—*I'm* sorry, honey, how *messed up* our healthcare system is. Michael Moore isn't everyone's cup of tea but he makes *wonderful* movies. All politics aside, the quality of work *is* amazing: they showed the hospital rooms on *60 Minutes* and they're all enormous *suites,* with stand-alone claw-footed tubs! You would die! (If they let you, which they *won't*.) Fit for maharajahs! And the *marble*. Marjorie, you cannot believe. And everyone's, like, a *registered nurse*. You know how in America no one cares? How they're all *surly orderlies,* with criminal records? (My husband was just in the hospital for a bunionectomy.) They actually *stole* from him! They stole Demetrius's iPod! I am *completely* trying to convince my mom to have her hip replacement surgery in Delhi or Mumbai. My mom's had 6 epidurals, 3 on both sides, and now they're shooting her spine up with Botox. Her back looks like Elaine Young's face! She has an *amazing* threshold for pain. *60 Minutes* showed this American woman in Delhi who was having it—they do this thing where they put a silver cap on the hipbone instead of sawing it off—I forgot what the procedure's called, it's only allowed in the States by experimental trial. That is *so typical* of the FDA! I mean, it's *all* about greed. If something's cutting edge—and Europe or *wherever* is *always* cutting edge—I mean, do you think the paranoid American doctors would try to sew a woman's face back on? That woman in France whose face got torn off by a dog? And now, she's a *fox.* Demetrius and I *love* her. She still *smokes her Gauloises*! How French is *that.* I'm telling you, that cadaver donor was a *hottie!* The Americans would be so terrified! Of being sued! But it's not their fault, it's the *system's.* Anyway, the hip procedure is *completely* legal there, and it *works,* and the recovery time is *so much faster* because it's *so less invasive.* Instead of costing 40,000, it costs 8. And they don't pressure you to leave! You know how in America, because insurance companies are *so crazed,* they're always hustling you out the door? I mean, it used to be when women had their babies they were told to stay in the hospital a few days to rest. Now they kick you out the same day! Like some Cambodian dropping a kid in the paddies! (Cambodia's a *great* place to go, by the way. *Super* tourist-friendly. Cambodia and Vietnam are totally our hottest destinations.) They were trying to get Demetrius discharged while he was still groggy from surgery! They wanted me to take him home! I said to that mean black queen, 'Mary, he's not going *anywhere.'* Got a sleeping bag and stayed right in the room. He was in *so much pain* and they only gave him a Darvocet! Until I did my Shirley MacLaine *Terms of Endearment* number. So I don't know, Marjorie, I just wanted to mention it in case you were thinking of having anything done, because the *best* part is that after surgery the lady we saw on TV was ordered by her doctors to go to a resort and lay on the beach! It was all part of the prescription! 'Go to a resort! Doctor's orders!' And the *best* resorts are only like $140 a night."

Nigel said October would be a good time, or January, to avoid the monsoons. You *definitely* want to avoid the monsoons. When the old woman mentioned the Taj Mahal Palace where she stayed as a girl, Nigel lit up.

"Oh my God, the Taj is the *best*. But you have to stay in the old wing. Demetrius and I were there and Cameron Diaz, Bill Clinton, and the Australian Prime Minister had just swept through. I think Wild Bill Hickock and Cammy Tell Me True maybe shoulda got somethin started! The Taj is *amazing*. The service is *unbelievable*. And the boutiques! They have a Louis Vuitton *and* a Burberry. I almost bought one of those 7,000 dollar cellphones—the Vertu? With the 24 hour concierge button? No matter what country you're in, you can ring them up and have a pizza delivered. They could probably get a slice to Elaine Young! Or tickets to a movie, DVDs, whatever. Demetrius was about to *die*. Do you use the Internet? Probably not, huh. My husband *loved* it, because we didn't bring our computers, but every room had *huge* flat plasma screens—just plunk yourself down on the bed and use the remote to get your E. The Indians *so* have the tekkie thing wired—we outsource *everything* to them. I heard they were so busy they were outsourcing *outsource* jobs! Oh! They're outsourcing *babies*! Women from the States are renting out their wombs! Marjorie, I am *so serious*. The Indians are *amazing*—more amazing than the Chinese. Well, maybe not, but damn *close*."

Marj asked when Trudy was coming back. He scrunched his face and said he wasn't sure; she was having health problems. "I keep telling her to go to India!" She didn't press. They talked some more about the Taj and Nigel went rummaging for something. He returned with a DVD he said was made by the hotel on its centenary. "But you need to give it back, Marjorie. Promise? They're really hard to get and it's the only one we have."

She took a different route to Beverlywood so she wouldn't have to pass Riki's store. She couldn't bear to see it locked up with all the wilting garlands and tattered memorials.

XXI.

JOAN

SHE was late, as usual. On the way to her appointment she must have passed 3 roadside tributes. They were all over LA now, commemorating places where pedestrians had been struck down, or fatal car crashes and robberies had occurred, and thus far the city had benevolently let them be. Some vanished within weeks, while others were maintained for years, carefully tended and refurbished by loved ones. (The mems lasting the longest were usually for kids who'd been run over near schools.) She was always dumbfounded by their simple eloquence—suddenly revolted by her own pimp-ride, high-end vanity project. She'd never be able to speak in the demotic language of the people; there would always be the arcanely contaminative architectural babel injecting itself like syntactic bacterium into what should have been simplicity itself. There was even a new crop of art photographers who tried to make a name for themselves by documenting the funeral venues, as if those sites were quaintly worthy of pretentious scholarship. It was exploitational, not Egglestonian, a bloodless catalogue of macabre, trivializing juvenilia. Meet the Folkers.

Joan was lunching with a group at Architects Without Borders, a nonprofit that built shelters for victims of the "Boxing Day Tsunami," now redeploying its efforts to New Orleans. Average White Band (which Barbet insisted calling them) had joined together with a slew of organizations—Shelter for Life, Relief International, Architecture for Humanity—to put up cement-block homes in Sri Lanka, a thousand or so for around 15-hundred dollars each. The gang had experience building in places like Bosnia, Afghanistan, and Iran (earthquake-stricken Bam, which Barbet said should now have an exclamation point after it, like a Lichtenstein). Ever since ARK lost a competition to design transitional housing in Kosovo to Gans & Jelacic, Barbet had chilled on altruism, sending Joan out as emissary—it was good for networking. Katrina itself had spawned a cottage *(shack)* industry of moveable "Southern venacular" crib prototypes from a pair who called themselves HELP (Housing Every Last Person). *Barf.*

Even Mayne and Libeskind (and MVRDV, Huff + Gooden, Hargreaves, UN Studio, ad nauseam) were getting into the act. "What a surprise," said Barbet. Shigeru Ban talked about making digs out of cardboard tubes and plastic beer crates, modeled after homes that sprang up after the Kobe quake; "durable prefabs" and "flat pack" Future Shacks were on the boards. Someone even dared to mention Prouvé's aluminum/steel Tropical House; Joan was ready to kill. She knew it was mostly PR talk and no action—starchitects and borefucks were good at that. The New Urbanists would prevail. Sketching out Sub-Saharan HIV clinic thumbprints or collapsible origami-like bungalows (*anything* but blue tarp tents or Fleetwood-trailered FEMA Village agglomerations) was a way for Joan to distract herself from the demands of the Freiberg Mem, and do something beneficial in the process.

S HE met him in his bungalow at the Bel-Air. Joan was a little nervous and had already played out the scenario of him wanting to fuck. She ran the loop in her head as if preparing for a court trial or presidential debate. She was pretty sure she'd be able to resist.

Lew was genteel, having slipped off the alpha E-ring he wore around groups. After cordial smalltalk, he asked her to watch something on television: an amateurish CNN-style montage of what the tsunami had wrought. The famous hotel pool getting flooded. A pasty-skinned old man clinging tenuously to a railing as the fatal waters rose. Crowded buses rocketing like skateboards into floating taxicabs. Assorted indistinguishable riverroar flotsam. Then, the iconic image of that body outside the Astrodome: incongrously spliced in, rank and spookily clownish.

A soundtrack, courtesy of Bobby Darin, accompanied the watery parade:

First the tide rushes in . . . plants a kiss on the shore—

"My son put that together. I guess it's his way of dealing—with whatever. It didn't make me happy."

"How old is he?"

"14."

"It's just that age. Teen angst."

"Yeah, well, I'm *my* age." He sighed. "It's creative, anyway. I think he got the clips from MTV. Burned them on his Power-Book. Or whatever they do."

"Was he close to his uncle?"

"Very." He ejected the disc. "Mr Darin: nice touch. Or maybe it was Kevin Spacey."

Joan changed tack, deciding to be heretical.

"I know this is a weird segue but it's something I wanted to ask. Architects are funny. Sometimes we work in a vacuum, and that's good. Depends on the client. We *like* vacuums; we like to fill them up. *(Oops. Wrong metaphor.)* But sometimes we ignore the obvious, and that's *not* good. Is there anything you envision for the Memorial, Lew? We've talked a lot, but is there anything that's persistently in your head? When you wake up in the middle of the night. Or when you're brushing your teeth."

He appeared to be musing. Then:

"Not really. Something . . . simple—elegant. Not too much bullshit." His mouth tensed at the word, before softening to a smile. "Big help, huh?"

"Yeah," she said, without irony. "It actually is."

He led her to the dining area. She sat at the table and he brought over wine. The fuck-loop streamed through her brain— she flashed on that hotel pool flood—before quickly shutting off.

"Joan—I see all these . . . Holocaust memorials, and . . . the *thousand slabs*. The thousand crosses in Berlin. Oklahoma: the 168 Chairs, the 168 Seconds of Silence. I *hate* that—*literal* shit. One of

the WTC things was only going to be open to the public from the
exact minute the *1st* plane *hit* to the exact minute the 2nd tower
fell. Another of the ... *proposals* had these *lights*—I don't know
how many—but it was the number of people in the towers that
couldn't be identified by DNA! The *92* trees native to New York
planted in the soil of the *92* nations the victims came from, the
wall with *92* Messages of Hope."

"I know," said Joan, simpatico. "Paul Murdoch. He's here in
LA. Flight 93 in Pennsylvania. A 93-foot-tower with 40 wind
chimes inside. One for each passenger and crew member. 40
groves of mixed maple trees the closer you get to the site. Then, 40
rows of—"

"*The 1,776-foot tower.* Make me wanna holler!" (The last, he
shouted like Eddie Cantor.) "And that's not even going to remotely *happen*. That's why I like Andy—Goldsworthy. Cause
he'll do something outside the box. Something *natural*. I'd like to
do Goldsworthy and someone ... something *else,* more permanent, or permanent-*looking*. Andy can do his cairns or his water
and stones and snakes—I *think* he's going to use water, which I
don't object to. We've got 400 acres and the actual Mem is gonna
be a pretty small 'footprint,' as they like to say. But I want it
churchy. Like stumbling across the ruins of a church. Now,
whether that's at the end of a grove, or an allée, or up on a hill—
fuck, I don't know, Joan. I just don't want to wind up with something honoring a quarter of a million dead people! You can't *do*
that shit with any kind of literality. Is that a word? I mean, *how?*
Did you know that a hundred thousand people died in Sumatra in
15 minutes? One of my guys said the quake was so strong, it actually affected the earth's *rotation*. How do you memorialize *that?*
You know what I'm saying, honey? What happened to my
brother and his wife, and their *kids,* and to *me* and my *family*—is
personal. And for that very reason, the scale should be intimate.
For *any* fuckin reason. A prayer. Let the world fucking carp. The
world is *always* going to carp and piss and moan. The world wants
Trump and Disney—America wants to sell tram-tickets to ceme-
teries with *bling*. Hallowed ground don't mean a thing if it ain't

got that swing! Do you know how many calls we still get about Katrina? To help with that shit? Where is George fucking Bush? My brother didn't die in *St Bernard Parish,* he died on the coast of India. I mean, is that *OK?* Does that not meet with everyone's *approval?* It's obscene. *Do I know what it means to miss New Orleans?* Maybe. But sorry! Samuel's in Elysian Fields—and *his* Fields ain't got a Looziana zip. Wanna hear a Katrina joke? My pilot told it to me—man, he's dark! A drowned horse walks into a Texas bar. Bartender says, 'Why the long, bloated, maggoty face?' Oh, you don't get it! Hey Joan, know how many people died over there? *230,000.* There's another *50,000 missing.* And those are only guesstimates. Know how many died in *Pakistan?* 80 thou. Know how many people swallowed water in Louisiana? What was it, 900? Losing the city *itself* was the fundamental . . . *that's* what's tragic. And everybody knows it. *That* makes sense. The money poured into the tsunami? They don't even know how to disperse it! There's such a surplus, they've been asking people to divert to *other causes.* That's how fucked up and confused everyone is. The relief agencies and the schmucks who run em are bankrupt, spiritually, morally, and every other kinda which way. A guy lost his entire family of 37 in Ban Bang Sak—send computers, Bono! You know, I have *zero* interest in donating PCs to all the little Sambos before they rape and burn each other. They *will* be raped and burned. I don't *want* to save rifle-toting black children! Let Bono knock himself out! Does that make me a bad guy? I *employ* people. Right? Thousands of fucking people. Families. I don't renege on healthcare *or* pension promises. Right? And I want to honor my brother and his wife and in so doing, honor those who died. You know what, Joan? I don't *believe* 'We All Have AIDS.' *I* don't—not so far as my doctor's told me. Sharon Stone can suck my 5,000,000,000 dollar cock and write a song from the coal mines of menopause and go talk about it on *GMA.* I *do* have a foundation, but it's not about *relief,* it's about *cancer research.* My mother, Mamie, had leukemia. When she died, that was worse than 200,000 people getting swept away, OK? Can you understand? I mean, how do you . . . *represent* that? This isn't 'We Are the

World,' this is she *was* my world. And now it's about *He Was My Brother*. Samuel Freiberg, RIP. Someone said I should put a plaque up for whatever we wind up doing. Joan, do we need a fucking plaque?"

"No, Lew. You don't need a plaque."

"FEMA can't even figure out what to do with the money *Congress* gave them. It's so radically fucked up that Congress is now asking for money *back*. Anyway, I got an email from one of my Inner Circle people at Guerdon—a sweet guy." He riffled some papers on the table, then quoted. " 'I have come into deep waters, and the flood sweeps over me. I am weary of my crying . . . rescue me from the mire, and do not let me sink.' I mean, sentimental bibleshit, right? So, I'm just gonna do my thing—with a little help from my friends. I think any other way would be arrogant. *My* thing. People *will* have their 'fuck that rich asshole' moment— they've *been* having it! 'He's only honoring 2 people!' The public won't be allowed to stroll around and drop their trash . . . *poor babies*. No iPod commentaries! No gift shop! They'll just have to sweat it out. Jerk off to the Iraqi civil war or the latest Amber Alert. Or see a Korean horror film instead. Cause all anyone wants is a gore fix. I sound like Howard Beale, huh? Great movie, *Network*. So *get* your tragedy fix, but not from me. I ain't no dealer! I'm not a healer either. *But why isn't Lew Freiberg helping to build new levees?* Because *Ted Turner* will take care of it. Leave it to the Three Stooges: Carter, Clinton, and funk-breathed HW! Leave it to Halliburton! You know what? My *foundation* sends money, but I funnel it to Humane Society International. They're the folks—a lot are Buddhists, by the way, like Esther was—who deal with animals. You know, animals saved a mess of people in the tsunami and wound up shit's creek, literally. *People* can *help* each other but *animals can't*. Animals are 'sentient beings' too, right? That's the big Buddhist phrase. My sister-in-law was a pretty serious practitioner of Zen-whatever. We had our moments, but Esther was all right. Helped stabilize my brother. So *that's* where I choose to send my money. To HSI! And if folks're gonna cry, *fuck em*. People *will* cry, that's what they *do*. That's what they're *good* at. But at the end of the day we got 400 acres. You've seen it, Joan. At the end of the day, long after we're dead and gone, there'll *still* be 400 acres and 'the ruined church.' What I'm calling the Ruined Church. And it's going to be a sacred space. Esther loved that phrase. 'Sacred space.' And that *sacred space* will speak volumes for all the suffering of people *and* animals. You know what else disgusts me?"

"Tell me, Lew."

"Newsvultures standing on some tsunami beach—those Big Wave anniversary reports are just nice excuses get some Phuket R & R—saying—*intoning*—'No one can explain why some areas have received *bounty* and others have *slipped through the net.*' Right. *Right.* Well, that's just *the way it is.* Same as it ever was. Always was, always will be. *That's* 'duality.' Buddhism 101. *No one can fucking explain.* Or *splain,* as Ricky Ricardo used to say. And guess what? No one should even *try.*"

He stood.

"Here's what I think."

"Tell me what you think," she said, girlishly.

"Let's get this party started."

XXII.

RAY

Ay left a message with the cop who sent the note, inviting him to drop by if he was ever in the neighborhood. 3 hours later, the detective knocked at his door.

He was in his early 50s, sandy-haired and red-faced. Funny, he reminded Ray of Robert Redford in that *Twilight Zone,* thicker and older of course, in a sport jacket instead of a uniform. Ghulpa seemed suspect of his visit and Staniel Lake ("My granddad was Daniel and my father was Stan, and yes, the kids called me 'cocker staniel' in school") picked up on it. He made it clear right at the beginning that he wasn't there as a representative of the department and whatever legal course Ray decided to take meant nothing to him. He said he was here for strictly personal reasons: though he didn't want to "talk it to death," he felt bad about what happened, plain and simple. BG made tea and offered to heat up prawns in grated coconut. The detective politely declined, indicating that he didn't want "to add to the paunch." He didn't really have much of a stomach, but his manner charmed them both.

Detective Lake kept it light.

Ray was again touched to hear he'd come to the hospital, and apologized for not being awake. "That was plain rude," he said.

Staniel laughed. "I was happy to see you get your rest."

He said that his father, a retired police officer, died about 2 years ago from emphysema in that very same place. Ray had a few choice words for the night shift's bedside manner and the detective mordantly chuckled. The assumption he already knew that his host was partial to the shield hung in the air; a tough old bird who wasn't litigation-happy. Nowadays, that was practically a miracle. Ray started to feel like a retired cop himself—one of the boys.

Staniel asked after the dog. The old man said he'd been to visit the Friar, who was on the mend and would probably be home in a couple of weeks. The guest was genuinely happy to hear it. "The night was a royal fuckup," he said, violating his own informal rule, once Ghulpa was out of earshot. (He dipped his voice so she wouldn't hear the vulgarity.) Ray thought that gutsy because anything the detective said might technically be used against him and his department. Not that Ray would ever break confidence, not in a million years, and Staniel Lake seemed to know it.

To be conversational, Ray said he used to live in Mar Vista, and how he once owned a miniature golf course; a magic shop; then a bigger place on Sepulveda called Ray Rausch's Game Emporium. How he'd lost everything in the slot-car craze of the late 60s after buying a miniature racetrack—Racer Ray's Indy 100. How he'd gambled away whatever savings he had. How he got divorced in '73 and lost contact with his kids. The grim years before going back to work at a hobby "hatch" in Montebello. (The old man covered a lot of ground. Even Ghulpa learned a few things she didn't know.) The owner of the place "up and died," leaving Ray the entire inventory, which he sold just in time: mostly trains and model planes. Kids were collecting different kinds of things now, computer-related. He couldn't pretend to even understand the gaming market anymore. But he'd done all right, he said.

By the time the detective got paged and had to run, Ray had been beating his gums for almost an hour. Later, he realized how lonesome he'd been for intelligent male companionship.

THAT night the old man had crazy dreams triggered by his pell-mell reminiscence. His bedroom got mixed up with the CCU, and the clinic Nip/Tuck was at. Joanie and Chester peered out from weird foliage, frozen at the ages when he left—3 and 7—and Ray began whimpering in his sleep. He awakened with a jolt when a lion sprang on his chest, and Ghulpa comforted him, fetching a cool, damp rag. He shook his head in dismay. With a sardonic smile, he told BG he had *her* to thank; she always regaled him with tales of man-eaters from the Gir Forest that she'd seen as a child at the zoo in Calcutta. She loved telling him the stories her parents recounted of lions that crept up on pilgrims who lay sleeping in camps, leaving only bloody saris behind. They'd walk right into houses and silently carry out children by the napes of their necks in the dead of night. Whenever there was something in the news about a little boy or girl who'd been stolen from her room, in California or Florida or wherever, then found murdered down the road or in a creek, Ghulpa's face darkened. She could never see the human hand.

"The lions," she'd whisper. "They are not stories!" She was defensive, eager to repel all argument. "It is still happening each year, in Bombay! In Delhi, in Calcutta!"

XXIII.

CHESTER

MAURIE kept leaving messages but Chess didn't feel like returning. He was moody and pissed. He still hadn't met with that attorney.

The bone doctor X-rayed and found nothing. He said Chess should probably see a neurologist for an MRI. He now had shooting pains in both hands and numbness in one of his thighs but wasn't sure if the numbness was "real" or some sort of byproduct of pain. He *hated* being a pain patient; when you spoke to doctors it was like you'd fallen down the rabbit hole—the *habit* hole—where all perception was up for grabs. In order to gauge your "distress," the nurses asked you to point to emoticons on a sliding scale: primitive renderings of faces that were smiling, indifferent, frowning, crying, screaming. It was infantile and regressive, demeaning and asinine. He saw his fellow travelers—the tired, poor, huddled asses of the waiting room—as losers, the low rung of doomed complainants in a new kind of hell. New to him, anyway. He was still a virgin, but pretty soon he'd be like one of those African girls forced into marriage that Oprah went to visit who were too young to give birth and wound up with fistulas from miscarriages, incontinent of feces and urine (Saint O gave them little purses with C-notes tucked inside; more than *he* would get)—soon he'd be turned out right and proper, gangbanged by the Ubangi pain tribe. Chess always imagined that if ever he got sick, it would be something definitive: a burst appendix, a kidney stone. Diabetes. Something *organic* that hadn't been *done* to him. As a joke, and for money! At least his jawbone wasn't rotting away from an OD of Fosamax.

WAITING for the neurologist, he thumbed a brochure that said 30,000,000 Americans suffered from chronic pain that was so bad they *wanted to die*. Then why was the FDA busy pulling meds? *Someone* wanted us to believe that if we took a vestige of Vioxx, a soupçon of Celebrex, a vial of vitamin C, a wicked wedge of Mom's apple pie, well, then, we were right behind the stroke/heart-attack 8 ball. Someone *really* wanted us to believe that iddy-biddy Bextra caused "fatal skin reactions"—what the fuck was *that,* terminal psoriasis? People just wanted to *feel* better. Had to be some Recondite Brand vs Generic showdown, with trillions at stake.

He flipped through *Reader's Digest, Metropolitan Home,* and *Surfrider.* Read an article about a woman on disability heading to a conference that she *organized.* Staying at the Grand Hyatt in Washington. Loved her room. Got vertigo and breathing problems from what she thought was the chlorinated water in the decorative pools. Wasn't the hotel's fault. Turns out she and who knew how many goddam thousands of others have something called *multiple chemical sensitivities* or *environmental illness.* Then there was a thing in *Elle* about a chick with "impingement syndrome" and decomposing cartilage. Her vertebrae were "slapping" against each other, bone spurs throttling nerve roots. Chess pictured barbed wire wrapped around fresh green stems from Whole Foods. The essay reinforced what he had learned: that chronic pain eventually became not a symptom but *a disease in itself.* Poor bitch wound up getting steroid injections right in the tailbone, which gave her "a faint beard and a kind of extreme PMS." Well, far out! The piece ended by informing the reader that an operation often created a worse problem than the one it set out to repair (thanks for the tip). In fact, there was new evidence that, in some cases, exploratory surgery *actually revitalized dormant cancers.* But none of it mattered to Chess, because by the time you were so miserably desperate that going under the knife seemed like a rational option, well, by then your central nervous system was already so welded to pain that nothing could break the cycle, not yoga, pot brownies, hypnotherapy, methadone, not beaucoup $, not *zip.* Even making love, as they used to put it, could mortally exacerbate whatever was wrong. George Clooney said he got the sniffles and leaked spinal fluid through his nose after getting injured on the set, but Chess wondered if he'd actually wrenched his back on a 12,000 dollar Lake Como Duxiana.

Chess had been online reading about useless surgical amphitheater interventions. Like the lady with bullet-proof pain whose bones kept crumbling; the drug she took cost $600,000 a year because her disease was so rare. Her joints broke like teenage hearts and they kept cutting her—the *doctors* were addicted—until she didn't want to live. Every putz and putter on the golf course had had a knee or back torpedoed—the drill and scalpel were supposed to be the last resort but greedy Hippocrats could never get enough. One guy's calcified endoskeleton was strangling a bundle of nerve-endings and the sonofabitch was still crawling to the bathroom 6 months after being carved. His blog said he was planning "death by cop"—get loaded, get naked, and run into traffic waving a gun. The Yahoo! watchdogs were probably gonna shut him down any day now. Could be too late.

When they called him in, the panic momentarily receded. The physician was a brawny, handsome guy of about 60 who looked like he could fix anything. They scheduled the MRI and Chess voiced some of his fears. "You have a very active imagination." He told the new patient not to worry, he'd dealt with far worse. Chess asked if in the meantime it was OK to get acupuncture and the doc said, "Sure, if it helps." What about a massage? "Nothing too vigorous." He even made one of those "happy ending" jokes but somehow it didn't grate. He gave him an Rx for sleeping pills, anti-inflammatories, muscle relaxants—and more painkillers. Percocet.

"And stay off the Internet," the doctor cautioned, smiling again as he left the room. "Sometimes too much information is *not* a good thing."

Chess put on his shirt.

XXIV.

MARJORIE

S HE watched the DVD that Nigel, "the travel gal," gave her—a *very* professional presentation, very *theatrical,* with the same high quality of those *Mystery!* shows on PBS. It starred a familiar-looking Indian actor (hosting). He was probably quite famous.

Marjorie was thrilled to see the hotel again. Sure, the interior had been modernized but *plus ça change,* as her daddy used to say; it seemed to have the exact same *feeling.* She remembered the name "Tata," they were like the Trumps of India, or the Rockefellers, actually, and still very much entrenched. (The Tatas were Zoroastrians, which the *Encyclopaedia Britannica* said was one of the oldest religions.) The family owned the Taj chain and even manufactured cars and trucks that bore their name. How divine it would be to rattle around in one's very own Tata! The film was interspersed with black-and-white stills showing how "the palace" looked in the 20s, 30s, and 40s—and how it looked in the early 50s, when she made her sojourn as a young girl.

Her mother had died of blood poisoning the year before and Dad thought it would be good to draw Marjorie out, salving the wound of premature loss. His idea, she thought in retrospect, was to draw them *both* out; such exodus being as essential to his emotional stability as to her own recovery and growth, a grandly dramatic gesture, the bold, father-daughter gesture of a lifetime, which she could never repay. (Revisiting their idyll was as close as she would come; sort of "interest" on the loan.) Marj knew he'd been to India twice before to buy fabric for the clothing and knickknack shop her parents owned in Massachusetts; the quality of Bombay silk was astonishingly good, the tailors like none others on Earth. In America, he could resell garments at a 10-fold markup. It was actually his wife who had the idea, and because he took Marj to places where the married couple had 1st shared so many intimate joys of discovery, the trip with his daughter was tinged with heartbreak. For Marj, though, it was the most romantic thing in the world. Now she knew better, but at the time, a widower's frisson of pain and pleasure never crossed her mind: as they toured in private cars, he'd remark, "This is where your mother loved to people-watch," "This is where Mom had her tea and watched the ships," "This is the museum she adored," "This is where your mother took her shoes off and prayed along with native worshipers."

The trip had such a dreamy quality that she'd begun to think she had imagined it all, until she saw the marvelous little film. Bless dear Nigel for that! (She had lived with it in her head for so long.) Not only did the clangorous sounds and smells of India waft back to her but those of her father as well, the wind-chime laugh and the clearing of his throat, the cigar smoke that permeated his woolly, pleated three-piece, and clung like the most comforting cologne, the size of his hands and look of his fingers (a slight indentation on one of the nails), the kindness and almost mystical sadness in and around the eyes, the punctiliousness of his dress, his unadumbrated curiosity, and thirst for experience, his solicitous manner toward others—he never turned a beggar down, marveling in a most uncynical way at the ingenuity of their "coin extraction techniques"—but mostly, his tenderness toward *her,* his dearest child, green apple of his eye, sassy replica of departed wife, his sugarplum girl, his Marjorie Morningstar, one day to become Marjorie Rausch Herlihy née Donovan. From all the terrible things she heard on the news, she was beginning to think her dad was the best who'd ever lived, or that maybe fathers were just different now. She even remembered clutching him close when the driver took them to the section of town, high on a hill, where Parsis—Zoroastrians!—brought their dead to an open room to be devoured by vultures. (It was impossible to see anything though, but the very *idea!*) She thought of that poor boy, suddenly bereft of Riki, dear, innocent Riki, and the tears welled up. Soon she would have to go to the wretched store, that claptrap mausoleum with its soggy, decaying shrines and relics, to find him.

T HE doorbell rang. It was a 30ish man in a stylish suit.
"Mrs Herlihy?"
She blanched.
Was it bad news about Joan or Chester?
"I'm Lucas Weyerhauser. Am I catching you at a bad time?"
"I don't think so!" she said, slightly agitated.
"Good. This is something that's a lot of fun for me—and I hope it'll be fun for you! In fact, I *know* it will. May I come in?"
Instinctively, she closed the door a bit, narrowing the space between them, not to be rude, but to let the man know she was a savvy city dweller, despite her age.
"Well," she said, with a small smile. "What is it?"
"I *completely* understand," he said respectfully. "That's *fine.* I can tell you from right here."
He turned and curtly waved to a fellow in a chauffeur's uniform who stood beside a dark sedan. On signal, the driver got back in the car.
"You play the lottery, don't you?"
"Why, yes."
"Now, how'd I know that?"
He winked. She was at a not-unpleasant-sort of loss.
"Because I work for *Mega Millions,* in New York, and it's my *business* to know. May I?"
She thought the young man was asking to come in again but instead he handed her a vest-pocket card with LUCAS WEYERHAUSER in raised gold letters. *Special Programs Division* was inscribed below, with an elaborate blue-gold seal, also embossed—the official seal for the State of New York.
"I won't take too much of your time, Mrs Herlihy. I know this is out of the blue but here's how it works: the Los Angeles Super Lotto and New York lottery systems—New York's is 'Mega Millions'—are sister programs. Just like Cannes and Beverly Hills are

sister cities. Not too many people know that Cannes and Beverly Hills are sister cities but it's an official truth. Now, the joining of East and West Coast lottery systems is something that isn't generally publicized but is of great and mutual benefit to the infrastructure of both states." Marj smiled, uncomprehending. "I didn't mean to make you dizzy! OK: let me put it simpler. For every hundred thousand Super Lotto tickets bought in LA, the state of New York buys, say, a hundred 'sister' or 'mirror' Mega Millions. What that means is, even if your ticket doesn't show you to be a winner in *Los Angeles,* you *might* be a winner in *New York.* If you *were* to win in New York, part of those monies would be used for many, many things—school lunch programs, filling potholes, even buying computers for police and fire stations. The long and short of it is that *you,* Marjorie Herlihy, just became a hero."

"Hero?"

"That's right," he said, grinning. (He reminded the old woman of a fresh-faced dancer from her favorite musical, *Oklahoma!*) "You are a hero because your Blind Sister ticket—that's what we call them—from the pool *automatically purchased by the State of New York,* the ticket you bought . . . is a winner!"

"But they haven't announced—"

"Nor will they. The Blind Sister lottos have 'shadow drawings'—that's *exactly* what they're called—and the 'heroes' (such as you) are *always* named within 24 to 72 hours before *home state* winners. Blind Sisters cannot be publicized, Mrs Herlihy. That is actually federal law. And that's why we ask you not to share this with the vendor of original purchase."

"Riki?"

"That's right. We've already been in touch—they are *very* happy campers—they'll be compensated based on a formula not all that different from the one California currently has in place. Of course, they *knew* about the shadow program, all vendors and merchants do. Again, something mandated by federal law."

Marj's door was fully open.

"And now," he said, with a deep sigh, "I have to disclose something that inevitably doesn't *thrill* our winners, be they residents of the Big Apple or be they residents of Lala-land." He leaned over to whisper. Marj felt strange and alive and discombobulated, as if all her senses were heightened. *"Unfortunately,* Mrs Herlihy, you won't be getting the amount listed on the winning ticket. Let me tell you what your share is, after taxes." He pulled out a small calculator. "Because you're over 65—you look 45 if you're a day!—the Blind Sister Superfund subsidizes half the IRS burden. *Your* piece of the pie is kind of a 'finder's fee,' Mr Michael Bloomberg's way of saying, *'Thank you, Mrs Herlihy.'* All right now," he said, focusing on the little machine as he punched its keys. "Let us now see. Let us now praise famous men and women. The formula is rather complex, but that's why they give me the big bucks . . . as soon as you fill out the paperwork, you'll be collecting approximately . . . Wow!" He playfully tapped the instrument, as if there was something wrong. "This looks like a Social Security number!"

He gazed into her eyes like a mesmerist.

"Mrs Herlihy, I have flown here on the governor's jet to tell you that you have just won . . . $6,483,572."

Marj felt as if she were falling. The young man rushed to her side, quick on his feet, the way Chester was around the time he was in college.

Mr Weyerhauser held her arm as they went in, turning a final time to the driver before closing the door.

XXV

JOAN

S HE sat at Starbucks, grouping people like an anthropologist. 2 subsets interested her this morning: the Nomadic Nesters and the Sidewalk Kings.

The Double Ns were spinsters who used the café like a personal drawing room. They spent little actual time *à table,* careful to bitchspray their territory with a clutter of computer, ceramic coffee cup, spiral diary notebooks, dog-eared New Age bestsellers, and peeled-off layers of outerwear. Nomadic Nesters were invariably female and may just as well have used the brackish blood of barren, precancerous wombs to delineate their turf. They hogged 2nd chairs for whatever overflow of detritus, even if the place were mobbed—a contradictory stratagem of the desperately gregarious—and in the rare moments they actually inhabited their space, waited like spiders for the victims who inevitably came along to ask if they might use said 2nd chair. The coquettish Double N would react to the request as if suddenly awakened from deep sleep, thinking her Marcel Marceau gape to be somehow attractive—the contrived and waifish acknowledgment of her own charming eccentricities, which she delusionally imagined others to revel in. Apologizing profusely for her absentmindedness, she would attempt to engage the poor soul who'd approached, with a flurry of cheery bullshit inanities before the seat got dragged to another table as she watched with an insanely intense grin and more marcelled tics, blinks, and twitters. Often the Double Ns begged a hapless neighbor to watch their things, batting Baby Jane lashes when the captive dupes reluctantly assented, rewarding them with a big-voltage desexed smile like a nun gone to rut. The Nomadic Nesters were so highly strung they could actually be seen examining thermoses and cups with Starbucks logos on shelves marked CLEARANCE. Joan feared that becoming N² was her fate.

The Sidewalk Kings were men, usually in their 40s, who strutted in front of the coffeeshop, talking into Bluetoothed air. Sometimes they rather delicately placed an arm behind them—little Napoleons pacing a ship's prow. They spoke just loud enough for practically everyone to hear; SK monologues were always about money. Joan had the idea of taking pictures with her Razr and leaving personalized Kinko's-pixeled records of their peacocky boulevardier preening on Porsche windshields with notes that said, "You think you're Warren Buffett but you're just a dickless wonderboy."

(Thom Mayne would never be on *Bluetooth* or *BlackBerry* or *any*colored toothfairy like that. At least that was Joan's idea. The churlish beanstalk was a Luddite who only used the phone when he had to. Who *cared* if he blabbed about His Favorite Weekend? Who *cared* if Richard Meier went on and on about his "cherished" Viking Ultra-Premium grill in the *New York Times?* Or if Danny Libeskind let everyone know he kept the complete works of Shakespeare, "in miniature," under his bed. *Barbet* cared.)

I shouldn't have fucked him, she thought, on her way to the office, venti latte plashing from the tiny hole of its cheap plastic lid onto her Olivier Theyskens skirt. *Never fuck a client. Never fuck where you hope to build.* She had the spiky fantasy of Barbet waiting for her with a messengered note from Guerdon LLC, Lew's holding company, stating that ARK was no longer in competition and thanking them for their "interest, energy, and enthusiasm." *Oh God.* She literally shook the thought from her head and groaned. When she got to work, she would scrutinize her memorial file to wash it all away. She'd been thinking about what Lew said about the Mem; anyway, it was time to do what Barbet called an "intuitive run," a mental jog through the labyrinthine realm of design possibility. She'd probably blown it sky-high by making wetspot Pratesi whoopee, but didn't care, or at least was telling herself that. So what if they lost the gig? Let Brad Pitt have it. Wasn't he part of Uncle Frank's "dream team"? Give it to Hayden Christensen or Lenny Kravitz—*who thinks Bauhaus is the bomb*—the true Rock Starchitects of Tomorrow.

I'll just give up my place and go live with Mom. Cave in to peri-menopausal loserdom. She was becoming indifferent and dismissive about everything, and knew that was a sign of depression—the knowing of which made her care even less. She felt soul and spirit ebb like a sewage tide of N-squared nutrient-sucked wombdead blood, Joan was over, and over it, she was all over herself. It was cold comfort when Pradeep pulled glibly Googled factoids from his ass to cheer her up: Brunelleschi was 41 when he entered the Florence cathedral competition, and "the great Donato Bramante was precisely your age when he was called to rebuild St. Peter's in Rome."

There was no message from the holding company when she arrived and after an hour at her desk, Joan felt less paranoid. She flipped through the gigantic orange Hermès leather notebook Pradeep gave her on her last birthday and reexamined Andy Goldsworthy's seraphic earthwork. How could she compete? For the 10,000th time, she looked at Donald Judd's aluminum Marfan boxes and concrete bunkers in a neat desolate row but rejected any similar concept because of Freiberg's grouping phobia. There was a xeroxed article about Michael Heizer's awesome Earth Art "ruin" in the Nevada high desert—it all made her queasy. Déjà vu vu vu vu vu: newspapers, slick city magazines, and Sunday supplements carrying the same tired layouts on an eroto-Escherian loop: Marfa/getaways, Marfa/land boom, Marfa/Chinati (*chinati* meant "raven" in Aztec—she wanted to gag), Marfa/Prada storefront *installation,* Marfa/*Giant,* Marfa/eccentric 50something heiresses, Marfa/renovated rundown Deco buildings and adobe fixer-uppers, Marfa/ocotillos and prairie dogs, Marfa/Dan Flavin/ Barracks, Marfa/"Mystery Lights" . . . the monthly piece somewhere, anywhere, everywhere about culinary auctions of black truffles from the foothills of the Pyrenees, or Masa Takayama's latest psycho-expensive sushi parlor, always "tucked behind an unmarked door" . . . the controversy over the use of "Kobe" vs "Kobe-style" . . . the Coppola family compound turned lodge-resort in Belize . . . *the Spiral Jetty (aerial shot)* and Andrea Zittel/A-Z Administrative Services/A-Z Raugh/A-Z Escape Vehicles and *Michael Fucking Heizer.* If she read one more thing about Smithson's Spiral Jetty (aerial shot) or the Lightning Field or Andi Joshua Tree (Mojave as Marfa) Zittel's schoolgirl uniforms and desert hiking trips or Heizer's cranks and idiosycrasies or *High Desert Test Sites* or *Center for Land Use Interpretation* or *Dia: Beacon* or *Lannon Foundation Earth Sculpture Installations* or for that matter anything about William T Vollman (who even *looked* like Robert Smithson; oddly, both Smithson and Vollman looked like Donald Judd without beards) and the Inland Empire or Imperial Valley—she was certain she would disembowel herself at the Basel Art Fair and take a few with her. There were other, *different* loops: the UCLA Live spring brochure with its dumbass hypey look-at-me names: *Chava Alberstein, Pappa Tarahumara, Tania Libertad, Astrid* (Zaha!) *Hadad;* the New Literary Hoaxes; the people compelled to amputate their own limbs; the affluent Manhattanites who got monstrous diseases and wrote tender trenchant diaries of their own demise . . . the Brian Wilson *Smile* and Elvis Costello classical-crossover/Metropole Orkest loop; the Walter Benjamin/Eva Hesse/Guy Debord loop; the Proust translation wars; the what-does-Steve-Jobs-who-is-always-standing-in-front-of-a-big-screen-image-of-himself-have-up-his-sleeve loop (one year it was a rare cancer). CEO porn: hedgehogs with half-a-billion-dollar cash payouts ("the new status symbol") and other assorted unjailed swine making 200,000,000 a year, retiring with guarantees of thousands of free hours on private jets (you didn't even have to be on the plane yourself, you could just send it for friends like a taxi) plus eternal use of company-owned skyboxes, bodyguards, chauffeured cars, and "home lawn maintenance." What irritated Joan most being that architecture was now firmly in the loop-the-loop consciousness of public domain. The same new bullshit modernist house in Santiago that was in *10 X 10_2* only took a month or so to work its way to *Vogue,* the smart-aleck

Details fauxfags, and the Travel Channel's oafish *Amazing Vacation Homes.* The Master Builder's emporia information orgy was like some Philip K Dick PR firm automaton regurgitating to the tick of a nuclear clock: loop-the-loop artists endlessly rediscovered-repackaged with ballsy new psychosex bios, *the Year of Bontecou, the Year of Goya, the Year of Arbus, the Year of Caravaggio* (it was always the Year of Gehry, Koolhaas, Piano, and Hadid), before beginning again, looped in on itself, sniffing its own fulsome shit and vomit. *Joan* wasn't even who she thought she was, merely a skin-sack of Diet Coke sugarwater and ruined ovarian eggs playing the *role* of Joan Herlihy, increasingly neurasthenic, bitterly nympho'd, aging mannequin *manqué.* Barbet, the playful playboy business partner and sometime lover of outsized libido and ambition; Pradeep, the debonair Delhian manchild who got off on hooking her up with a richie; Freiberg the satyr Medici, a Jack Palance in her customized version of *Contempt.* It was all some big dumb *telenovela:* even the sheer *observation* was "loopy"—Starckly unoriginal, banally incontestible, radiantly reliable. It was scary. Like the sage once said, we are not living, we are being lived. *I don't want to hear about Marfa anymore. I want Marfa to die like New Orleans. I don't care about 60-lb Didion and her brave, beautiful Broadway-bound deathmarch. (The producer's coup would be to fix it so she expired on the day of the premiere, like the* Rent *guy.) I just want this Mem. Please God let me do*—In the file lay more taxonomized, staggering memento mori that could never be hers: the templelike Taiwan earthquake mem with its 2,455 lotus-blossomed inscriptions representing each victim; pedantic WW2 memorial—lowered Rainbow Pool and wallfield of 4,000 stars for every hundred soldiers dead; sunken, doomed, watersheeted voids of Arad's footprints; canopied Arizona Memorial and ghostship of 11-hundred-and-77 souls (survivors of the attack are allowed to have their ashes interred within); Ando's floating Fort Worth museum, and grassy skylit subterranean repository on the solemn lonely island of Naoshima; the 2,711 undulating Art Spiegelman cartoon steles of Eisenman's mem to the Murdered Jews of Europe; Yad Vashem's domed Hall of Names hovering like a deathstar over a bottomless well; Anouska Hempel Design's buried Bahian resort within Itacaré's verdant, vertiginous cove; Calatrava's avian Sacramento River span, and Vebjørn Sand's da Vinci footbridge in Norway (& those of Robert Maillart as well); the small, elegantly winged 9/11 altar on Staten Island honoring its 260 residents who died on that day; a Princeton student who won an Archiprix for his virtual *Wave Garden* just off the Pacific coast—torn veil mirroring electrical grid generated by waves and surfers; the churchified "hooded tower" of the Aires Mateus brothers' orthogonal limestone Rector's office at New University of Lisbon (unforgiving unblinking slits like those of Thom Mayne) with breathtaking attachment of banked Epidaurian steps; Testa's gorgeous carbonfiber skyscraper, woven like a basket, airily billowing naked except for elevator shafts; that burnt gnome Louis I Kahn's unbuilt FDR mem on Roosevelt Island, linden trees leading to open stone room at the end of a finger that touched the sea; Michelucci's meditative Chiesa di Longarone rotunda near Belluno; Johannesburg's inner-city apartment block with Babel-barreled core, a hollowed-out basement filled with 3 stories of rubbish—*Pawson's anthology: ancient spiral tower at Samarra. Watery silence of Barragán's magisterial Los Arboledas. Mexican grain silos. Neutra's chapel at Miramar Naval Station. Noguchi streams and boulders. Dreamtime moonview platform, Katsura Palace. Smithson's Spiral Jetty! Spiral Jetty! Spiral Jetty! Spiral Jetty! Spiral Jetty! Spiral Jetty! Stone enfilades . . . Shaker chairs . . . Orkney standing stones . . . Aqueducts . . . Pyramids . . . Bowls . . . Boxes . . . Balance . . . Pools . . . Harmonics . . . Reduction . . . Walls . . . Ramps . . . Mass . . . Economy . . . Ascent . . . Infinity . . .*

    She sat like a dazed animal.

    She could still feel Lew's come inside her.

    The office hummed with undepressed interns.

    She wanted to leave before Barbet arrived.

    She decided to go visit her mother.

XXVI.

RAY

H E was thinking about his kids. Ghulpa said, with a kind of wonder, that he'd never spoken so much about them as he had to the visiting cop. He shrugged and stared at her teeth, which seemed to have found tortured new angles in their effort to escape her mouth and view the world.

BG was right. (Thankfully, she never judged him on that, or any account.) He'd done wrong by them and it pained him to talk of the past. Sure, things had soured between husband and wife, but was that any reason to excommunicate his own children, his blood? Cut them off at the root? They were good kids. Tough times back then, economically—a lot of keeping up with the Joneses. It killed Ray not to be able to provide: the Don Ho vacations, the once-a-week to Chasen's, the new car every year and whatnot. God bless, but Marj was a ballbuster, she was rough on him for not being a bigger breadwinner, bitched him out right in front of the kids. That hurt. The bottom line was, no one could hold a candle to his father-in-law. That sentiment was always front and center. Ray actually liked the guy, which made it even harder.

He used to take the brood miniature golfing on Robertson just to get away from her. That's what got him on the entrepreneurial kick. He secured a loan against the house her dad bought for them so he could buy in to Kidz Links, a 9 hole course that Chess and Joanie loved. $15,000 was a shitload of money back then. (He thought he could make it work but his partner was a thief.) The Links had bridges and tunnels and little windmills that swatted the ball away if you didn't time it right—all kinds of fun things. The children played for free, of course, and got popular at school. Finally, it folded. Ray wanted so much more for them than he could give. It never sat well with him the way he treated his boy.

When he was 5 years old, Chester used to ask for money every time the ice cream truck came. For a while Ray said the truck played that tune only when it was out of stock—the ice cream man's way of saying "sorry" to the neighborhood. His thieving partner got a laugh out of that and played along. They told Chess to stay inside until it went away so the driver wouldn't feel bad. It worked for about a week until he got wise and bawled his eyes out. Now Ray wondered, *What was in my head?*

He wondered plenty: where they were: if his children were even alive. You never knew. People had accidents and abductions (he crossed himself reflexively). Maybe Chess was in prison for torching an ice cream truck ... the girl would be close to 40 now. He called Joanie his "princess." Back then all the dads called their daughters Princess. Chester, he called—*what*—Chesterfield. (That's what Ray used to smoke.) Occasionally, he thought of trying to get in touch with Marj. He couldn't remember who told him but the old man knew she had remarried, a wealthy guy, one of those country-club types. A real-life duffer with no time for kiddie links. A *breadwinner.* He wondered if they'd had kids themselves. Maybe so ... or he could have had some from another marriage. *Eight Is Enough. Yours, Mine and Ours* ... anything was possible. Ray imagined large family gatherings in La Jolla or Oceanside or Carlsbad, seersucker Sunday brunches on the yacht. Champagne and Eggs Benedict. Probably a corporate man. Someone his ex father-in-law would approve of.

Maybe Ray was even a grandfather now, the thought of which compounded his remorse. At the same time, the possibility made it easier to distance himself. There were so many chasms to cross. He could do some of that in his head, too old for the rest. What was the point of raking himself over the coals? There was a whole horde out there just like him: the gimpy fellow you passed on the sidewalk, the lonesome-looking lady boozer waiting for the light to change. Everyone had a history. Still, a divorce or even the death of a child was one thing but the deliberate amputation of a life, 2 lives, a wounding of innocents through absence born of self-indulgence, cowardice, or plain perversity was a cardinal sin. You heard about those sort of people but mostly they were mentally ill, vagrants or jail faces. At the end of his tug-of-war, Raymond Rausch considered himself an ordinary retiree who'd grown insular, dependent upon his dog and a woman from a country that was as exotic as whatever high tone beachside town he fantasized harbored Marj's new life. Maybe the kids lived in Europe, where they'd been to boarding school, and learned other languages. They could have become doctors or lawyers. Chester might even be working for the ACLU! Wouldn't *that* be something . . . Or maybe Marjorie was dead—again, he crossed himself. Joanie and Chester would probably spit if they saw him on the street. Not that they'd know who he was. He'd have to be wearing a sandwich board saying JOAN AND CHESTER RAUSCH'S FATHER, WITH THE DNA TO PROVE IT.

Ghulpa sensed his reflective mood and let him be. He sat in front of the TV eating lentils and rice. A great *Cold Case* was on. Somewhere in California. Marine has a fight with his pregnant wife. Leaves the house to go to Jack in the Box and cool off. 10 or 11 at night. Only gone about 45 minutes but in that time, a serial killer breaks in and bashes his old lady in the head. Rapes her. Later, neighbors say the Marine and his wife fought a lot. The swabbed semen belongs to just 15% of the population—the Marine being in that group. (The days before DNA.) Wife loses the kid but survives. Her short-term memory isn't so good but she remembers all the trouble between them and tells police that he did it. They lock his ass away. After 4 years in San Quentin, the guy says one day his body begins to shake so violently that he decides to throw himself off the tier and end it. That's when the lightbulb goes off: he's in prison for a reason, and everything will sort itself out. 16 years go by. It's friggin *Papillon*. The *Cold Casers* finally get on it. Track down the real killer, currently in the penitentiary, a black sonofabitch who bashed in ladies' heads. That was his MO—bash and rape. Killed about 7 of 'em. The Basher and the *Cold Casers* have a heart-to-heart. They tell him he's done a lot of bad things in his life that he can't make good. But there's *one* case where he still can make a difference. Ask him about the Marine.

Turns out the Basher's a Marine too. Tells the cops it was the only one of his crimes that ever really bothered him—because a fellow Marine had been falsely accused. Semper Fidelis! He confesses, and they release the husband. State gives him a hundred dollars a day for all the years of incarceration. Something like that. Comes out to $600,000. He cuts a check to the lawyer for 200 grand and blows the rest in the stock market. "If God wanted me to be rich, I'd win the lottery. So it's not that big a deal. But paycheck to paycheck that's my life back, my prayer. And that's what I got." He's free.

Ghulpa joined him for the last 15 minutes of the program.

"They broke in your house too," she said sagely, before collecting his bright orange bowl for a refill. "Just like that monster. Don't you forget it."

Ray said he wanted to visit Friar in the morning.

He was going to take him home, no matter what the doctors said.

XXVII.

CHESTER

CHESS enjoyed not returning Maurie's calls.

Laxmi came by a few times, with raw foods and various herbal concoctions. Shit like Gaba, Traumeel, and L-Tryptophan. They smoked dope together, and in the back of his mind he always thought something sexy might go down. (He let her rub the Traumeel on his shoulders but nothing "happened.") He told her not to tell Maurie she was visiting and Laxmi seemed cool with the request. Not because they were doing anything illicit—it just wasn't anybody's business. Though maybe he shouldn't have voiced that; he doubted if she'd already blabbed but wondered all the same. (Maybe his remark would give her an incentive.) Chess didn't even really know if she and the Jew were still "together." Since Laxmi hadn't said anything to the contrary, they probably were. He could just see them patching things up—if the guy laid another half-grand on her, she'd chill right out.

That isn't fair. Laxmi wasn't like that. She's a good girl. Must be the pain talking.

It wasn't until after she left that Chess realized he hadn't been turned on by the minimassage, and that spooked him. Could be the fistfuls of vikes he was taking . . . or maybe it was nerve damage. *The nerves that feed my dick.* It was so fucked up.

Some functionary from *Friday Night Frights* called to ask about getting the tape back. He couldn't believe they'd be that cheap—maybe it was a legal thing. But the guy was asking about a *2nd* tape, the one "sent by mistake." The dumbfuck asked him to leave it by the door for a messenger to pick up. Chess didn't even get the chance to say what the fuck are you talking about.

He searched the big envelope the compilation DVD and his "audition" tape had arrived in, and there it was, overlooked. Chess remembered clocking the 2nd tape subliminally, then being so thrown by the veterinary clinic clip that he forgot it was there.

He popped it in the VCR.

There was Maurie, in-studio, talking to camera in the role of Perp—laying out the patsy game.

> I've known Chester a long time. We're buds. I'm a director and I usually have him do all my location scouting. I think lately his life is on the dull side—I don't think he'd mind a little spicing up.

"On the dull side." *The motherfucker.* "Buds." *What did* that *mean? Like some word out of* Fast Times at Ridgemont High. "I'm a director." *Right, you're Ridley fuckin Scott.* "I usually have him do all my location scouting."

Mah nigger!

Tʜᴇʏ met at a patisserie on Doheny called In Conversation. Mr DeConcini was early and stood to greet him at a tiny outside table, sympathetically watching his client move slowly toward him, clearly in distress. They shook hands and Chess winced from the strength of the grip. He got a stabbing pain. The attorney apologized.

Remar was bald, black, buff, and gay, one of those aggressive queers in delicate, rimless glasses that you don't want to tangle with. Chess was right—the lawyer confirmed he'd been tipped by someone on the show. They chitchatted before the plaintiff gave the waiter his order: orange juice, latte, chocolate croissant. He knew the breakfast was a freebie.

Remar asked for an egg-white omelet, and red Tabasco.

"You know, this is really a growth industry in terms of recent litigation. Some of these shows are just outrageous! It's not just the injuries—which many people don't even report, because they wind up, for God knows what reason, still consenting to be on the broadcast. That's America—we *love* to be on television! The fame game. Born and bred for it. I think it's *one* thing if you're a 19 year

old kid and all your friends watch this garbage and somehow it's
cool to be made a jackass. When you're 19 you've got a whole different mind- and body-set, you're out there on weekends in-
dulging   in   dubious   activities   anyway—I   know   I
was!—skateboarding, gettin concussions, whatever. So you're
used to being knocked around. But it's something else *entirely* if
you're an adult person, *fully grown,* awakening each day with the
reasonable expectation one's privacy is not going to be violated in
an egregious, frivolous manner, for the sport of others. How old
are you, Chester?"

"41. I'll be 42 in 3 months."

"You're 41—you've put away childish things. Now, I don't
know what in the *world* your so-called friend had in mind to
think that you would somehow enjoy a hazing. Which is what
this *was.* A *dangerous, unregulated* hazing. It's actually worse: at
least fraternity kids know what to expect, to a degree. This is
more equivalent to an act of terrorism! I am not exaggerating, my
friend. This sort of thing is a cultural fad that is going to have
major legal consequences for the networks and their parent companies. It already *has. We will not tolerate bloodsport,* Mr Herlihy.
We are not living in Roman times—*yet,* anyway! All of these cases
are *landmark,* because they will help reverse a horrible trend, a low
cultural watermark. Collectively, we are beginning to deplete
their pocketbooks, and that is the *only* way to get their attention.
So I see this as an opportunity, Mr Herlihy. An opportunity to
make you *more* than whole."

Chess liked what he was hearing. "Aren't there limits on this
sort of thing? 'Ceilings'? Isn't that what they call—I mean, if it's
tied to income . . . if you need me to put together tax returns for
the last 5 years, it's *not* going to be pretty. I don't know if I've even
filed."

"Those 'caps' only refer to noneconomic damages involving
medical malpractice. This is *not* that, my friend. This is close to
criminal negligence. We ain't *got* no cap. In my experience, claims
like these can generate jury verdicts in the high 6's—that's *without*
punitive damages! No guarantees, of course."

"What about Maurie? I mean, would he be part of the suit?"

"Might be."

He removed his lenses and methodically cleaned them with a fine-knit cloth. Chester thought it was a move he probably made while in court, for the benefit of a jury.

"Depends on how you feel. We could do him for fraud. Intentional misrepresentation. Intentional infliction of emotional distress. Go after his savings—pension, whatever. You need to think about that. But I'll be pursuing *Friday Night Frights:* the entity that provides the venue, the *superstructure* so to speak, that makes it possible for folks to wake up in the morning with the bright idea that evoking public spectacle by putting their friends through emotional and physical hell is somehow a *wonderful* gift to the world. *FNF* and their *parent company* are at the top of our food chain. Oh, *believe* me, they'll make us an offer we can't refuse. They do *not* want to go to court—though we may very well want to take them there! The tabloids settle *every day,* and the amounts are impressive. Most of the time you don't hear about it because of provisions for confidentiality that are built in to the settlements. They're kept under seal, and for good reason. People would be *amazed* at the kind of numbers we're talking about. We are *absolutely* playing in that ballpark, Mr Herlihy, because we are *beyond libel.* We're in a whole different universe! We're talking personal injury, negligence, and intentional infliction of emotional distress. Hell, if they ever broadcast that—and I wouldn't put *anything* past these folks—add 'false light invasion of privacy' to the brew—then shake n bake!"

They took a breather as the food arrived.

Remar spoke of other things. He'd just paid $3,000 for the right to drive through a gated community off Mulholland, "which reduced my commute by 40 minutes." He said how wonderful Barry Manilow's show in Vegas was ("I'm a sucker for Barry, always have been"); how he and his partner were thinking of buying a house in San Miguel de Allende; his pro bono work with a Venice literary foundation where established authors mentored kids from the inner city.

He stabbed a forkful of bloodily spice-soaked eggs and looked up.

"Chess—I want to ask you something that may seem a little off-the-wall. Were you a bedwetter?"

"No."

"OK, great. Because you peed your pants, didn't you?" Plaintiff nodded. "Do you remember when that happened? Exactly? Because it's going to be important to establish this involuntary response—perfectly normal under the circumstances—but we *will* need to establish that it happened at the *exact moment* you felt your life was over. *Note* I am not saying the moment you felt your life was *threatened,* I'm saying, *over.* There's a difference. That is going to be part of my strategy, and I think it's going to serve us *very* well. So if you don't recall right now that's fine. And by the way, *I* would have done more than just pee! I've seen the tape. I'd have definitely made myself 'a sandwich.' So just think about the moment you *thought* that happened, Chester, see if it comes back, and if you can't recall, think about when you *imagine* that it happened. And I'll do the rest." He put the now cooling eggs in his mouth, savoring the taste. "And another thing: I don't want you speaking with *anyone* from that show."

"They actually called again."

"Uh-huh."

"They wanted to pick up the tapes they sent over."

"You didn't give them back any material?"

"No."

"Good. Great. You played that *perfectly.* I can see that we're going to *excel.* As a *team.* All right, Mr Herlihy, I'd like to have those—*today.* Will you be home?" Chess nodded. "I'll send an intern from the office."

"What about my friend? Maurie?"

"Maurie Levin."

He uttered the name as if a dossier had already been compiled, and it made Chess slightly uneasy. He didn't want to be a rat. For all his raving, he really only wanted restitution, not revenge.

"He's been calling but I don't feel like talking."

"Nor *should* you. I wouldn't recommend it, Mr Herlihy, but if you happen to have a conversation—keep it light—do *not* say you've spoken with an attorney. You're going to doctors every day for your pain, that's all anyone has to know."

"What about his girlfriend? I mean, she was kind of in on it. But I don't want her involved."

Remar smiled as he slurped his latte.

"She's been over a few times—just to visit. She feels bad about what happened."

"That's OK. But the same thing applies—keep it light. In case she's doing a Mata Hari number!"

Chess didn't exactly get the reference, but strenuously shook his head.

"She's not."

"I'm sure she's *very nice,* Chester, but you never know. People get *weird.* He may have a bigger influence on her than you think. *No talk of an attorney or pending actions*—simply put, it's none of their business. And it *is* business." He patted his mouth with a pink napkin. "So: am I officially hired?"

"Yeah! Absolutely."

"*Terrific.* I'll send some papers for you to sign when the intern picks up the tape. Very standard." He smiled. "And make sure it's *my* intern, and not someone from *FNF!*"

They shook hands, but this time Remar used a gentler touch.

XXVIII.

MARJORIE

S HE woke up and the world was different.
    She felt young—her body felt young. This would be, had already been, a year of great change.

They still delivered the *Wall Street Journal* and she hadn't the heart to end the subscription because it was Ham's favorite. She usually threw it out but today, Marj opened the paper to a full page ad for financial planning and investments.

Maybe your next retirement party won't be your last.
Maybe all a gold watch tells you is the time.
Maybe bingo doesn't appeal to you.
Maybe today is the day you wake up and say . . .
Hello future.

Yes.

She was a rich woman now.

As if to signal the auspiciousness of this time, her daughter stopped by. In a tenderly fractured moment, she thought that perhaps Mr Weyerhauser had contacted Joanie to ask her if she "knew." Then Marj realized that *of course* he hadn't, and *of course* she didn't, it was probably a federal law not to inform loved ones until a specific time; and just an apt coincidence, felicitous, that Joanie was there, *now,* looking so beautiful, standing before her after so many weeks. It took everything she had not to tell her youngest of the astonishing sea change. (The old woman was planning to share the wealth, as any mother would.) She'd wait until Mr Weyerhauser gave the "all clear."

Her head was in a whirl. She thought of going out on a limb and inviting Joan to the Taj Mahal in Agra, traveling like royalty on the Deccan Queen like Judy Davis and Dame Peggy. Her daughter was stubborn and finicky yet why wouldn't she assent? The windfall might alter her view, not in the sense of greed, but in the spirit of sheer life's-too-short celebration. Besides, for an architect, seeing that tomb was a busman's holiday. Before she could work up the courage to ask, Joan got paged from her office and had to leave. She'd only been there half-an-hour but told her mother she would phone in the evening to make dinner plans. Marj decided to extend the invitation then, at an Indian restaurant: perfect.

The last few days it was hard to sleep, even with her trusty Halcion. Around midnight, she made herself chocolate pudding and a festive Baileys Irish Cream, then watched the hotel DVD a 3rd time. After the viewing, she still wasn't tired, and pored over a historical book from which she used to read to the kids—captivated by the familiar tale of the Taj. (Her beloved hotel's namesake.) The Mughal emperor built it as a monument to his wife who died in childbirth. It took 22 years to put up; each day, elephants laden with marble and precious stones formed 10-mile processions. When all was done, the emperor plucked out his architect's eyes—or cut off his hands, depending on the version you were reading—so as never to be able to replicate such a thing of beauty. As if it were possible! Thank the Lord her Joanie wasn't prey to such barbarities! There was some anecdotal confusion over the fate of the Taj Mahal *hotel*'s designer as well. Her father's account had him jumping into the sea when he saw his dream built backward; others said he shot himself through the heart.

The most interesting detail about the monument in Agra was something she'd read long ago but forgotten: the emperor Shah Jahan intended to build a *2nd* mausoleum, for himself, just across the river, made of black marble instead of white. (The memorials were to be linked by a black-and-white bridge.) What amazed Marj most was that this unbuilt crypt was often referred to as a "shadow" monument. Wasn't that glorious? It must be divine providence, for *shadow* was the very word Lucas Weyerhauser (it gave her pleasure to say his name aloud, like an abracadabra to all

countries she would one day visit) had invoked to describe the
source of her newly minted Mega Millions.

   The shadow drawings of Blind Sisters.

M R Weyerhauser was precise in his instructions.
          She would go to Wells Fargo and obtain a money order
for $11,492, made out to the State of New York. This would be a
"marker" to secure her winnings, demonstrating to the State Attorney that she had been officially contacted and was in full agreement with the magnanimous terms of her godsend. (With Lucas's
help, she had already completed several pages of the calligraphic
onionskin contract.) Before he left, he gave her an ornately beautiful cashier's check, of a kind she had never seen: modern yet somehow reminiscent of 19th century currency. Like something out of
the Wild West! It was embossed, covered over with all kinds of
gold and delicately woven ink scrollings. Lucas said it was done
that way to avoid counterfeiting, and the paper these sort of
checks were written on alone cost in the proximity of a hundred
dollars.

   The draft was in the amount of $1,863,279.47. He said, with a
gleam in his eye, that leaving it "wasn't really kosher, but I know
you won't go out and splurge." There were taxes to be paid before
the monies could be collected, and though his bosses in New York
were real sticklers about it, he often left these checks with his "sisters" anyway, because it was *fun*. (The 1st payment of what would
be a total of 4 over the next 6 months.) It had become his "signature" to put them in the hands of the winners, prematurely; he
had the feeling his bosses knew, but looked the other way because
he was good at what he did and had been doing it a long while.
Lucas understood how "damned exciting" the whole thing was
and "if it were me, I'd want someone to do the same."

   She went to Wells and got the money order (he told her not to
"gossip" about what it was for, especially if the teller was
"chatty"). Lucas said he'd come back sometime in the next few
days. He wasn't too specific about *when*—there were other win-

ners to contact; one lived as far away as Ojai, and the federal rule was that he had to greet the winners himself. She dialed the number on his business card and got a recording: "You have reached the State of New York Blind Sister Beneficiary Hotline." She quickly hung up, thinking that perhaps she'd violated some sort of protocol. It made her feel silly, yet glad everything was on the up-and-up. She almost broke out the Baileys again.

Marj left a get well note in Cora's mailbox. She knew Cora and Pahrump were at the hospital, and wrote on the card how bad she felt, and that she hoped—*was certain*—Pahrump would soon be better. (She didn't want to mention leukemia. She didn't even know how to spell it.) Enclosed was a check for 25-hundred-dollars that she requested be given to any place that helped dogs and other animals who were "having a rough go." Cora was well-off and she purposefully left the Payee space blank, rather than filling in her name, in the chance the neighbor might take offense and think she was offering money for Pahrump's care, which certainly wasn't the case.

Then she strolled to Riki's.

She'd uncharacteristically forgotten to get a receipt for her balance while at Wells, so she went to an ATM a block away from the liquor store. Paying the cash machine fee was a luxury Marj could afford: her savings, CDs, and money market were in excess of $925,000. That was her worth—excluding Hamilton's monthly pension and Social Security checks, excluding the value of her house (about a million), excluding the recent, salutary generosity of the magisterial State of New York.

They were open for business. Flowerpots and blackened, stuttering, or gutted half-broken votive candles still lined the sidewalk. The handwritten notices had increased in number. There was no one in the shop but Riki's son. Marj smiled, albeit painfully, and he said hello, a little painfully too. She was worried about what to say—she'd made a few dry runs in her mind but no words had come—and the old woman began to involuntarily tremble. He was a kind, good boy and, seeing her distress, approached. Marj hadn't planned to be the party who needed comforting but so be it. They looked in each other's eyes and she told him how sorry she was. *It was that simple, and thankfully the right words had come, without effort. God had given them to her.* He asked if she wanted something to drink. An elegant, haggard-looking woman in a sari emerged from behind the curtain of the back room. *She must be Riki's wife; the poor boy's mother!* Marj smiled, steadier this time, walking toward her. The widow wasn't as welcoming as her son but not unfriendly. *A different generation, and a creature far more shattered by the loss.* Mrs Riki's head bobbled back and forth in greeting, just as her husband's used to. They took each other's hands, eyes starting to brim. Marj reached for her pocketbook and took out the envelope with the 2nd money order she'd gotten from the bank. She pressed it into the silently protesting widow's hands. With the fortitude of a good witch in a fairytale, Marj made it clear she'd brook no refusal and perhaps because of her age, or simple aggrieved and grievous exhaustion, or because Marj was physically frailer than Mrs Riki, the widow acquiesced. Now there were freefalling tears all around. As the old woman left the store, she thanked the widow and son out loud. Later, she wondered if that was an odd thing to do—not the pressing of the money into her hands, but the thanking of them— then she thought, no, that was absolutely the *right* thing, God had given her words again, to thank them, to thank the spirit of the husband and father for the kindnesses he had showered onto the entire neighborhood in this small corner of the world, a corner so far from the one they knew. The State of New York would soon be thanking them as well, she was grateful to have played her part, and Marj wondered if the widow had been formally told. She'd forgotten what Mr Weyerhauser—Lucas—had said about that, but the notification of vendors and merchants was probably a duty left to someone other than the young man.

He couldn't, afterall, be expected to do everything.

XXIX.

JOAN

Lᴇᴡ asked her to meet him where he lived. He actually said, "I really had a nice time with you" (she remembered a sweet jock once saying that), and he wanted to go hiking. *Anilingus at the Bel-Air; now hit the hiking trail. Uh-huh. OK. Muy bueno. Muy bueno Sierra Club sandwich.* He suggested they go to the Lost Coast; she thought that meant somewhere in Sri Lanka but no, it was apparently near his home up north. A rugged place without roads, the last of its kind. She'd never heard of it but that was appropriate. She was lost, with a capital *L*.

She packed flacons of Halla Mountain green tea and Chanel face creams, her favorite (and only) Yohji dress-up dress, blue jeans, Patagonian fleece and silk long johns, and went to Van Nuys where his jet was waiting. The thing was empty and looked like it sat 60 people. She'd deviously asked Barbet to come along, knowing he wouldn't, and of course no invitation from Lew had been extended. (Her lame way of being *inclusive.* Or maybe more like having the pimp on watch outside the motel.) Joan was sure he'd already intuited that she and Lew had slept together—a ballsy roll of the dice. The irony was that in her eyes she had merely been careless; God's way of giving her a shove off-bounds during the *El Zorro/Fountainhead* game. She never thought, deep down, that the fuck had bestowed any kind of competitive edge; if anything, she'd blown it. What was she doing, then? *It's a longshot but I want to be spoiled.* Thanks for the *Mem*ories but just I want to be mobbed-up and married to a moneykiller. *Does that make me a bad person?* Barbet and Pradeep spoiled her but they weren't proper pirates—they were little boys. Shit: any girl'd want to know what it felt like to storm the (bill) gates of billionaire heaven.

His company employed 15,000 people. He lived on a thousand

acres in Mendocino. He was in the middle of a Promethean house-proud rebuild. The temporary contemporary was a cloud of colossal tents where he camped like a Bedouin king. The nomadic compound was designed by the same architects who put up similar ones for a resort in Rajasthan; each module 30 feet tall, full plumbing and heat-radiant tiles with the same floral inlay of *pirtre dure* that adorned the cenotaph of the Taj Mahal. (Other billowy canvasses had been modelled after Karl Friedrich Schinkel's 19th century Schloss Charlottenhof.) A retinue of servants reminded her, in their thin ties and closescrubbed style, of everything she'd read about Howard Hughes's Mormon entourage. Freiberg owned 2 mountains: *Motherfuck:* Joan wanted to know what it would be like to own mountains and streams and the fauna and flora without and within. *To own the very molecules....* Lew said he was changing his design ethos. (His word.) He was learning. He was eager. He was childlike, charming, autocratic, guileless. He was without mercy. He was openfaced and closehearted and mysterious. He was volatile and babyish and hedonistic, petulant and homely, but some days unspeakably, mystically handsome. She could be one of his aesthetic teachers. (His phrase.) *Just like Anne Bancroft and Patty Duke. Ha.* He kept saying how he wanted to buy houses in LA—he never bought just one of anything—with Joan as guide and muse. That's what he *said*. He'd already looked at Gary Cooper's classic A Quincy Jones; a complex in Holmby Hills with a Turrell skyspace; a cozy villa in Palos Verdes with *Mudejar*-style ceilings, based on computer software that mimicked the Alhambra palace's geometries (recent tenant: Julio Iglesias); and a 2,000 acre working ranch high, or as high as you could be, in the Malibu Hills, with an underground Turrell (*oy vey*) Olympic-size swimming pool. He had this big "churchy thing"—that ethereal side. He wanted to make a copy of E Faye Jones's Thorncrown Chapel in the Ozarks. And he was absolutely *obsessed* with Louis Trotter's Bel-Air folly and final resting place—LA COLONNE. (He knew Louis's son Dodd.)

His brother Samuel's death in Tamil Nadu had frightened and galvanized him. Lew Freiberg was 48 years old and had only recently embarked on creating one of the epoch's great art collections. Before the 1st year anniversary of the tsunami had passed, he'd spent $300,000,000 raiding fiscally challenged museums of their French Impressionist art. He had inherited Sam and Esther's vast trove of Buddhist antiquities, the Goyas, the Fra Angelico altarpiece, Rothkos, and Pollocks (Lew's favorite "spatterfuck" was *Full Fathom Five*), and their quintet of fine art modernist armchairs, at $100,000 apiece. He gave Joan a tour of the 15,000 square foot cave tunneled into a mountain that would eventually contain 2 kitchens, 6 sleeping rooms, and a computer-retrievable 200,000 bottle wine reserve. Excavated 50 feet beneath the earth, it was a kind of medieval, meditative humidor—aside from the mosaic'd, brightly lit ballroom that was to be a replica of Moscow Metro's Komsomolskaya station, complete with subway cars as lounges. There was going to be a grotto down there too and because of dampness vs delicate electronics, a corps of engineers had designed a system to completely recirculate the air at least once a minute. That would cost 2,000,000 alone, the side benefit being that people could watch Lew's favorite Capras while soaking in a lava rock pool. Sylvia Sepielli and Michael Stusser (of the Osmosis spa and meditation garden in Sonoma) and one of Spielberg's production designers were building a Kyoto-style *ryokan* and authentic bathhouse within, to which Guerdon planned to import an authentic full-time *okami,* or lady innkeeper. There was the half-built observatory; what really interested Lew at the moment was "an outlaw star" that had been ejected from the heart of the Milky Way. He loved the idea of an outlaw star—that's what *he* was—and sang Joan a sweetly off-key "Desperado." A chef and his wife lived in one of the tents, cooking for Lew and the children, when they weren't with their mom. The new house would be built with virgin old-growth timber, deadhead cypress, and pine from rivers in southern Georgia, handhewn logs dredged by divers from lakes where they'd been submerged for centuries. Cold, river-bottom wood didn't rot and was exceptionally beautiful. It was 10 times more valuable than ordinary planks.

3 hours after her arrival, Lew's 10,000,000 dollar twin-engine Bell/Agusta AB-139 faerie'd them away at 200 miles an hour. He leaned close—their faces touched and his hand lightly gripped her thigh—to peer out one of the huge cabin windows on Joan's side. There it was, the Lost Coast: coniferous forest of fetid adder's tongue giving way to melancholic, barren swatch of no-man's-land—like the smudged, empty margin of a book where a crazed scholar's pencil notes reside—then rocky drop-off of hyper-graphic de-illuminated text into foamy wind-tossed void where the rest of the pages of the Infinite are buried. Lew said it was the longest stretch of undeveloped shoreline in the States. (Naturally, he was one of the few "inholders" to own private land within a federal reserve.) The desolation made her shiver. As the fog rolled and the helicopter banked, her head slowly cleared.

She was finally starting to get ideas. She wanted to visit the site in Napa before going back to LA. (Joan knew what he was up to and wondered why he hadn't already jumped her back in the *Cirque du so-so lay* Mogul Tent. It was better for them to keep their mitts off each other anyhow, until the Mem issue was settled—like boxers before a match. She was having a reptile brain moment: if they got intimate again, what of the tenuous sap now suddenly rising?) Without pen and paper she mentally grafted her thoughts onto the primeval grid, mnemonically marrying them to the mossy, fuzzy, scary-crazy-ecstatic carpet below.

They landed. They walked a mile or so, passing the lean-to of a sculptor Lew had befriended, a Robinson Jeffers type who famously worked with wood and was allowed to lease a parcel of land out here. He wasn't home. They poked around his frontyard, if you could call the stupefying cauldron of the Pacific a yard. Lew said the guy's work reminded him of "Andy" (she'd heard enough of Mr Goldsworthy, thanks very much). As they hiked, conversation segued to the furniture of Nakashima and Noguchi—Lew had just bought a little postwar table for $800,000, at auction— Strange, Houshmand, and Walsh. He spoke of the sundari where the body of his sister-in-law was found, without mentioning Samuel; she wondered about that, and remembered what Pradeep had told her about the "spirit tree." Maybe the topic of his brother was just too painful. They talked about the tidal wave catastrophe in general, which proved amenable enough to an ocean that seemed to roar, hiss, wallop, and sting for its supper. Lew shook his head and laughed about the shrinks who'd flown to Banda Aceh as grief counselors. It was so loud that he had to shout. He asked Joan if she knew about the supplies sent over in bulk: shipping containers with hair conditioners and gel, bikinis and disposable pink razors. Another riff on the obscenity of corporate America's largesse. (His phrase.)

He told her how "Sam and Esthie" were in Kerala and Kochi—he had all the emails and digital photos his brother sent from the trip (there weren't too many)—how they'd visited a place called Jew Town with an amazing 16th century synagogue, "the Paradesi," its roof strung with dangling oil lamps and crystal chandeliers. Sam said that most of the Jews had gone to Israel, and only a few were left: " 'black Jews' and 'white Jews' (orthodox) but today we saw a deeply taciturn woman sewing who went by the unlikely name, or likely, if you wish, of Mrs Cohen." *Deeply taciturn.* His brother was a good writer, with a droll, subtle way. Lew had culled from the computer correspondence to make a booklet for the family service.

He recounted by rote how the couple were in Chennai before heading south to Mahabalipuram, where they perished. When the waters receded at the place their lives ended, ancient carved elephant heads and long-buried running horses were miraculously uncovered. Not many died there besides Sam and Esther. They were among "the lucky ones," said Lew sardonically—of ¼ million, only a few hundred Americans were killed. He'd come to believe it was their fate, their appointment in Samarra. With a doff of the cap to his Buddhist sister-in-law, Lew wittily amended: appointment in *samsara*.

(A conjuration of Buddhist stuff had been on Joan's mind from day one and she envisioned a sand mandala Mem, with a nod to Kyotan Zen gardens. A walking labyrinth, like that September 11th installation in Battery Park—something akin to Roy Staab's arrangement of reeds and knotweed in the Hudson River would, like a mandala, be obliterated in mere days' time, but she dismissed its transitoriness as too "Andy." *Damn him.* {As Jon Stewart might say.} She dredged further from her mental file: the 93 WTC granite shrine, and small stubborn chunk that still remained after 9/11—a memorial of a memorial. She thought of all these things and it was excruciating to realize that her "sappy" frisson had been spurious and she didn't have an original idea in her semen-filled head. *Zaha wasn't Zaha for nothin.*)

Then he said something heavy that she hadn't been aware of.

The body of his brother had been recovered then misplaced by authorities. Only the cremains of his pain-in-the-ass sister-in-law—that said with a smirk not devoid of warmth—would be buried on Napa grounds.

"You know," said Lew, philosophically. "Memorials are hilarious. I mean, the *idea* of them. A grave is a grave. But . . . everything we *do* is a memorial. *Eating*'s a memorial. *Shitting*'s a memorial. *Fucking*'s a memorial. Do you know about Malcolm Forbes?"

"He rode in balloons and laid Fabergé eggs. He took Liz Taylor on a Harley and threw *Brokeback* chopper parties."

"Right! And he's buried on an island in Fiji—only a few people know this. Mel Gibson wound up buying in the same neighborhood. He just had an 8 lane bowling alley shipped over, by the way: not Malcolm, *Mel.* A man has to bowl . . . the passion of the Mel! Gotta hand it to the guy—I mean you *better* hand it over, or he'll *take* it. Mel's crazy, but I like him; I've been to his father's church. Been to Mago too. But the *Forbes* place—the most beautiful place on Earth. (Aside from where we are now.) The Forbes family actually had a written contract that said when they sold the island, they would *come pick up the body.* Exhume ol Talcum'd Malcolm, Fabergé balls and all! What if Malcolm-*Ex* thought he was going to be spending an eternity under white Fijian sands— oops! Sorry! You're in purgatory now—Malcolm in the Middle.

"Remember that Jap who bought a Van Gogh? What'd he spend, a hundred million? For a Dr Gachet? And that was back in the 80s. Or 90s. I think he was a 'department-store king.' Super Salaryman. Did you know that when he died, he was gonna have the painting cremated along with his body? I'm serious! *Never happened.* I think he was in debt and the banks took it back. Poor little slope. Hell, I'd pay good money to watch a Gachet burn. Nothin lasts forever. My brother sure didn't.

"So much for memorials and the wishes of the dead."

B y the time she got back to LA, Joan had a name for the Freiberg Mem, even if she couldn't quite summon the thing itself.

She went to ARK and rushed to her portfolio—this time scanning the Esther/Buddhist section. She reread the *sutta,* Buddha's words to a god who had tried in vain, by ceaselessly running, to reach the end of the world. (Maybe Joan would just wind up forging a great and beautiful prayer wheel, to signify "mindful" running, or turning. *It could also signify spinning my wheels.*) Samuel was a marathon runner, so it was a good thematic fit:

> *Thus have I heard: The end of the world can never be reached by walking. However, without having reached the world's end, there is no release from suffering . . .*
> *I declare that it is in this fathom-long carcass, with its perceptions and thoughts, that there is the world, the origin of the world, the cessation of the world, and the path leading to the cessation of the world.*

How beautiful—that this tireless, needless runner should be covered over by waters, turbulent then still. Receding. . . . It reminded her of Lew's "running horses," freed at last from the Great Wheel of Rebirth.

That's what she would call it, and she couldn't wait to tell Barbet: *Full Fathom Five.*

XXX.

RAY

SHE told Raymond—most of the time she called him "Raj" or "Bapu," but it was Raymond whenever something weighed heavily on her mind that she had trouble giving voice to—she told him she'd awakened with the smell of monsoon in her nose.

Ghulpa often wore a fragrance called ittar that smelled like the 1st monsoon wetness of parched earth. The old man lasciviously said *he* felt a bit parched, and could do with a little "moisture"; her overbite twisted and she called him a lunk. He was only joking.

Her mood grew dark and he didn't understand. She wept and padded around the house in Target flip-flops then took to her bed. Ray guessed she was hormonal, or sensing the ebb of womanhood, because she was that age. He prided himself on the sudden insight, feeling more worldly and knowing than he'd been accustomed.

Big Gulp wanted sweets and Ray promised he would "make a run" to her favorite shop in Lakewood. She gave him a list: mango ice cream with elaichi, and mishti dahi, sweet yogurt made with jaggery. (She knew he wasn't strong enough yet, but acceded to make him feel better.) She hankered to watch a Bollywood movie. He said, well, they should try and go before the Friar came home because then they'd have their hands full. A theater near the bakery showed all the latest, Dimple Kapadia and Rani Mukherjee—or he could pick up a DVD. BG spoke of getting a big new bed, one that was "fantabulous." The Indian ladies were always talking about beds. Ray thought maybe she had a fever.

She recalled her days with the Consul General. Ghulpa cried inconsolably, saying how she missed caring for the 2 little ones. The life of a CG was glamorous but tough. She sympathized with Pradeep's wife, Manonamani, who hated "going on the town" or even entertaining at home, especially after the 1st child was born. Ghulpa used to commute with the family to LA, looking forward to those trips because in San Francisco she was a gilded prisoner of Pacific Heights—like Manonamani herself. She would visit her cousins in Artesia, and it was almost like being home. She could dare to flirt with the gentlemen and feel a bit alive. (She knew Pradeep had been having an affair with a "wicked Hollywood woman" who was a builder, but it was easy for her to look the other way. Her employer was good to her, and she was of a mind that terrible things came to those who judged another.) Ghulpa was grateful for the opportunity she'd been given, grateful to Pradeep and the Mrs for bringing her to this country, but still she saw her life passing by. Sometimes she even longed to return to Calcutta. She yearned for the great Kali Temple there—as a girl, she climbed upon it until guards chased her down. She was brave in her own fashion, and one day did the unthinkable by running away from Pacific Heights. She left Manonamani a note saying she had not taken anything except her own money and the clothes on her back, begging her not to call the police or immigration and begging her not to worry, that she was so sad to be leaving them and the children like this but feared for the stability of her own mind! She added that it would be "no problem" for them to find someone to replace her.

And then she took a Greyhound to Los Angeles . . .

WHEN Ray and Ghulpa arrived at the surgical center, there was a woman in the waiting room whose dog was having chemo. She struck up a conversation and was startled to hear that their "baby" had actually been shot, but was too timid to ask any details. Her face relaxed a bit when Ray, noting her discomfort, said it had been accidental and "the Friar" was going to be just fine. In fact, they were there to pick him up. The woman showed off a picture of Pahrump, a feisty-looking King Charles with a tumor. She confessed she'd been telling friends and family he had leukemia because a tumor sounded "so awful." Ray assured her this was the finest institution of its kind in the world, and they'd patch up Pahrump as sure as they'd patched up his Friar. She listened as one would to an oracle.

"I'm sure of it," he said, fully convinced.

This time, the Friar was well enough to greet them in a visiting room. He was weak and limped but showed signs of his old self. Ghulpa fussed over him while the technician spoke to Ray about aftercare. She gave him a roster of places that provided hydrotherapy; one was in Covina—not so far away. The woman even suggested a therapist who could "support" Nip/Tuck (that's what the hospital staff now called him; they got their jollies from his AKA) reacclimate. "He'll need some help with PTS—post-traumatic stress." She warned about loud noises, sirens, cars backfiring. All were potential problems. She wrote down "www.dogpsychology-center.com" on a slip of paper. (BG took it from her to examine.) There was a man named Cesar who could help. If Ray wanted to call for an appointment, the hospital would "facilitate."

He asked if they could take him home but the gal said he needed a bit more time. Maybe by the end of the week. The old man was crestfallen. He was embarrassed because all he'd been talking about was how he wouldn't leave without his boy. BG stroked Ray's neck.

As they left, they passed Cora on the couch.

"Where's your baby?" she said, expectantly. She was agitated, as if something dire had happened.

"Oh, they want to hold on to him awhile longer. They're pretty thorough folks! He *could've* come but they want to give him that extra boost. If you ask me, they've gotten plumb fond of him, and don't want to let him go! But he'll be fine," said Ray, with a wink. "He's a champion. And so is—"

Ray pointed a finger at the photo Cora still held in her hand.

"Pahrump," she said, with a sickly smile. Then her lip began to tremble. Ghulpa rushed to hug her. He knew what the woman was thinking: *No one gets out of here alive.*

At home, there was a message from the ACLU, saying it was urgent that Mr Rausch call.

XXXI

CHESTER

OFFERS for work came in that Chess had to turn down. That was harsh. He made sure to pass each one to Remar; proof of income lost. It wasn't the pills that precluded him from working—it was more the actual driving, turning his head this way and that, getting in and out of the car. Even holding up the camera or pumping gas exacerbated the pain.

Remar also wanted him to round up whatever tax returns he could get his hands on. Chess repeated how that might open a can of worms, but Remar was blasé.

"We'll see. We'll reconstruct. No harm, no foul."

MAURIE came over, without warning.
"How you doin?"
"All right."
"Listen, Chess. I know what happened was fucked up. But that wasn't anyone's plan. You know that, right?"
"I know that."
"I mean if I had a *clue* it would have gone down like this there is *no way* I would have involved you. I thought it would be a goof. A way for us to pocket some bread." He reached out and touched Chester's arm. "I'm really sorry. OK?"

It felt like a ploy—Chess wondered if he'd been put up to this by *FNF* legal, or even a lawyer of his own. He was probably just being paranoid. He actually missed his "bud," and wished things could go back to how they used to be. *That's how sick I am.*

Maurie said he got a gig to shoot a commercial for an Indian casino in Morongo. Was Chess up for scouting? 3 days that'd pay around 4,000. It sounded too good to be true. Chess knew Remar would never give the go-ahead—it was short money and a bad move, the type of thing that might scotch his whole case. Maybe that was part of the Jew's master plan. The Protocols of *FNF.*

When he said he couldn't because his neck was torqued, Maurie turned on him with a fury.

"You're really being a fucking ham! Get back in the *saddle,* man! Where's your sense of humor?"

"I don't *have* a sense of humor about possible nerve damage to my *spine.* Should I be laughing, Maurie? Does that sound, like, Comedy Central?"

"You're kidding, aren't you? Is that what the doctor said?"

"They don't know yet."

"I can't believe this! Who've you been seeing? *Mengele?* These people are *friends* of mine."

"These 'people'? At *Friday Night Frights?*"

"They'll give you *work,* man—I already spoke to them. You could work *full-time,* get your union hours. You could buy a new car. *Total medical coverage.* Why are you being such a dick?"

"You know what, Maurie? Maybe you should split. I got a headache."

"Yeah. I'll split. I don't like to be around old women."

"Right! I'm an old woman. Now go buy flowers for all your *close personal friends* at *FNF.* Flowers and K-Y."

"You gonna *sue* these people, Chess? Cause that is about the most *fucked-up thing* you can do. Karmically."

"Oh, are we Hindu now, Maurie? Did you convert?"

"I've been there, that's all. I've sued and *been* sued and it's a motherfucker. Turns you upside down and sucks your life force. But hey: what do I know? *Go for it.* Get Tom Mesereau on the phone. *I'm* the guy who sued Home Depot after I tripped over a rubber hose in the gardening department. Took *3 years* and you know what I got? *22K*—60% of which went to lawyers and taxes. By the time it was over, I was popping benzos like Altoids and my self-esteem was in the shitter. But *go* for it." He scuttled toward the door then turned, theatrically. "Know what I think, Chess?"

"Tell me, Maurice."

"I think you should do some yoga and call it a day." He paused.

"I can *seriously* get you on staff at *Frights.* I told you, I *talked* to them. It's *done.*"

"They throwing me a *bone,* Maurie? Are you the *bag man?* What is this, a pity fuck? Or are they running scared?"

"Whatever." He rolled his eyes.

"I think they're *running scared."*

"Man, this thing has really twisted you! I don't know who's whispering in your ear, my friend, but this is *not* going to end with you sipping daiquiris on your own tropical island. I'll *tell* you how this is going to end: with your *body* healing way before your *head* does. Cause it's a self-perpetuating thing—the more paranoid you get, the more 'pain' you're gonna be in. It's all about pride, Chester. Ego. Is your ego so fucking *fragile* that you couldn't take a little practical joke? Couldn't *laugh* at yourself and have a good time? Be on *television,* with a steady fucking *job* and a *new car?* Healthcare? And maybe a *girlfriend?"*

"A girlfriend? What does that mean?"

"I think you need to get laid."

"Get the fuck out, Maurie."

"You need a little *kundalini,* bud. Channel your energy *elsewhere.* You need a *chick* to fuck, not a *lawyer.* News Flash: the lawyers are gonna be fucking *you.* Or didn't you know that."

"Sayonara," said Chess, now standing.

"If you think you're gonna win the lawsuit lottery and hump Kellie Pickler, cool. Knock yourself out. Be the Payback Poster Boy. But remember: chicks dig guys with *jobs.* Chicks dig guys with jobs and *new* cars who *don't* sit around their apartment smoking weed and popping pills like Lenny Bruce, building their case against the world."

"Fuck you!"

"I get it," said Maurie, backing down. He was halfway out the door now. "That's cool. *Namaste,* Chester," he said snidely. *"Namaste. Gassho.* Call me when the swelling goes down—of your *ego.* In the meantime, try not to leave any severed fingers in the chili at Wendy's. Though there's big money in that too, if you don't get caught."

T_HAT_ night, Chess watched a tsunami doc on MTV. Surfers and real MDs went over to help. Their T-shirts said MALARIA SUCKS. Rock songs played during amputations, to hold the attention of the demographic.

He switched the channel: another Big Wave Anni show, with the same recycled shots of killer tides engulfing the infamous hotel pool. (Some guy really must have got rich off that footage.) There was a segment on these nerdy bureaucrats in Hawaii who kept saying they wanted to warn people but didn't know how. One of them said they probably *could* have if they'd been able to find phone numbers of the embassies. Chess thought that was sort of funny and disarming. The pinhead suddenly gets a "miraculous" call in the middle of the night, "a real lifesaver," from the State Department—and *then* he thinks to ask, Can *you* give me the numbers of the embassies? By the time he starts his round of wake-ups, it's too late. Not that it wouldn't have been anyway. The documentary was pretty engaging but they eventually ran out of stuff to say and it got crazy. People began theorizing about 50-story waves being generated by simple landslides or how a volcano blowing its top in the Canary Islands could basically wipe out Manhattan. The nerdwatchers said the chances were "slim" but such events were "imminent." Basically, the whole Pacific coast, from Vancouver to San Diego, could be wiped out as well. Each time, the size of potential waves grew: from 100 to 200 to even 300 feet. Why didn't they just say the waves would be a mile fucking high? You'd have to be in a goddam 747 to be safe. They kept cutting back to this butched-up pseudoseismoscientist dyke saying, "It could happen anytime. It could happen . . . *today.*"

Right. About the same odds as you going down on Anne Hathaway. You fucking whitehaired diesel. Weasel diesel crock.

Chess swigged down Percocet and Soma with a diet Dr Pepper. He flipped to a series on AMC called *Film Fakers.* The premise was a bunch of unknown actors cast in lead roles in genre films (there'd been a similar thing a few seasons back starring people who got famous on reality shows), the reveal being that everything was bogus, from script to director to crew. An extended, low-rent version of *Punk'd,* except with unfamous people. Kinda funny.

He lit a joint. Maurie's words stung and Chess wondered if he was being a poor sport. Maybe the pain *was* in his head. *But how could that be?* In grade school, he was "a whiner." Even his kid sister called him that. No, this was different. It wasn't an ego thing—he'd been injured for real. Take these *Film Fakers* kids: they were all young, desperate, aspiring actors, and however pathetic it turned out, happy to have the exposure. Whereas Chess was a grown man, just like Remar said, fighting the good fight against getting older, struggling to pay bills and join the union. No, *fuck* that—fuck Maurie Levin and his manipulative bullshit. *Fuck* your bosom buddy *madres* at *Friday Night Frights.* I'll sue the shit out of em and slap a suit on your kinky-haired ass if I have to, Superjew! *Fraud and misrepresentation. Emotional* fuckin *distress.* You *blew* it sky-high today, Rabbi! Comin over here runnin your *namaste* mouth. Try to buy me off with your chicks-like-guys-with-jobs-and-new-car-smell fucking *horseshit. Chicks like chicks with dicks!* he thought, laughing out loud. *I'll fuck your pimped-out hippie girlfriend too.*

SHE dropped by again, and gave him a New Age bookstore pamphlet about Ganesh, her father's patron.

Laxmi said that years ago her dad broke his back and finally had something called spinal fusion, where they screw a metal rod in your spine. The surgery was done in New Delhi. Chess thought she was sharing the anecdote to make him feel better—as if whatever was wrong with him would never be that bad. Her heart was in the right place. *Her pussy too. But I wouldn't know.*

After she left, he went online. He was stoned and curious. Fusion stuff was all over the place. The technology had recently been in the news because the doctor who invented it won a patent suit against some manufacturing company for infringement. He was going to get a settlement of one-point-3,000,000,000. In a peace-and-love prescribed press release, he said there were no hard feelings—he really liked the company that tried to steal from him, and even announced he'd be doing business with them in the future. *Well who the fuck wouldn't.* A lot of experts said that half the

250,000 spinal fusions done in the States each year were totally un-necessary; statistics said that instead of fusion, you could have the far less invasive laminectomy or even no surgery at all and do just fine. A little Pilates or even a walk around the block went a long way. But Medicare had bought into the game big-time and every-one was brainwashed into thinking that the more money a proce-dure cost, the more effective it was. The American way: $$$ = Best. Docs got kickbacks, free trips to Hawaii, and 6-figure con-sulting fees from whoever made the hardware, and hospitals quadrupled their fees, leaving the crippled, infected, and dead in their wake. Money kept talking even if it didn't end up walking.

Chess went into some of the blogs and chat rooms. People were beginning to wake up and smell the litigation. But you had be careful: a lot of class action suits had fraudulent underpinnings: big drug companies were being extorted, and they were starting to fight back. Reading about this shit was like staring at one of those Bosch paintings. Gave him the willies. He would *never* let someone cut into him, that's for damn sure. He'd be on a beach somewhere counting his money before *that* would happen.

Slurping daiquiris.

Watch me, Maurie. Watch it happen. Fuckin Jew.

XXXII.

MARJORIE

Lucas Weyerhauser was late.

He laughingly asked if she'd spent the $1,863,279.47. She told him she had the money order, the 11½-thousand-dollar "marker." He thanked her and said he'd be sending that to the New York State Attorney by special courier, the same folks who flew out jewels for Academy Award presenters, and "trucked" Federal Reserve gold bullion. "Your money order," he said with a smile, "might very well be sharing a 'pouch' with Scarlett Johansson's Harry Winston tiara."

He asked how it went at the bank, wanting to make sure she hadn't "shared" with friends or family members just yet. (She decided not to tell him about her close call with Joan.) He showed the old woman the contracts she'd signed, now notarized and stamped with official-looking seals. Marj asked when she could expect the 1st payment and he laughed again, sweetly, and said sometime in the next 6 weeks, as soon as the tax was paid on her winnings. That was standard, he said, showing off a cashier's check—not the "marker" monies, he clarified—from the family in Ojai who "were unfortunate enough to win a bit less" than her. The amount was for $335,000, which meant, he said, they'd be able to "liquefy" within the next 10 days. Mr Weyerhauser didn't think Marj wanted to "cash out" that quickly but if she "so desired," arrangements could always be made. A minor hassle but he'd do anything for his Sisters. She said no—she didn't want to be pushy—and the young man thought that prudent.

He'd be back on Friday. He urged her to stop calling him Mr Weyerhauser (she toggled back and forth between Lucas and the former) "because it makes me feel a bit beyond my years." What a smile he had! Then he pulled a box of expensive chocolates from his briefcase and said, "Of all my Blind ones, you're the teacher's pet. I'm not supposed to say that but I don't think I've broken any federal laws."

After walking him to his car—the nice black chauffeur stood in readiness—she went next door to check on Cora. She was always slightly concerned that her neighbor would see Lucas through the window; the old woman hadn't yet concocted a story to explain him.

When Cora opened the screen, she began to babble, without Marjorie having said a word.

"Oh, Pahrump's just fine! The clinic is *wonderful*. It's like the Mayo! They said he won't be there but a few days . . . did you know that as little as a few years ago, the *poor veterinarians* used to sneak sick dogs into UCLA at night to use the radiation machines? Those men are *living saints*. You don't have any idea what goes on, Marjorie—but everything's different now. The world has *completely changed* when it comes to animal care. Thank God! There is an entire *oncology department,* and the *nurses*—angels from heaven!"

She invited Marj in. As they settled onto the living room couch, a toilet flush startled. Stein came in from the bathroom, still drying his hands.

"Hi, Mrs Herlihy," he said.

"Oh, hello!"

"I oughta get you a Toto, Ma." He turned to their visitor. "They're from Japan—I just got 3 for the house. They're like carwashes for your tushie."

"Oh, Steinie!"

"How are the kids?"

"Fine!" said Marj. "They're fine."

Cora gave her son a look, telegraphing that "the kids" never came around, and the topic might be best left unexplored.

"I was just telling Marj about the marvelous hospital Pahrump is in."

"The tumor's out and they don't think it's spread."

"Tumor?" said the guest.

Cora shot Stein another look.

"Let's not talk about it! My son has already taken me to a variety of boarding schools, for when Pahrump gets out."

"Boarding schools?" said Stein, with an indulgent smile.

"He's not coming home?" said Marj.

"Well, no—not right away."

"He's going to need close looking after for a few weeks," said Stein. "I didn't want to put Mom through that."

"You should *see* the place we went to, for my Rump!"

"Watch your language, Ma! It sounds like you're talking about my Toto! But it *was* pretty amazing. It gives that convalescent home in *The Sopranos* a run for its money. You know—the one Paulie put his mom in? I think she turned out *not* to be his mom. They go so long between seasons, I get confused. Anyway it's like a palace."

"The dogs watch *television.*"

"On plasma. I kid you not. There's even a little beauty salon, and a *spa.* It was written up—in *Los Angeles* magazine, I think."

"And if you pay *just* a bit more," said Cora (her son playfully interjected, "You mean if *I* pay just a bit more"), "those wonderful people sleep in the bed with them! If that's what your dog is *accustomed* to . . ."

Marj couldn't get a grip on what they were talking about.

"Each program is individually customized."

"If the pet is lonely or frightened the 'tenders' climb right in!"

"Yeah, they tenderize. Our insurance picks up a lot of it."

"Insurance?" said Marj. She was getting an education.

"Oh yeah. It's only a few hundred a year. You can get coverage on potbelly pigs and chinchillas. I'm serious. Google employees get it automatic. A lot of big companies are doing it. One of the partners at my firm has insurance on his *gecko. I kid you not.* He has a gecko called Gordon. By the way, Mrs Herlihy, that check you gave my mother was above and beyond."

"Oh! Yes!" exclaimed Cora, silently clapping her hands. "You dear heart! I didn't even thank you! But we can't accept it."

"You must," said Marj.

"Mom, I already told you. We'll give it to the Humane Society."

"Yes," said the old woman. "That would be *marvelous.*"

"But you *shouldn't* have, darling."

"*Very* thoughtful and *very* generous," said Stein. "The donation will be made in yours and Hamilton's name."

"That is lovely! Whatever you feel is best."

"Maybe we should use the money to buy Pahrump that bed," said Stein, in jest. "Or a Toto!" He turned to Marj. "These doggie palaces have custom mattresses. They're Posturepedic, or what-ever—made from that NASA material that 'remembers' body shape. I mean, it's like a miniature of what you get at the Penin-sula. The last place we visited had a bed that looked like a Mies van der Rohe—you know the chaise Amber and I have in the den, Mom? I asked them and they said it cost 2 grand! I kid you not. These dogs live better than *we* do."

"Pahrump loves his own little bed *just fine,*" said Cora, worried that Marj might think her son had been serious about how they were going to apply her donation.

"Just don't be surprised if he comes home spoiled. Amber and the kids dragged me to that store where Paris Hilton outfits her Chihuahua. You can get a Sean John sweatie with your dog's name spelled in diamonds. 25 hundred. But the *best* is what we're going to do for Pahrump when he's back home with Mama."

"No, no, no," said Cora.

She was spirited now, enjoying her son's antic attentions.

"We're gonna get him a *masseuse.*"

"We are *not,*" said Cora. "He's *teasing.*"

"Mrs H, I kid you *not.* There's a pain management clinic for dogs with the Big C. I'm talking certified canine massage thera-pists! The hospital referred them. Ma, I am tellin ya, *we are gonna do it.*" He turned to Marj. "Mrs H, do I look like a kidder?"

S HE heated some chicken soup.

Marj didn't know what Stein did, but thought maybe he was some kind of attorney. There was a piece on *20/20* about a lawsuit against the sweepstakes company Ed McMahon worked

for, and the old woman remembered Cora saying her son had
something to do with that. Evidently, they were no longer allowed
to send letters to people saying they were winners when they
weren't really winners at all.

She wondered why Joan hadn't phoned like she said she would;
she'd probably just gotten busy. After the encounter with Stein
(who she thought was a ruffian) Marj considered giving her own
son a call but held back. She hated crowding her kids. Though
this time she had a reason to call Joan—she could say she was worried she hadn't heard back—but decided to wait a few days before
getting in touch. Instead of making her daughter feel guilty, Marj
idly wrote a scenario, out of pride: she would ring up and say she
"didn't want to miss her" before leaving on a little jaunt to the
desert; that Cora invited her to come spend the weekend at her
son's house in La Quinta. She'd probably just get Joan's machine,
but that's how she decided to handle it.

She rehearsed the lines in her head before drifting off.

XXXIII

JOAN

SHE was about to call Marj when she checked her messages. There was her mother's voice, nervously hesitant, going on about La Quinta (where Hamilton liked to take her; they used to stay at the eponymous resort, in "Frank Capra's former bungalow"), then something about the Taj Mahal. She knew it was a ruse, and it didn't make her feel great; she had promised to call, then everything went out the window when she got her marching orders to go up north again. That's what kind of whore she was. And, not to worry, Lew wound up fucking her in his brother's house in Napa, on the *Forbes 400* memorial acres, fucked and sucked her hard, left her sore as a week's full of downward dogs, bruised and yeasty and burnt.

She thought some more about *Full Fathom Five.* The story of the couple left hanging in the branches had unhinged her but Joan wanted to avoid any treehuggers' on-site plantings; best leave that to Sir (Sri?) Goldsworthy, the Dumfries shaman whose "Garden of Stones" Holocaust Mem at the Museum of Jewish Heritage, with its dwarf oaks emerging from holes within 18 13-ton glacial granite boulders (18 = the Hebrew alphabet correspondence with *chai,* the Jewish equivalent of *ch'i*), would be hard to beat. (In the future, the acorns born of the dwarfs would be planted by children of Holocaust survivors. For real.) It was out of her purview and Joan knew there was always the danger a wily Lew might interpret such a gesture, from anyone else but Andy, as cliché. Still, she circled the idea of a vast reflecting pool; talk about cliché, but it was pretty hard not to go there. If she could do something "new" with water, if that were even *possible,* if she were *good* enough—a flat green slate pond engineered to remain at perfect ground level in the staggeringly elegiac meadow he'd selected might achieve the timeless, anonymous effect that had subsumed since the Lost

Coast rumination. (Brilliant alternate working title: *Lost Coast*.) She'd immersed herself in the tsunami—ancient legend come to life before the contemporary world. In some ways she felt privileged, because whether one knew it or not it was the defining event of hers, Lew's, and everyone's lifetime, like being on the planet during Vesuvius, Pompeii, Krakatoa. And maybe Hiroshima. (She knew it was all wrong and that it didn't make sense, but in her mind the death of New Orleans was closer to the disappearance of the WTC.) She thought about the dogs and elephants that nudged people to higher ground, dolphins urging fishing boat captains to the relative safety of deeper seas, and afterward, when scarred, sentient pachyderms lifted detritus from the injured, or aided in the disinterment of the dead . . . All her life Joan had felt a strange closeness to that region, as her mother did, now racking her brains for this idiot's assignment, something asinine and collegiate about it, civic science fair, building the Perfect Memorial, though if she had her way, not just for richies who got tree-bough-hanged but for everyone who died and everyone who lived, all the walking dead and miracle folk, the incognizant motherless children, a monument to the broken and unbreakable—impossible! How to memorialize a myth of such potency? Now was the Time of the Memorial. It was *her* time. Yet to note absence and the void—to *note* it—was a philosophical conundrum. There wasn't syntax for such a challenge, architectural or otherwise. *What would be the point?* Was she capable of erasing herself, of banishing hubris? Only from Silence could the semblance of such a thing be born. Maybe that's why she rode Freiberg bareback, subconscious thought being that life growing inside her was the only answer, an antidote to egotism. At least it would be a starting point. *Womb to tomb.* What was a grave, anyway? Something to mark the memory of a spirit. And what was spirit but the embodiment of Myth? (She laughed as she suddenly thought of Pradeep telling her how his favorite, Ali G, sang the last phrase of the national anthem as "your home in the grave.")

Sri Lanka was called India's teardrop: only this morning she read something in the paper about a killer convicted on the strength of DNA—tears the little girl had shed onto the seat of his car. *We are all made of water*

and again the images seized her, being fucked by Lew, fury of *his* DNA, her fury as well, he'd gripped her long hair, it had been 20 summers since some rough Berkeley Romeo did that in back of a stationwagon; mournful Napa wind howling through reconnoitered memorial grove as she got rimmed rattled and rolled (rimmed Koolhaus, rimmed reaper) in that haunted house *lea,* it began to rain, great blackwater sheets of it, then, Joan embarrassed at her own wetness, hoping it wasn't a turnoff, it had been a turnoff for some of the men in her life but they were babies, that's just how she was physically wired, she got so wet sometimes they'd assfuck her by mistake—there it was, so true, body as earth and tsunami, crass dumb analogy, fucking as access to Myth, fucking *was* Myth, recession and floodwater, corporeal heat and gaseous gale force cuntfart wind, magnificent oblivion as tears, secretions, and semen dissolved and commingled, the blacking out, animal rush of hearts and minds to higher ground, eyes opening, closing all veils, thresholds akimbo, atremble, reflecting pools reflecting ambient absence, sounds and swells and swelling, screams and shadows, gorge and engorged and failure to outrun the deluge, system collapse, that's how we were wired, that's how we vanished, kicking and screaming in sepulchral acquiescence, all the same, the sacramental memorial of 2 bodies as they rutted their way to birthing and deathing and grubby celestial silence. *I'm a Mem. Yes I am, and I can't help but love him so.*

She wished those 2 had died in the Maldives because that thousand-mile-long sea-level spine of atoll lent itself more readily to earthen monument making. How awful she had become! A leech in the architectural house of God: slutty 2nd-rate talent who'd ceased to know herself even through multiple readings of her Vedic astrological chart; it comically, macabrely ordained that she caretake *others,* her rising sign in codependence, moon in the House of Enabling—she especially knew how to make *men* feel good, as she roiled and withered, washing away from the inside, her cervix a village brittle with seabranches, vertiginous seahorses, tumbling mothers, and drowned wide-eyed children gone saltwater ass-over-heels. She *was* that woman in the Andaman Islands, paid 2 rupees—4¢—by the local government in compensation for the tidal wave death of her babies, there she was, there was Joan, Joan of ARK, Joan of the disastrous, diaphanous moon-pulled tide, parasite of Melville's "Maldive Shark," riding the predaceous Wave:

. . . sleek little pilot-fish, azure and slim

—that was she—

How alert in attendance be.
From his saw-pit mouth, from his charnel of maw
They have nothing of harm to dread,
But liquidly glide on his ghastly flank
Or before his Gorgonian head;
Or lurk in the port of serrated teeth
In white triple tiers of glittering gates,
And there find a haven when peril's abroad,
An asylum in jaws of the Fates!

They are friends; and friendly they guide him to prey,
Yet never partake of the treat—
Eyes and brains to the dotard lethargic and dull,
Pale ravener of horrible meat.

She picked up the phone to call her mother.

XXXIV.

RAY

EVEN Ray couldn't dismiss the propitious omen of the City of Industry's offer arriving at the very moment Ghulpa announced her pregnancy. (She said she was certain of her condition when she could no longer smell the monsoon.) The Rite Aid kit had confirmed it.

They both cried.

He was waylaid and astonished.

He saw himself at the end of his life now, all wrongs, failures, and misgivings mitigated by this bloodied crumpled thing soon to join them in the world. He could see the pink coverlet of its flesh, almost smell it as once he had smelled his lost children; felt wornout fingertips caressing bakery-fresh dermis, inhaling the luminous, wispy penumbra of hairs on its head—old man to new old man—and saw his BG come alive again. God, he loved her. A good and worthy woman who'd been premonitorily dreaming of monsoons, saturated in their majestic, superabundant, terrifying memory.

For the last week, as he watched his *Twilight Zone*s, she talked from the kitchen, half to him, half to herself, of the storms' flat-headed mushroom clouds and bridesmaids of crows, dust, and dragonflies, muttering stories of Durgā and the man-eating tigers that her parents had passed on. For the last week, Ghulpa had been all about water, Kwality ice cream (or mango with cardamom), flooded lullabies, and bedtime tales. She rinsed her hair in coconut oil and stitched a tiara of jasmine for her "Raj"—she laughed and cried like a spinning weathervane and nearly brought Bapu to exasperation. She spooned down chikko and spoke of immersion as an impish girl in the Hooghly River. For the last week, newlywed to her fetus, all washed back to Mother India, her water broke from blackholed skies, all was sweetmeats and sandesh, all was Durgā Puja, statues of the goddess straddling fearsome papier-mâché lions loaded onto slow-moving trucks with Little Gulp jumping on, hooded by a green centipede of banana leaf, on the way to the ghat for submergence. Now Ray peaceably drowned as well in those fluid recollections and Taj Mahal–themed *pandals,* Durgā and Ganesha in carriage, illuminated by fierce neon, he sunk like a treasure in her tears, sunk in his private old man sobbings, the couple's lachrymose communion incubating beneath the sacred folds of her almond-skinned belly. Raymond Rausch experienced a teleological rapture of the days, and a feeling most merciful that there had been a purpose to his smallest and even largest abdications, and that he had been forgiven.

WHEN he got lonesome for Nip, he watched that wonderful fellow on National Geographic's *Dog Whisperer,* a gentle warrior who healed the worst of the worst, even a pit bull named Half-Dead with scars around its neck—the owner, a homeless pimp, kept it tied for weeks to a pole, with barbed wire. At the end of the show the Whisperer told the animal's stunned and grateful suburban parents, "The beauty is, they move on. Your dog is no longer living in the past, he's living in the present. That's why years of trauma can be reversed in an instant."

THE amount the city offered for the wrongful break-in was $308,000. A funny number, so precise, but Ray didn't want to ask how they'd come by it. The fewer the details, the better—he didn't want to be the jinx. Now that there was a figure, he felt less combative, and friendlier to the concept. The lawyer on the phone quickly said they could do "far better" but Ray thought it just fine, even though Ghulpa frantically motioned that they needed to discuss it amongst themselves. BG was frantic about everything these days and who could blame her. Ray nodded at her, hanging up congenially.

"Bapu," she said almost gravely. "Think of the little one who is coming."

She wanted to give the little one everything. She wanted the little one to have the finest clothes and a rockinghorse bed. More than anything, Ghulpa demanded—in strict compliance with Bengali tradition—the finest in education for their child. The little one would become a scientist. He would go to Caltech. (He was never a she.) He would go to Harvard. He would go to Oxford. Ray assented, on a mellow, natural high. In the space of a few hours, in the winter of his years, he'd become a father and a wealthy man. He even allowed himself the thought:

I will be her husband. She will be my wife.

Detective Lake called to say he was in the neighborhood. BG prepared mint tea while the men visited. Of course, not a word was said re child or settlement, but it was obvious to their guest that Ray was in fine fettle. The mood of the house was buoyant.

When Ghulpa came in with the tray, the detective asked what part of India she was from. He said a merchant told him of a festival that honored whatever tools people worked with in their livelihood. Writers had computers and pencils blessed; musicians, their instruments. On this particular holiday, the merchant said that priests even anointed the weapons and ammunition of local police. He asked if it was all true and she smiled, bobbling her head like a sleepy cobra before a snake charmer. Yes, she said, the festival of lights, the festival of Diwali, in this Puja all "ammo" is blessed, the bands play, and the people chant *Om Jai Jagdish Hare*. Then she covered her mouth the way she did prior to a laughing jag. She went abruptly to another room and Ray just smiled because he knew she would soon begin to weep with the amniotic joy of housebound, baby-fevered mythos.

Their own private festival of light.

XXXV.

CHESTER

THE pain was really getting to him.

He didn't have medical insurance and Remar reiterated his offer to find doctors willing to see Chess on a contingency basis. It was called being treated "on a lien," or something like that. The lawyer compared his situation to having been in a crash—you could rent a car while your own was under repair without shelling anything out. Vendors and insurers usually had good-faith agreements re restitution that sometimes applied to doctors as well. It was important that Chess begin to create a papertrail of medical bills. "This isn't a self-esteem issue," said the lawyer. "You should find the help you need, *pronto.*" He would "procure" a list of clinics the firm had worked with. On the strength of the facts of the case, Remar felt reasonably confident Chester could get quality care for nothing or at least pennies on the dollar. He even offered a cash advance. "Don't let your pride work against you. Again, that's not the issue here."

His landlord, Karen, Don Knotts's daughter, stopped in with soup and sandwiches to commiserate. She was rangy, red-haired, radiant, and big-boned, with a gangly, generous smile. (She was an actress who used to do theater with her dad; Chess loved hearing stories about Life with Don.) She told him that a friend of hers who didn't have health insurance woke up in the middle of the night with chest pain and went to the ER. They put some kind of stent in there and by the time he left—12 hours later because he was so freaked out about how much everything was costing—he'd racked up $47,000 in bills. She was surprised he didn't drop dead right then and there. Karen said the guy was suing the hospital for what attorneys were calling a 600% markup.

You didn't need a whistleblower to tell you how vulnerable you were in the U S of A: *with* or *without* medical coverage. The uninsured (all 45,000,000 of em) were circled like enfeebled prey, while a corporate syndicate of turkey buzzards sought out the soft anus of the dead and dying. Hospitals had Mob-style accountants keeping 2 sets of books—one for scum, the other for bluecrossed bull's-eyes. Paradoxically, the *uninsured* were the schmucks who got jacked. Ripe for some homecooked-style fucking, with all the trimmins. You didn't even have to be in possession of a scabby street person profile; you could just be some poor slob Coffee Bean & Tea Leaf manager going through tough times who can't afford the few hundred a month for so-called coverage. Even if you *had* coverage, they found a way to shit in your mouth. The hospitals added insult to injury by calling themselves "not-for-profit." What a joke!

Let's say you wanted to do the right thing and spring for the premium. Be a good boy and all that yadda yadda good citizen horseshit. Well, *tough*—rates had gone up 70% in just 3 years. *60 Minutes* said 50% of all personal bankruptcies could be traced to overinflated medical bills. Hospitals kept the costs of their procedures secret, so you couldn't even comparison-shop; accounting departments sent out drone missile invoices left and right, blowing up middleclass houses like piece of shit Shiite temples.

It was a marathon rape everywhere you turned. Didn't matter if you were an enlisted person *who died in the line of duty;* there was *still* a cap of 12K. They knocked on your door and forked over a "military death gratuity"—that's what they called it—like a restaurant tip. Raping Private Ryan. The government dunned amputees for costs to replace cheap body armor. Deduct it from the gratuity! Chess read in the paper how they didn't send soldiers home anymore by special transport, with flags draped over the coffins. *Fuck that*—they shipped em in cargo holds, commercial air, wrapped in plastic.

You couldn't actually sue for malpractice anymore either; there were more caps than fuckin West Point on grad day. If a strung-out surgeon snagged the wrong kidney or a Down-syndrome RN accidentally switched your nametag with Joe Prostate Cancer and the next morning they murdered your hard-on and you had to be diapered the rest of your life, it was Eat Me Time: damages were capped with a capital C. The gameshow was rigged—everything had its price but the price was *wrong,* and it didn't matter whether they blinded you or left sponges in your pussy that tortured you for 6 years before someone figured it out, if they figured it out at all, or they transfused the wrong blood. *We're sorry!* capped out at a few hundred grand. Deal or No Deal! *That* was the law and it was *global:* even Holocaust reparations were paltry. Let's say your gonads got irradiated by the SS and for the next 50 years intermittently balloon-bled like pomegranates, or your nips were carved off by *der Weise Angel,* or you got twappy and phthisical from chemical injections—the most you could get was 3 to 8 Gs. End of story. *Finito.* Cap City. *Capo di tutti Capo.*

Done fucking No Deal . . .

He'd settle, all right, but only for what was *fair and balanced*—one thing Chess *did* know was he didn't plan on being 60 years old and still in court. Eventually, come payday, he would have to sign off on future-related medical procedures. The trick was, he needed reasonable assurance he'd physically *recover* and not blow whatever money they gave him on potential surgeries, extensive rehab or whatever. He had to think worst-case scenario. That was the new fun zone, right? The *Worst Case Scenario* game? He knew the drill from fender-bender whiplash—you had to sign a waiver once they cut the check, releasing the big boys from liability if anything went hinky down the line. He knew that much, and Remar confirmed it. The *Li*-ars had the *ability.*

Still it was kicky to do a little fantasizing about the jackpot. He didn't want to get his hopes up but what was the harm? Probably healthy. Chess lit a joint and let his mind drift toward insane riches. The Catholics were really cleaning up. The Church was running scared; at least people were seeing results. A couple million here, a couple million there—in most cases, it was altar boys who got blown on '70s camping trips. How tough could *that* be? A sleeping bag by the fire, marshmallows on sticks, hot and hale Marys around your dick . . . but everyone was so *traumatized.* That's what kind of weak fucks Americans were. Put em on the wrong end of preachercock at a tender age and they become simpering snitches, queers, and serial killers. If he knew it'd make him a millionaire, Chess would have let *los padres* bite the wafer to their hearts' content. The men in collars could fist him at Roger Mahony's Bar and Grill for all he cared—just throw another few hundred thousand in the kitty.

❋ ❋ ❋

Dear Mr Chester Herlihy,

As a responsible citizen, you've paid taxes most of your life, and that's why I think you have a right to be profoundly concerned *by what I'm about to tell you.*

Until recently, there was considerable confusion over who pays the high cost of nursing home care... Medicare, Medicaid, or you??? With the passage of the Health Insurance Portability and Accountability Act of 1996, our federal government made it clear who is primarily responsible for the cost of long-term care, and it is you!

Don't take chances with your future!!!!!!!!

You were pre-selected to receive this special long-term care insurance offer from Mutual United Evergreen Capital Assurance Company—

XXXVI.

MARJORIE

"You look so thin. Have you been eating enough?"

"I'm fine. I'm sorry I didn't make it last week. I had to go up north—the Memorial. How was the desert?"

"The desert?"

"You left a message. La Quinta."

"Oh! No—I didn't feel like driving."

Joan raised an eyebrow.

"I don't like the idea of you driving to Palm Springs, Mom."

"Cora's dog got sick. That's why we couldn't go."

"The little King Charles? What happened?"

"I think he has cancer."

"Poor thing!"

"She said leukemia but her son said a tumor. Joanie, I didn't think dogs *got* leukemia."

"They can. But promise you'll never drive to the desert, OK? It's too far."

"I promise. He's being treated by some pretty good doctors though."

"What's his name again? The dog?"

"Pahrump. I hope I get that kind of treatment!"

"God forbid. So how ya doing, Mom?"

"Oh! Not too badly. Not too badly. A little lonely but pretty well. Pretty well."

"I wish we could see more of each other."

"Oh! We can! I know how busy you are. We had a terrible thing happen here."

"What?"

"An Indian gentleman—a lovely man—someone shot him in his liquor store."

"You're kidding."

"Just around the corner."

"Where you buy your lottery tickets?"

"Such a *ghastly* thing. A wonderful, wonderful man. The neighborhood was really shaken."

"Mom, maybe we should move you elsewhere."

"Oh, that's silly, Joan!"

"Maybe Century City—that gated place. It's close to the mall. You wouldn't even have to drive."

"That place? Oh, it's like a prison! This sort of thing can happen anywhere. The police had a meeting with all the neighbors. They said it was unusual. I don't think we have much of a gang problem, and there hasn't been a burglary in *any* of these houses for as long as I can remember. Except maybe kid stuff. Vandalism."

"That is so scary. I mean, just a block away."

"Oh! I clipped something from the paper that I thought was cute."

"What is it?"

She handed her daughter the article. Joan scanned it.

"Well," said the old woman. "The CEO of Domino's Pizza went to India for the opening of their hundredth store. I didn't even know they had pizza shops in India! They landed in Delhi then chartered a helicopter to Agra to see the Taj Mahal. Just like something Hamilton would have done! And when they got there, a whole herd of elephants was waiting with 'Domino's Pizza' painted on them in red and blue."

"How disgusting."

Marj ignored the remark. "The elephants were a big help in the tsunami—they have a 6th sense like you *wouldn't believe.* Maybe you could use them as part of your design."

"That's a good idea, Mom, but I think the client wants something a little less representational. I don't think he's an 'elephant' kinda guy."

"Well, I thought you'd be tickled."

"It's very funny. Those CEOs really know how to live."

"Joanie—I was thinking that when—if you have the time— when you finish your project—I was thinking we could maybe go see it."

"I don't know if we're going to be chosen, Mom. But if we are, of course we'll go up. It'll be a pretty big deal."

"No, no—I meant the Taj Mahal. Do you remember how I used to read you the captions from that picturebook? So did your father. I always thought you became an architect because of that building. Was I wrong?"

"I think that probably had something to do with it," said Joan, with generosity.

"You used to talk about how beautiful it was. You called it a cream puff. Or a Foster's Freeze. I can't remember which."

Marj brought out *Mumtaz of the Taj Mahal,* which she had stashed nearby in anticipation of the visit, a worn portfolio of paperdoll cutouts—the ornate costumes of Shah Jahan and his favorite wife. The pages were well scissored, each clipped getup stored between bindings with a curator's fastidiousness. Joan was touched that her mother had treasured the childish keepsake.

"I haven't seen this in 30 years."

"One Halloween, Raymond dressed you like Mumtaz."

"Kinda morbid!"

"You were *darling,* absolutely *darling.* You had a little sequin stuck on your forehead. A bindi."

"You never got India out of your system, did you?"

"Oh! I don't see how one can! The hotel we stayed at in Bombay was like a *palace.* In fact, it is called the Taj Mahal Palace *to this day.*"

"Yes, Mother, I know. I've been hearing about it since before I could walk." She saw that the stupid remark had wounded her. "You know," said Joan, "now that you have the time and the money, I think you *should* go. I really do! You're in *great* physical shape—probably better than I am!—and a trip like that would do *wonders.*"

"Well . . . I *did* stop off at the travel agency."

"You're kidding!" Joan got morbidly excited by the idea of being let off the hook. She didn't want her mother driving to the desert but somehow it was all right for her to go to India on her own. "Mom, I think it's an *amazing* idea."

"But do *you* want to go?" said Marj, eyes sadly glinting. "You've worked so *hard,* Joanie. And I have plenty of money . . . we could use Bombay as our base! I have all the brochures Nigel gave me—he knows *everything about it.* We could ride elephants! I've always been frightened of that, same as I am of horses. When Ham and I went to Israel and Egypt—long ago, when it was safe—you couldn't get me on a camel for my life. But when I saw that little girl being saved by the baby elephant—"

"What little girl?"

"The one I was *telling* you about—I saw it on CNN."

"You didn't tell me . . ."

"She was going for a ride on the beach. On the morning of the tsunami. Was it Thailand? On a baby elephant. What is that place called where the tourists—you know, that in all the newsreels . . ."

"Phuket."

"Phuket! She was going for a ride—her parents were still sleeping. And suddenly, the elephant turns and *races* to the hills. It *knew* a big wave was coming. *Sensed* it. The *dearest* thing. And ever since I saw that, I've had the picture of both of us atop an elephant! The Kipling Girls!"

"It's a really lovely idea, Mom, truly, but I'm not sure how practical it would be for me to go on a big trip like that. It's like 24 hours just to get there, no?"

"Nigel said you can stop in England or Germany to rest."

"Not 2 of my favorite places."

"Or Tokyo—we could stay in Tokyo, if we go the other way. A 3-day lay-under!"

"Layover. I don't know, Ma. It's kind of mega."

Marj didn't know what she meant.

Her mother smiled and grew quiet. Joan handed her the book. Marj tucked the colorful illustrations—Mumtaz in an orange sari, carrying a rifle to assist the shah during a tiger hunt—back inside.

"Are you hungry?" asked Joan. "There's a great Indian restaurant I read about in the *Weekly.* Gitanjali, on Crescent Heights. Do you feel like Indian, Mother?"

XXXVII.

JOAN

THAT night, she dreamed of elephants.

Her father was in there too, face a blur—she really only knew it from a few old photographs. There was an image of them standing by a windmill on a miniature golf course. *Jesus. The kiddie golf course, just south of Cashio.*

She wondered about him awhile.

She carried the awareness of herself as one of those adult children with a parent who had disappeared. *Los desaparecidos.* Sometimes she thought she could still feel herself in his arms. He *had* read to her from that Taj Mahal book—the Taj, her first memorial, Koranic verses tattooed upon its delicate devastating sandstone skin, watery, Foster Frozen tomb everlasting. Emperor and wife. *Shah Samuel and his Esther.* Where was the difficulty in all this? Why was she such a cunt? Why was it so hard to envision traveling with Mom? The woman who wished her everything? How many years did she have left? She felt like one of those amphibian worms Barbet told her about that eat the skin off their mothers' backs. The looking-for-daddy thing was *so* trite, especially when she-who-gave-you-life sat forlorn and elegant, deep cataract well of chocolatey eyes asking to give of your heartstream. *Still looking for daddy:* when the being who nurtured you lay undone, besieged and beseeching. Joan felt the sting of it— what she *should* do is let Dr Phil ream her out in front of a live studio audience. Do a deathdance with Ellen DeGeneres . . .

How had she gotten herself into this? She realized now that the Freiberg Mem would be her final commission—or attempt. The blood of ambition, once boiling, had pooled out. She was anemic and gone reckless in her arterial, architectonic imaginings; her vagina was the only thing that gushed. Perhaps that was a good thing. Everything sickened her—restless and reckless. She'd al-

ways wanted to screw a billionaire and for that she remained un-
apologetic. Joan liked to fuck and titans usually fucked pretty
well. She saw Kirk Kerkorian cross the street once, in front of the
Regent Beverly Wilshire and thought, *He looks like a lion.* Not a
single bodyguard, no entourage, *nothin.* Double K made Lew
look like a squirt, though Freiberg probably had more money.
She'd *love* to climb a snowcapped mountain like K2. Lew was OK
in the sack but tended to say dumb things like "Love is a sexually
transmitted disease." Or "Health nuts are going to feel stupid
someday, lying in hospitals dying of nothing." Or "My ex called
our waterbed the Dead Sea." (After their last rendezvous, he'd actually said, "I love the smell of Napa in the morning!") She had a
feeling he memorized them out of those Yiddish humor books
people keep in the shitter. He had a serious side but liked to
karaoke to "In A Gadda da Vida" and the McGuire Sisters' "Picnic Morning" and tell creep-out jokes like the one about the Iraqi
woman whose doctor told her he needed blood, urine, and a pap
smear. "Here," she said. "Take my chador."

Seemingly, the oaf gene *and* the saccharine one ran deep in the
Freiberg clan. Lew revealed how Samuel and his wife loved the
poetry of Mattie Stepanek, the dysautonomic mitochondrial my-
opathy pinup who took forever to die. One day Joan was on the
treadmill at the gym watching a bunch of Mattie clips on *Oprah.*
(It was on the very day she saw the "Oprah Goes to Auschwitz"
billboard on Olympic.) The anniversary of his death, something
like that. A rerun of a rerun. There were firemen in the audience
and everyone was crying, including John Travolta and Joaquin
Phoenix. (The theme of the show was Heroes.) Snot was flying.
Oprah cried so much she wiped her chin with the heel of an open
palm like an old pro who knows that tears on the face sometimes
don't "read" for the camera. They panned off O to Mattie's mom
sitting in a special wheelchair because she had the same thing her
son died of. Passed it on to him and her other kids. There she was
in the motorized peoplemover with the expensive black leather
headrest that looked like something from Virgin Airways Upper
Class. O asked Mom what Mattie's last moments were like and

she said, "Well, each breath was agony. And we couldn't give him painkillers because that would be like giving him death. And he said he was ready to go, that he'd seen heaven, and heaven was nice, and he was ready. And I guess I wasn't"—sniffle, sniffle—"I guess I was kind of *selfish* but I said, Mattie, you have to hang on! And he said, OK, Mom, I will, cause I love you. And after *2 weeks of this*—I was bribing him, Oprah! I'd say, Mattie, where would you like to go? *We can go anyplace in the world. We can go to Disney World.* And he was *so weak*. Finally, I thought, I can't torment him anymore. I told him: Mattie it's OK, it's OK for you to go. And he just *gasped*. He was too weak to say anything but I think he was saying thank you."

Then, the suckerpunch. She said:

He had that same look my other 3 kids had when they went.

This would be Joan's last hurrah—that's how she thought of it—and she knew the phrase to be vaguely delusional, grandiose, because she'd never really had a 1st. There would be nothing to remember her by but the veined dome of her barren uterus. *Brunelleschi's Dome, bewitched, bothered, and unbuilt . . .* she would never be asked to design MoMA knickknacks or water-front condos; never be asked by Miuccia Prada to conjure the splintered jewel of a flagship; never be asked to lay out city master plans with Wolf D Prix/Coop Himmelb(l)au; never collaborate with Thom Mayne on government-subsidized wastewater treat-ment plants; never go pub-whoring with Tracey Emin or be in-vited to the Finnish Lapland to carve ice art alongside Future Systems, Tadao Ando and Rachel Whiteread, *El Zorro* and Yoko Ono, Kiki Smith and Isosaki; never be thrown on the Holocaust Memorial boxcar bandwagon (the latest, in Farmington Hills, an-nounced itself by emailed précis: *It's a new Holocaust museum that resembles a death camp. Its brick walls are surrounded by wire remi-niscent of the electrified barbed wire at Auschwitz. The building's top half is painted in blue and gray vertical stripes, as if it were clothed in an inmate's uniform. A tall elevator shaft looks like a crematorium chimney. Steel tubs resemble gallows. The trees surrounding the mu-seum are stunted and wiry, to suggest starving inmates*); never be

asked to star in magazine ads, like Matteo Thun balancing a maquette on his head for Canali, or standing inside a box, on Audi's
dime, like a gunsel in a roadshow Mummenschanz with the
Nike-esque slogo *Never Follow.*

> . . . the first architect to be given the Hiroshima Art Prize for work
> that promotes peace, is relentless in his vision to create spaces that
> are positive responses to the brutalities that surround us all.

Daniel Libeskind   *Never Follow*

*Never follow a relentless pussywhipped kike in python boots and a
Yohji trench who gets off on pouring rusted ☺'s into concrete Shoah
tribute troughs.* She saw Cowboy's recent design for an add-on to
the Royal Ontario Museum: it looked like a Sony Aibo robot dog
taking a bite out of a lovely old cathedral. An aesthetic train
wreck—you couldn't take your eyes off it. Maybe that was the
whole trick . . .
Some of the condos the starfuckitects were being asked to
design—aside from containing wine vaults and massive screening
rooms—literally had minimuseums of their own work! Meier
was putting up a building whose units were called "limited edi-
tions," signed and numbered acrylic models of each apartment
presented to the proud new owners as "closing gifts."
No. That would never happen to Joan Herlihy—

BARBET asked her to attend an opening at the Gagosian in
Beverly Hills.
And there he was again: the Renaissance Meier showing col-
lages or constructions or whatever at 10,000 a pop. *Pop goes the
easel.* Faux Cornellian boxes with artful effluvia of the great man's
double helix pasted within: a First Class (naturally) boarding pass
(JFK to LAX), a subscription label peeled from a magazine with
RM's name and address (East 57th), a *placement* card for some

fancy dinner—*Richard Meier* in High Society hand-inked cursive. The starchitect himself greeted all comers—tufthunting toadies—in a corner like a silver-fox cardinal fresh from a papal conclave. To Joan, he looked like a well-heeled dentist, the type with something questionable on his hard drive.

She'd met him before and he had always ignored her but this time, when Joan said how much she loved the "constructions," he looked her square in the eye and seemed to connect. Maybe he was horny. He probably wasn't such a bad person. She actually admired that church he did in Rome. He was no Thom Mayne—balling Ricky Meier wouldn't be a walk in the (memorial) park—but who knew. She thought she could probably do it if she had to.

XXXVIII.

RAY

THEY went to Little Indian Village on a drizzly day. She glowed with the life inside her. She never stopped smiling.

"You're feeling your oats."

That's what Ray liked to tell her, though BG hadn't a clue what he meant.

He wasn't feeling so bad himself.

They sat in a window booth of Ambala Dhaba grazing curried goat and Mysore bonda, spring dosa, and payasam. Then they went to market for spices and she bought zebra rice, tiger biscuits, Ovaltine, and a case of Manila mangoes. At a curio shop, he got her a small statue of Durgā on a wooden base, nicely detailed. The goddess strode a lion and possessed 8 arms; one held a trident, one a sword, another a lotus, another a conch shell, another an arrow. . . . Ghulpa said that when Durgā went to war she lopped off heads while trumpeting a conch—a one-woman band, for sure. He bought an emerald green sari to commemorate the pregnancy. Man, she was pretty. He told her she made him "prouder than all get-out."

They were late to the film. There were subtitles but some of the phrases were in English. At 1st, Ray thought it was silly. The story was about a wealthy man (he recognized the bearded, aristocratic actor from a poster she kept in the living room) who learned he was dying. He had a handsome son, a wastrel who'd recently married and moved with his wife into his parents' palatial home. The living room looked like the atrium of a Hyatt. The daughter-in-law was soon pregnant and the father wanted his son to get a job but the kid was too lazy; he had some damn-fool acting competition on his mind instead, a fantasy longshot that would make him solvent. Now that he'd been secretly diagnosed as having a terminal illness, the dad belatedly realizes he's ruined his son through a lifetime of coddling. He decides his legacy will be to force the boy to grow up—fast. So he kicks the newlyweds out of the main house and makes them stay elsewhere on the property (some punishment!), a kind of luxury Quonset with no electricity. Dad proceeds to generally torment his heir—already in his late 20s—until he has no choice but to earn rupees of his own (soon there will be another mouth to feed). The kid realizes how tough it is out there in the world. He tries his hand at being a movie stuntman and gets chased by a wild pack of dogs, then inadvertently set on fire. That sort of thing; slapstick but effective. The producer is impressed by the kid's bravery because he knows he's an amateur. When he asks what he is called, the young man won't say. "I am trying to make my name," he says. "When I do, you will hear it." The plot was dopey and Ray was surprised because it actually engrossed the hell out of him. (Every now and then there was a vigorous dance number and the actors stood and gyrated. The show would have been fine without it.)

Then came intermission—these Bollywood deals were *long*. A slideshow of advertisements: Indian lawyers who could get you out of jail, Indian tax lawyers, Indian immigration lawyers, Indian realtors who sold mansions right there in Artesia, Indian wedding planners, Indian haberdashers. After the slides there were a bunch of trailers for upcoming extravaganzas, with most of the actors looking suspiciously like the ones in the feature Ray and Big Gulp were sitting through.

The film resumed and the whole thing got very amazing. Ray thought it "damn fine." *Damn good.* It turns out that the dying rich guy (who was incredibly charismatic and looked like he was 55) is a famous toymaker and all he wants is to live long enough to see his grandchild born—and continue to strengthen his weak-minded son by being a major hardass. The tough love routine was heartbreaking to keep up and heartbreaking for his boy to endure, but it was what the "doctor" ordered. Finally, the kid has enough of Dad's bullying and tells him he was at fault for raising him too leniently! That all he ever wanted was "a finger to hold on to but you gave me an arm, all I wanted was to stand with my own 2 feet on the ground but you always hoisted me on your shoulders to get the royal view." He was eloquent and Ray had to admit the spoiled sonofabitch had a point. The kid said that when *he* became a father, he would *never* treat his son that way—nor would he ever banish him from his house or deprive his daughter-in-law food for the fetus—if *his* son stumbled, he'd be patient and give him time. (The dad said, in an aside, "I would give time if I had time"—but his progeny couldn't hear.) He was laying the guilt on pretty thick and Ray was worried the old guy would drop dead on the spot. He told his father he would *never* let him see the grand-kid. He was damned pissed and there didn't seem to be any way out of it. Things got more and more complicated, this and that happened, the boy managed to make the finals of the cockamamie talent show, suddenly he was odds-on national favorite—and if he won, the stakes were enough for him to become completely in-dependent.

On the night of the televised competition, they rush the sallow patriarch to the auditorium in some kind of beautifully appointed private ambulance. The arena's packed; even the producer that hired the son as a stuntman shows up. By mistake, he learns that his father is actually dying and finally understands the ruse. He stands onstage distraught and basically relinquishes his spot, telling the millions of people watching that the famed and beloved toymaker is on the ropes, and he doesn't give 2 shits about winning the damn contest, all he wants is that everyone should take a minute out of their lives—right then—and pray that his dad lives long enough to see his grandson, that his fate is in the au-dience's hands. He tells everyone that the toys his father made were responsible for millions of babies' 1st smiles—the word he used was *design,* his father "designed babies' 1st smiles"—that the old guy manufactured the big, cushy, friendly, forgiving toys that helped children learn they could fall down and get up again. Be-fore the transfixed mob, a shaky father and son meet onstage. He wipes his dad's tears away. "At last," says Pop, "you are a man! You, who caused so many to cry, now wipe away others' tears."

Just when Ray thought it couldn't get any more rollercoaster-emotional (Ghulpa was stifling sobs), the old guy clutches at his chest, the daughter-in-law goes into labor, and they're both rushed to hospital! The grandson's born and the father is discharged but has only a short time to live. Now he must give the baby a name: with a last breath, he christens him with his *own*. Ray finally got the whole Indian thing about rebirth—the child is father to the man.

The cycle would begin again, and that was how it should be.

It was damn fine. Damn fine.

On the way out, Ray looked at the poster for the film while BG used the restroom. It said, COME TO LAUGH, COME TO CRY, COME TO TERMS . . .

When they got to the car, Ghulpa, eyes still wet, told Ray he must christen *their* child. Without hesitation, he said Chester— she knew about his kids but had never been told their names— and she smiled her bucktoothed smile, repeating *Chester* under her breath, and it pained and startled him that he'd blurted out such a thing, that it would be seriously considered; it honored and frightened and overwhelmed him that the whole event was even happening. But life was like a dream and now he understood why, in the midst of melodrama, there was suddenly singing.

XXXIX.

CHESTER

ATTENTION: Business Owners & Individuals
Healthcare for the Entire Family
Medical Dental Rx
As Low as $54.95
Per Month.
ALL **Pre-existing conditions accepted!**
No **limitations on usage!**
YOU **cannot be singled out for rate increases or cancellations!**
NO **age restrictions!**
Limited Time Offer Good Through Friday!

⁂ ⁂ ⁂

He was seeing a lot of Laxmi and didn't know what to make of it. He really didn't want to analyze too much. He smoked pot for his pain, and Laxmi smoked along. Sometimes she brought her own. She could roll it too.

He showed her the healthcare fax and she said it sounded like a scam. He knew that, but wanted to know what she'd say. He liked that Laxmi saw through it. She said lately *everything* seemed "scammy."

"Did you know the Enron guys were trading futures on the *weather*? That's what it says in this documentary I got from Netflix. I'm not even kidding." She segued into a thing about how cigarettemakers were behind a campaign to send free coasters to young people because they knew kids tended to smoke when they drank. The tobacco industry "positioned itself as antismoking," and even teamed with drug companies to create inhalers for people with breathing problems. "The people who lobby that shit are among the most obscenely fucked-up dysfunctional entities on the face of the planet."

The way Laxmi talked cracked him up, even when they

weren't stoned. She took a megahit from the joint and they both guffawed.

She was writing a book about her "molestations." Her expat father had been in on that, though he wasn't "primary." She couldn't remember exactly what he'd done but there was inappropriate stuff for sure. Chess had a feeling that whatever went on with her dad might have had something to do with why a sensitive hippie chick like Laxmi would get involved with a crass guy like Levin. Another thing that made sense about it was the Jew Factor: the heebs tended to get *mucho pussita*.

So Laxmi sat on the couch and *journaled* in her Moleskine (he called it Molestskin) while they smoked dope and Chess watched TV. When they got hungry, if she hadn't brought food, they walked over to Ürth Café or a tea place on Melrose with a garden in back. He was attracted to her but didn't have much of a sex vibe going these days, probably cause all the painkillers had done a number on his testosterone. She didn't seem to care. In fact, he thought she might be relieved in light of her diary and all—being a port in the storm was OK by him. Still, he got Viagra samples the last time he saw his doctor, just in case. For that rainy day. The potential listed side effects spooked him: you could get a headache or your heart might start hammering or in rare cases, V-men went temporarily blind. He knew most of it was bullshit and maybe his pride was the only thing preventing him from giving the blue pill a whirl. (The shape reminded him of a baseball diamond.) Chess wasn't sure she was all that interested anyway. He didn't want to rock the vote. He liked her company. They were happy campers.

One afternoon they got *completely* out of their skulls and watched something on television about "assets forfeiture." There was a stretch of highway in Florida where cops pulled people over for burnt-out taillights or whatever—everyone from rapper-types to single moms with babies onboard. The cops acted all friendly but just when they were giving folks the greenlight, the pigs would say, *Oh by the way, do you happen to be carrying any contraband or firearms, and would you mind if we have a look?* The question was so left-field that it kind of blew people away, especially since they'd already been softened up for the kill. The cops then "confiscated" their money, peeling the lettuce right out of their wallets and purses! Told em whatever amount of cash they had was "suspect" and would, like, grab $300 from Mom while her 2 year old bawled in the backseat. The trippy thing being—Chess and Laxmi went from seizures of stoned-out laughter to slack-jawed silent awe—that the whole deal was full-on taped by police car camcorders! That's how above the law they were! You could go to court and try to get your money back (one guy had 9 grand taken off him, a builder who later proved he was on his way to buy a used tractor) but that *alone* would cost 20 or 30K. The segment bled over into other forms of corruption and the one that really stuck in Laxmi's craw was the 60something Grace Slick lookalike now facing 8 years in federal prison for sending Hillary Clinton a New Age "dreamcatcher," one of those Native American feather-things people hang on their rearviews. Eagles were under an endangered species protection act and even though the woman said she found the feathers while hiking, the motherfuckers were going to put her away! The last thing on the tube was about a kid who'd been raped and murdered. A guy abducted her from school. They finally figured out how he did it. The little girl had been told never to go with a stranger unless he used the codeword *Unicorn,* which only the family knew. What happened was, the parents got divorced and the husband told a friend about how clever they'd been. So the guy drives up after school and says, "It's OK, come with me: *Unicorn."* Then he takes her to a creek and fucks her in the ass and crushes her head in and they only catch him when he does the same thing (sans codeword) 10 years later. He confesses, sittin with the cops in the interrogation room, and tells em he's just like an alligator, he comes up and feeds then sinks to the bottom of the river for another 10 years or so, "digesting." That's just the way he is, he says, and nothing can ever change im. Laxmi cried hard at that one. Unicorns were the new bogeymans. Jesus! It was grimmer than the grimmest Grimm's.

* * *

REMAR phoned to say the parent company "was willing to settle for 50,000." Chess would have to sign a general release
(like he thought) "holding them harmless" from any future medical bills he might incur. Remar said it was a joke but he was obli-
gated to pass on the information. "They can eat their release and
shit it out in front of a jury too." Chess liked Remar; he made him
laugh. Hang tough, he said. The *Friday Night Frighters* were in for
a major scare of their *own*—and damn well knew it. Things were
lookin *good*. Parent company can rim my black ass. You heard of
Meet the Parents? Well, we gonna *eat* the *parent*.

LAXMI continued to give him nonsexual massages. She
poured her heart out. She wanted to be an actress, and write
books too, like Shirley MacLaine, a dream her mother once had.
Mom was a "major depressive." Laxmi read aloud from an incredibly moving article in the *Wall Street Journal* about an American boy who'd been abandoned in Nepal "back in the day." His
mother, originally from Beverly Hills, was named Feather (in his
stonedness, Chess misheard *Father* for Feather). His dad was a
Jew and an artist, just like *hers*—this was during the 60s—and
they lived on a commune in New Mexico before making the hajj
to India. (Laxmi said the parallels were weird: she'd been raised in
Beverly Hills before living with her parents in a "tribal family"
north of San Francisco.) The couple split Sebastopol and went to
Europe. Feather got pregnant and had their kid—the boy—in
Switzerland. She and her husband, who was kind of crazy,
wound up in Dharmsala, where the Dalai Lama makes his home.
Feather decided to become a Buddhist nun but the dad couldn't
hack it without her and snapped, begging on the streets of New
Delhi until the authorities sent him back to the States. Feather left
their child at a monastery. She was this ice queen whose own
mother had committed suicide and later, when he was grown,
half apologized for making certain choices and told her son the
only thing she ever wanted was to give him the *dharma*—a path
free from suffering. That was so tragically ironic to Laxmi be-

cause all of the woman's actions had only *caused* suffering. It made her cry (she cried a lot when she hung with Chess) because she thought of *her* father, alive and rich and mentally sound, and *his* abandonments and pretensions of detachment. He didn't have schizophrenia as an excuse! Schizophrenia would have been better than narcissism. Laxmi kept the saga folded up in her journal and reread it about a hundred times because it was so resonant. Her mom was long dead from an accident that Laxmi had an inkling was a suicide—the car swerved into a tree on a street called Lasky in the middle of the day—and now her father was in Pune, India, a wealthy, high-functioning guru capitalist. The story of the boy and his parents had motivated her to write the Moleskine memoir of her upbringing on a Sebastopol commune that was later branded a cult. Yes, she was young but so many youngish women now wrote stories of their adventures as drunks and seekers, addicts and adepts. She would do something different, something epic, she would finally be *understood,* she told Chess that's what women really wanted, and Laxmi hoped she could manage it without self-obsession. It was so *hard.* She cut photographs and epigrams from magazines and pasted them in her diary. She made little drawings too but most of the time felt completely lost.

They bonded over the fathers they never really knew. 2 hurt people tilting against the injustices of the world. And all that. She liked listening to what she dubbed Chester's "love rants" (so named, he thought, because he got so passionate; she called him Chester, never Chess). The latest was on class-action suits. There were apparently attorneys who specialized in suing banks for the clever little wrongs regularly committed against customers. Judges forced settlements—5,000,000 here, 10 or 20 there—and the lawyers took half. The rest was distributed, minus a mysterious calculus of deductions, to X number of the public, who never even knew they were involved in a class-action suit to begin with. That would explain how one day he got a check in the mail for "Zero and 23/100 Dollars"—23¢. (Laxmi went on a mucousy laughing jag when he dug through a drawer to show her the perforated stub.) The Internet said if you didn't cash it, the 23¢, or whatever, would go to a shadowy "charity," the beneficiary details of which the banks refused to disclose. He spent an hour at Washington Mutual, standing there while pain shot up his leg, just so he could endorse his 23¢. (Laxmi went on another jag.) Worse than that, Chess was convivial with the teller, who was some kind of mongrel bitch that wouldn't even joke along through the bulletproof glass; the microphone system was so fucked that when he wasn't cupping his ears from feedback he was practically doing sign language.

(Laxmi nearly crapped her pants.)

He dared to wonder how much he could squeeze out of *Friday Night Frights*. There had to be a formula to it, one of those statistical templates accountants dispassionately applied and attorneys rubberstamped. Had to happen each and every day. Buyouts and hush money settlements made the world go round! Shit, they were still giving so-called falsely accused Rampart scandal cops 5,000,000 apiece—and they'd *already* compensated the bad guys to the tune of 50 or 60 mil. Chess thought it would probably be hard for *him* to get a mil, but you never knew. He wasn't even *close* to plumbing the litigable depths of his physical trauma, no real diagnosis seemed on the horizon, plus Remar said it was the type of thing juries would automatically be sympathetic toward because "plain folks" could definitely relate. Everyone could see themselves in exactly this kind of unjust situation; for reality shows (like frequently sued tabloids), settlements were the cost of doing business. The popularity of the genre was definitely on the wane and jurors would probably want to sock it to em, for fun. Nobody liked to be made a fool of for free—it was unAmerican. Besides, Remar said he'd scored with a bunch of similar cases. Chess hadn't yet had the giddy conversation with counsel about how much he might expect monetarily. The lawyer would take a 3rd but hadn't even clarified if the award was taxable. Part of him didn't want to know. Part of him knew that whatever anyone got in this world would be chopped off like that knight in the Monty Python movie, arm by arm, leg by leg, until only a dancing torso remained.

He just needed to make sure his slice of the piñata had enough cash stuffed inside: if it was ¾s of a million, then Remar and the MDs could *take* the arms and legs. ¾s of a mil was a lot, as long as you made sure to move your ass out of the country. Go subtropical and comport yourself like a king. Set up shop in a walled compound in San Miguel de Allende, right next to Remar and his gay caballero's homo hacienda. Laxmi told him that in Costa Rica you could get a hundred acres easy, plus servants, chef, and private yoga instructor—for the rest of your livelong days.

For now, he had other concerns. He needed about $5,000 until mind and body were wrapped a bit tighter. Something to float him for the next few months. He put the call in to Marj. She had plenty of bread and he'd never asked for much; that had to count for something. He didn't want to give too many details about the *FNF* fiasco (the whole thing embarrassed him—an authentic part of the pain and suffering angle) but would think of an "alternate history," as Laxmi put it about various aspects of her journal.

XL.

MARJORIE

*I*T'S *some kind of bone spur but they don't think I'll need surgery. It's pressing against a nerve—the sciatica. Yoga's really helping. I know a girl, a real yogahead. She takes me to this studio and we do Bikram. They keep it over a hundred degrees. It's a sweatbox but you feel a thousand times better when you're done. I've been doing some Pilates too, but it's costly. They have these beautiful machines, beautifully designed. One of em's called a Cadillac—leather padding, gorgeous wood, nice straps. Elongates the muscles. No, they work with injured people all the time. I think they were originally designed for people with injuries. Anyway, it's not an injury, Ma, we're not really sure what it is yet. An "inflammatory process." That's the big phrase. The main thing is it's limited the amount of time I can spend in the car. Which is where I spend most of my time, as you know, because of the nature of my work, which was going very well until a few weeks ago. I didn't want to bother you about it. I'm holding off on an epidural. I've already had an MRI and X-rays, and the epidural is next. I've talked to a lot of people who've had em and they're pretty successful. They can really pinpoint the pain. Usually you need 3 of them and there's one they do that really targets the problem, they go in real deep. It's all outpatient. No, no, the last thing I want is surgery. The insurance thing is hard right now but I got a great attorney and we're working that out. Oh yeah! I had to get an attorney. I'm not looking to make a killing, Ma, I'm just looking to feel better. So I'm spending a helluva lot less time in the car, which is a good thing. But how are you doing? You look great, Ma. You're in better shape than I am! The good news is, I'm about to get a chunk of money. A serious chunk. A settlement. You know my friend Maurie? Remember my old friend Maurie Levin, Mom? Well, he finally got it together to make a feature. He's been kicking it around for years. A dark little comedy. He cowrote it with the guy who did* Million Dollar Baby. *Did you see that film, Mom?*

Million Dollar Baby? *With Clint? Clint Eastwood? Was Ham still alive? Maybe not. Ham liked to go to the movies, didn't he? Didn't Hamilton like to go to the movies? He would have liked that one.* Million Dollar Baby *was the Clint Eastwood, and the guy who wrote it directed a movie about LA that made a lot of money.* Crash. *That's what they called it. Did you hear about it, Ma? Did you watch the Academy Awards? It got the Academy Award. But I'm talking about the other movie the guy did, the boxing movie. I know you like Clint Eastwood, but I don't know if you'd like this one—*Million Dollar Baby. *I can bring over the DVD. You have a DVD player, don't you, Ma? It's about a girl boxer. Probably not your thing. That girl Hilary Swank, the one who kind of looks like a guy though every time you see her in a magazine she's all done up to make you forget it. Good lookin woman but her bread and butter seems to be the roles where she's a tomboy or a cross-dresser or whatever. I don't know if* Million Dollar Baby *would be your thing. It wasn't really mine either, but it was well done. Very well crafted. Good script. Dark. Hilary won an Academy for it, her 2nd. She must be the luckiest person in the world. She finally dumped that dipshit husband. Pardon my language. Jeez, what a cipher. Pretty good movie though—old Clint knows his stuff. A pro. Been doin it forever. Anyway, Maurie's going to direct a film from a script he cowrote with the* Crash *guy and yours truly is going to produce! That's* right. *I think Haggis is a Scientologist. You know, there's so much bullshit written about Scientologists but they must be doin something right. They always get bad-rapped but how come so many of em are so successful? And* happy. *How come? I'm going to go down to the Celebrity Center and check it out. There's just too many famous, rich, happy Scientologists! It can't be a coincidence. They hate shrinks and so do I. Useless carbuncles on the ass of society. What, is it going to be any crazier than* Islam *or the* Kabbalah *or* Christianity? *I don't think so! Our movie's fairly low-budget—these days, 15,000,000 is low-budge, Mom!—so I'll get a nice chunk of change around the end of the year. Be able pay you back without a problem. I know you're not worried. No, Ma, I insist. Have I ever not paid you back? I'll even give you* interest—*I have it all printed out in one of those accounting programs. QuickBooks. My assistant did it for me. Very official. Ma,* *you're not a bank. No, no, no. Are you serious? Because it's not neces-sary. I mean, that would be amazing. You know, all I needed was 5 but 10 is fantastic. 10 will really, really help, Ma. A check is great or a transfer—what do they call that, a wire transfer?—however you want to do it. I'm ignorant. Whatever's easiest and whatever makes you com-fortable. I'm still at the same place. You've never seen it? I can't believe that. Yeah, Don Knotts's daughter! Yes, it's sad. Very sad. One of the greats of all time. Karen is amazing. When she found out what hap-pened, about the bone spur, she dropped by and brought me soup and stuff. She's the best. But 10 is great—that'll really help with car insur-ance, rent, all that good stuff. I'll make it last, Ma—it's not like I'm shopping at Barneys! But how you doin? Seriously. You OK? You sure? You look good. You look great. I love that jacket. What is that, Chanel? Or is that a Tremayne Clothiers original! How's Joanie—she OK? I haven't talked to her since Ham's memorial. She's a little—you know Joanie, the air she breathes is sometimes a bit rich. That's her, al-ways was. I don't like to judge but I'm a tad more working class. Not so fancy. I could live for a year on what she runs through in a week. But she's talented, a very talented gal, I'm not running her down. She's my little sister. Very, very talented. I just hope she gets her due. She should have a kid already. Wouldn't you like to be a grandma? I might sur-prise you on that score myself! If she doesn't make you one, I will, how bout that? Do we have a deal, Ma? But she should have one, seriously. Meeting men was never a problem for Joanie! Unless maybe she can't—have a kid. They're all adopting now. Meg Ryan got one from China. And look at Angelina Jolie—I always thought she couldn't, but there ya go. Shiloh. That kid's gonna be a heartbreaker. Can you imag-ine having Brangelina's genes? I'd like to be in her jeans. And fit in Brad's! You know, I'm really sorry I haven't been to see you, Ma, but I've been swamped with preproduction stuff and trying to sandwich doctors in between. I've had so many scans I feel like one of those air-port luggage machines. I ran into Cora outside. Yeah, of course I said hello. Her son was just leaving. What's his name, Stein? Anyhow, Franken-stein was pulling out. That's my pet name for him. He's got a black Rolls, I couldn't believe it. They're like Jewish mafia pimpmo-biles. I'm kiddin, Mom. But it's like a tank. A 400,000 dollar tank.*

You couldn't give me one of those. Well, maybe if you gave it to me! Stein—that name! Frankenstein waved, and off he went. I chatted with her a minute—nice lady—and she said her dog got sick. Then she started talking about her fatass son. Sorry, Ma. Excuse my language. I'm not running him down. Probably a good guy. Treats his mom right. That's how you have to judge a person. Lucky guy though. You don't drive a car like that without having some kinda killer karma. Pardon the pun: car-ma. *You know Cora seemed a little out of it but she's smart as a whip. I asked her what Stein did—for a living. Know what he does, Mom? Did you ever talk to her about it? It's so* crazy. *I didn't really even understand what she said. The guy distributes drugs—prescription drugs—to pharmacies. He stockpiles em in warehouses. And she said that every January the drug companies jack the prices of the pills or whatever and her son collects on the difference! It sounded like stock futures or . . . the racetrack! I don't* know *what it sounded like. I couldn't figure it out but my brain isn't so big. That's why I don't drive a Rolls! I'm glad you and Cora look out for each other. You do, right? You have her number pasted on the fridge? Neighbors have to look out for neighbors, especially in your age bracket. Widows are a prime target. I was watching* 60 Minutes. *Those telemarketers—ever get a call from a telemarketer, Mom? Promise to let me know if you do. Do you promise? Do you promise, Ma? Let me know if someone calls and wants you to invest in gemstones, OK? Or "reverse mortgages." Whatever that is. Mike Wallace was all over that. Jesus, I think he's older than Don Knotts, and Don Knotts is dead! Seriously, the guy looks better than* I *do. Maybe he's got pain too, who knows. Sucks it up and lives with it. Probably's had 14 epidurals. Different generation. The Great Depression generation. Different mindset, stoical. My generation, we're just* depressed! *Mike Wallace—now there's a guy who could afford a Rolls. All* those 60 Minutes *people. There's like 12 of them, right? But you let me know if somebody calls and says they want to put your money in "guarantee bonds." They call them the "8 Gs of senior softspots": guarantee bonds, gambling, gardening, golf, gourmet food, grandchildren, groups, and Greyhound bus trips. These people are professionals at gathering information. They trick you into giving them your Social. Don't* ever *give anyone your Social—OK, Ma? Promise? You know how they say never to use an ATM at a 7-Eleven? You never heard that, Mom? You don't ever do that, do you? I mention it cause I know you buy lottery tickets. Never use the ATMs in those places. Or a liquor store. You don't do that, right? Only use ATMS inside your bank. Cause these other ATMs are information gatherers. They're like spybots in computers. Spyware. I read all about it. If you're at the mall and they're giving a car away and you want to be a contestant or whatever and you fill out a form, these guys are in a consortium—it's like* The Sopranos—*and they wind up buying all the names for like a hundred dollars a pop. That's how they get their victims. They call em mooch lists. Don't enter any contests, Ma! Dentists are supposedly the easiest targets cause they've got issues with self-esteem. That's what I read. Isn't that funny? I think it was in* Time *magazine or something. Somewhere. Dentists are big losers—they're prime. I'm saying this as your son. Thank God you don't have a computer! I can't tell you the solicitations I get over the Internet. From Nigeria. From Johannesburg. I got one from a guy who said he was handling the estate of an entire family that went down in Lockerbie! I barely remember Lockerbie. He wants my help. I can become a 25% beneficiary—for a small fee! Me, Chester Herlihy, of West Hollywood! Good luck, buddy. I told him I had back problems and had to reboot. They're always from Africa. The blacks are the blacks, I don't care where they live. And I'm no racist. Anyhow, I keep getting these stickers in the mail with my name and address. They come once a week. They're from charities, legit charities, harelip-fixers, that think you're supposed to be thrilled they've printed out your name. I never throw em out because what if someone picks them from the trash and uses em? I can see why people become packrats. You know, anyone can fill out a form and have your mail changed so that you go to pick it up one day and suddenly it's being delivered someplace else! I mean, the post office hasn't figured that one out yet! It's like the whole cargo container thing. Can you imagine? I think you can do that with a driver's license too. You just drop by the DMV and tell em you lost your license, give em a name and they pump it out. See, you could never do that with a credit card. The credit card people are all over that. If it doesn't involve money*

*though—a fraudulent little address change or a bogus driver's li-
cense—it's easy! Party time! I got an envelope the other day that said in
this fake kid's-pencil-scrawl computer font:* I JUST DON'T WANT TO BE
HIT ANYMORE—HELP ME PLEASE! *Inside was a letter saying how some
kid was beaten with a stick because his uncle made him do "bad
things." Can you imagine the scams, Ma? I mean, the* scope. *That
Palestinian bitch who lured the little Jewish kid off the Internet? Said
she wanted to meet him for sex? After they shot him, all she had to say
was, he was "cute." We're never gonna beat the terrorists. We can't
compete. If you* ever *get a fireman or a cop or a whatever who comes to
the door,* do not answer. Cops *never* come to the door. And if they do,
you are not required to let them in—*it ain't the law. OK, Ma? You
don't legally have to provide access. They need a* warrant. *That's
right—just like the movies. Ask for their card and their phone number,
then* call me. These guys impersonate *cops. And they're not just
blacks. The really good ones are lily white. They impersonate cops and
firemen and whatever, the BTK guy did that, told people he was checking the phone, for chrissake. Oldest one in the book. That guy in Manhattan did it, set a fire in the hall then knocked on some chick's door and
of course she let him in. So if that ever happens, unless the neighborhood is being attacked by Al Qaeda and everything's going up in smoke
or there's a* serious *earthquake, or unless it's someone you know, you
give me or Cora a* call, *or call 911. OK? Even the* government's getting into the act. The government is targeting the elderly, Ma! If you
get on a "list of felons" they* will *make your life miserable. They'll
threaten to take away your Social. I'm talking about maybe a traffic
ticket you forgot to pay* 30 *years ago. Or a ticket* Hamilton *forgot to
pay. I'm talking about some felony your "alter ego" committed—the
other Marjorie Herlihy. Marjorie Herlihy, the Pomona welfare fraud
queen! But they don't care! They'll come after you, Ma, even if you're
disabled! And I won't be able to help, financially anyway, till I get my
settlement. So if you ever have something like that happen,* call me. I
*know a terrific guy, one of the top attorneys. Remar DeConcini. Tough
as they come. Remar's A-one. He's black, by the way. Now: are you
hungry, Mom? Why don't we do Indian. Oh! I brought you some
books and DVDs. The DVDs are an* Oprah *compilation. The money*

goes to charity. And I got you 2 books. One is exercises you can do for arthritis. The other's called Die Rich and Tax Free! *Kind of a morbid title but I thought you might like it. Might give you some helpful hints, though I know you keep up on this stuff cause Hamilton was good at it. He taught you stuff, right? You're not offended, are you? It's funny, isn't it? The title? Yeah, I laughed too! We can cross out the "Die" and write "Live." "Live Rich—or Die Tryin!" Come on, let's go, I'm starved. Yeah, I got the check, I put it away, and thank you. Ma, it's right here, in my wallet. You want to see? It's already deep in my pocket.* Thank you, Mom*—that's really going to make a difference. I love you. Now let's go have Indian. And you gotta let me treat. OK? You promise? You promise you'll let me treat?*

XLI.

JOAN

S HE hadn't heard from Lew and that didn't feel right.
Pradeep was in town. She fucked him, over at the Four
Seasons. He went to the bathroom and shut the door. This
time he didn't light incense. A minute after he settled back in bed
the smell from his offal wafted out like half-burnt oatmeal.

When Joan told him she'd had an affair with Lew, the consul
clucked and laughed. He wagged his finger and said, "Naughty."
She was about to get pissed when he reversed himself and told her
it was probably a *good* thing. Pradeep really had a gift—the unctuous diplomat through and through. In this case, she needed
someone to sponsor her insanity.

"You know," said Pradeep. "It's actually quite a smart move—
he likes a 'raider.' He hobnobs with the corporate raiders, no? So
he admires bravado, especially in a brainy woman. Look, this isn't
a guy who gets threatened by men *or* women. So don't beat yourself up. And you know you're toe-to-toe against Rem and God
knows who else. Because Lew's not going to *tell* you. I agree, he
will use Goldsworthy either way. Goldsworthy is not your concern. It's the *secret* ones who are your concern. But I don't see this
'alliance' as a problem. This *grande affaire*. The odds were *always*
stacked against you, Joanie, and you know it." He pronounced
against like an Englishman, which had a way of comforting her.
"Did you hear he was going to do something in bronze?"

"Who?" said Joan.

"*Andy*—Goldsworthy is going to do something *bronze-*
worthy."

"You're kidding. Who said that? Lew?"

"No . . . I don't know where I heard it."

"If Goldsworthy's doing something in bronze, then I am *so*
fucked."

"But why?"

"Because he's supposed to be working in *rock* or *leaves* or snaky little *arrowheads*. Anything that's built *to last* is going to majorly threaten me."

"*Don't* be threatened, OK, Joanie? It's not *worth* it. Maybe I was dreaming."

THEY went to Barneys and she offered to buy him an extravagant pair of shoes. He declined, so Joan tricked him into waiting for her at the restaurant while she closed the deal. She was going to get him Barker Blacks but thought the skull-and-bones thing kind of lame. She settled on a pair of Berlutis, fashioned from scarified cowhide; the marks were made when the animals rubbed against barbed-wire fencing. The salesman warmed to this macabre embellishment with the inverted pride of a car salesman talking about the efficiency of hybrid engines. The loafers were almost 13-hundred dollars.

Pradeep drove them to the Coldwater Canyon park where all the rich ladies took their newborns.

She'd had enough of herself and asked about his life, something she usually avoided.

"How is Manonamani?"

"I think she is well." Then came a sly, sad little laugh.

"Do you like having kids?"

"Yes. I *love* it. Even when things aren't going so wonderfully. It's hard for her, more than me. She doesn't leave the house when she's here—in the States—it's gotten worse. I think it's a phobia. We don't even go to the opera anymore. It is 100 times as bad since we lost Ghulpa. Our runaway nanny—our runaway *bride* only she had no groom as far as we could tell! It has been *hell* finding a replacement. Also Mani's father is ill, and her mom not far behind. Sometimes it is a bit 'parlous.' So she is there now, with the babies. In Delhi. I go when I can. There is not much between us, body to body. For events at the house, she no longer comes out. She stays 'in quarters.' It isn't easy and will affect my next post.

They hear about everything in Delhi, believe me. But all's health is good. And this is what is important."

He knocked the wood bench with his knuckles.

"How much time do you have left?"

"As consul? A year, maybe 14 months. Then: back to Delhi. I am afraid I will become Tony Bennett. I will leave my heart in San Francisco." He put an amorous hand on the ridge of her hip. "I hope to leave my loins *here*."

He winked and she groaned. He laughed.

"Then?" she asked.

"Then? Who knows. Maybe a desk job. I am a corps man to my core! Perhaps Sydney. Or Tanzania—Dar es Salaam is very close to Mauritius. We *have* to go, Joan; Flic en Flac. Iceland! We could have a frigid rendezvous and *slowly* melt away. I hear there's an *extraordinary* B&B carved from ice, courtesy of your *El Zorro,* Queen Hadid!"

"That's *Finland,* you ass."

"We could have that special dish," he said mischievously. "You know: rotting shark! This is the delicacy Björk's husband told me of at the BAM dinner. You can be poisoned if you don't let it rot *long* enough. Did you know this, Joan? But the same is true of anything, no? We could eat smoked puffin with skyr and fly back to Delhi for goat fetus."

He could see she was in a mood. He laughed and did the diplomatic dance that came so naturally, stroking the nape of her neck, saying he was "just making jokes." He "more than valued" their time together and said she shouldn't worry about Lew Freiberg, "not at *all,*" and that he'd do his best to "counterspy and lobby" on her behalf. He *was* a sweet soul—the only man she'd ever been able to share bed and friendship with, which said more about him than her. She liked to tell Pradeep that she was a "tough nut."

As they strolled to the car, past runaway mommies, nannies, and absurdly expensive perambulators, he spoke seriously of a "getaway." They both knew it wouldn't happen but his tones were so enticing, so dulcet as they say, so *diplomatic,* that she let hands and voice wash over her. He wanted to show her the ashram in Pondicherry, where Antonin Raymond and even Lew Freiberg's favorite "interior decorator," Nakashima, had practiced as devotees of the Hindu mystic Sri Aurobindo. She'd heard of the place and of course was interested—for professional reasons. You needed special permission to even visit Golconde, as it was called: never a problem for her "connected" friend. She'd seen pictures of it, filled with teak, walls of crushed-seashell plaster and burnished limestone. Pradeep was the consummate consul; he seduced by getting under the world's pearlescent skin.

WHEN Joan got home, a couple of packages were waiting, one large, one small. The labels said GUERDON LLC. The part-time doorman brought them up.

The handwritten card said: "Let's Get Lost (Coast)." A hastily scrawled PS asked if she'd be available to come up again next weekend for his birthday. His kids were going to be with him in Mendocino and he wanted to "show them off." She opened up the boxes and here's what was inside: a diamond Piaget watch on a knobby shagreen strap; a WW1 gold and ruby-studded powder case with her initials (it once belonged to Jean Harlow); a vast, silk-embroidered Nurata Suzani she had admired in his bedroom; and a crate of blood oranges.

She thought, *I am in for some kind of ride.*

XLII.

RAY

THE Friar came home.

The old man cut up tiny bits of filet and fed him from the end of a sharp plastic fork. He went to sleep beside his master, as Ray watched that *Dog Whisperer* fellow do a stint on Oprah. Then Ray popped in a *Twilight Zone* DVD.

The lawyer was stopping by in the morning to discuss the City of Industry's offer. Ghulpa had a sleepless night. She'd been disturbed by some items in the Indian papers they'd picked up while in Artesia. One said that the number of Asiatic lions in the Gir Forest had risen in the past few years after a crackdown on poachers; another, that every single tiger in a Rajasthan sanctuary had been illegally slaughtered. The conflicting stories (Ray didn't understand how they conflicted, because as far as he could gather they took place in different regions) had distressed BG immensely, and he could do nothing to assuage her. The dog snored at the foot of the bed, his dream state deep and placid. He was still under the influence of medication.

At 3 in the morning, she riffled papers on her nightstand to show Ray a clipping about attacks on human beings in Bombay. (Funny how the Indians lumped lions, tigers, and leopards all together—they seemed to mean the same thing.) The cats came at dusk and crept into tin shanties and orphanages to steal their prey, just like in the stories her parents told her. 14 people had been killed since the beginning of the year. Ghulpa was particularly bothered by the fact that some fatalities were the result of leopards leaping onto victims from their perch in trees. It made her shudder. That detail wasn't particularly alarming to the old man; what got him was the part about folks being snatched while they "squatted outside, answering nature's call."

A well-to-do lawyer had been half-eaten while jogging near

Film City, where the Bollywood movies were made. Evidently, the pitiless beasts liked hanging around the backlots. Big Gulp looked toward the poster in the living room, as if suddenly worrying about the safety of the famous "Mr B," her supercoiffed matinee idol. (She sometimes called Ray "Mr B" too, but the *B* was for "Bapu.") Ghulpa spoke of their child, averring she would never "show it" India. "Either you are eaten by devil-tigers or washed away by monsoon," she said, and Ray wasn't sure if she was altogether joking.

He almost told her that cougars ate people right here in LA, then thought better. The bones of a boy had just been found in Big Bear, a 9 year old presumed killed by a mountain lion; they could tell by the bite marks on the skeleton. The theory was he'd been attacked in the woods then dragged to an isolated area. In fact, Ray had just read about some rangers who were monitoring pumas not so far away—about a hundred miles. They heard pitched cries for 3 hours but couldn't tell if it was fighting or breeding. (The rule is they're not supposed to interfere.) "The mortality beep" came at dusk—the collar around the animal's neck emits a sound when there's been no movement for 8 hours. The rangers hiked over and discovered that the male had killed his mate, who was in heat; she was probably just protecting her kitties. He weighed almost twice as much but she put up a helluva battle. Sometimes, the rangers said, males kill their own sons, just because they consider the turf—all hundred-and-35,000 acres of it—to be theirs alone.

Finally, Ghulpa slept. He padded to the kitchen with the offending *India Post* and fetched some cold filet from the fridge. He sat at the small Formica table and got carnivorous, throwing some of his favorite ruffled potato chips and Heinz 57 into the mix, washing everything down with a can of Coke. He felt good—like a big old mangy cat himself. His dog was back, his woman had the seed of life in her, *and* the city was going to make him rich. Raymond Rausch had his hundred-and-35,000 acres but was in no mood for a kill.

What did it matter that he was a lion in winter?

It's good to be the king.
He flipped through the paper, ending at the classifieds.

BRIDES WANTED
JAT SIKH PARENTS
Invite correspondence for their handsome son.
Seek U.S. citizen, family oriented bride
For their 28 yrs, 5'9" son, family well settled
In California.
Son is working on H1.
Please reply with biodata
And photo must
Caste no bar
Contact P.O. Box No. 79-M-145
c/o India Pacific

Caste no bar—neither cast ye your pearls before swine . . .
The winds were at it again, and the trees outside, such as they were, shook like false prophets. He fell into troubled dreams himself—he'd placed an ad for a bride and felt guilty to be disrespecting Big Gulp. She was his partner, had been loyal, selflessly nursing him through hard times, she'd pressed his feet and laughed at his bad jokes. So why was he advertising for a bride? And why was one of the candidates already sitting in a new home he'd bought with their settlement, high in the hills where the pumas keened? He had used the City of Industry monies to acquire land, behind her back, and a ranch house up in Angeles Forest—knowing Ghulpa was terrified of wildcats, and knowing that was where they grabbed kids off their Schwinns. What had she done to deserve this? Why had he treated her this way? The doorbell rang. Another bride arrived. Ghulpa belligerently served lukewarm tea to the growing crowd. This time, the bride was a man, and Ray had mixed emotions. He got queasy and tried to remind himself he was dreaming. Then the old man felt better for BG's sake, because her mood lightened. She was jealous no more. But Ray was bewildered: the white-veiled newcomer was his own

son—the bride was Chester—and that made him cry softly in his sleep, tears keeping him in the shadowland of awareness, as a febrile knight held hostage by a moat. He was worried about waking Ghulpa though not actually awake himself.

THE lawyer arrived and Ray was surprised when the Friar bared his teeth. He was ready to be called Nip again, adjusting to being back home. (Come morning, he vomited, peed, and trembled nonstop. Thank the Lord he would soon begin rehab.) Ghulpa had to put him in the bedroom behind closed doors, because it looked like he was about to attack between fits.

The meeting was short. Mr ACLU was upbeat. The city's offer had "bumped" to 375,000 but he still felt they could do better. Ray turned to Ghulpa and she grew morose, the way she did while contemplating matters of a serious nature, such as monthly budgetary concerns or the troubles of a cousin, be they astrological, physical, or romantic. She asked the attorney if any harm could be done by "going back on the table." He seemed happy with the query and said, "Absolutely not. If you're asking if we're in danger of them rescinding the current offer, I can tell you the answer right now: No. They will either agree to pay more, or stay at the same place. *I* think they'll go up. It may take a few weeks, but things are moving pretty quickly—that's indicative of the open-and-shut nature of this case. So even if they say they *won't* pay more, my hunch is it'll be a bluff. Let's keep our poker face awhile. Trust me, they will *not* want this in a courtroom."

Ray cut the folderol.

He asked the gentleman what he recommended.

"I *recommend* that we do as Miss Ghulpa suggested. You are wise beyond your years," he said, in a complimentary aside. "I recommend we go back to the table. We have nothing to lose and everything to gain. It is my *asseveration* they'll step up. This isn't about being aggressive. This isn't about greed. The issue at hand is the city making *right* a rather reprehensible *wrong*. They have the resources for this sort of thing, Mr Rausch—you won't be picking anyone's pockets! If you like, we can even designate some of the monies to a charity, say, an animal fund. The Friar Fund— how does that sound?" he said, with a wink. "A scholarship for veterinary students . . . it's win-win. *Everyone* can win, and that means the city as well, because they are admitting to a large mistake, and in this country, people need to be accountable. We seem to have strayed from that notion—accountability has become a dirty word. In some circles. My own personal feeling is that mistakes need to be admitted to, corrected, and compensated for. *That's* democracy. We concede culpability, then move on. That's the moral imperative. That's the high ground.

"So: how's everyone feeling? Do I have your permission to return to the table?"

XLIII.

CHESTER

THE chick from "My Favorite Weekend" called, right while he was sitting on the couch trying not to panic about the spastic bundle-bolt of electricity shooting from his elbow to the middle of his biceps. Also, he'd taken 3 Percocets and was just starting to get a buzz, but hadn't eaten anything, so there was nausea attached.

He popped 2 Compazines. She asked if he got the email and fax she sent. Chess told her his computer crashed, and he never got a fax. (Both of which were true.) The thought occurred that he might have blown it. She said she would fax him again. He wondered if she was hot. *Maybe I should ask her out. Maybe she's the type who likes to blow stoned, crippled location scouts.*

Did he mind if they did some of the column as "a phoner"? *Not at all. We could do it as a boner.* Where did he like to eat? Caught off guard Chess said JAR for brunch (he'd only been once, with Levin and Laxmi) and that he loved the way it looked since it was redone. (That's what *Maurie* said, anyway—Chess hadn't been there since.) The chick responded with something that implied *too many* people liked JAR for brunch and he kicked himself. OK. He liked L'Ermitage—"always lots of rappers"—and the new Ivy at the Shore. Even though it wasn't as great as the old Ivy at the Shore. The little breakfast place across the street from the Viceroy. *Blah.* He was rambling. She asked if, being a scout and all, he'd discovered any new or far-flung places (translation: funky/interesting), still within city limits of course. *Dipshit! You forgot the angle—the below-the-line location scout angle. Why the fuck else would they care about how you spent your shitty, pain-ridden weekends? Do you want to be in the* Times *or not?* He managed to dredge up The Bucket, in Eagle Rock—a burgerstand "classic." (Thank God it came to him.) And Clifton's, downtown (a genuine fave). She loved all that. Just what the bitch wanted to hear. He began talking about Laughlin Park, the grand but little-known gated hood in Los Feliz where he sometimes scouted commercials. He told her that's where David Fincher and his wife lived, in the old Lily Pons house. (He forgot exactly who Lily Pons was. Maybe he never really knew. The chick didn't ask.) Chess wondered if she thought he was a loser and a name-dropper, but figured the *Times* liked that sort of anecdotal embroidery. Besides, now he was really feeling the Percocets and chattily segued into Guide to Forgotten LA mode. She seemed to warm to the new tack—Jesus, you couldn't talk restaurants forever. He even mentioned the old train store on Sepulveda his dad used to take him to when he was kid; the place was actually still there. She thanked him and said she had to run.

He was sure he'd missed his chance but an hour or so later, the fax machine rang while he was sitting in the can. Did its whole antiquated spewing-forth number.

The weird thing was that his pain had dissipated during their chat—a kind of epiphany because at the moment "My Favorite Weekend" called, Chess was in a world of hurt. Lately, the prescribed witches' brew hadn't been too effective. Karen Knotts told him about a friend with some kind of arthritic deal going on in her back; the docs slapped on a time-release drug patch that was supposedly stronger than heroin. (Sounded like the same thing that poor bastard attorney from New Jersey finally got from his jailers—the so-called trafficker on *60 Minutes*.) Chester had actually begun to think along those lines, almost the way depressed people start fantasizing about suicide. As relief. The stuff that scared him most was reading about pain that couldn't be touched by *any* narcotic, organic or synthetic. The cases where snipping off nerves didn't even do it, the "phantom" shit. There was a big ol blogworld out there about victims of Ménière's—ringing in the ears—who eventually offed themselves. The lucky ones were research freaks who stumbled on the perfect guy at whatever obscure hospital who turned out to be the Ménière's Muffler King. But if you didn't go that extra distance, you could wind up on the end of a rope or an exhaust pipe.

You could wind up on the bike path of the Golden Gate.

There was this girl who was driving along the freeway mind-
ing her own business when something fell off the pickup in front
of her. A scumbag with his Best Buy home entertainment center
lassoed to the truck bed. Piece of debris went through the windshield and took out half the chick's face. Guy never even stopped.
Her optic nerve was obliterated and now she couldn't taste or
smell and peed all the time and the MDs were fuckin helpless. A
permanent throbbing in her head that all the fentanyl in the world
couldn't *patch*. Refuses to learn Braille because she thinks one day
she'll be able to see. *Oh God*. Chess thought maybe *he* was like that,
delusional in thinking one day he'd be pain-free even though the
shortlived diminution epiphany had given him a ray of hope. Still,
that was the saddest part: Halfhead didn't want to learn Braille.
Her "My Favorite Weekends" were dead and gone.

Maybe it was all about being distracted. Could it really be that
simple? It made him wonder if the mind-body stuff Laxmi had
been hyping had some truth in it. Maybe he *would* hit Remar up
for bread (he didn't want to waste the money Marj had given him
on anything medical). It was probably a good idea to go see some
of the practitioners his fake girlfriend recommended: hyp-
noshrinks, biofeedbackers, Feldenkreisers, whatever. It couldn't
hurt—not any more than it did at the moment. He didn't want to
become addicted to pain or the idea of *being* in pain. He had to nip
that in the bud before it was too late.

L AXMI came over, crying.
      He put her on the sofa, lit a joint, and put the kettle on.
"Chester, I really need your advice about something!"
"Anything."
Maybe she was finally breaking up with Maurie and wanted to
talk about it. *Far out.*
"I got a job offer—and I *really don't want to take it,* but I *really
need the money.*"
"OK. So what's the problem?"
He put on his neutral, "mentor" uniform as he grabbed some
teacups from the cupboard.

She took a deep breath. "Here's what's happening: those people from *Friday Night Frights* called to ask if I'd be one of the actors who set people up. I mean, it didn't even come through Maurie, as far as I know. And it's like kind of a *regular* gig. And I said *no* . . . I just felt so *creepy* about what happened to *you*—but then they called *back*—and it pays really good! And I just needed—I just wanted to ask you—your *advice*—because I *definitely* don't want to hide something like that if I make that decision . . ."

"It's a no-brainer," he said, coolly macho.

The kettle was whistling and she joined him in the little kitchen. She always brought her own tea.

"I think you should *do* it."

"Really?"

Laxmi seemed genuinely surprised. He could tell she was relieved.

"You need the money, right?"

"I *so* need it. And it's like a *lot*. I do *not* want to ask Maurie for a loan."

He could tell she thought that was something he might like to hear. She was right.

"And I'm really—things are going *really well* right now with my journaling. I'm starting to paste together sections for the book and I just feel I have kind of a *momentum,* and—"

"That totally makes sense, Laxmi."

"—the money would so help! And the thing is—part of what I wanted to talk about—I could probably get a job at Ürth—I filled out an application—or the Bodhi Tree—they're hiring in the 'used' store—but I think my hours would be *really bad* at 1st—I'd make more at Ürth but nowhere *near* as much as on *FNF.* I mean, for me, it's 'crazy money,' but I'm just so *conflicted*—"

"Listen, Lotus Girl"—she smiled when he called her that—"believe it or not but I've actually *watched* that show, and everyone seems to have a good time. Even the so-called Vics. I think I was kind of an aberration. An anomaly, whatever. Shit happens. Right? So don't get your hippie head in a lather—just *go for it.* If it's gonna help you finish your book, do what's necessary. TCB. Elvis out. Do what you gotta do."

"Oh my God, Chester, that is *so understanding* of you." She hugged him close. "That is so *heartfelt*. I would *never* do *anything* to hurt you. You *have* to *know* that!"

"I do, honey. I do."

He poured water over the teabags.

"And I just didn't want to lie. I *had* to talk to you about it."

"It's totally OK." They sat on the couch. "And *thank* you."

He took some more pills. They relit and smoked the joint.

He took her to dinner that night at the Polo Lounge. Brett Ratner, Jake Gyllenhaal, and Jay-Z were there, at separate bar booths; it was kind of a scene. (She wanted to go to the Dime but he didn't think they could get in.) He was doing all right with his pain. Chess ordered an expensive bottle of wine to celebrate her getting the gig, and him getting the 10K from his mom.

XLIV.

MARJORIE

"ARE you Marj?"

"Yes."

"I'm Bonita Billingsley—a friend of Lucas's."

The woman was dressed in YSL. She was in her early 60s.

"Oh! Hello!"

"I'm from Ojai. I'm a Blind Sister!"

"Oh! Dear! Yes! Lucas said he drove up to see you."

"He did, and made me *very* happy. So: how does it feel to be filthy rich?" she said, eyes agleam.

"Well, I don't feel filthy just yet . . . but I'm looking forward to it!"

The woman had an easy laugh.

Marj invited her in.

She looked all around. "What a beautiful house! Is your husband here? I don't want to interrupt."

"He passed, about a year ago."

"I am *so sorry*—mine did too. On the 18th, it'll be 3 years. '18 holes,' " she said, whimsically. "He *loved* to golf."

"So did my Hamilton."

She admired Marjorie's wedding ring, which the old woman never removed—a fire opal surrounded by diamonds that reminded her of "the color of my beloved India." Once she said it, she sounded hopelessly pretentious. Marj realized how nervous she was; she wasn't used to being social.

"You've been?" asked the visitor, with eager respect.

"Oh yes—but not in a while."

"I've always wanted to go, but I guess I've been a little scared."

"I'm planning another trip."

"Well, maybe you and me should hit the road!"

Marj smiled—maybe so.

"My friend Cora and I call this 'Widow Street,' " she said, bringing them back to commonground. "Cora lives next door. And there's a gal across the way whose husband died just a few months ago—we're not that close."

"Fred had stomach cancer. The kids were there—all 4 of em, at bedside. But I was working, back east. I'm a sales rep. Well, I *was*. Not anymore! I really kicked myself that I wasn't with him when he left us, but then *Lucas*—Mr *Weyerhauser*—read me something a great guru said. Yogananda. Have you heard of him?" Marj looked quizzical, but reflected back that same sort of civil curiosity the woman had earlier demonstrated. "He wrote *The Autobiography of a Yogi.*"

"Oh my, yes!" exclaimed Marj, involuntarily touching her visitor's arm. "The Self-Realization Fellowship—I've been to Sunday services there. *Beautiful.*"

"*Aren't* they glorious? Krishnamurti lived in Santa Barbara— that's where we're from, originally. Lucas showed me a passage in the book where Yogananda said that he wasn't at his guru's side when he passed and felt just *awful* about it. But *then* Yogananda *realized* it was the *grace of God* that allowed him *not* to be there at the end, to spare him the suffering of seeing his teacher die. (That's how I think of husbands and all *kind* of folks—our own personal gurus, warts and all.) Well, when I read that, poof! It made *everything* all right. I felt *100%* better. The guilt just *washed away.* And I don't mean to be sacrilegious, but I think it's by the grace of God that we were selected for this marvelous *gift.* I just wish Fred were here to play with some of my new toys. He would *love* the new Lexus. My gosh—when you back up, a little TV shows how close you are to the car behind. Warning whoops and everything! Fred *hated* the way I parallel-parked!"

How strange—Marj recalled her neighbor going on about the very same thing. That's how we seemed to advance, in America; if you heard about enough people having something, why, eventually you just had to have it yourself.

Bonita went on to say that she'd won an "enormous" amount in "the shadow" and there was a great big party being thrown in New

York for the "Sisters"—in about 2 weeks' time. Hadn't Lucas mentioned it? (She made no bones about having a crush on him.) She said the Blind Sisters was the most exclusive "country club" in America, and the State of New York was chartering a jet to fly in the winners. Everyone was "bunking" at the Four Seasons here in LA the night before, so "we can all get to know each other."

"There's going to be a fancy dinner at Spago."

"I hadn't heard," said Marj, with a smile.

"On Saturday! Did you apply for the Expedited Award Program?" The old woman was nonplussed. "I gave Lucas a check when he came up—for the Windfall Tax. Almost *killed* me to write it. But within 72 hours, the 1st payment was wired directly to my account, *just* like he said: *$1,140,000.* Marj, I nearly fainted!" The women cooed like pigeons. Then Bonita asked, "How much did you win?"

Marj didn't want to say; a shyness born from her upbringing when it came to things like money.

"I hope my question wasn't impertinent!"

"No! Not at all—"

"Oh, I understand!" she said, patting Marjorie's hand. "I didn't want to tell *anyone* about it—in fact, Lucas warned me not to, he was *very serious* about that—until I actually drew the money out. That's when it became . . . *real.*" Her eyes teared up and Marj handed her some Kleenex.

Then, realizing she might have appeared vulgar, the guest grew contrite. "I'm sorry if I busted in on you."

"It's fine. It's really fine!"

Now it was the old woman's turn to feel sorry. The last thing she wanted was to come across as "hoity." She reached out and patted Bonita's hand.

"It's just that I've been so happy!" said her visitor. "So *excited*—and I haven't had anyone to share . . . ."

Marj wanted to "open up," but felt constrained for a tangle of reasons. She let Bonita talk, grateful for the compensatory rush of words.

"It's just—I know miracles *happen,* but I never thought they would happen to *me*. I'm not a young woman but I'm not ready to die either. I want to *go* places and *do* things and *meet* people I would *never* have gotten the chance to meet. Do you see that car?" She pointed out the window. "It's an SUV *hybrid*. I paid for it in *cash*. I have never paid cash for *anything in my life*. Can you understand? Do you know where I drove it today? To Children's Hospital. I sat in the lobby awhile and just listened. I learned more about suffering in those few hours than I have in a *lifetime,* and *my* life hasn't been a cakewalk. But I've never—knock on wood—had to suffer through the sickness of a child. I went to the bank and came back to the Ronald McDonald's—where the families stay while their kids have the chemo—that same afternoon. Gave out little packets: $5,000 each. And the nurses who work so hard got their packets too, oh yes. They are unsung! You cannot *imagine* how that made me feel."

Marjorie was moved, and quietly wept. She shared with Bonita what had happened to the liquor store owner and how she had tried to do her part; and given a gift to Cora when her dog fell ill. She felt a little awkward blowing her own horn—the sin of pride was on her mind—but the visitor was so full of life it was contagious. Bonita proclaimed them "kindred spirits," old and wise enough to know how to spread joy with their great, good fortune, not to squander it, and that was a blessing from the Lord ("and Lucas") Himself.

"I guess people like us, who were relatively comfortable before the shadow drawings, well, we tend to think, 'Why did this happen to *me?*' That *nagging feeling* that someone else was more deserving."

"Yes! Yes, it's true."

The woman hit a nerve, and it was nice for Marj to be able to air things out.

"But it's God's way. I think that's what Yogananda would have said. And it is *God's* way how we choose to disperse those monies—we are His instruments. Well," she said, standing, "I don't want to preach at you! Or take any more of your time. I'm so sorry I barged in—"

"It's all right, Mrs—"

She searched for the name.

"Billingsley. *Bonita.* And I *certainly* hope to see you at the Four Seasons—maybe before! I'm gonna give you my cellphone number; don't know how to work the damn thing, but here it is, it's a '917,' don't ask me why. (The area code.) Oh: you *should* talk to Lucas about the Expedited Awards Program—he's not the pushy sort—well, he *is* but in a *good* way—because he knows how overwhelmed his Sisters can get at the news—the '1st blush'—it'd overwhelm *anyone*—and Lucas doesn't like to foist things on people till they *ask*. And as much as he *does* tell us, I sometimes think he believes we're supposed to find out the rest by *osmosis*. But I'm telling you, gal," she said racily. "We are going to have *one helluva time* on that plane!" She reminded Marj of a character from an old movie—like a saloon girl, or some loosey-goosey roommate of Claudette Colbert. "I, for one, plan to get *extremely* drunk. I'm going to *get* drunk and *stay* drunk—for a month! On Baileys Irish Cream!"

"*I'm* a Baileys girl!"

"You are?"

"Keep it right by the nightstand."

"Well, then!" She gave out a hoot. "We are going to get along *gangbusters,*" said Bonita, making her way to the front door. "But if I *don't* see you, give me a call—here's the number in Ojai too. Though I *shan't be there* for long. My kids're all grown and I have a *very funny feeling* it may be time for a Roman spring. The Roman Spring of Mrs Billingsley! I'm having my 7-year itch, only I waited awhile—it's my 28-year itch!"

The women exchanged profuse goodbyes at the door, and as soon as she left, Marj ran to the mahogany bureau and took out the check to scrutinize it. There it was: *$1,863,279.47.* She was proud of herself for not having divulged the amount. Lucas Weyerhauser's business card sat on top but this time she dialed his cellphone instead of the State of New York Blind Sister Beneficiary Hotline.

You have reached Lucas Weyerhauser. If this is regarding the State of New York Blind Sister Shadow Drawing, please press 1. If you'd like to leave a message for Lucas, please press 2. If you are a federally sworn merchant or vendor, please press 3.

She smiled like a schoolgirl then cut herself a piece of Marie Callender's rhubarb pie.

XLV.

JOAN

AXEL was the boy who'd done the tsunami/Katrina edit with the Bobby Darin soundtrack. Joan thought it mordant, and not unclever; Lew said that ever since his son had read a story about teens doing good for others, he was stoked to come up with his own way of helping, but a devilish streak kept getting the best of him. He was that kind of kid.

His father told her that Axel got acutely strung out on *People* magazine's Make-A-Wish PR porn: the adolescent with acute lymphoblastic leukemia who created videogames for other badass baldies where action figures zoom around on skateboards zapping cancer cells and collecting shields against chemo side effects . . . that one really got him going. There were a hundred more Leuk Skywalkers where *he* came from, all dying to get into the weekly rag, *any* rag, itching to join the *American Idol* deathrace decathlon. How we love to manufacture little saints—Stepanek set the bar pretty high. Then came the budding entrepreneurial altruists, cataclysm whores and parasites, their sinister stageparents hoping they'd be noticed, lauded by the Gates Foundation, invited to DeGeneres or GMA, everyone would somehow get their funky fame fix, teens and tweens healthy in body but inevitable burnouts by the time they hit their 20s—like the 9 year old who raised ¾ of a million to build water wells all over Africa . . . the snobslut from Maryland who donated 27-hundred prom dresses to seniors living in the Big Uneasy.

Axel Freiberg had higher aspirations.

Lew had 2 others, Drea and Fanny, but at 13 Axel was the oldest. (Joan confirmed, to her horror, that he was named after Axl Rose.) The boy had been obsessively into the tsunami charity thing, even though Banda Aceh & Co. had long since been upstaged by Katrina, and more or less forgotten. His own father wanted to tell him *both* causes were passé—too many cooks had spoiled the largesse—but how could he, there he was lavishing time and money on an upscale minimalist grave, and besides, anything to stitch the boy into Family, anything to ground him, was golden. The "pimpy" therapist of course concurred.

After watching Willie Nelson and a bunch of unknown losertypes do their part on MTV for the 200,000+ dead, Axel wanted to pull a Geldof and organize a concert but was having trouble focusing when it came to Indonesia vs New Orleans. He didn't want to dis Dad re *wrong tragedy*. (The boy was half hoping, half waiting for another catastrophe to come down the pike.) He wanted Lew's help getting in touch with people like Mark Cuban and Russell Simmons to coproduce an event. Axel's shrink conferred with Lew and they decided he wouldn't make any calls on his son's behalf but would agree to enlist someone at Guerdon LLC to support Axel's efforts. Seemed the healthier thing to do.

But then Lew found another stash of DVDs, more tsunami/Katrina footage, with a fresh soundtrack. Axel had lifted lyrics from the MTV special and put them over horrific images of floating bodies. Willie Nelson jauntily sang:

Still is still moving to me
And I swim like a fish in the sea all the time

—the last ending with the body of a tiny corpse being wailed over by its mother. Then came *I'm drowning in a whiskey river, bathing my memories in the wetness of its soul*—more bodies, putrefaction, stupefaction, and flood.

Lew confessed to Joan that it got much worse; his son was sick. He had downloaded Russian kidporn off the Web and this time used a creepy a cappella version of an old standard to accompany the image of an unseen fat man raping an infant.

You must've been a beautiful baby
Cause baby! look at you now—

The discovery put the kibosh on Axel's plans to be a world-class concert promoter. Lew canceled delivery on the mega-toy International 7300 CXT—the world's largest pickup truck (he admitted it was partially for himself)—and the 45,000 dollar Opus foosball table being hand-delivered and assembled by a technician from Edinburgh, both gifts for the boy's now-canceled birthday celebration. The foosballers had tiny 3-D heads of Axel's friends and family, fastidiously customized from photographs. The shrink said the boy was starting to cross boundaries—Lew: "Duh!"—and that interactions with his sisters should be closely monitored. Lew was getting ready to ship him off to a wilderness camp for psycho kids, something even his ex agreed on.

He was having 2nd *"and* 3rd" thoughts about the efficacy of the therapist, whom he was paying $20,000 a week to be on call for his son, and whose main clients in the last few years had been highly profitable, highly dysfunctional rockers trying to get it together for reunion tours. Lew vilified the man because he was part of a group of psychiatrists who'd rushed to Phuket (*and* New Orleans; another scam—"hurricane counseling appropriations" were now above the 200,000,000 dollar mark). Freiberg scoffed at the presumptuous, demoniac do-gooders, "disaster bastards" he called them, hating that sort of hubris: Western *professionals* who thought they could help those who'd lost mothers, fathers, sisters, brothers, dogs, houses—all through the magical art of talk and handicrafts. He also knew that part of the reason the shrink went to Tamil Nadu was to ingratiate himself with Lew, but it had the reverse effect; all that hidden disdain for indigenous healers and outlandish fixation on PSS made him puke. Oh, he'd learned a *lot* since his brother's death—that's why he was helping the *animals.* Calamity Jane already made 3 trips to the 9th Ward and was probably cheating on his wife with other trauma-chasing funhouse hotzone narcissists. Lew even read an article saying the Jungian high priests were having nervous breakdowns themselves, sobbing as they went door-to-door in Plaquemines Parish, distributing self-help guides and getting *paid* for it. Bunch of pussies.

"Did you know there is only *one* fucking psychiatrist in the entire country of Rwanda? *Right on.* Tell me what some analytical *asswipe* could do to *restore the self-esteem* of a woman whose baby was torn off her shoulder and thrown against a wall? By her own *brother.* And now she's got a *cow.* That's all she has left. A cow. 5 dead wall-slammed babies, you know, machete'd or stomped on, a dead hubby, she's got AIDS from the daily Hutu gangbang, or the Tutsis, the Tutsi rolls, *whoever,* and now all she's got left is a fucking *cow.* Oh yes! Call in the Antioch-trained grief counselors!"

Lew was captious—Joan knew better than to engage. Just ride it out. Besides, she liked to listen: it was only his juicily fractious *ch'i* talking, and he had a surplus. *Ch'i* was sexy. Soon it would be dusk and they'd start to drink and she'd fuck it all out of him, out of herself too. All that overt/covert energy would be put to good use.

D REA and Fanny were adorable. They were 9 and 3, with their own wing and handlers. Joan was glad that he wanted her to meet them, regardless of the brevity of the encounter. *(Though maybe it doesn't really mean anything.)* She was a bit nervous around the girls, and at 1st they barely glanced at her. They were probably nervous too—not nervous, shy. That was natural. *But what do I know.*

The nanny supervised while Drea read aloud from *The Adventures of Mark Twain.* Lew said it was a special dumbed-down version all the schools were using now. Originally put together for kids with disabilities, the book had caught on and been approved for the larger student body.

J OAN thanked him for the gifts he sent to LA, murmuring they were "beyond extravagant." She didn't know what to give him in return (full well realizing her shorthaired pussy was enough)— but still, she had to bring *something*—which wound up being a silk-wrapped piece of blood coral she got 10 years ago, scuba-diving on the Great Barrier Reef. It had always been precious to her, alien and astonishingly beautiful, a bony, corpuscular vessel, and Lew was dead-on when he said it looked like something Damien Hirst wished he'd come up with. Watching him stare at it as if it were under a microscope, even Joan began to doubt the "realness" of its provenance and thought maybe the object was something she'd dreamed. An aborigine told her it didn't come from the world of vocabulary (it was like a letter in the alphabet of the nonverbal) and there was no need to describe it—but if one was determined, it could simply be called "the 3rd Unit." The 3rd Space. *The 3rd Twirl. Man likes codes and alphabets. This object is part of the code of a dreaming place called Red Sands. We regard language as an emblem. A word stands for something and then we fall in love with that word. This object is meant to pull you back to Energy, not Word.* It was a thing that stood outside *a pair;* it was the "C corollary to A-B." She didn't understand. All Joan could tell Lew was that "it came from the ocean" and suddenly she felt like a liar, an impostor, impoverished of ideas, famulus to the Wizard of Oz. When she dutifully regurgitated the shaman's explanation, it sounded like a crazy person's verbigeration.

On that weekend of Lew's b-day BBQ...not a barbecue, strictly speaking, because the chef frivolously served up deliberately kitschy Sara Lee (still in the supermarket box) along with the bison and foie gras, hearts of palm stuffed with fava beans and pistachios, blood orange gelatin, "McSweetbreads" and columbine, snapdragons and cornstarch paper and edible soyabean stamped with the flavorsome logo of *Guerdon LLC;* they drank deconstructions of Bloody Marys—that's what the chef called them, thinking everyone would be amused—Joan just thought it was stupid. The man only dug himself deeper when sharing that he'd recently attended a bachelor party in Vegas where after-dinner drinks cost $2,000 apiece. For dessert (the cake sat in its cardboard vitrine like an objet d'art) they ate marshmallows infused with lavender and a kerfuffle of "Kentucky Fried" sorbet that tasted like, well, chickenskin. A gustatory crew watched from cameras in the kitchen so they'd know when to clear, and when to proffer the next cryovac'd course.

The girls were sent to bed. Supporting cast and crew discreetly vanished. They were deliciously alone as evening fell. Over glasses of Belondrade y Lurton verdejo, Lew rambled on about black holes and bursts of gamma rays burning brighter than a trillion billion suns—but lasting only seconds—and one-square-inch star cubes weighing more than however many quadrillion planets put together. He made his usual racist jokes and ruckus, outright drunk now, pawing her chest, softly, absurdly goosing the crack of her ass through Kate Hepburn capris, and getting contemplative about plaque the doctor said he'd found in his carotid (right-side only) before railing on a fresh bevy of pet peeves. Then he gifted her with Zai skis, and the craziest thing she'd ever seen, called a Henk—a 30,000 dollar carry-on suitcase he'd bought in Vegas, at Wynn's. Lew said it was made from the same material used for rockets. A briefcase was attached, of horse-hair and rare wood (no doubt). The monogram: JHA. She wondered how he found out her middle name was Alice. She'd always hated it.

I N the morning, on the way to the airport, Lew drove past the gallery site where his brother's bequest of paintings and artifacts would be showcased, and where he planned to build a studio for his own modest artistic pursuits.
Lew Freiberg, billionaire sculptor.
Also, he said he needed a place to house his "curiosities"—like Clyde Barrow's bullet-ridden blood-stained shirt that he'd bought at auction for $125,000, and a collection of 3-century-old books, accounts of murder trials bound in the killers' skin. Richard Gluckman was designing it. She knew Richard and didn't take it as a threat; a studio was one thing, a memorial another. Still, she was well aware that her New York friend had built spaces for Chuck Close and Richard Serra, and suddenly, that nagged—what if Gluckman had put something in Lew's head to have Serra do one of those rusted jillion-ton Cecil B De-Mille cookie-cutter Ss for the Mem?
All Joan knew was what she'd been told—ARK was seriously in play, along with Rimjob, Andy G, and other unknown soldiers

of (fame and) fortune. She was on the short(hair) list; Lew confirmed it late last night. For the life of her, she couldn't decide if letting him slurp the meat between her legs had strengthened or weakened her case.

But maybe those days and legs—bridge of thighs—were coming to a close, and soon she wouldn't be capable of getting men to seek the peyote button visions of her clit. Maybe she was already on her way to excommunication—like the ex wife, the son, and the traveling roadshow shrink—all of them wilderness campbound. Soon she would be dumbed down, just like the Twain text; sex and hormones and Memorial gone, dumb and dumber.

Dumbed down, rubbed out, and old.

Old.

XLVI.

RAY

HE took Friar Tuck to the park, where he promptly bit a dog and its owner.

The old man hadn't expected that, because the Friar was weak and sluggish. He was really just bringing him there for sun and fresh air. But when a Weimaraner came along and sniffed his hindquarters, the Nipper nipped, then attacked the woman as she jerked away her pet. Luckily, no blood was drawn on either side. The gal—a big, stocky type—was peeved, but softened when Ray said his friend had been shot, and this was his 1st "constitutional." Ordinarily, he wouldn't have played that card but the immediate situation seemed to call for some ham. (A lawsuit was all he needed.) She asked what happened and Ray said the sheriffs shot him by mistake. As it turned out, the woman had actually read about it, and softened even some more. She nodded in sympathy, commenting on the Friar's sutures. Ray apologized again, and that was that.

He was going to leave but felt winded after the encounter. He sat on a bench on the outskirts of the meager greens. The Friar lay down and closed his eyes. The old man took the letter from the veterinary hospital from his coat pocket, put on his glasses, and gave it a read.

Dear Mr Rausch,

As you know, "Friar" was brought to our hospital approximately 2 weeks ago after sustaining a right radius fracture secondary to a gunshot wound. X-rays of the chest and abdomen, as well as a complete blood panel, were within normal limits. Because there were open wounds to the right front leg, and because the fractured bone pieces were still in excellent alignment, we did opt to treat Friar's open leg with a splint. We have been changing the bandage every day. We are very pleased to see that the wounds are healing nicely, and the leg continues to have excellent alignment.

At home, it is imperative that Friar be kept as calm and quiet as possible for the next 4 weeks while his leg continues to heal. This means no running, jumping, playing, or roughhousing. Initially, we would like to see Friar back at our hospital every 2 days to change his splint. This will require a light sedative, so please do not feed Friar breakfast on the morning of these visits. If at any time you notice that this splint becomes soiled, please call us and we'll be happy to change it immediately. A water-soiled splint can result in a serious underlying skin infection. In approximately 2 weeks, we will take a new X-ray to assess the healing progress of Friar's fracture.

We are sending Friar home with a pain medication and antibiotics. Please give these medications as directed.

Thank you very much for the opportunity to help Friar. He certainly remains one of our most popular patients. Please don't hesitate to contact us with any questions or concerns.

It choked him up—he was proud of his little warrior. Getting shot was a big deal. He'd rather have a heart attack any day. Nip still wasn't sleeping too well; he was way off his game, crying out in the night at faraway sounds. He shook and puked during the day but the docs didn't seem to think that would last. Ray was anxious to get him in the water, soon as he healed enough to swim. He lifted the submissive animal, cradling Nip in his arms as he hobbled to the car; 2 invalids. Then he laughed. Still had the gumption to take a bite out of a sonofabitch—and that fatso too.

That's my boy.

THE next day, he cruised Sepulveda after dropping Friar for a splint change.

The boulevard had changed. It used to be ratty-looking but around Washington, he noticed all kinds of new places—

coffeeshops, boutiques, upscale malls. He slowed at an elaborate building that actually seemed to resemble a railroad station. He circled around and parked, for a closer look. The sign said AL-LIED TRAINS. He threw a quarter in the meter.

The store must have covered about an acre. A couple of employees loitering at the front gave him a deadpan greeting. He asked if this was the same shop that used to be over by Pico and Veteran. They said it was, but had moved to this location in '86. "Really brings back memories," said Ray. The men were young, and not up to kibitzing with a codger. They went about their business without asking if he needed help.

Every 10 feet or so was an elaborate, enclosed "city" with a train running through. A multitude of signs read DO NOT TOUCH, KEEP YOUR MITTS OFF, etc. (Ray thought it overkill, and a tad un-friendly.) He sure got nostalgic, though. Remembered buying Chesterfield his 1st set—must have been the early 70s. He could still feel the cold steel heft of the engine in his hand, a Lionel, and see the wonder in his son's eyes when he opened it Christmas morning. White puffs came from the smokestacks, and when you pressed a button the train whistled. Toward the rear of the store, Ray looked inside a case and saw the very same model. The vin-tage engine wore a price tag: 13-hundred dollars.

He stopped one of the clerks. "Is that just for the engine or is that for the whole train?"

"Buy it!" said the clerk.

"But is it for the engine or all 6 cars?"

"Cash or credit card," said the clerk. "Buy it!"

"OK, stop playing around," said Ray.

An older clerk came around the counter.

The whippersnapper got lost.

"We bought that directly from the owner. It's probably from about 1961."

"Looks just like the one I gave my son."

"Usually, the engine and caboose are what you're buying— in this case, we're just throwing them in. It's the cars in the *middle* that you're paying for. See that aquarium? That's $600 right there. And the scraper on the flatbed—scrapers are rare, but this one's rare-on-rare cause the flatbed is *black* instead of *red*. So that's 400. See? So we're actually throwing the engine and caboose in."

Ray pointed to the set below, a string of Pullman cars with an observation deck.

"That's not the California Zephyr, is it?" he asked.

The clerk looked at him blankly.

"Well, of course it isn't. It says 'Pennsylvania.' "

The tag on the Pennsylvania said 45-hundred.

The whippersnapper darted past.

"Cash or credit card! Get in! Get it! Get in and get it, right now!"

The old man scowled at him as he disappeared.

Maybe when the city paid the settlement, he *would* come "get it." That punk was really getting Ray's goat.

As he left he thought about his own defunct emporium, and miniature golfing with the kids—then it occurred to him *another* son might be on the way. He'd do right by *this* one, see this one through. He'd have the money to, anyway; it certainly cost a chunk o' change to raise a kid. Besides, he was a different man now. He wouldn't walk away. He had Ghulpa, and she was no Marj. She was no ballbuster.

Ray headed back to the hospital. He wondered how a place like that—they sold *toy trains,* for chrissake—managed to have such a lavish building. How in hell did it stay in business? The owner must be rich: only explanation. A computer geek probably bought it on a whim, for his own personal sandbox. That's why the folks working there were so rude. Didn't matter if they made a sale or not.

Yes, I will have a son. Not "Chester." I couldn't do that again. We'll call him Lionel . . .

He would tell Ghulpa it was an honorable name, and came from "lion." Well, it did, didn't it? In a way. Not such a good thing, though, come to think of it, when it came to his BG. She *might* allow it, because the hearts and souls and strength of lions were so important to her, even though she feared them. Didn't her beloved Durgā, her bloodcurdling Kali, ride atop one?

They would have a lion for a son. What more could she ask for to beat back her terrors than a lionhearted boy?

XLVII.

CHESTER

CHESS and Laxmi went to the zoo. Though she didn't like the idea of them being caged, she wanted to show him "the Ganeshas." They smoked weed before driving over, and he dropped 2 Inderals and 4 vikes. They took her car.

He read aloud from the newspaper as they wended their way through Griffith Park. They were laughing so hard it was tough for Laxmi to steer. Chess had the full-page ad in his hand and declaimed from it, telling Laxmi she should use it for a monologue in her acting class:

What does Mc® mean to me? Everything that I love ... to me, Mc means McDonald's®. So I'm cool with Mc and Mc is cool with me.

Mc is cool with me!
Underneath the Golden Arches, it said, "I'm lovin it."

"Oh my God!" said Laxmi. "McDonald's is selling fruit salad with yogurt now! I'm so sure the fruit is cloned!"

"*Look* at this chick," said Chess, staring at the graphics. "Here's what she's saying: 'I don't know who loves this salad more. Me? Or my fork.' Fork *this.*"

"It's *so creepy.* And the *drawings.* They're like from *chick-lit* novels! Anorexic girls in stilettos with chihuahuas—the chihuahua accessory is *so over*—they're just *staring* at you, and, like, sitting in *Eames* chairs."

"Are we spending too much time thinking about MickeyD's?"

"Yes! Yes! They've won! They've totally won!"

Laxmi laughed in that abandoned, guttural way she saw Cameron Diaz laugh on reruns of *Trippin'*.

Chess did some more dramatizing.

" *'Having one makes even a bad hair day feel good.'* That's what it says! I'm serious! Having one makes even a bad hair day feel good!"

" 'I'm lovin it'!"

"What the fuck do they mean, 'I'm *lovin* it'?"

"They *are* lovin it!"

"Love *this,*" said Chess, grabbing his crotch. Theme of the day.

Laxmi whooped then Chess winced and *ouched* from a shooting pain. She was laughing so hard she almost swerved off the road into a girl on horseback, which seemed *totally* surreal.

"Oops," said Laxmi. Then: "Bad hair day!"

"Do you *see* these people?" said Chess, holding up the ad so Laxmi could cop another look. "They're like in some *loft,* a *hip loft* with Levelor blinds and red brick—"

"The Pacific Electric Building!"

"—some marketing fool's *idea* of a hip loft! It looks like a bad comedy-club set. Check out the shag carpeting! It's *lime.* And, what is that, a *turntable?*"

"They don't even sell those at Restoration anymore. I went in. I really wanted one. But you know who still has LPs? Amoeba, in Hollywood. They even sell *8-tracks.*"

"This fucking ad looks like it was production designed by UNICEF! See the kids on the couch? One's a spade, right?"

"Kate Spade! And her brother!"

"A cuddly-assed *African-American.* And there's a Latino on the end who looks like she's ready to have her burrito McMunched. *Munch munch, munch-a-bunch o' Fritos* . . . a TJ donkey's gonna give her oral—a McBurro! Waiter! Bring me a McBur*r*ito, smothered in underwear! And special sauce! Bring me the head of Alfredo McDonald! Laxmi, look at this! It's the fucking Jesse Jackson Rainbow Coalition munch-a-Latino-for-lunch bunch!" The driver split a gut, futilely waving her hand that she could take no more. "And the guy in the middle? Check out his hair! It's *long.* A Filipino mix who thinks he's hot! Like a reject from *Project: Runway!*"

Laxmi peered over at the page.

"Wilmer Valderrama, look out!"

"Wilma *who?*"

"He's, like, everybody's boyfriend—"

"Fred and Wilma?"

"—from *That 70s Show?*"

"Hey, Laxmi . . . you better be *glad* you're doing *FNF* and not print ads for Ron McDon. This shit is *low.*"

"But their Dollar Menu is *hot.*"

They were already near the end of Zoo Drive. Their high-frequency stoner jag petered out but Chess still scanned the paper, looking for residual laughs. He read aloud a small item about how some pharmaceutical company admitted harvesting pituitary glands from dead kids in Ireland without their parents' consent. *There's a horror film for ya.* Used em to make human growth hor-mone; the hospitals got "just a few dollars for each."

"The luck o' the Irish!" he said, with a demented leprechaun accent. Laxmi lost it again. "Gland of the free! Johnny, we hardly knew ye—*or* ye pituitaries."

Some of the cadavers had been *"hollowed out"*—any and every organ that was market-redeemable had been removed.

Laxmi shook her head. "That is *so totally surreal.*"

"I just saw a movie on Sundance," said Chess. "What a fucked-up channel—they'll, like, put *anything* on. I mean, this fuckin *car ride* would be better than *Tarnation.* Anyway, it's about this Jewish guy from New York—Maurie Levin!—who flies to Austria after hearing about some old doctor on trial for experimenting with disabled kids back in the 40s. Killed em and took out their brains. His name was Dr Gross."

"Of *course.*"

"The guy gets there—"

"Dr Levin!"

"Right. Dr Levin the documentarymaker gets there just in time for this public ceremony called the Burial of the Brains . . ."

"Of *course.*"

"*Laxmi, I shit you not.* It was *so lame.* I thought it was a Chris Guest movie—you know, the guy who did *Best in Show?*"

"I loved that! Isn't he married to—"

"The chick from *Psycho*'s daughter."

"She died, right?"

"The mother. The one from the shower."

"*So creepy.* I heard that guy Hitchcock *really hated women.*"

"He's like a duke or a lord or something."

"Hitchcock."

"No, the guy who's married to—the Guest guy."

"Sir Maurie! Lord Levin!"

"I *think* he's a duke. Duke Guest. Guest Host. Patty Duke. Whatever. I read it in *People.*"

"*People* . . . people who read *People* . . . are the *loneliest people in the—*"

They passed the kiddie train you could ride on, and it triggered a meditation on his dad. *Maybe my father is rich—a rich man. Maybe my father is a public figure and knows who and where I am but is hesitant to contact me. Maybe my father has been in touch with Joan and Marj all along. Maybe it was actually my father who loaned me the 10K through her auspices. Maybe my father is a CEO or COO or CFO of a major media corp. Maybe my father is the key shareholder of the parent company that produces* Friday Night Frights . . . she saw him zone out and let him be. According to Laxmi *her* father was rich but Chess wondered if she had some fantasy-exaggeration element goin on. *Maybe my father is her father,* he thought. Seeing it for the still-stoned musing that it was, he shook his head and laughed. He'd keep that one to himself.

L AXMI said they should rent go-carts because they had a lot of ground to cover before getting to the elephants, some of it up-hill, and she didn't want Chess to be uncomfortable. Much better than the tram. He was surprised at how easy it was; for 20 bucks, anyone could trip around on a handicapper scooter. *Even a fucking terrorist.* There wasn't paperwork to deal with (all they needed was your John Hancock) because evidently the San Diego Zoo had already been sued by some pioneering class-action gimps who said it was demeaning for them to sit there signing full-on legal disclaimers before being allowed to ride. That's what the person who gave them the single-page form said, anyway. Still, it was refreshing that you didn't need a doctor's note. They could only go so fast but were actually pretty smooth and efficient. And Laxmi was right—no way would he have made it walking.

Once they got going, Chess looked at her as if to telepath, *This shit is getting weird.* She vanished in a puff of hippiegiggle.

Laxmi zigged and zagged and had a grand ol time but Chester was self-conscious as he steered, feeling a touch of the paraplegic, wishing he had a military outfit so it would at least look like he'd survived some roadside blast in Fuckistan, but the hiking pedestrians that they slowly overtook didn't seem to give a shit. The pair was invisible as they navigated sundry paths and This Way To The Reptile House tributaries. He took more pills. He wanted to make sure to have a little something in his stomach so they stopped at one of the multicultural shacks for some Mex (triggering another series of McBurro riffs). The nascent panicky mindset that the pain might never end was almost as bad as the pain itself, that he was now one of *those people*—or at least in the process of getting his membership approved—on the torture rack till the end of their days.

The Inderal lasted 24 hours and was used primarily to quell the fear of public speaking; another shriven skull the witch doctors said to throw in the cauldron. One of the brainiac medicos Chess saw at UCLA told him there were lots of new "management stratagems." He rattled off a bunch of meds and the eager patient went home and did his search engine thing. Scared the *shit* out of him. There was something called Pamidronate, for sucky bone cancers like Paget's disease, but you had to *inject* it. That *really* freaked him—that the guy'd even *mention* it, unless he was showboating. Is *that* where he saw Chess heading? Shooting up some exotic cancer drug in the bathroom at JAR (for brunch)? Who knew: maybe these types of injuries *did* eventually lead to the Big C—what used to be laughable, myth and folk wisdom, had hardened with Sweeps Week logic into unassailable doctrine in the clinics' hallowed halls. Made perfect sense. People weren't enrolling in medical school because of DeBakey or Albert Schweitzer—they were being recruited by *House, Grey's Anatomy,* and *CSI.* There were antiseizure drugs for stumpers and something called gabapentin for the neuropathy that went with renal failure or diabetes. The whitecoated putz looked at Chess like he was a fool for not having already gotten his epidurals; the needles they used were Tommy Lee–gauge. The "epi" delivered morphine or bupivaicaine directly to the spinal cord, so you didn't have to do that zombified painsoaked stiffwalk anymore, but all Chess thought about was a 1st-year student hitting a nerve and infecting him, botching the very procedure little old ladies sailed through. He saw himself on a zoo scooter 10 years hence, his own motorized pushcart, covered with KEEP IT GREEN stickers and cannabis logos, diapered, wheeling through Whole Foods for fish oil and Centrum—

Not gonna happen . . .

THEY found their way to the enclosure. He used to come with Joan and his mom. Laxmi thought it *so cool* that Marjorie was "into Ganesha." She said there was no way elephants should not be in the wild, and Chess concurred, after mulling over the double negative (his brain wasn't working too well), realizing she meant they shouldn't be caged. They stared in silence at a family of pachyderms (that Fleetwood Mac song "Tusk" went idiotically through his head), cute and anciently weird and even spooky to apprehend, before disgust at their voyeurism washed over. The couple was still high, seized by intense reefer outrage re captivity that quickly segued to melancholia.

Laxmi said there were a thousand myths about how Ganesha was created. While her husband Śiva was away, Pārvatī created a boy from her "scurf"—the flakes and scales of her skin—so he'd keep away nettlesome visitors and guard her bedroom door. When Śiva came home, Ganesha didn't know who he was and wouldn't let him in. Śiva cut off his head. *Those gods don't fuck around, huh.* When he realized it was his own son he had decapitated, Śiva freaked and restored the kid to life by giving him the head of the creature closest by: a white elephant.

Soon my body will be a white elephant—scurf's up!

They stared at the hairy beasts, tripping from the vantage of their go-carts. Laxmi giggled that Ganesha was the guardian of the *anus*—she actually read that in some Bodhi Tree book—and a man's cock represented his trunk. *Jesus,* thought Chess, *the motherfucker guards* everything. *Was Laxmi trying to tell him something? He flashed on his Viagra stash.* She said the reason she loved Ganesha more than any other god was because he'd transcribed a famous poem by breaking off a tusk (*fuckin Fleetwood Mac again and those dumb drums and horny USC cheerleaders; Jesus, that was 30 years ago*) and dipping it in ink. Chess told her he thought that was far out. *I'm really starting to talk like her. Soon I'll be a vegetarian. A Viagratarian.* That's why she kept a statue of the elephant on her desk or in her purse, wherever she did her journaling. She said Ganesha gave her "writing *ch'i.*"

THEY turned in their scooters and smoked more weed in the car. Poor little Dumbos. Ratty, dusty, and dry. On *display.* They were *gods* and people didn't have a clue.

"Did you know," said Laxmi, "that elephants *communicate?* I mean, they *talk,* but it's *subsonic.* They can die of heartbreak. And they go *crazy* in captivity, they always say it's this thing called 'musth'? You know, this male hormone thing? And that's *true,* but it's *triggered.* Musth is like this testosterone secretion that makes them very aggressive. It's stinky and drips into their eyes and mouth."

"I can relate."

"It has something to do with ketones? My dad used to tell me about all this. He's really very knowledgeable about certain things—I mean, he's not a complete pig. Like if you blow into their trunks, they'll remember your scent for life. Did you know that when they die, the whole herd lingers over the carcass? My dad didn't tell me *that,* I already knew it. Chester, it is so *sad* and so

sweet. They *mourn.* And the heads of the tribe are *female.* It's a ma-
triarchy! There's like this *70 year old female* who's running the
show! I love that! That's why it's so sad to see them in cages . . .
and they mate for life? You knew that, right? They are *so special.*
They can feel *the whole world* through the bottom of their feet—
that's how they wound up saving all those people in the tsunami.
They could *feel* the waves coming—"

Chess felt a wave, and leaned over to kiss her.

She kissed back.

XLVIII.

MARJORIE

LUCAS phoned.

He was glad Bonita came to visit. Surprised, but glad. He hoped it was all right that he gave out Marj's address. *Of course it was.* He said Bonita was a good lady, didn't have many friends, and wanted to "share the joy." Implicit in his words, to Marj anyway, was that Bonita was lonesome. Lucas had performed a small, cogent act of kindness. The Blind Sisters—and Lucas—were family.

Soon he'd be on his way to Texas to inform a new batch of shadow winners ("Oh yes, the Lone Star State is a *major* participant in the drawings") and asked if she wanted to have a bite before he left. "That's what one vampire said to another," he joked. "Let's go have a bite." He told her not to primp, that he liked the natural look. They had a laugh and he added, "I've never been an aficionado of too much makeup." "Well, I won't primp if you won't primp," said Marj, coyly. They laughed again and set a time. He wanted to eat somewhere at the Grove. He said he liked the Grove.

SHE went next door to check on Cora and Pahrump.

The dog looked weak. Cora said he was sick from the chemo. Marj tried to distract her.

"How 'bout I pick up a lottery ticket for you and Mr P?"

"You're still buying tickets? From that *place?*"

"Oh! *My* yes. It's *very* important. The son had to leave school to help out—they're not going to sell. They're marvelous people. I spoke with the widow. She *will not* let this destroy them. God knows it would have destroyed *me.* Something like that happening to my Ham? She said she still believes in the goodness of people. Isn't that marvelous? Perhaps it's cultural. We Americans tend to be so cynical. We used to have more of the rugged spirit."

"Well, *I* think they should *string them up*. Have they caught them yet, the blacks?"

"I don't think so. There weren't any witnesses, so no one knows if—"

"The *schvartzuhs,* always a *schvartzuh*. Why don't they just kill their own? That's what they do, you know. Steinie told me. *Whites* don't kill them: the blacks do a very good job of it themselves."

Marj stroked Pahrump. The animal growled unconvincingly.

"Now you just *stop,* Rump. Don't you *dare*—that's Marj Herlihy, *my dear friend* and *your* guardian angel. She's going to take away your trust fund if you don't stop misbehaving! We're going to take it away, aren't we, Marj? You really should have *seen* that hospital. It's on Sepulveda, just behind where Steinie goes to the gym. And the *people* who came in! They should make one of those TV shows about it. Someone brought a lovebird they'd left in the sun—it got dehydrated. Oh Marj, the *care* that is lavished! You could probably bring in a *cockroach* and they'd know what to do. But it *costs a fortune*. I met a couple who had a dog the police shot by mistake."

"Oh Lord," said the old woman, flinching.

"The police are out shooting *dogs* when they should be shooting"—she paused, voice lowering to a susurrus of contempt—*"blacks."*

L ucas's driver dropped them off at a Chinese restaurant in the Grove, across from the dancing fountains.

They spoke of this and that, how glad and lucky he was to have found a vocation which had allowed him to make so many people happy. He said most of the time he felt like the star of "an amazing reality show." She wasn't exactly sure what that meant, but he was *such* a sweet young man, just the kind of boy she wished Chester had turned out to be. Though it pained her to even be thinking that way.

"So: are we going to see you at Spago?"

She looked at him inquisitively, then remembered the lady from Ojai's words. Marj needed her memory jogged.

"We're having a gala for the Blind Sisters—well, half the winners are men, but they don't seem to mind the appellation. In fact, they get a kick out of it! Shall I RSVP for you?"

"Your friend said—"

"Bonita has called me *10 times* about what she's going to wear. What am I, Isaac Mizrahi? Hello! I know *someone* who needs a *Xanax!* One day it's *Chanel,* the next it's Oscar—*de la Renta.* Bonita is *a hoot and a half.* Did she tell you the State is putting everyone up? At the Four Seasons?"

"Yes! But I wasn't sure—"

"Pardon the 3rd degree," he said, in whimsical self-reprimand. *"I'm* the one who's supposed to be minister of information! All right, Marjorie Morningstar (her father used to call her that), here's the skinny: dinner at Spago, on Saturday night in Beverly Hills. Lots of luminaries and friends of the mayor are going to join us: Phyllis George, Merv Griffin, Joan Collins. RJ Wagner and his wife . . . you will *love* Jill and RJ. Chief Bratton might even stop by—his wife's a *pistol.* We have the top 2 floors of the hotel reserved, all penthouse suites. Nothing but the best for my Sisters! If we're a little tipsy, into the elevator we go. I don't think the cops are making arrests for riding elevators under the influence—not yet! The next morning, it's breakfast in bed before everyone boards Mr Bloomberg's GV. Then, *straight to JFK,* smooth as silk! Fasten your seatbelt, Marj, it's going to be an *unbumpy night."* She was having a little trouble following. "Oh! And *then"*—he made the sound of a trumpet fanfare—*"off* to Gracie Mansion for the triannual Blind Sisters luncheon, with all the trims! Want your picture taken with Hillary Clinton? *Your wish is my command.* And you will *love* Mr Bloomberg. *And* Mr Trump. Personally, when I meet a billionaire I think: What's *not* to love?" He laughed, and it was absolutely infectious. "You know," said

Lucas, growing serious, "the whole 'Sisters' program is actually Michael's baby. So: are you with us, Marjorie Morningstar?"

"Why yes, I would love to be able to come."

"Your presence is *required.* I *will* need that check from you."

She searched her mind.

"I gave you the money order . . ."

"You certainly did, as a marker that lawfully secured your spot as a Shadow Drawing fundwinner. But the New York trip is only for those in the EAP—the Expedited Award Program. Marjorie Morningstar, I am *remiss,* and for that I apologize. I'm not sure what got into me. The New York trip certainly isn't compulsory, by law. This award comes with no strings. And I didn't bother explaining it because you seemed so comfortable here in Beverlywood, and to be honest, I wasn't sure you'd be interested. Didn't think you'd want to hop on a plane and go all the way to New York, which is a bit cold right now. I should never have assumed—"

"But I *am,* Lucas! I really would like to go."

"Well, that is *great.* Because I for one would miss having you. Bonita's coming, as you know, and it's a pretty big and wonderful bunch—we're gonna have ourselves a world class blast. Top o' the world, Ma! Now, here's precisely what it all means: those who've elected to participate in the EAP are entitled, again, by federal law, to receive their monies *early,* i.e., technically, at the *exact moment* wheels touch down on the runway in the great state of New York. By charter, those monies—*ceremonially*—*must* be given to you once we hit the tarmac. Because *then,* as our lawyers love to say, you've reached 'sovereign soil,' triggering what is called an 'enrichment'—oh, they love having names for everything!—and all *kinds* of penalties accrue to the state if they do not make you 'whole.' I like to call it the Carpetbagger Clause! It's actually a *good* thing, not just for the taxpayers of the State of New York but for the Blind Sisters as well. The tax implications are complex but I assure you favorable. The bottom line is that it's contingent upon everyone who elects to enter the EAP to give the Superfund a check, *pro forma,* for a % of their windfall. It's literally called a Windfall Pretax. Didn't Bonita say—I'll bet she did! she was about to burst!—didn't she say that she was suddenly a million bucks or so richer?"

"Yes . . . I think she told me something had been wired—"

"$1,140,000. That came within 24 hours, by the way. And when we get to JFK—we *might* be dropping anchor in Newark this month, I actually need to make a mental note to check on that so the fleet of limos doesn't go to the wrong FBO—wouldn't *that* be a bungle—the minute we enter Big Apple airspace, Bonita Billingsley will receive a check for 12,000,000 more."

"But she already *got* something—"

The old woman struggled to make sense of all the formulas— the forms and formulations. She didn't want Lucas to think she was the slow one in the group.

"You *bet*. The amount of which is *completely* at my discretion to draw upon, as long as it does not exceed the tally allotted to the Windfall Pretax Fund, a number arrived at by a rather Byzantine series of accounting equations with which I promise not to bore you. But they *do* give me wiggle room, that's one of the perks of my job. Again, Marjorie Morningstar, here's the bottom line. If you give me a check for the amount of"—his thick pen had a calculator embedded within, and the slender fingers worked it like a pianist's—"$563,789.53 . . . if you give me that check *tonight,* or even tomorrow morning, but tonight would be preferred—I'll bend the rules, whatever makes you feel comfortable—if you can give me that check, I will hand *you* a negotiable instrument and bill of exchange for the amount of *$2,790,591.57* in a special toast at Spago on Saturday night. A pack of Rolls-Royces—they belong to the hotel—will then ferry the Sisters to their suites at the Four Seasons. Suite Sisters! We'll have a small afterparty, attended by the likes of 'unknowns' such as Maria Shriver, Laura Chick— she's the City Controller here in LA—and Ray Romano." He was losing her again. "You'll sleep the sleep of a babe in the woods. In the morning, you'll have a lovely bath and breakfast *en chambre.* Then you and the Blind entourage will be whisked to a private airport in Van Nuys where our sky chariot awaits. Now, if you are

opposed—you don't even have to give me an answer just now—
that's fine. No pressure. We can enroll you in the expedited
process, or not. I'll tell you one thing: at the moment we speak, 3
others are vying to be EAP enlistees, but I only have *one more slot.*
Marj, I want you to know *absolutely* that it doesn't matter to me,
either way—of course, I'll be a *little* sad—and I know you might
not be able to get your hands on that kind of money with such
short notice. Unfortunately, the figure I quoted is the least I can
accept without jeopardizing my job. It's kind of a silly catch-22:
you may not have the money *now*—but in 90 days, that number
will be *insignificant.* Cause you've got 6,000,000 coming down the
sluice! So, it's important for you to hear that I won't be upset, *even
though you're one of my favorites"* (he winked) *"and that if you're not
with us, I just may curl up in my private bedroom on the G-5 and cry
like a baby as they pass the caviar!* But seriously, Ms Morningstar, let
me know. You have my cell. You have my soul. You have my
heart. Give me the word and ye shall be heard."

The waiter came with fortune cookies and the check.

Marj cracked hers open, tucking the wish into her purse.

XLIX.

JOAN

CHESTER made a lunch date with his sister at a place Laxmi recommended in Venice, called Axe. It turned out that Joan was a regular, because it was over on Abbott Kinney, near ARK.

They hadn't seen each other since their stepfather's funeral. When Chess called to say he wanted to "talk about something," her antennae went up. He said on the phone he had visited Mom, and that clinched it—Big Brother needed a 2nd helping. She didn't ask if Marj had already *tithed*. She didn't want to know.

He was thin and drawn, and walked with a hobble that struck her as slightly theatrical. *Oh boy. I'm gonna get hit up for a bundle.* He gave the place a once-over and said he hoped the menu wasn't "minimalist." (A lame dig at Joan's aesthetics.) She told him he'd been pronouncing it wrong. It was *ah-shay,* she said, not *axe.*

"Well, *you* look like you've been eating!" he said, with a smile. (In secret sibling language, that meant: 1) You're rich and you're lucky; 2) I'm poor and I'm fucked; 3) You're a middleaged whore; 4) You've gained weight because you're a rich, lucky, middleaged whore.) He launched into the ballad of how his old friend Maurie Levin set him up on a reality show and got him injured. She literally shook her head, bemused. Chester was always putting his foot in it. There was something endearingly pathetic about him: he was some kind of classic, dipped-in-shit, dyed-in-the-wool fuckup. Her brother went on to say he was suing the company that produced the show and that his supercharged lawyer, "Remar" (even the name made her chuckle), was "extremely optimistic" things would "settle out" before a court date was set. Might take a year, though, maybe 2. Joan had already done the math and decided to give him 5 grand; she ran the figures in her head when he 1st called. *5,000 and not a penny more.* That was OK. She had enough in the bank right now and it'd actually been a few years since he'd asked. He had the pride thing going but that wouldn't last forever.

The waiter took his time. It was that kind of place. Both staff and clientele seemed like smug California dreamers, New Age grifters. When the guy finally came, Chess asked for a Coke. He said they didn't *have* Cokes, they didn't have *soda*. Like Chess had asked for yak urine. (Which they probably *did* have.) Joan just smiled. She ordered tea and tofu. Her brother had a bowl of rice and chicken, and a jug of weirdass juice.

He made some cursory stabs at catching up. *How are your projects, are you seeing anyone,* bip bop boop. Even threw in a zinger about Mayne winning the Pritzker.

"Since when do you keep up on the life of Thom Mayne?"

"I do *read,* you know. My landlady gives me her *New York Observer*s."

"Well la-di-da."

"And *LA* magazine."

"That's a restaurant guide, right?"

"I'm telling you, Joanie, I've been to so many doctors' offices, I'm up on all the zines. I just sit in waiting rooms, reading. Mayne's doing the Olympic Village in New York, right? *Tough*-looking fucker. Supposed to be kinda nasty, you know, nasty to his clients. I *hate* that shit. I wouldn't last 2 seconds if I was rude to the people who hire me. Ever meet him? Doesn't he look like that French guy? That actor? The guy from *The Da Vinci Code* ... Reno! Jean Reno. Mayne gives a pretty good interview. Doesn't he live around here? He did a 'My Favorite Weekend'—the *Times* wants me to do one of those. Seriously. Anyway, I was reading this interview where Mayne said an architect's career doesn't really begin happening till he's in his 50s. So your clock hasn't officially started to tick."

(In not-so-secret sibling language, that meant: 1) You haven't made it in your field and probably never will; 2) You are likely to achieve career success only by consenting to be sodomized by an already established architect—and should maybe just shoot for

Thom Mayne; 3) If you're gonna "build" anything, it better be a kid, before you go barren.)

Joan was beginning to wonder why she had agreed to see him. She'd forgotten how gallingly passive-aggressive her brother could be. Maybe she wouldn't give him the money afterall.

"You know," said Chess. "I was thinking. I was wondering. About Dad."

"Dad?"

She suddenly—wonder of wonders—realized he was stoned.

"Yeah. You know, Maurie told me he heard a story about Michael Bay—that director? He did *Pearl Harbor* and *Armageddon*. Maurie said that Michael Bay—and I don't know if this is bullshit—Michael Bay found out his dad was John Frankenheimer, the guy who did the original *Manchurian Candidate*. He died last year or whenever. Supposedly he and Burt Lancaster were banging extras in their trailers during *Seven Days in May*. That was '64 and Bay was born in '65. Do the math. You know, I did some scouting for *Path to War*, this TV movie he did. Frankenheimer. He died on the table, I think, in the middle of surgery. They were operating on his spine—probably what's going to wind up happening to *me*. I'll kick, right on the table, with the bozo anesthesiologist snoring away. Do you have any idea how often that happens, Joan? I've really looked into this shit! They just *kill* you. End of story. You can be healthy as an ox and they accidentally kill you cause they had a fight with their girlfriend or they're daydreaming about which satellite radio service to get or they're pissed off because the guy at Cingular fucked up and deleted their BlackBerry addressbook. Anyway, I just thought the Michael Bay/Frankenheimer thing was weird. Maybe it's one of those 'urban movie myths.' Like the gerbil. I don't know if it's true but it got me thinking about Dad. I mean, Bay and Frankenheimer are both action guys and they're both alleged to be pricks. I mean, I don't even *know* Michael Bay, and I really like his movies—not as much as I like the Scott brothers, but he's fucking *good*—though I never heard anything great about him, *personally*. Not that that means anything. You always hear bad things about people then one day you work with them and they're pussycats. So I don't put all that much stock in gossip and shit. Still . . . I saw him over at the Sports Club LA and he seemed like a nice guy. I mean, he wasn't going off on anybody. Very unassuming. Or maybe I saw Renny Harlin. No—it was definitely Bay. You know, come to think of it, Michael Bay kinda looks like Thom Mayne!"

"Oh Chess, come on," she said, mildly exasperated.

"He *does,*" laughed Chess. "I swear! Not that making movies is a popularity contest. Most directors have prickly reputations. The good ones, anyway. But, Joanie, don't you think that's *strange?*"

"What are you saying, Chess? *What's* strange."

"Frankenheimer supposedly denied paternity to the bitter end—which would be cold, if it turned out to be true. Bay shoulda stole a cigarette or a coffee cup. They can extract DNA from that shit. Anyhow, it just made me wonder what the chances were that Dad was still in this city. Maybe even in the business. And he just doesn't want to contact us."

"Yeah, right. *Maybe Dad's George Lucas!* You finally unraveled the secret, Chester! Our father is George Lucas! Or Frank Gehry! Maybe Dad's Frank Gehry! No—" (time for her to get in a zinger of her own) "—he's a *location scout.* That's it! Dad's the Location Scout King!"

"OK, Joanie. Chill."

"*You* chill. I just don't understand what you're trying to get at. I mean, you're stoned. Fine. It's a weekday and you're limping and you're loaded. Look, if you need money, why don't you just ask? Just come out and ask. You could have asked me over the *phone,* Chess. You didn't need to spend your precious gas money to drive all the way to Abbott Kinney."

The waiter brought the food.

She thought she might have been too rough on him. Then her sympathies quickly waned. *Oh, fuck* him. *I'm not going to feel bad about his crazy shit.*

Chess seemed humbled and began to eat. He let some of the smoke clear before he spoke.

"It's just that you reach a certain age—I have a few years on you, Joanie—and you wonder, or *start* to wonder, what your origins are. The medical thing's important too. I mean, what if our father had—or *has*—medical issues that are relevant?"

"What difference would it make, Chess? What difference would it make?"

"I've been talking to this friend about her dad. They're estranged. (She's not really a girlfriend, but I have my hopes.) Anyway, they're estranged but she knows where he is and occasionally they talk. And my friend—this girl—she thought it was weird that I never at least tried to find Raymond."

He waited for his sister to say something but she didn't.

"Isn't it weird that we never sought him out?"

"No. Not particularly. Why would we?"

"Here's a guy who really impacted us. Our *real father,* right?"

"Impacted? How?"

"We're both searching for a home. We always have been."

"What do you mean?"

"Jesus, Joanie, look at what we *do.* I'm a *location scout*—could it be any more on the fucking nose? That's what I do for a *living:* I *look* for places, mostly *houses.* I'm out there every week, *looking for the perfect house.* But what is it I'm *really* searching for?"

"You are so stoned."

"Having this injury has given me time to think about shit, Joan. We take a lot for granted . . . and look at what *you* do. *You build houses.* Or at least you're *trying* to. It's not even like a *metaphor* with us, right? Do you see what I'm saying? And our *relationships*—or lack of them—I think, can be traced to this guy—*Dad*—leaving. I mean, neither of us can *commit,* right?" She grimaced, struggling to chopstick a tofu cube. "I don't think either one of us has been with someone for longer than 3 years. Am I wrong, Joanie? Cause if I am, *great.* But I don't think so. It's all that abandonment shit, right? That's the paradigm."

"You've been watching way too much *Oprah,* Chester."

"Maybe. Maybe so. Great woman, by the way. But I think—I think I'm going to look into it."

"Go for it," she said, aloof.

"I kinda have the time right now. And I guess I just wanted to get together and see if that—resonated."

"I said: *go for it,* Chesapeake."

That was the nickname Mom gave him. Raymond called him Chesterfield.

"Chesapeake," he said, misty-eyed. She felt sorry for him again. "She hasn't called me that in a *long* time. Anyhoo: I'm not asking for your blessings, Joanie."

"No blessings, just cash. Right?"

He shook his head. "I don't need your money. I'm fine. I just want to keep you in the loop."

"Great. Perfect. Consider me in the loop."

Maybe she had embarrassed him into rescinding his request. If that were true, she was prepared to feel minorly guilty. Joan didn't know what to make of her brother's oratory. He sort of had a point, bordering even on eloquence, but she just didn't have it in her to care. It was his soap opera, not hers. She spent little time thinking about the man who walked away when she was 3. She knew their mother had loved Ghost Dad more than Hamilton— she'd tearfully admitted as much to Joan one night, after too much *vino*—but the daughter never probed further. *Fuck Raymond Rausch.* If he could live without *her,* she could definitely live without *him.* But things hadn't turned out so well for Chess and it made sense, particularly in the throes of maudlin midlife and what sounded like a new love, to root around in that particular cellar. *Rock on, Chesapeake Bay. Rock on with yer bad self.* She thought his fantasy of Ray Rausch being a Master of the Universe was sad and hilarious. Money was always in there for her brother, one way or another.

Money shouted. Money sang. Money talked.

Money *walked.*

She remembered how Raymond used to read to them from *The Jungle Book.* One Halloween, he gave Chess a wig and red Speedo; the little boy trick-or-treated as Mowgli while their father comported in a raffish Baloo jungle bear number. (Maybe that memory wasn't even her own. Maybe it was Marj's, as-told-to.)

2 months later, just days after Christmas, he was gone.

JOAN got a call from Trudy, the original Travel Gal. After a light skirmish of *How are you?*s, Trudy advised Joan she had just returned from "a little vacation," and heard from a coworker that Marjorie had expressed interest in going to Mumbai. Trudy said she tried Marj at home but couldn't reach her, and was "just checking in to see if everything was OK." She had tagged along with her mother once when the Travel Gals arranged an anniversary cruise to Alaska; her adoptive father was sick and Joan offered to help with planning, along with lending moral support. That was back when she was seeing more of her mom—she felt to blame for being somewhat of a stranger since Hamilton's death. *Add that one to the list.* It should have been the other way around—she should have seen less of Marj while her husband was still alive, and more of her now. Whatever. It was all moot. She told Trudy she'd get hold of Mom and they'd come in together. Frankly, she was irritated the woman had phoned. She hated the folksy hard sell.

Besides, Joan had no intention of going to India with her mother, Pradeep, Thom Mayne, John Frankenheimer, Salman Rushdie, or anyone else you could think of. She needed to bag the Freiberg Mem and get her ass in *gear,* finish the maquette, have Barbet sign off, then fly it on up to Lew. The whole high-dollar dog-and-pony thing. She needed to wash that Mem right out of her hair and soak up the world press that would accompany her honor, propelling her to new worlds: the tony gallery rep for gouaches and watercolors, the crazy-cool furniture line, sex-sizzled signed and numbered condos, Sunday-magazine profiles, Robert Wilson collaborations, Taschen/Rizzoli *Joan Herlihy: Builder* book pub parties, and international university master classes. If everything turned out like she wanted, she wouldn't be able to *sleep* for the next 10 years, let alone travel for pleasure or familial obligation.

Maybe her brother was on to something when he brought up the ticking clock. She had stopped taking birth control pills like her gynecologist told her to every few years, and hadn't had a period in nearly 3 months.

Which was normal.

But now she had that same feeling she'd had years ago with Pradeep, a few weeks before she miscarried.

L.

R A Y

Through Lawyer, Deputies Issue Apology for Wrong Door Break-In

By **CHARLTON WOOLTON,** *Times Staff Writer*

8 deputies who broke down the wrong door of a City of Industry residence, mistaking it for a narcotics distribution site, apologized Friday through their lawyers for the damage, including the shooting of a family dog. Doctors said the early-morning break-in was a contributing factor to a heart attack suffered by the apartment tenant Raymond Rausch, 76. He was hospitalized for 5 days. Both Mr Rausch and the dog, "Friar Tuck," have since recovered and been released from their respective caregiving facilities.

"These fine deputies that stand with me today wish to offer their unqualified and sincere apology to Mr Rausch," said attorney Emmerich Pitori, general counsel of the Los Angeles County Professional Sheriff's Assn.

Sheriff Phin Oldwalder said he could not recall any other law enforcement officers in Los Angeles delivering *mea culpas* for a controversial police action. "This has never happened in this county and this speaks well for the integrity of these deputies."

The apology came at a news conference at the Los Angeles Athletic Club, called after an outcry from the ACLU. Mr Rausch has so far declined to take legal action, and somewhat colorfully characterized himself as a longtime supporter of "police and firemen."

"Sometimes we simply do not have the time, when the safety of the community is concerned, for due diligence when it comes to intelligence sources that have in the past been tested and deemed reliable. Each one of the deputies, to a person, wishes things would have been different and certainly wish the information they had been given that night had been more accurate."

Hours after the break-in, a correct address was verified, and deputies made an arrest just blocks from Mr Rausch's Mercantile Road residence. Washington Lamont Birdell III was taken into custody for possession of narcotics and firearms.

IT was "all good," according to the ACLU attorney.

Ray hated that phrase. It sounded juvenile and disrespectful.

2 members of counsel showed up at the apartment to cynically explain the timing of the Oldwalder press conference, saying it was "no accident," and how the Sheriff was "well aware" they

were "smack in the middle" of negotiations. But the old man didn't find anything *Machiavellian* about it, once the 10-dollar adjective had been provided. To the lawyers' silent consternation, Ray said he felt the police were being sincere. The legal team was really hurting because Ghulpa couldn't provide necessary backup, seeing as she had to wrangle the Friar, who'd been chasing his tail, throwing up, and crying all day—stopping just long enough to viciously curl his lip at the suited men. Ray felt like doing a little of that himself. She finally got Nip to the bedroom and slammed the door behind them.

The offer had gone from 3-seventy-five to half a million, but they were almost certain the city would settle out at 7-fifty. To Ray's and everyone's surprise, the unseen Ghulpa shouted, "We'll take it!" The visitors looked at Ray, and that was that.

Sold, at half a mil.

After a moment of readjusting ties and briefcases, the men were compelled to say it would be wise to go to jury, yet also acknowledged the wisdom of a settlement, for the sake of closure. Ghulpa emerged. The lawyers reiterated their position, this time more convincingly detailed and commonsensible, but she held ground, reaching out for her partner's hand. He squeezed it in solidarity. Then one of the fellows said, "Good! Great! Terrific," and Ray began signing a stackload of papers. BG made everyone chamomile.

There were so many documents, at one point Ray took a breather and sat back in his La-Z-Boy with a grizzled, sleepy-eyed grin. He had cadmium-yellow curry in the crook of his mouth and Big Gulp reentered from the kitchen with a damp cloth to roughly wipe him while she affectionately clucked. 30 minutes later, the whole crew hustled their happy asses out of there.

After they left, Ray told her how he'd visited Allied Trains while Nip/Tuck was getting a bandage change—the memories of bringing Chester to that place. He cautiously broached the name Lionel as a possibility, if they were to have a son. "Chester" didn't feel right; she understood, and quietly agreed. (The cousins would probably wind up doing the christening anyway.) Ghulpa softly repeated: *Lionel*. What does it mean? she asked. Well, he said, inadvertently bobbling his head the Indian way—it's the name of a *train*. His eyes widened and he smirked like a big, sweet clown while she kept the same blank look. "It's the name of a famous toy train! But also," he added, with utmost gravity, "the name of a *very* legendary actor: Lionel Barrymore. You know, come to think of it, Gulp, Lionel Barrymore was actually the American 'Mr B.'" He was improvising, but had to admit that was a pretty good one. He probably should have thought it all through beforehand. Ghulpa didn't seem entirely convinced.

That's when Ray pointed out that *lion* was the name's root. She didn't react—which was good.

"Doesn't your friend Durgā ride on one of those?"

"We'll see," she said. "And if it's a girl?"

He waited a moment, then said, "Lioness."

She scowled, then laughed in spite of herself.

She went to let the dog out. He'd puked on the rug. She swore at him then soaked a towel to daub it up. The old man pushed PLAY on his *Twilight Zone*.

STANIEL Lake stopped by and was promptly bit—the Friar actually broke skin. That didn't make Ray happy at all. The detective shrugged it off but Ghulpa was mortified and brought out alcohol and cotton swabs. The detective said he was fine and asked if he could wash his hand in the kitchen sink. The old man felt even worse because when it happened, he'd instinctively swatted Nip's butt—the dog yelped and pitifully shuddered, even though the hit was nowhere near the wound.

"Don't worry about it," said the kindly Mr Lake.

Ghulpa put the dog back in the bedroom, where he began to shriek and howl. She shushed at him and somewhere a neighbor said, *Shut it! Shut that crazy motherfucker up!*

"Sorry about that," said Ray. "He hasn't been himself. We're

gonna get some help—Friar's got 'mental' stuff. You sure you're
OK?"

"I'm fine. Not the 1st time. Hell, I was raised around dogs.
He'll have to do more than that to scare me off."

"He just might! Had your tetanus?"

"Don't even worry about it, Ray."

"I may have to give a press conference myself," joked the old
man. Then he thought the remark sounded cavalier. He tried to
balance it out. "You know, I really appreciated that—the words of
those officers. I know they're good men."

He felt bad. He wasn't sure if he should say they had reached a
settlement; maybe it wasn't kosher, legalwise. He forgot to ask the
attorneys about that. He didn't want to do anything to upset the
applecart. But he made a note to eventually explain the decision to
Detective Lake, why he'd agreed to accept the City's terms, and let
him know for the record there were no hard feelings—he was
going to be a new father soon, that's all, and worried about the
child's welfare and what the future held, plain and simple. He
wanted to take the detective and his colleagues to the Pacific Dining Car when the money came in but didn't know if *that* was allowed; again, if it was kosher. Oh, the hell with it, he'd do it
anyway. He'd do it *before*—before he got a penny. He wanted to
convene, explain himself to the cops so that when the news broke,
they wouldn't think he was a hypocrite or a greedy man because
afterall they had the best intentions and he didn't consider it to be
their fault that things went wrong (like things sometimes/always
do), they put their lives on the line each and every day, and they'd
spoken from their hearts, and hadn't been Machiavellian. He
wanted to say all of that right this minute but BG kept shooting
him looks, he understood those kinds of signals, she was telling
him to bite down, button up, zip it, upset as she was about the dog
chomping on their guest, she still wanted to protect her own, protect her man and the bump in her belly. She subtly glowered each
time she sensed Ray was weakening, wanting to share his sappy
thoughts with Mr Lake.

The detective stayed about an hour, watching *The Twilight*

Zone on and off, before going his way. Ray asked if he'd like to have a meal one day soon and Ghulpa seemed fine with that—it was the right thing to have said. He apologized for the Friar's uncivil behavior and again, the detective shrugged it off.

Ghulpa and Ray watched a *Larry King* rerun. He was interviewing the model who lost her fiancé in the tsunami, a beautiful girl who clung to a palm tree for hours before being rescued. She spent 3 weeks in the hospital with a broken pelvis.

Ghulpa shuffled in from the kitchen with food, staring spitefully at the screen.

"I will *never* return," she said, as if suffering a fresh insult.

"But that's *Thailand,* not India," said the old man.

"My child will *never* see that terrible place. I don't care."

"Suit yourself."

LI.

CHESTER

THE kiss at the zoo surprised him.

It had stopped there, aside from a little groping, which was fine and dandy, because Chess didn't think he was up for anything else. Too heavy. But it was obvious they were becoming more than just friends and he worried about getting too dependent. He didn't need another drug in his life. Still, winding up as the neutered companion, like on some TV sitcom—standing on the sidelines while Ganesha Girl got involved with another Maurie-type—would be rough. (Though he knew he'd probably settle for anything; she was definitely nice to have around.) He was *super*-attracted. The idea of Laxmi even sitting on his toilet was a turn-on—just thinking about it gave Chess half a hard-on, which was all he seemed capable of lately. But for the life of him he couldn't see *her* side of it.

Why would she be interested?

He got paranoid, occasionally wondering if it was a new setup involving Maurie, some meta–*Friday Night Frights* mindfuck. (Maybe his old pal was doing another reality show that even Remar was in on.) Chess started TiVo-ing *FNF* because Laxmi had become a semiregular. Apart from the thrill of watching her—she was usually scantily clad, as they say—he enjoyed it. One episode featured a clever show-within-a-show. They recruited a Vic, telling him he was going to "do some stunts" on a *Punk'd*-style series called *The Fright Club*. A *real* stuntman pretended to be fatally injured during the filming and the police came; the kid who'd been hired *completely* freaked. It was pretty sophisticated, kind of like the Michel Gondry version. Whenever Chess felt particularly vulnerable, usually after smoking weed, he thought Laxmi's attentions might be part of an elaborate hoax. He knew it was crazy, and was usually able to talk himself down fairly quick.

Chess was convinced that his fears were only a function of all the physical bullshit he'd been experiencing: bouts of room-twirling vertigo in the morning being the latest. His doc ascribed it to the voodoo of various meds but Chess made an appointment to come in anyway because there was evidently some sort of "non-invasive procedure" they could do right in the office to equalize the fluids in the ear. From everything he'd gathered off blogs and chatrooms, dizziness was a bitch to get rid of. (People usually got the cookie-cutter diagnosis of BPPV—Benign Paroxysmal Positional Vertigo.) There was a widely accepted fix-it called the Epley Maneuver; like everything else, how-to diagrams were all over the Net. It seemed kind of hillbilly. The nurses took hold of Chess, yanking him this way and that until his eyes jumped and jittered in their sockets ("nystagmus," said the regal RN), thus dislodging debris or "ear rocks"—literally what they were called. Sometimes it worked, sometimes it didn't. You had to sleep semi-recumbent for a few days after the mad teacup ride or risk undoing any salutary effects. If the vertigo didn't go away after 2 or 3 Epleys, they left you twisting in the wind, in a thunderstorm of vomit.

Like lots of things—chronic pain being Numero Uno—no one really took it seriously, not even putative professionals. MDs just kept writing scripts for antihistamines and Dramamine, generally categorizing repeat offenders as fags, drags, and whiners. If the problem persisted, they were legally compelled to rule out MS, Parkinson's, compression of vertebral arteries (that's what was worrying Chess), or Ménière's. People with vestibular disorders were called "wobblers"—sometimes you could be sent to permanent vertigo jail from the side effects of a virus or something as routine as a run-of-the-mill antibiotic. There were surgical treatments for BPPV but Chess didn't even want to go there. The idea of someone cutting into his spine was bad enough but plumbing into notoriously delicate aural canals and fluid reservoirs or tinkering with weensy ear bones sounded like an invitation to suffer the consequences of illustrating Mohammed. So for a while, he took to propping himself up while he slept, which wasn't easy. He spent $400 on special formfitting bolsters at Relax Your Back. Sometimes, on top of the painkillers, he needed 4 Klonopin (1 mg) and 3 Ambien CRs (12.5 mg) just to get him through the night.

He dutifully passed on his recent Job-like travails to Remar De Concini LLD, AKA the Gay Pit Bull.

A FTER the make-out session in Griffith Park, Chess shared some memories of his dad. Laxmi enthusiastically echoed how *The Jungle Book* was a favorite of hers too, from girlhood. (She meant the version with John Cleese.) A few days later, she brought over a Netflix of the original Disney. They did hash brownies and Baileys Irish Cream: a killer combo. Laxmi said she used to watch the one from 1994 with her mom when they relocated to a rental on Tigertail Road in Brentwood Hills. From the commune.

The odd couple sat on the couch munching magicsnacks, and got all snuggly and captivated. They wrapped themselves up in each other's arms, grooving on the night's activity. (Chess didn't become aroused and as usual found that both worrisome and copacetic.) When it came to the innocuously clever, charming scat song of the old hipster orangutans, Laxmi exclaimed it was "totally racist." "I mean, all they're really *saying* is, *they just want to be white.*" Chess wouldn't give an endorsement; he didn't relate to the politics of it. She must have realized she sounded over-the-top, adding that "The Bare Necessities" was "amazingly perfect and Zen."

Chess remembered more of the movie than he cared to. He used to call Daddy Ray "Baloo." They got to the part where Baloo wanted to adopt Mowgli as his son but the panther said it wasn't right because Baloo was a bear. That was always a downer. *Still* was. The panther said the "man cub" had to be returned to the "man village" and Baloo got all sad and Chess, under a goodbye hashish-Baileys moon, grew teary-eyed as well. Baloo told

Mowgli he couldn't stay in the forest and it broke the bear's heart. The boy ran off. When Baloo the bear said, "If anything happens to that little guy, I'll never forgive myself," Chess thought of Raymond. *What a shitheel. A remark like that would never occur to that old fuck.*

A wave of dizziness washed over him and he braced himself to barf. Chess began to cry, the tears somehow stanching nausea. He full-on sobbed. Laxmi held him and they rocked together, then both began to laugh. That was cathartic and good, and what was special about their relationship. That funny-sad thing they could tap into on a dime. They lit up a bong.

George Sanders was the voice of the man-eating Bengal that kicked the shit out of Baloo when he tried to protect Mowgli, and suddenly the old bear lay on the ground without moving. Chess had forgotten this part: he couldn't remember if Raymond died or not, and in his stonedness, got briefly freaked. Then, ever so slowly, the bear opened an eye—of course. Of course he was OK. Those were the days before wholesale bloodbaths and glimpses of hell had worked their way into animated kid stuff. But actually, now that he thought of it, Bambi hadn't had such a far-out time.

"You know what you should do," said Laxmi, "if it doesn't work out with that lawyer of yours? You should get an *Indian* guy. My dad could probably help."

"For an attorney?" he said, confused. "But he'd be . . . in *India*. Right?"

"You may not know it, Chess," she said, taking a deep toke, holding it, then coughing a mite. *"Every*—or at least *lots* of American law firms outsource to Indian firms. Rebar probably has a whole—"

"Remar."

"Remar probably has a whole fleet working for him *already*. They call them 'chutney sweatshops.' My father said that even *Du Pont* farms it out. It's like a *10th* of what they'd pay in the States. Why *wouldn't* they?"

The phone rang—it was Maurie. Chess gave her a furtive Freemason heads-up.

Maurie mentioned the Morongo casino gig again and how Chess should lighten up so they could go make some bread. *What the fuck. Yeah, I'll go.* He probably wouldn't have assented if Laxmi wasn't there but her secret presence lent a nice *Fuck You* to the conversation. Maurie was surprised, and glad to hear it. Laxmi got up to use the head, walking on giggle-suppressed exaggerated tippy toes to drive home the fact of her satisfying private life with Chester. That titillated him, there was something payback pervy about the 3some going on a trip without that arrogant piece of shit knowing what was happening behind the scenes. Not that there *was* much happening, not yet. Just a little huggin and kissin and smokin.

Chester hoped to change all that. He went online to order Viagra. (He'd thrown the original free samples away out of pride, and didn't want to call the doc back for a "refill." Anyhow, the dick-stiffeners were expensive.) It was easy. They even had a "special"—like a clearance. He got Oxycontin, Xanax, and Ambien CR at a discount. Sweet.

LII.

MARJORIE

SHE bought her daily ticket.

A funny feeling, because the notes and flowers that decorated the liquor store *in memoriam* were down now, and you had to look hard to see the wires, mostly gone themselves, that once held bouquets in place.

The devout son was behind the counter and the mother nowhere to be seen. The young man smiled and went about his business. It was strange to Marjorie, not that it should have or could have been any other way, but she had the unsettling feeling that Riki had somehow died in a different way—the violence of it had conveniently receded, and now it seemed as if his death had been natural, or he'd gotten the flu and would soon be back, or he'd simply returned to India for an indeterminate amount of time. Marjorie knew it would be poor form to share her little wish-fulfillment fantasy-observations. What right had she to smalltalk about such a thing? Besides, it wasn't part of their culture to endlessly hash over death; death was so much a part of their world that no one had the need to "kibitz" about it (as Hamilton would say). The Indian people embraced the cycle of life—karma, death, and rebirth—and didn't need to be inoculated or familiarized or talked down to, or have their noses rubbed in the obvious by meddling, mawkish Westerners. That would be ignorant and presumptuous. But part of her still stubbornly wanted to reach out, and she remembered hearing something on a talkshow, maybe Dr Phil, where an expert said that in times like this, the worst thing a person could say was "nothing." That had really stuck. Well, she would just have to get over it. She had done her part and given the widow an honorarium and anything else at this point would be self-indulgent. Marj would continue to patronize the shop, as usual, thus actively demonstrating her support. The side benefit being that the old woman could help restore a sense of normalcy, not that it was even possible. And she mustn't forget: they would soon reap the benefits of her Blind Sister winnings. She needed to ask Lucas when they would be told, and if an exception could be made to inform them earlier. She wondered what % they had coming.

Ever since she gave them the money, the grieving family treated her with what sometimes felt like an awkward obsequiousness, which was perhaps cultural as well. The son slipped small gifts into her hand that his mother had delicately wrapped, packages of sweets or modest scarves of silken fabric. When Marjorie came in, the young man warmly greeted her and never let her leave unescorted, not only for safety reasons but it seemed from deep respect and gratitude. (Another facet of Indian society was to respect the elderly, which was wonderful, because lately, with all the excitement, Marj Herlihy sometimes felt her age.) She had the means to lighten their heavy load, which she did, and Bonita helped her to feel humbly ennobled. My God, look what Bill Gates does with his billions! Say what you like, but he gives away more money than any other person on planet Earth. By helping Riki's family, she was nurturing her connection to Mother—Mother India, whose arms in which she would soon be embraced.

S HE had given a check to Lucas for the Expedited Award Program and when Marj checked her balance at Wells it reflected the 565,000-dollar debit. She was surprised the State of New York had cashed the monies so quickly but Lucas said he was the court-appointed caretaker and after he explained, it made sense that the faster the check was "converted," the faster the "upstream" of "shadow monies" would "flow" through Marjorie's account. It was nervous-making but exciting as well.

There was a message from Bonita on the answering machine asking if she wanted to "do a little New York shopping," and to "please place a call to the *darling* bungalow—22B—where Ms

Billingsley *is currently residing,* with her *retinue of shirtless manservants,* at the very *pink* and very *posh* Pink Palace." She went on to say—it was a *long* message—that "a little birdie" told her Marj had enrolled in the EAP and after shouting "Congratulations, Moneybags!" reminded her of the dinner at Spago on Saturday night. "Your 1st check should be in by then and *honey,* let's *splurge!* We have *got* to get our rich asses over to Hermès!"

She used salty language but Marj didn't mind—Bonita was a fun new friend. How long had it been since Marj had a new friend? She couldn't even think when. And what in the world was the Pink Palace?

She had planned to stop by Cora's: though now her heart was racing! *Manhattan* . . . she was dying to tell *someone* but had been warned of "interstate (*intra*state?) disclosure penalties," something like that, she probably had it wrong, yet there *definitely* were consequences. Even Bonita told her not to "gab" until she got that 1st installment. Marj didn't want to jinx anything.

She dipped her hand in the mailbox and tore open an envelope with a check for $150,000 from a company called Amerimac. At 1st she thought it was a Blind Sister copayment but then she looked closer and stamped across was THIS IS NOT A CHECK. She read the attached letter; she'd been prequalified to consolidate her debts. Well, she didn't *have* any debts. It said *One Low Payment,* and *No Equity Required,* and *Refinances Also Available.* She decided to show it to Lucas—it was the kind of thing that would make him laugh. He'd come up with some witty remark to put those junk mailers in their place.

Another letter was from *Who's Who.*

Dear Our New Member:

    Congratulations, MARJORIE HERLIGHY. May I take this moment to personally congratulate you as a new United America's Who's Who in Families and Professionals member? You will be pleased to learn that we have formatted the publication to make it even easier for our members to produce beneficial business relationships with other United America's Who's Who people, so that you might contact others of your immense professional status.

United America's Who's Who in Executives and Professionals takes great pride in formulating as successful a directory as possible each year.

We appreciate your support and look forward to a continuing relationship.

Very Truly Yours,

Randall Wolcott-Jones, President

The old woman presumed the invite had been triggered by her recent admission into what Bonita called the "country club" of Blind Sisters; or maybe it had something to do with the EAP. The puzzling thing was that no one was supposed to know about the prize yet—though organizations like *Who's Who* probably had some sort of inside track. That would be something *else* to ask Lucas. (Even Hamilton had never been solicited to join the august group. Marj always wanted to be in the Blue Book but it seemed you had to be born in Pasadena or San Marino to make the cut.) It said there was a fee, which Marj assumed covered printing costs. She put the "congratulations" in the drawer, with the Amerimac check.

The phone was ringing—

My, am I popular this morning!

"There you are!"

"Who's this?"

"It's Trudy! Trudy Gest. Now *what's* all this I hear about you wanting to go to India, Mrs Herlihy? Did you find yourself a boyfriend?"

"Oh heavens no!"

That was the sort of thing Trudy liked to say, even when Ham was alive. It was her style, and reminded Marj of Bonita, though not quite the class act. Then it occurred that she was only thinking of Bonita as "classy" because she knew how wealthy her new friend was; and *that* just wasn't fair. *Shame on you, Marj Herlihy.* The old woman asked after her health. The Travel Gal responded that she was still "putt-puttin along"—an area she obviously didn't feel comfortable talking about (again, the reprimand: *What a busybody I've become*). Trudy probably suspected Nigel had blabbed, and Marj hoped he wouldn't get in trouble on her account.

"If you want to go to India, I'm going to have to start calling you Mother Marjorie—as in Mother Teresa!"

Trudy went on about how excited she was with the potential itinerary, before interrupting herself.

"Guess who *I* talked to?"

Marj thought she was going to say Lucas but she said Joan instead.

"My—daughter?"

"She still is, the last time I checked! I couldn't get *ahold* of you, sweetheart, you're *a very busy girl.* Out painting the town red, no doubt—or whatever color they're using now. *The merry widow.* You don't have to tell *me.* And Joan was just *thrilled*—she wants to help us plan. Now, I understand Nigel had a *very* lovely conversation with you about Mumbai. Nigel tends to get a *little enthused*: if you're not careful, you can walk away with a severe case of TMI . . . that's Too Much Information!"

"Is Joan coming?" she said, a bit flustered.

"She'd be a fool *not* to! But you know our *Joan.* A little stand-offish—Lord, she's even busier than you are! Bless her heart, I wish *my* children were that busy. But, sweetheart, you have *got* to let me talk you out of spending too much time in Mumbai! Especially if you're going to travel *alone.*"

Overwhelmed, Marj went on default.

"When I was a girl, my father took me to the Taj Mahal."

"Oh yes, I know!"

"I want very much to see that place again."

"It's the one place you *must* see if you go all that way—but the Taj Mahal is a 'far piece' from Mumbai, sweetheart. Why don't we put you in Delhi, Mother Marj? We'll get you a bed on Singapore Airlines. *That airline is marvelous.* Next time you're at the market pick up *Travel + Leisure,* or *any* of those magazines: Singapore Air is consistently rated the *absolute highest.* Par excellence. Did you know they will even come *right to the house* to pick up your bags for check-in? Now, I think it's a 17 or 18 hour flight, but—"

"I meant the Taj Mahal *Palace*—the hotel, in Bombay."

There was a pause before Trudy horse-laughed.

"Oh, *I'm* sorry! Of *course* you did! *Now* I remember . . . Nigel's notes are a *mess*—he's been out sick for a week. The Taj is *lovely*—the old wing. Bill Clinton's absolute favorite, by the way. But don't you want to go to the Taj Mahal? In Agra?"

"Only if Joanie comes."

"I'll talk to her again." Before Marj could raise an objection to that, Trudy said, "Now, if you *do* stay at the *Taj Mahal Palace and Towers* in Mumbai—I want to make sure I have that straight!—I wouldn't recommend *leaving!* Marjorie, the city is a *horror.* If the *taxis* don't kill you, those *street urchins* will! We *have* had people run down by cars. Oh yes. The *filth* and the *smells*—I personally don't have the stomach. I think you may be romanticizing! Which is what our memories do . . . my friend Florence was *just there.* She gave one of those little beggars a single rupee, and *made a friend for life.* They will *not* leave you alone! They chase after you for *miles.* The Indians! *One step outside the hotel* . . . they're all petty thieves!" (Marj winced, thinking of Riki and his family.) "Flo had a pregnant girl come up to her and when she tried to give her a few coins, the girl said she didn't *want* any money, all she wanted was *milk.* Flo kept saying, 'I'll give you *money* and you can *buy* milk.' But the girl *insisted.* Flo said she looked like an *angel.* It was *very convincing.* How can you turn down an angel who's asking for milk instead of money? The land of milk and money! The little criminal pointed out a place where Flo could buy the milk. Well, by now my friend's curiosity was piqued, Flo is *very inquisitive,* and hard, may I add, to get the better of. You've got to wake up pretty early to do that, and let me tell you, these Indians are early risers! So Florence buys the angel-faced girl milk then walks away and hides; 10 minutes later, she sees the girl go back and return it! She's in cahoots with the people who own the shop! Flo said she wasn't even sure she was *pregnant,* that she thought it might be *padding.* Do you see, Marj? It's a sham! The merchants pocket the money and get the milk too and the whole thing begins all over again! Florence was *extremely impressed.* The Indians are *the most extraordinary bunco artists.* That's why they use them in the call centers. They learn English *perfectly* and the next thing you know they're phoning at dinnertime—with perfect American accents!—and you think you're getting someone from AT&T! When they're 10,000 miles away! Oh, the companies that hire them here in the States are *no fools,* I assure you. But are you *certain* that you and Joan don't want to go to Italy? Or Spain? Or Scotland? Scotland's *wonderful* this time of year. We'll put you at the Balmoral. There's a *marvelous* train that beats the *pants* off the Orient Express. Hands down. It winds through the countryside and during the day, you picnic with royalty, right in their castles. It's a 4 hour layover in Newark and you're there the next morning. *That's* what *I* think you should do, Mother Marj. *That's* what I think you should do."

LIII.

JOAN

JOAN and 3 interns tweaked the maquette of the Freiberg Mem. It was huge—about 10 by 4—and Barbet kept saying how amazing it looked.

The finely detailed creation comprised the valley void itself, ringed with artfully xeroxed leaf cutouts of weeping spruces and blue elderberry. The "water grove" of green-veined marble was a rectangular trough, theoretically difficult to apprehend unless one were very close—not to the model, but the eventual elegant gutter itself—the set piece's formal entrance being a walkway through a pair (representing Samuel and Esther) of yew-carved rooms. The tub was just 18 inches deep; through a complex computer-calibrated system of ducts, drains, and siphons, it would always remain level with the meadow floor, after, or even during, minatory Napa downpours. Joan got the idea from a book on the Ajanta caves in Western India—an early, stalwart survivor of her messy Freiberg archive—where 2nd and 3rd century artists used sunlight caught by centralized pools to illuminate the recesses of honeycombed darkness so as to be able to make filigreed paintings of gods and goddesses (the scholars' theory, anyway). Barbet occasionally had a numbskully idea—like the notion of the grand groove periodically flooding over, à la human tears—something so asinine it made Joan question the forces of nature that had adroitly conspired in favor of their partnership, in both business of design and sexual congress.

Lew called from a bungalow at the Bel-Air.

She went right over.

MORE gifts—bangles and cuffs made from exotic maples and milo wood. Lew muttered that the Indian government had officially denied his request to uproot and export "the hangman's (spirit) tree."

He muted the TV. The tsunami anniversary was upon them, and CNN was rerunning *Larry King*s.

"Larry's such a horny old fuck! And he *farts*. I know people who've been on that show—he farts during breaks! Just lets it rip!" He rang room service for drinks and steak. "Look," he said, pointing to the silent screen. "It's that supermodel whose *fiancé* died in Phuket. Larry just asked if she was in the *shower* when the wave hit. The shower! Dream on, Larry! That musta got him farting, big-time! So Miss Supermodel says, *No*. She's trying to be dignified. And Larry says, 'I understand the force of the water *tore off all your clothing.*' Look! Watch! He says *'You're nude during all of this?* . . . nude out in the sun 8 hours. Did you have skin damage?' " Lew slapped his knees in jubilation. "Not only is ol Larry farting like a goat but now he's got a righteous furry goat hard-on! Then he specifically asks about her *pelvis.*"

He was relishing his role as Human Subtitler.

"She says, *'Vell, yes'*—she's got that supermodel accent—*'but, Larry, you don't even* sink *about being nude.'* So she's in a palm tree, in her birthday suit, and these guys come along and she says they try to lift her but she's in too much pain—did you read about this chick, Joan? Remember her? She was all *over* the place, cover of *People*—really milked it. Broke her pelvis. *Shattered* it. Wrote a *memoir,* formed a charity—'Give2Asia Happy Hearts.' I'm serious. *Give2Asia Happy Hearts!* Give to Larry's Happy Farts! Brilliant, huh? A real Vassar chick. So Our Lady of the Martyred Supermodel says the guys leave and she doesn't think they're coming back. She's nude in a tree, looking the way she looks, probably shaves her bush, waxes her poo-hole, and she doesn't think they're coming back! *Fuck* no, *course* not! Why *would* they? They're gonna go rescue some fatassed village women instead! They're going to go save some *babies*. They're gonna dig a *cow* out of the mud. So Supermodel says, *Lo and behold*—the guys come back! And she's *so shocked* at their fucking kindness! You know how teary-eyed and grateful supermodels get when someone lends a helping hand. But *this* time, she says, not only *Thai* guys, but *Swedes* and *Bulgarians* and *whomever* show up! Like, a whole *brigade*. You know what's funny, Joan? This stuff I always find fucking interesting. Larry asks about the fiancé, if they had a wedding date set, and Supermodel says no. But they *talked* about it, she says, on the night before the tsunami. *The night before.* Supposedly she says in the memoir that when the 2 of them met on a photo shoot, 'there was no bolt of lightning.' Like, a dead connection. Then, 6 months later in Majorca on *another* shoot, she suddenly realizes they're soulmates! Soulmates, Joan! Did you ever notice how in big tragedies people always seem to be talking about really important shit *the night before?* Planning out their whole fucking lives together. Like that couple who died in the earthquake in Iran . . . I don't know why this crap sticks in my head. That's how whacked out I am, bet you haven't noticed, huh. The Iran thing: this American couple—I think they were from the Bay Area, maybe that's why I remember. Both kind of eccentric, not so young, been dating awhile, have a little money between them, love to travel, they're on one of their chic weekend getaways strolling along the Champs-Élysées and one of em sees a poster in a travel shop. For *Iran.* So. Being the intrepid soulmates that they are, they decide to go to *Iran* for a fucking holiday. Where do they go? To the quaint city of *Bam,* right when the earthquake hits. And in every single interview—it's all about the interviews, honey!—the woman—she's the one who survived— why does it always seem to be the woman who survives? though I guess sweet Esther would argue with me about that one—the woman, in all the interviews, says that the guy proposed to her *the night before.* There it is again: the night before! Of course, the next *day,* the quake hits and a ceiling fan goes right through her fiancé's chest. But at least he got the chance to get down on his knees and propose! I mean, it's like all these *victims* have the same fuckin publicist! Look! Joan, look!" He pointed to the screen like a 10 year old on a sugar jag. "There's Larry, asking Our Lady of the Martyred *Shtu*permodels about the funeral for *her* fiancé and she says—Joan, you gotta look at her! Dumb as a fuckin pony!—she

tells that horny farting goat about the funeral. In her memoir, she
says they toasted the deceased with some drink called a Slippery
Nipple! Jesus! That's what her memoir says, I am not shitting
you! The guy is fully ignited and she writes about how she's getting 'tipsy'! I guess that's what you call a Polish cremation! And by
the way, I think she *semi* cops to being addicted to laxatives (I can't
believe this *diarrhea* is actually in my head) which her *soulmate*
was in the process of detoxing her from right before the wave took
him out! And the funeral's in London or wherever and she's going
on about how Superfiancé wouldn't have wanted anyone to be *sad,*
he'd want everyone to have a *good time*—I *hate* that. When people—if you can call a *shtup*ermodel a person—when people make
that bizarre fuckin leap in their heads so *they* can feel better, you
demean the dead by projecting how instead of *mourning* they'd
have wanted you, you know, to have the *big celebration* and fight
for your right to party! So they all go out and dance. I don't even
want to *think* about the motley crew who showed up for *Shtup*er-
fiancé's burial. That's *too* fuckin horrible. They dance through the
tears! The poignance of it all! Yeah *right,* I'm *sure,* that's *exactly*
what Sir Soulmate would have wanted! 'I died drowning, getting
thwacked by garbage and dead babies breaking the bones in my
face as I screamed and my lungs sucked in animal feces and gaso-
line—but *party on!* And now I'm in some kind of waterworld
Dante-esque *hell,* but you should be *dancin,* dancin, dance the
night away!"

He looked back at the TV, finally unmuting it.

He was drunk.

Joan was drunk.

"You *dumb cunt,*" he said, staring at the model. "Oh! And people are calling in to *ask* her shit. I'm telling you, Joan, I have this
fucking show memorized!"

"I can see that," she said, with a smile.

"It's on my hit parade! I had someone at Guerdon burn DVDs,
I'm serious, I'm givin em out for Christmas. (Don't tell Axel!) She
keeps talking about the garbage, crushing her pelvis! Look, look,"
he said, raising then lowering the volume. "One of the callers—a

guy, of course—is asking *Shtup*ermodel if she'll need 'further sur-gery' on her hips! On her hips! Loose lips sink shtuperhips! He was just like Larry, a horny motherfucker, you could tell all he re-ally wanted to know was *When can you get back to spreading for cock.* A woman calls and says, 'Think you'll ever fall in love again?' and Shtuperwhore says something like, '*Ya, ya, it's too soon,*' blah. 'Ya, it's too soon, but I am looking for the future, what-ever it brings.' Bringing up baby! Coming soon to a theater near you! Coming soon on her shattered pelvis! Another guy has trou-ble spittin out a question but finally says he was a *survivor*—that's why Larry's people probably patched him through—says he was just up the beach from where Slippery Nip *Shtup*mod was stuck in the tree, but oh! Larry's a hardass! Toughass Jew. *Man,* he was *rough* on this call-in motherfucker! Ol cardio-fartin Larry keeps cuttin the slob off, saying, 'What's your *question,* what's your *question?*' just like he was at Nate 'n' Al's with the gang—then he *hangs up* on the guy! See, Larry doesn't want any *fellow victims* bonding with her, she's *his,* he wants that wet, fractured pussy all to himself! *The answer my friend is blowin in his wind!* See, Larry doesn't dig the idea of some guy who was on the *same beach* when the wave hit—he don't dig it *at all.* So Larry's passin gas under the desk, sounds like fucked-up muffler, soiling his jock, marking his turf! Surf and turf! I'm tellin you, look at him, he's got new suspenders—look!—new suspenders, a fresh hair-cut, and horny as hell! I look at that bitch and all I can think of is my sister-in-law, impaled on that sundari. I guess God smiles on the beautiful. Esther was no prize. And let's face it, *Shtup*ermodel Fiancée *is* beautiful. Up in the tree for 9 hours, it held her in its arms, that's what she said—*Esther's* whorefuck tree wasn't so benevolent. At least they found the boyfriend's body. Poor Super-fiancé. Samuel wasn't that lucky. Maybe if he had a manicured bush, the bureaucrats wouldn't have 'misplaced' him. Stupid fucks."

Joan brought up a Faulkner story she'd read in college about a Mississippi River flood. A pregnant woman, stranded in a tree. (Indirect reference to Katrina, which she always tried to avoid

around him, but she was inebriated and couldn't help it.) A con-
vict rescues her.

Then Joan blurted out that *she* was pregnant, she, not Faulkner's lady, not Esther, not Superwhoever, but she, Joan Herlihy,
and Lew was quizzically, quietly uncomprehending before
soberly nodding his unsober head. She hadn't expected such
speedy, almost elegantly impersonal acquiescence, but that was
why he'd made billions, he could reframe and conform his energies to the wildly brand-new. His expression became that of someone listening to a confession of illness, humbly attending the
details of what could or couldn't be done to effect a healing.

She didn't stay much longer. He asked her not to leave, but suddenly Joan got nauseous and emotional and didn't want to be that
way around him, not now, not tonight, and didn't want to hear the
inevitable question: whether she was certain, but more, whether
she was certain it was *his,* didn't want to hear that now, not
tonight. Joan knew she would have to take a paternity test, both
parties would demand it—she would reserve the right of dignity
to beat him to the punch and suggest (she would need to move
soon: tomorrow morning) what she knew his attorneys would require anyway—she was going to keep this child, Joan knew it was
his and she wanted to raise it, but not tonight, she did not want to
discuss any of it tonight, did not want to feel anything more, no
strength or will or heart or bowels to engage in dialogue, spoken
or unspoken—not tonight.

A T home, she dreamed of the Lost Coast. It was carpeted by a
macadamized boulevard that morphed into Eisenman's
Mem to the Murdered Jews of Europe, pillar after pillar, slab after
slab, until the touristy petrified forest resembled a jail for villains
in a Marvel comic. But the vast necropolis had a teeming underground life—in her netherworld, things went topsy-turvy, the
dead lived aboveground and the living, below—as in some bad
Czech sci-fi novel, dark figures clambered amid the labyrinth,
scavenging among darkly crosshatched monoliths, fudgey tooth-

some mugwumps, extraterrestrial carpetbaggers and the like, deaf and dumb silhouettes floating in mimed and weirdly gesticulative dreamworded rotomontade, the whole memorial metastasized in stop-motion, slowly unfurling red-carpet black-tie Gehry gala, a granite, boulder-holed, dwarf-oaked Ajanta unfurling, dripping slate-gray basins and ornamental asphalt bodhisattvas that crushed the populace and drove them to grottoes, besotted dilatory shadowclumps futilely attempting to outrun the cubist tsunami lava that slowly and surely advanced over all the acreage of this gob- and Godsmacked earth until every living-now-deadthing was sheathed in stone, hardcloth'd dandified forest curated by Lagerfeld, incapable of nourishment yet paying blackened homage to that which once had nourished and been nourished in return: now everything in static, ecstatic haute couture, a dynamically moribund gorgeously abstract iron maidenhead machine. Somewhere in the nightmare came Rem and Zorro with their shticks and dirty tricks, and somewhere came this *baby, their* baby, Baby Jane Doe (née Herlihy-Freiberg), and the Faulkner treehouse woman's—and Larry King, and her mother Marj, and the Taj Mahal and Domino's elephants, and the city of Madras AKA Chennai where Esther Freiberg was gutted and pilloried by a spirit tree whose roots, having giddily performed their sacred dilatation & curettage, now covered the entire universe itself (Joan would scribble it down best she could upon awakening), the 18-inch-deep inverted sarcophagus of Napa too with its inconceivably expensive, minutely calibrated pumps and drains overseen by mean old Calvinist Thom Mayne, his no-foam latte dispensed from her Impressa at Pritzker High in Diamond Ranch; woven into the somatic tapestry like cheap golden thread were all of Joan's failures and all of her lusts and all of her loss of desire.

All there:

The Perfect Memorial.

LIV.

RAY

THEY took Friar Tuck to a rehab center in Covina.

BG said the place looked like a resort. The woman at check-in was expecting them. Ghulpa confirmed they wouldn't be "outlaying any monies" and their greeter said yes, she was correct, the City of Industry was taking care of everything. The couple were treated like VIPs.

The Friar snarled at Rahul, the assigned trainer, then spat out a beaded necklace of coughs, in nervous spasm. The unruffled therapist in swim trunks, flip-flops, and medical smock bent down and stroked his new patient, telling him how brave he was. Without taking his eyes off Friar Tuck, he told the owners this wasn't the 1st dog he'd worked with who had been shot. The old man was surprised yet glad the helper was experienced. Rahul gently drew his hand over the injured hip to assess pain and mobility.

He asked "Mr and Mrs Rausch" if their dog was a "water guy" and Ray said yes, "Nip" liked chasing after waves in the ocean and had been known to jump in a pool now and then. (That's when he told Rahul the alias—Nip/Tuck—and the therapist had a laugh.) Today's session would be short. He liked to start his clients out slowly, to acclimate them to their new surroundings.

They watched him lower Nip—now the preferred appellation—into the water, steadying the wounded warrior onto a special, brightly painted treadmill that Rahul called "the yellow submarine." After a few minutes, he suggested they have a walk around the facility; "overprotective parents" sometimes impeded progress. He said there was a waiting area where they could have snacks and coffee.

A staff member escorted them to a patio café called Starbarks. She got Ghulpa a tea and Ray a soft drink, and the Rausches settled into a gingham-covered picnic table with bowls of carrots, cauliflower, and ranch-dressing dip. Against the old man's mild protestations, the staffer made him a cappuccino, sprinkling it with cocoa. In the future, she told them a shuttle could pick the Friar up at home, saving them the trip; but of course they were more than welcome to "tag along" whenever they liked. There was a treatment package that included acupuncture and massage. "The meridians are exactly the same as with humans," she said, when Ghulpa asked about the needles. "We always recommend it whenever there's been surgery or bone injury. I'm pretty sure the city will pick that up." She winked, as if it was already a done deal. The Center even had a Saturday yoga class called Upward Dog that was "a hoot."

"You should see our 'kids.' They can hold all the major poses. It's really a wonderful holistic workout—and great for the owners too. All species are invited!"

"Well, hel-*lo*," said a lady, trundling over with a King Charles in her arms. She beamed at Ray and Ghulpa but they didn't recognize her. "How *are* you?"

She reintroduced herself as Cora, who they'd met at the hospital on Sepulveda.

"And *this*, I'm sure you remember, is the famous Mr Pahrump!"

They were happily reunited, marveling not only to find each other again, but in this wonderful place as well. Comrades-in-arms, in the war of recovery.

"It's our 1st time," said Ray.

"Isn't it *marvelous?*"

"The Friar's having himself a little 'submarine' therapy."

"He's on the treadmill?" She put down Pahrump—who was sniffing at BG's Vans and pant cuffs—and clapped her hands with glee. "Now, isn't that *fabulous?* I'm going to get one for the house. My son Stein bought me an 'ellipis'—I have arthritis—but I *never* use it. Of course, you can't just dunk it in the pool! You need a special kind."

Ray gave Pahrump a caress. You could still see the tumor. The dog had a tremor and Cora said it was from the effects of chemo and the various pills he was taking, all of which were making him stronger each day.

"He's got something for his heart and for 'cognitive dysfunction' as well. Whatever *that* is! Since his surgery, my Rumper's been having a little trouble recognizing Stein and the grandkids. They say that's perfectly normal. There's a period of readjustment, and it's longer or shorter, depending on the animal." Her eyes welled with tears, but just for a moment. "I cannot *imagine* how he's suffered . . . he is a *hero*. Aren't you, baby? Aren't you my hero? They have him on Percorten-V for Addison's disease, and Eto-Gesic for his osteo. I'm telling you, after all this is over, I'm going to be ready to hang my veterinary shingle!" She boastfully rattled off the inventory of curatives. "There's a *glorious* antidepressant, Clomicalm—a miracle drug! He's practically back to his old sleeping patterns. Which is more than I can say for *myself*."

The ordeal had taken its toll. A few days ago a well-meaning staffer suggested that if things got too difficult, there was always a 30 acre avocado ranch up north, "the only retirement home for the white-whiskered set in the entire western U.S." She cried at the thought of banishing King Charles from his kingdom. ("I might decide to go live there myself!") Still, the thought of Pahrump living amongst sycamores and rosebushes with a cadre of caregivers and retired show dogs *did* provide comfort, and warmed her heart during dark nights of the soul. The staffer told her that the upscale "spread" even had its own newspaper, *The Muttmatchers Messenger*. "Isn't that darling?"

Cora had begun to like the whole idea.

"The most *amazing* place I heard of—now shoot, who told me about it?—the most amazing place is a home that takes in your pet, should you 'predecease.' I'm having Steinie look into it. My son is most definitely *not* a dog person. He's a businessman, doesn't have *near* the patience. And I love my grandchildren but they make Pahrump skittish. Always have, don't know why." She stroked beneath his chin. "Maybe they're not dog people either, huh. My baby is *very* special—aren't you, bubblehead?—and *very sensitive*. And now with this cancer . . . poor thing, it's laid him so low." Tears flooded her eyes. "But this *extraordinary* place takes our *children* in—should something happen to us *before,* or we become incapacitated . . . I think it's $25,000—maybe 50 for a horse or a llama. They have llamas, isn't that lovely? They do, they do, they do. My, I think they even said they would take an elephant! *That* way you have peace of mind knowing that if you were gone, *God forbid,* your little one would be cared for till the end of his days."

BG nodded sympathetically. As she spoke, Cora took in the fact that Ray's companion was in a different age bracket than her elders but the young Indian woman was reserved and polite and attentive. Besides, she was busy speechifying now, her main theme being that the world wasn't the awful place the news depicted it to be—the world was filled with caring people who loved all manner of 4-legged angels who couldn't fend for themselves. We were all God's children, wasn't that right? Talk turned briefly to Saturday yoga, and Cora spoke of a class at the Center held on Sundays ("by a psychologist") that was meant to foster a closer relationship with one's pet, especially during the healing process. "They call it Unleashing Your Inner Canine," she said, with a titter. "Isn't that darling?"

Just then the therapist arrived in a blue terry-cloth robe over his wet suit, with Friar Tuck on a kind of muzzle-leash. Ghulpa was pleased to note the dog had been blown dry, making him look silly, handsome, and endearing all at once; they really were very thoughtful and thorough. Cora encouraged Pahrump to do a bit of socializing but "Nip" growled, looking as if he was prepared to live up to his sobriquet (that's why his mouth was strapped shut). Rahul tugged on the leash and told him to sit but the Friar went wild, and Cora nervously gathered up Mr P. The poor woman retreated as the dog redoubled his fearsome lunges; the therapist soon got him in hand.

Ray waved a wan goodbye but wasn't sure if Cora saw.

"He did very well today. You know, we often see this kind of aggressive behavior when a dog has sustained the type of trauma yours has. Not everyone takes a bullet and lives to bark about it! That's a pretty big deal."

BG watched the Friar's eyes lock onto his handler's, as if in appreciation of the comment.

"I'd like to give you a number to call—someone who might help speed along the process." Ghulpa immediately asked who would pay, and while he was reluctant to commit, Rahul said he *did* know something about their case and that he'd be *extremely* surprised if the City of Industry didn't cover "any and all charges" that came up; the center had special social workers who "interfaced with the city" and would handle billing issues for the couple. The person he had in mind to hasten Nip's recovery actually worked with all kinds of animals, he said, quite a few of them owned by celebrities.

LV.

CHESTER

THEY took their Cabazon road trip—to the Morongo resort.

Chess packed his full pharmacopoeia: a grab bag of painkillers, tranquilizers, muscle relaxants, antivertigos, anti-inflammatories, stool softeners, sleep inducers, and the like. And some fall-on-the-floor weed. They were only staying overnight but he didn't want to be caught unprepared.

Anyway, he wasn't the designated driver. He sat in the capacious backseat of Maurie's Mercedes 500, wondering where his erstwhile friend had baked the *short*-bread. You could smell the leather even with the fucking windows down. Maurie said he got it at one of those police auctions. "The car was a steal." He laughed and ran some bullshit about how the ride probably belonged to a dealer, "if these seats could talk," yadda yadda, but Chess was suspect. *Police auction, my ass.* Maybe Maurie was about to direct a feature or something, produced by that Haggis guy who was supposed to be his big bud. *Perfect. 2 fuckin hacks. 2 fuckin Haggasses.* Maybe Maurie Levin was a "silent creator" of *Friday Night Frights,* had been from day one.

Chess scoped the blond hairs of Laxmi's legs; her bare foot was resting on the dash. *Jesus.* He could see where the razorwork ended.

Her iPod sat in a dock, playing tunes Chess didn't recognize. It made him feel fuckin *old.* He watched Maurie pretend to be hiply familiar, hands rhythmically beating the steering wheel like he'd heard it all before. *Bullshit artist. Fuckin scammer.* Whatever. It was a beautiful day and Chess was buzzed. The vertigo had receded but that was the maddening thing about inner-ear stuff: it was always in the back of your head (or the sides of it) that suddenly you could be tossing your tostadas.

So far, so good.

Maurie prattled on about Morongo and how rich the Indians were, goddamn thieves and sociopathic drunks, worse than Gypsies, and how the 3 of them should come up with a way to hustle the BIA. Fuckin Injuns—nothing but black-braided bitch-parasites and ultraviolent alkies. Maurie said they should legally declare themselves Native Americans, like that leftie professor who got fired for saying everyone who worked at the World Trade Center was a mini-Eichmann. "Didn't that asshole say he was fucking Cherokee? Yeah, right. *Jeep* Cherokee." Maurie had that blustery Jew thing going, he could make you laugh in spite of yourself, that's probably what drew Laxmi to him in the first place—opposites attract—Chess *prayed* they weren't still fucking, though they kinda sorta acted like they were, but not as much as they used to, not so demonstrative, not around him anyway. Maurie liked to grope her but didn't do that shit anymore; now and then he body-spammed or reached out to touch and even though there wasn't anything too pervy about it, she swatted his hand anyway—Chess hoped she did that for his benefit. The definitive conversation about the Maurie issue was long overdue. They'd danced around it but Chester always wimped out.

What was he afraid of? He was afraid of hearing Laxmi say that it was *nuts,* and she was *sorry,* but she just couldn't shake the kikey SOB; that Levin had some kind of psychosexual stranglehold on her. He was afraid of the pathology—too much of a daddy thing going on. Maybe Maurie and her old man even looked the same, *smelled* the same. . . .

Chess pushed the bad thoughts from his head and watched the desertscape zoom by. His backpack was filled with dope, and books too—Laxmi had picked up some "spiritual volumes" for him at the Bodhi Tree a few weeks back. A nice surprise. Chess was pretty sure at this point the relationship between them was still secret, and that made him feel all warm and fuzzy inside. *Fuck that prick.* He enjoyed having the books along, he'd stowed them away like a taboo treasure trove, thinking of them as love letters. He was "holding," and it gave him a little goose—suddenly, he remembered the Viagra. Not that anything was going to happen. Not on this trip, anyway. You never knew.

T HE casino was a slick dumb orange building looming out of nowhere like a humungous stereo cabinet from Circuit City. They dropped a few dollars at the tables before checking in. The Indians were stealing their money already.

Laxmi dragged them to the spa and the Jew reserved 3 late-afternoon massages (evidently, they weren't so busy). He said to charge them to his room. *Big man.* Chess couldn't even believe she was staying with Maurie—he was more stunned than pissed—and when Laxmi took him aside to whisper something about "twin beds," like that was supposed to make it all better, he just shrugged. The *FNF* conspiracy theories swept back over him . . . but why should he care? It was none of his business and he didn't want to feel foolish. He didn't want to feel foolish about anything anymore. He was gonna sue the motherfuckers, and if Laxmi wanted to drop by the pad and smoke his dope and let him look at the hair on her legs, fuck it.

They had 4 hours to chill before getting rubbed. Maybe he'd check out the pool or the gym or go take a nap. Chess wondered if the masseuses gave hand jobs. He figured there was a pretty good chance because the place was new, and it might be part of a secret corporate policy to keep guests coming back. He reminded himself they were there to location scout for a commercial, but it felt kind of bogus, and he couldn't shake the idea that Levin was out to grease him so he'd drop his lawsuit (which he already might have blown) and join the *FNF* payroll. He didn't trust the Jew for shit.

M AURIE said they could wake up early and scout on Sunday morning before brunch. He told Laxmi she could sleep in. Then, around noon, they'd drive to "Las Viagras." That wasn't part of the plan and Laxmi hated the idea. One casino was enough. Maurie said cool, they could hang at Morongo or get stoned in Joshua Tree or have "supper" at the Viceroy, in the Springs. Laxmi wasn't into it. She said they should go back to LA after breakfast, but then she got to thinking about Joshua Tree and how that might be trippy. Chess couldn't see himself spazzing around in the high desert but kept his mouth shut. He'd just stay in his room—he was in pain most of the time anyway, still fine-tuning the medley of meds that mellowed him out. That's how fucked up it was: he'd become some housebound geezer, cozily experimenting with milligram'd combo-plates.

At a certain point, they wound up alone in the elevator. He told Laxmi he'd brought the *Kārma Sūtra* she gave him (the other Bodhi Tree books were weirder, and he hadn't yet delved into them) and she smiled, without enthusiasm or innuendo. When he made a move to kiss her—he was just stoned enough—she backed away, saying, "We shouldn't." He tensed up. His neck and shoulders stung and throbbed. *OK—cool. That's cool. I can live with that. Probably not such a great idea. Fuck it, we'll always have Griffith Park.* If he had to stretch the truth a bit, he actually liked that she was being prudent, or prudish, or whatever. Besides, if they did the deed, the Viagra might interact with other drugs he was taking and give him vertigo again. Just what he needed: Laxmi goes consensual then he pukes on her during the Tantric Tortoise, the Pair of Tongs, the Splitting Bamboo.

The Jew and the Lotus retired to their suite to "rinse off" and lie down. Did that mean they were going to fuck? What else *could* it mean? He was the lowest of the low—a cuckold without a wife. His rage at Maurie boomeranged. He decided to hit the casino. Walk it off. He checked out the losers at the slots then went to the spa and had a few words with the proprietress. Then he rode the elevator to 1508, replaying the *other* ride, with Laxmi, in his head, his failed minimove rocket-to-nowhere. It had embarrassed him. On top of it (and he knew this was sick) was the part that felt guilty about his behavior—that he'd betrayed his friend, the man who had caused him grievous injury! *At least,* he thought, *I'm lucid enough to know that it's only the irrational thoughts of a depressive mindspace.*

Chess sat on the bed, lit a joint, and flipped through the trove. The pages actually smelled like her—that patchouli vibe. The ludicrous thing was, the *Kārma Sūtra* had a whole section with the rubric, "Other Men's Wives," detailing how a man had the universal right to fuck a married woman! There were entire lists of what made hapless brides "eligible" for adultery: like if a gal was neglected or scorned, or had married someone beneath her caste, or even if her husband happened to have "many brothers." (Laxmi was a strong candidate—Maurie had neglected and scorned her, and was *definitely* beneath her caste. Plus, the Jew used to refer to Chess as his "brother.") He laughed aloud at the following passage: "Just as medical science explains that for certain diseases one should eat dog meat, similarly, in special circumstances, an individual may find himself in need of sleeping with other men's wives, and he should put it into practice only after a serious study of the *Kārma Sūtra*." Well, right on! Let the serious studies begin! He flipped through another book, the strangest in the litter, and this one offered conflicting views: if the spouse cheated, why, then she should "sleep in a trough of cow dung for a year," and be paraded through town on a black donkey. *Hey, whatever gets your Ganges wet.* This particularly *sizable* volume was *way* harsh, declaring that if a man poured the pork to his brother's wife, it was thereby proclaimed he should rip out his own cock and balls (a neat trick! whoa!), cup em in his hands, and walk in a "southerly direction." *Right on. But my personal opinion is the dude ain't gonna feel up to no stroll.*

Chess returned to the enlightened pages of the *Kārma,* to the addendum called "Justification for Seducing Other Men's Wives." Thus it was written: if a guy had insomnia "for thinking of the object of desire," or if he is *obsessing,* well, then, that was enough of a reason. *Shit. Jesus.* This is *crazy.* The book was really growing on him . . . then came the *coup de grâce:* "weakness leading to vertigo" was in there too! If you were feeling vertiginous, you could get jiggy with your neighbor's Mrs! Vertigo! It *said* that! The ultimate Epley Maneuver! Now, *that* was freakish. He realized how stoned he was, and wound up masturbating to the book's X-rated illustrations, suffused with Laxmi's smell.

A BOUT an hour before the massages, everyone met for drinks in a lounge off the casino. Tanqueray and Vicodin had Chess seriously toasted. Maurie was on another roll about the "shitfaced brownskins" and Laxmi *shushed* him. Chess began to riff about a white-collar con he'd read about that made the Sioux look like pikers.

"Ever heard of whistleblowers? You know, those guys in big corporations who snitch to the government?"

"Like *The Insider,*" said Maurie.

"I *love* Al Pacino," said Laxmi.

"Right." He felt in the groove, and flashed on the chapter of the *Kārma Sūtra* that said married women liked to be seduced by good storytellers. "There's this whole *confidence game* where people *whistleblow,* but the shit they're exposing isn't *true.* The government has whistleblowing laws—some of em guarantee 30% of whatever money is recovered. So there's this guy who whistle-blew—"

"Whistle blow-me!" said Maurie, and Laxmi giggled.

The remark was indecorous, not the usual thing she laughed at, which made Chess fleetingly paranoid. Maybe that was what Hippie Slut dug, that was the *hook.* Maybe her dad was like that— a captivating Jew with a dirty mouth. *Lord Ganesha, guardian of the anus.*

"The feds wound up giving him a hundred and 26,000,000!"

"Jesus."

"He goes on *Oprah* like some kinda hero then retires to a gated community. A few years later, they find out everything he told em was just some kind of *half-truth.* But it's *too late.* They dig a little further. The so-called kickbacks and price hikes he ratted about *never fucking happened.* So a federal jury convenes and declares the defendants—"

"Whistle blow-me!"

"—*not guilty.* The employees *all get off.* But the whistleblower doesn't have to return the fed's thank-you money!"

"You mean the fed's *fuck-you* money," said Maurie, with a leer. *"Everybody* should *get off."*

"The moral of the story is, *the government can be hustled.* I mean, it's like those sex harassment suits where companies used to have to pay people just to go away."

"Don't go away horny . . . just *go away.* That's what Laxmi's been saying."

"It's the modern-day version. And it doesn't even have to *be* a bigass company. Let's say some poor shrink—"

"You mean there *is* such a thing?" interjected Maurie, looking quizzically toward Laxmi, who giggled and choked, the drink fizzing through her nose.

"—overcharges someone a hundred bucks. For a hundred-dollar overcharge, the feds can ask for a fine of like *60,000,000.* Restitution under the False Claims Act."

"You've got *way* too much time on your hands, Desperado." Maurie shook his head and threw Laxmi a what-the-fuck's-he-talking-about look. Then: "You're like a fuckin *expert.* You're like *Lewis Black,* without the *humor.*" He belched, chirped, and cooed (while Laxmi laughed, convulsively), then theatrically scrunched his face to look at Chester sideways—like some tweaky owl out of Harry Potter. "You sound like a . . . what do they call those people? Magpies? No—agitators? Agent provocateurs! Nah, that ain't it either. Gadflies! That's what you are! You're a fuckin gadfly!" He screwed up an eye, and whispered conspiratorially. "Now: you don't suddenly know so much cause you've been busy researching *Herlihy v Friday Night Frights*—is *that* why you know so much? Look out, world! Mr False Claims Restitution is about to wreak havoc! Godzilla? Meet Fraudzilla!" (Her laughter diminished.) *"Bionic ethics!* You want to be on *Oprah* too, don't you! *That's* what this is about. You want to be in a million little pieces! You want to make a million little dollars! Or maybe have your own show like Dr Phil! Dr Chester! Dr Chester the Restituted Molester!"

Laxmi put a hand on Chess' leg, though not in any overtly sexual way—closer to the knee. She probably just felt bad she'd laughed so hard, at his expense. Her way of letting him know it was nothing personal and that mostly she was just stoned.

Maurie grunted, stood, and went to the head. Chess paid the bar tab.

When he returned, they strolled past the noise of the slots to the Sage.

A sullen silence overtook the 2 men. Laxmi walked between them as a buffer. She stared straight ahead, pretending all was well, now and then glancing at one or the other peripherally. Maurie's appointment was half an hour before the others'. He was getting Deep Tissue and Chess was having Sacred Stone. Laxmi had signed up for the Desert Volcanic Fango Body Mask/Sage Body Polish.

He hung back while his friends went to shower, and confirmed the arrangement made earlier. Because Maurie requested a woman, Chess had been stuck with a male therapist, a sweet-faced black masseur he bumped into that 2nd time at the spa— while the happy couple were upstairs doing their rinse-off. That's when he got his brainstorm. He slipped the girl a hundie to ensure a "mix-up," telling her it was his friend's 40th and they'd been playing practical jokes on each other all week long. Luckily, she was game.

The only thing that would ruin the prank was if Maurie had a tantrum, and walked out.

But Chess didn't think that likely.

LVI.

MARJORIE

THEY went shopping at Saks and Neiman's.

At 1st, she felt abashed—Marjorie couldn't remember the last time she bought clothes for herself, and was still in a period of mourning Hamilton. But her new friend did much to raise her spirits. They tried on everything from frocks to 35,000 dollar gowns. Bonita said this would be the party of their lives, and they should just say *the hell with it.* Marj wound up with an aristocratically festive suit by YSL, but her Sister was more daring: a Céline cherry bouclé jacket, and a, well, interesting ensemble by an unpronounceable Japanese designer.

At the last minute, Bonita said she'd foolishly left her pocketbook at home. Marj offered to put the 85-hundred dollar charge on her Visa—Bonita would have nothing of it. When the old woman finally said she wasn't going to leave the store without the dresses, the Sister almost tearfully relented. She said she would bring a check to Spago tonight. As they left the Fifth Avenue Club, they sang "High Hopes," arm in arm, followed by a darling young man who carried their things. It was like out of a movie or a dream.

MARJ was so excited she didn't know what to do with herself. It was only 3 o'clock and the dinner was at 8. She bounced around the house, singing, "Oops, there goes another rubber tree plant," and whispering under her breath, "Dinner at 8! Dinner at 8!" She decided to burn off energy and stroll over to Riki's for a lottery ticket.

Home again, she languorously picked through a bookshelf in the den while running a bath. She hadn't seen *this* one in what seemed like a century: a moss-green copy of *The Jungle Book*

with a faded Piranesi-style arch *ex Libris:* RAYMOND RAUSCH
pasted inside. She *loved* Kipling, as had her father (the writer was
born in Bombay, so Marj felt an immediate kinship. She always
imagined he looked like Sean Connery, who played one of
his characters in that glorious movie *The Man Who Would Be
King*). She was almost certain Rudyard had stayed at the Taj
Mahal Palace—maybe she'd ask Joanie to look it up on her
computer.

Marj flipped through the pages as she soaked in the tub, careful
to keep elbows above water. She remembered her ex husband
reading to Chester at bedtime—especially "Toomai of the Elephants." Oh, Chess *loved* that one! It was the story of a little boy
who was told about something no man or *mahout* had ever seen:
clearings deep in the forest called elephants' ballrooms where the
ancient creatures went to dance. Could anything be more delight-
ful? She reread it, and the sound of Ray's voice rushed back to her,
as if seizing the words: one stormy night, a noble bull called Kala
Nag ("black snake") broke free of his ropes and galloped with Little Toomai on his back for miles and miles, to the legendary, mysterious bacchanal. There, the elephants partook of doum and
marula, mgongo and palmyra, fermented fruits that made them
drunk. And dance, they did! When the terrified, delirious boy returned at dawn to tell his tale, the hunters were skeptical until
they finally went and found the place he'd described, in the heart
of the jungle—a vast "ballroom" of trampled wood, with trails
leading to and from and every which way. That night, in a very
human celebration, Little Toomai was rechristened Toomai of the
Elephants, and the magnificent brawny beasts raised their trunks,
trumpeting in joy for the new King of *Mahouts*.

She read the opening verse aloud:

I will remember what I was. I am sick of rope and chain.
I will remember my old strength and all my forest affairs.
I will not sell my back to man for a bundle of sugarcane . . .
I will go out until the day, until the morning break—out to
the winds' untainted kiss, the waters' clean caress—

*I will forget my ankle-ring and snap my picket-stake. I will
revisit my lost loves, and playmates masterless!*

S HE put on her "lucky" Schlumberger peas-in-the-pod and
parrot-and-feather Tiffany pins, plus a necklace she hadn't
worn in years made of tourmalines, peridot, and aquamarine
stones. (They set off the fire of her wedding ring opal.) It crossed
her mind that Cora might look through the window and see her
wheeling the suitcase she'd packed for New York; Marj wasn't up
for any explaining. In fact, she rather enjoyed the idea of Cora
guessing her whereabouts. The *mystery* of it. The old woman
smiled to herself, feeling like a double agent—a saboteur! It was
very Graham Greene! She could always say she'd been to the elephants' ball . . . but when she thought of Pahrump and how tough
a time her neighbor had been having, Marj felt a little less "cock-
of-the-walk" (an expression Hamilton liked to use). She scribbled
a note saying she was on her way to La Quinta with her daughter
and stuck it in Cora's mailbox. The suitcase was small but the old
woman had trouble lifting it to the trunk. She slid it into the backseat instead. She would get help once she got to the restaurant.

M ARJ drove right past Spago. For a moment, she didn't have
a clue where she was. Why hadn't she hitched a ride with
Bonita? *Dumb, dumb, dumb.* She circled Rite Aid a few times before coming back around Wilshire to Cañon. There was sidewalk
construction going on but then she saw the valets.
    She felt glamorous making her entrance. The pretty Asian
woman looked up "Mr Weyerhauser" then asked if the party
might be under a different name. Marj said, as if intoning a pass-
word at the Magic Castle (she'd been to that place in the Hollywood Hills years ago, with Ham), "the Blind Sisters." The hostess
seemed puzzled but a confident Marj added, "It should be a large
group." The gal checked again, under "Weyerhauser" and "Her-

lihy" and "Blind Sisters," but came up blank. She couldn't remember Bonita's last name, not that it made much sense that it would have been used for the reservation. She nearly blurted out "State of New York" and "lottery winners," but thought that unwise. (It might even be illegal.)

The hostess never stopped smiling. She made the old woman feel comfortable that there had been a mistake, and her party was certain to arrive soon. She led her to an empty table for 2, opposite the bar. She was lovely—and my, there were so many people there, yet she had been so personable! No wonder Lucas had chosen this place.

She ordered Perrier and after a few minutes pulled Mr Weyerhauser's card from her wallet. Stupidly, she'd left the cellphone Joan gave her at home. (Her daughter would have been mad about that. She told her never to leave the house without it.) Marj asked the server if there was another Spago and was politely told there once was, but no more. She waited almost an hour. She left a kerchief on the chair so that no one would claim it, then went to the bathroom, passing parties of beautifully dressed diners who seemed to stare at her with respect—Marjorie Herlihy knew that tonight she exuded elegance, wealth, sophistication. The old woman splashed her face and the water felt good; she had diarrhea from her nerves and wondered how much longer she should stay. She found a payphone to call Lucas but didn't have any coins.

She sat down at the bar for another 40 minutes—a gal her age, sitting in a bar! Ham would have laughed—nursing a glass of red wine. She wondered if there had been an invitation, and searched her mind. Did Lucas give her something with an address, something for the party? She *told* him she was coming—didn't she?—but there wasn't anything to RSVP. Usually, for a grand gala, there was a number you could call to RIP . . . no, they were probably careful about that. This sort of thing, if you had it on paper, was too easy to "leak." Still, she imagined those federal people had printers they worked with who were bonded. It was probably her own damn fault for being a late enrollee in the Expedited Award Program. There wouldn't have been time to send something out.

When she finally left, she made deliberate, old-world pains to thank the attractive hostess, one of those marvelous professionals trained never to make assumptions or judgments nor to condescend. She told Marj she was sorry, but nothing, not a scintilla, of her demeanor made the guest feel foolish, and for that Mrs Herlihy was grateful.

Perhaps she'd made a terrible mistake and the plan had been to meet at the Four Seasons all along. She needed to drive over, right away—where *was* that hotel? On Doheny? The thought crossed her mind that something awful might have happened to Lucas; or, more reasonably, the dinner was canceled due to a sudden emergency, and both he and Bonita had been trying to call. (Not that it mattered, because the damn "mobile" was at home. Anyhow, the old woman wasn't sure she'd ever given them her number—and how could she? She didn't even know it herself. Joanie kept saying she was going to tape it on the back but never did.) Wait. No! Now she remembered . . . Bonita saying she would give her a check for the dresses she'd charged "tonight at Spago." So even if there *had* been a last-minute change, Bonita—Billingsley!—would still have met her at Spago—*someone* would have— then proceeded, arm in arm *High Hopes,* to the Four Seasons or wherever it was they had settled on. She kicked herself for remembering to pack everything in the world—everything except that stupid phone.

She went to Rite Aid for coins to call the special State of New York Blind Sister Beneficiary Hotline. Everything was so brightly lit that she felt herself coming out of her skin. The cashier was a surly Mexican who said, "I don't have no change." (Marj expected Rite Aid to have a higher caliber of worker, at least in Beverly Hills.) The girl wouldn't even look at her and Marj knew that she was lying. Maybe they'd be kinder in the Rx section but it was so busy she would probably have to wait 20 minutes just to talk to the cashier. (She needed to use the toilet again.) The only place to sit was at the machine that took your blood pressure but right when she got close a little boy clambered onto the seat. Marj smiled and turned to leave. She was at a loss.

Up front, a raucous pack of youngsters jockeyed for ice cream, and she remembered how she used to buy Chess and Joanie cones and sundaes at 31 Flavors, kitty-corner to the drugstore (which back then was called Thrifty's). Ray didn't like it but she enjoyed taking the children on excursions to Beverly Hills, she thought it was good for their character to be exposed to wealth. She wanted them to see the large and orderly houses tended to by gardeners, homes she knew one day they could live in. More than anything, she had the desire for her children to attend Beverly Hills schools, the finest in the nation. (Ray never knew it but on Sundays, when Marj said she was with a galfriend, she went apartment hunting, just south of Olympic. But the prices were beyond their ken.) There was a huge pond on Santa Monica Boulevard and Beverly Drive and she sat with the kids on its stone borders, watching the big colorful fishes. Occasionally Marj even spotted someone that she recognized from television or the movies—she swore she once saw Fess Parker and Joan Fontaine but couldn't get Raymond to believe it. To this day, she retained the habit of walking around the city, and a few weeks ago actually passed by "31" on her way to get bunion medicine—it amazed, but the parlor was still there, one of the few surviving landmarks from that time. There used to be 3 theaters in the neighborhood, and 3 bookstores too—all gone now. She remembered vividly that the Beverly movie palace was literally in the shape of the Taj Mahal, it had become more important to her through the years, after the children had grown she parked nearby just to look. (Best to see its dollop of a roof from a block or so away.) It hadn't been a working theater for decades, enduring a series of drab transformations from clothing stores to banks, yet rose like a creampuff cloud above storefront commerce, visible only to the delighted cognoscenti, until finally, only a few months ago, they tore the icon down. It was almost proof there was a God that it had managed to stay for so long. Bless 31 Flavors, and bless the memory of the Taj Mahal too. She took the kids there for Saturday matinees. Ray didn't like that either.

"Ain't Culver City good enough?" he used to say. His English was perfectly fine but he liked to goad her by talking like a yokel. "No," she would answer. "It isn't."

She was surprised when the Mexican shouted at her. She thought the cashier was being rude but instead she gave Marj 4 quarters. The girl must have felt bad about how she had treated her, and the old woman thought, *See that? Everyone has a conscience.* Maybe the man who shot poor Riki dead was in a motel room somewhere, a tormented soul thinking about turning himself in. She thanked her then made the mistake of asking where the phones were and the cashier got surly again, pointing outside with disdain. Marj cursed herself—*of course they were outside.* She already knew that. She hated being the helpless old lady. The girl probably thought she was a refugee from the expensive new Assisting Living condos that had recently gone up around the corner. She probably resented her because here she was working for minimum wage and this wizened crone, this witch who lived in luxury and came and went as she pleased, was pestering her for coins. Still, the cashier showed she had a heart.

The pack of ice cream kids had migrated outside (they all looked Persian) and were being so noisy that Marj had trouble concentrating on dialing. Their cars were just sitting in the lot with the doors open and music blaring. She called the toll free hotline and left her name.

Then she found Bonita's number and listened to the strange message: *Thank you for calling. Unfortunately, the person who gave you this number does not want to talk to you or speak to you—ever again. We would like to take this opportunity to officially reject you. If you would like to order personalized rejection cards with this number printed on them, please visit our website at www.rejectworld.com. Our certified rejection specialists are standing by to serve you in this time of need.*

She winced in confusion. Some sort of joke? Bonita *did* have a quirky sense of humor. She tried the number again, and got the same recording. (Now her coins were all used up.)

She took a few steps and threw up. Like everyone her age, she had been trained to ask, "Am I having a heart attack?" but decided it was only the wine and her nerves. ("High Hopes" and "The Days of Wine and Roses" were catfighting in her head. She missed Jack Lemmon.) Joanie said, *If you think you're having a heart attack, breathe deep and force a deep cough. Keep doing that, then call 911.* The music from the cars drowned out "High Hopes" and one of the rowdy kids yelped, alerting his friends to the old woman who puked. "That's disgusting!" said a girl. Another girl said, "It's *sad*. Maybe we should help." Another wandered closer and said, "Lady?" Marj didn't have the strength to respond. Another said, "Just call 911," then boisterously broke into peals of laughter. Marj kept seeing the face of Jack Lemmon in his little hat; he would see her through. A boy said, "Call the pound!" A girl said, "That is *so mean*." A boy said, "She just threw up. She ain't *dyin*." "Maybe she's been partying." "She looks really rich." "It's a Senior Moment." "Is she a junior or a Senior?" "Hope she's wearing her Pampers!"

The pack moved toward the alley, laughing and smoking and remonstrating, then disappeared.

SUDDENLY Marj was driving south on Robertson, without any memory of having gotten in the car. She was lightheaded but seemed to have her wits about her. She resolved to call Joanie in the morning; her daughter would help sort things out. She felt something was "off" but wouldn't allow herself to believe she'd been done wrong. *No, that could not be.* She would get to the bottom of it in the morning but for now it was important to just get home and get to the bathroom (she was cramping badly from holding it in), take a tub, and climb into bed. She'd just leave her luggage in the trunk, where the valets had transferred it, and snatch back the note from Cora's mailbox. Maybe there were messages from Lucas on her answering machine or cell. She didn't know how to retrieve messages from the cell.

When she turned the corner onto her block, a car with dimly flashing white lights was parked in front of the house.

She pulled into the drive and got out.

A man approached.

"Mrs Herlihy?"

"Yes. What is it? What's happened?"

"I'm Federal Agent Marone, from the antifraud division. I'd like to speak with you about a person who goes by the name of Lucas Weyerhauser. I know it's a late hour, Mrs Herlihy, but— may I come in?"

LVII.

JOAN

THEY made love and he cooked for them, but Joan didn't think she'd stay over. She was worried about Mom. Maybe she would "camp" with her a few days, at the house in Beverlywood.

She told Pradeep she wasn't sure if it was age or loneliness, but there was something she couldn't put her finger on, a difference in the way her mother had been acting. She mentioned Marj wanting to take her to see the Taj Mahal (Pradeep enthused, "You should go! You should do it!" just like she thought he would), adding with a smile that Mom was more interested, "to put it mildly," in the Taj Mahal *hotel* than the monument in Agra. Pradeep laughed, informing that the Tata family—who owned the Taj Mahal Palace and Towers in Mumbai—were in talks to take over the management and renovation of the Pierre in New York. He was a fount of that sort of trivia. It was kind of his job.

Then a strange thing happened.

"You're a Rausch, right? Isn't that your birth name?"

"Why?"

"Before you were adopted." She nodded, perplexed. "And isn't your biological father's name Raymond?"

Pradeep knew all about Joan's family tree; perhaps it was his diplomatic nature, or a lover's genuine interest, that made him inquisitive of personal histories, which he was, to a fault. He retained names and dates as well, also part of his well-honed professional acumen, no doubt. From her end, she never asked about Manonamani and the kids—it didn't feel appropriate, and the truth of it was she hadn't much interest. But Pradeep was solicitous when it came to her own family members, listening with charmed, rapt attention, as if she were reading tales aloud from a storybook. Something about his earnest, guileless curiosity actually moved her to share things she wouldn't have with anyone else.

He fished out an article from the LA *Times*. An old guy had gotten a settlement for having his door mistakenly broke down by the police. She read the article.

A Mr Raymond Rausch (sans photo) lived on Mercantile Road in the City of Industry with a dog named Friar Tuck, who took a bullet during the break-in. He was 76 years old—same her dad would have been—and had suffered a heart attack. Joan wouldn't have given it much heed, if not for the coincidence of Chester recently bringing up his fantasy of progenitorship; seemed a bit eerie. And the fact that Pradeep was the one to call it to Joan's attention lent a certain gravitas.

She put it aside for now. Whatever "it" was.

Pradeep had actually done a sneaky thing. He suddenly announced that his consular term was ending earlier than he thought, and he'd soon be returning to Delhi. She vaguely knew this was coming, that commissions were recycled every 4 years, but the timing of his disclosure was canny—ever the diplomat, Pradeep softened the blow by deflecting, or deferring, to the mystery of her own family matters. He wanted Joan to have something else to focus on, beyond the trauma of his imminent departure. It was the part of him she resented and the part she found irresistibly compelling too, this nomadic yet grounded man, at once calmly present and peripatetic in the absolute, responsive, and responsible to so many. Sex with Pradeep was always intense because she knew he was "on his way," a moving target that appealed to her own emotionally itinerant nature; she felt like a consort at a consular feast, the pretend Devī of a pretend Śiva. Nothing could touch them because they were divine gypsies, abrim with the jittery ambrosia of adolescence which they'd managed to catch in a bottle, hormonally undistilled—they were built for speed and tender abandonments. She could never stay mad at Pradeep for long because she knew he'd be long gone, yet there for her, forever. What other man could she say that of? He insisted she call him, in any time zone, for any reason, no matter what he was doing, or who he was with—wife, child, head of state—he'd escape to terrace or anteroom and give her all the time in the world. Pradeep was like a brother that way, a colonial with the cologne of incest.

She stuffed the article in her purse and left the suite without showering. He would return to San Francisco on Monday morning to begin packing up. Manonamani and the kids had already left; in 10 days, he'd be gone. They pretended they would somehow see each other before his departure—that they'd make the effort. (Moving targets.) He told Joan that if she came to India with her mother, they must spend part of the time in Delhi. He would feed them diamond-shaped almond burfi and deep-fried pretzels, kathi rolls with pomegranate syrup, carry Marj on a palanquin for a *sirodhara* treatment in Kerala, visit goldsmiths at Calcutta's tea stalls on Ganguly Road—why, they'd even make a pilgrimage to the Taj Mahal! Wasn't that your mother's dream? (He laughed as he said it, knowing the backstory.) It is quite warm in Agra, he said, but Marjorie will adore the peacocks and trishaws, the dancing monkeys and bears. Joan knew he was dead serious, albeit in that urbane, diplomatically manic fashion.

THE model of the Freiberg Mem was done. She had given her creation—for it was Joan who was captain, and to Joan that her partner ceded the last word theoretically, in all ways—the unofficial title of the Pollock painting, *Full Fathom Five*. Barbet (who still preferred *The Lost Coast*) debated whether they should attach a name, finally intuiting the touch to be nicely dramatic, at least for the presentation. The superstitious compromise being that he would inform Lew that *Full Fathom Five* and *The Lost Coast* were "conceptual titles," without Joan having to broach them. The billionaire would either like them or not. Wouldn't be a dealbreaker.

He could tell she was a little down. They went to an early dinner at Locanda Portofino then took in a Chinese movie at the

Aero. She nudged him halfway through and said, "Let's go to bed." He was surprised.

Barbet lived in a leafy, asymmetrical house in Rustic Canyon, bought with an inheritance from his father. She waited until they settled into the living room with their drinks before telling him that Lew Freiberg had knocked her up. He laughed. She said she was serious. She looked downcast and ethereal. He said, "OK." He asked if she was sure it was Lew's. She said yes. She hadn't yet gotten the paternity test, that was coming, but yeah, she was sure. "Then you're going to keep it." Half question, half declarative. *Yes.* "He knows about it." Half question, half declarative. *Yes.* He asked if Freiberg (that's what he was calling him for this conversation) knew she was planning to have it. *Yes.* He asked if they'd spoken since she'd told him and Joan said no. Oh boy, he said, without any real vibe. Just, *Oh boy.* A suitable response. Then he sipped his drink and took some breaths and readjusted himself on the couch before saying he thought it was "actually pretty great." He said he'd been reading a lot of Indian philosophy—research related to the tsunami, of course—and there was something called Advaita, a school of thought promoting the idea that things just happened, without rhyme or reason, it was all beyond one's control, there wasn't even cause and effect, and though most of the time we had the *idea* of free will, free will was really just a fallacy, an illusion, the details of our lives had been predetermined, right down to our moods and illnesses and the color shirt we buy, everything was a *happening* and everything had already "happened," following a cosmic plan that included our genes and social conditioning—and that it was useless to feel guilty or egotistical about anything that transpired. My interpretation anyway, he said. That didn't mean you couldn't feel bad or glad or fucked up about something but the minute you accepted that the event *had* to have happened, "and that you were not *you,*" a weight lifted off, removing it from the realm of whatever egotism Westerners (Easterners too for that matter) had grown so accustomed. She told him he was full of shit and he roared with laughter. That was one of the things she found irresistible about *Barbet*—both these

men, Pradeep and Barbet, were defiantly, uniquely irresistible—
he knew he was full of shit, yet it was a quality in which he managed to take resigned delight. Naturally, he tortured himself like
everyone else, but he was a hedonist at heart, and Joan wished she
had the same "predetermined" backhanded joie de vivre.

As if on contrary cue, he began his Business rap. Barbet, now *un
peu* drunk, wanted to "deconstruct" the pregnancy through the
lens of the Mem commission—repercussions and ramifications, et
alia. He wondered aloud, and conscripted Joan to wonder with
him: *Is it a good thing, or a bad thing?* Are you a good witch or a
bad. That depends, he said, answering his own query. (Enjoying
the Socratic moment.) He asked if she thought the pregnancy was
something Freiberg "would leave his wife behind," using the annoying vernacular of the '60s. Joan said they were already separated and Barbet said he knew that, the real meaning of his
question suddenly becoming obvious: did she think he would
"pull an Ellison," and get hitched. Joan laughed, mildly contemp-
tuous—it was typical of Barbet to presume that was something
she might be angling for. She told him her intention was not to
make "a public offering," and that she doubted if Lew was head
over heels about *any* of it. Barbet didn't have an immediate response, he looked thoughtful and bemused and slightly peeved: it
didn't jibe with his jag. He asked if Freiberg had been "freaked"
and Joan said she doubted that but had left pretty quickly after the
announcement and didn't have time to assess. Barbet questioned
whether the ensuing silence was Freiberg's way of sending a message (sure seemed that way), then brought up the "very real possibility" of getting a call from Guerdon—and *soon*—saying ARK
had run aground, now out of the running.

Silent running.

Out of the rutting.

Full fathom five thy career lies . . .

Joan had thought of that, and confessed she was worried. (She
felt a percolation of whorishly melodramatic tears.) She told him
those very concerns were the reason she'd so urgently shared
"Mama's delicate condition."

"You mean, you wouldn't have anyway?"

"Have what."

"Told me."

"Of course I would have. But not so soon."

"Oh. So now I'm your confidant—with qualifications."

"Remember: it's all predetermined."

They laughed—thank God—and drank some more and loosened up, hashing the whole mess over amid the panicked hilarity and absurd rampant impossibility of it all. He said it probably wasn't Freiberg's, it was probably Thom Mayne's, or Rem's. Or maybe *El Zorro*'s!

Now she wanted to go to bed and she'd never seen Barbet more turned on. He put it in her rear end, that's where she wanted it, but missionary style, she knew the fact of her being pregnant, especially by someone other than him, would be arousing, to both of them, and she also knew in his Socratic depths that Barbet thought her indelicate condition might give them the edge in winning the Mem, he was fucking the gift whore, the unTrojan'd arse, the spirited muse-cunt/Mem-brane, storming the cathedral of meadow that stirred that mournful flatbed trough, spading and turning over bread and loaves and loam of fishes and flesh, freshly planted mons, scrubbing Joan's rough tendril'd scrubs and all the fine young elderberries, Western burningbushes, sharp-toothed and hairless, salt- and brittlebush, skunkbrush and devil's club, horned milkwort and poisoned oak, venus maidenhairs and licorice ferns, wormwoods and stinging nettles, purple loosestrife, clustered broomrape, lady's thumb, black-eyed peas and Susans too, blanket flowers and butter-and-eggs, hooker's evening primrose and sticky cinquefoils, hairy angelicas, gossipy horehounds, queen's cup, death camas, and ladies'-tresses, *Yes,* he would spruce up the yew turns and pimpride her processional pyre *if that's what it took whatever it took he would take*—and in their stroboscopic, solemnly strident, madly staccato ceremonies of this Temple of the Golden Pavilion, this Notre-Dame-du-Haut, this black and white Taj Mahal, Our Lady of Flowers and Latter Day Full Service Postmodern Postmortem Architectural Churchscrew, in this muskytear'd keen and keening—their nappy, Napa'd, soon-to-be-famous memorial of skin and stone—they duly performed ecclesia, preeclampsia, invocation and offertory, doxology and indulgence, until reaching the vaunted, founted promontory of grace.

LVIII.

RAY

GHULPA was spotting and the OB-GYN said that because of her age and cervical configuration, she would have to stay in bed for the remainder of her pregnancy.

Since she announced her condition, the Artesian cousins came and went more often then usual (they arrived in shifts), and frankly, it looked to Ray as if they were planning to stay. That was a good thing, because the old man hadn't got all his strength back, not by a longshot.

A sidebar dustup was the Friar's post-op peccadilloes. He lashed out at visitors, puked, whimpered, and barked nonstop. He guarded his bowl as if fiendishly possessed; if you didn't get your hand out of the way quick enough, you were in danger of getting fanged or defingered. Ray tried to keep the Friar on his lap when the cousins were around, but that was useless, and the muzzle made him even crazier. Ghulpa's family put up with it, surreptitiously kicking him every now and then. It was clear something would have to be done—they could never have a newborn in the same house with that animal. Nip remained pretty much under bathroom arrest. Ray made a bed for him in the tub.

Since the settlement, the cousins treated the old man with great regard. He'd evolved from being, in his mind anyway, a semi-seedy character to a bonafide breadwinner, and while BG never had such fears, it was obvious that her cousins felt because she was unmarried, her legal grounds for sharing the wealth were shakier than the extended family would have wished. Marriage was hinted at almost daily and while Ray wasn't opposed, he somehow wanted Ghulpa to suggest it. Hell, he'd already drawn up a will leaving the whole kit and caboodle to her; the ACLU fellow did that for free. (Ghulpa probably hadn't told her cousins, out of sheer mischievousness.) Ray enjoyed the currying *and* the curry.

It's good to be King. He began to feel like the dying, debonair toymaker—Amitabh Bachchan—from the Lakewood matinee. Ghulpa's people were apeshit over "Mr B," who had now added television to his résumé, having recently become the host of a version of *Who Wants to Be a Millionaire* that was a huge hit in Bangalore. The cousins actually called Ray Mr B (for Bapu) in jest, when they weren't using Raj or *"Sri Ray."*

The shuttle service came for the dog 3 times a week and the old man usually went along. He liked getting out of the house, and not having to drive. The apartment was too crowded with women and their smells. (Ghulpa was already talking about a duplex "investment property" in Cerritos. The stairs would be hell on his legs.) He couldn't even watch his beloved *Twilight Zone,* because the cousins played Bollywood movies and pop songs at full volume while giggling and shrieking their gossip. Besides, the Friar got spooked; all the commotion wasn't great on his nerves, which were shot anyway. He'd become nearly impossible to handle. The ladies made no bones about wanting to "disappear" the dog by the railroad tracks; one of them got so angry with Ray that she smarttalked him and he had to let her know who was boss. She backed down pretty good. The women locked themselves in the bedroom, and at least he had some peace and quiet for a few hours. But the poor mutt frightened people and was in constant pain. Even some of the folks at the Center told him Nip was "unmanageable." Ray didn't want to be selfish or cruel, but he loved that guy and couldn't bear to part with him. Big Gulp was shrewd enough to remain silent. It showed her man respect, and he liked that. She had a soft spot for the Friar as well, but knew Ray would never put their child in harm's way. He found himself starting to think about the place that Cora woman had mentioned, a rest home for broken creatures, out in the verdant boonies.

The staff at rehab told Ray they were pretty sure Nip's problems were behavioral, because he seemed physically and neurologically on the mend. Again, they brought up a resource of which he might avail himself. Because the "case" had been relatively high-profile—a police shooting, and all—they had taken the liberty to speak with a famous expert, who was very much in demand. They got lucky: Cesar was amenable to a consultation. Ray was touched they'd made the effort. Everyone was hopeful "the Dog Whisperer" could find the time to work with Nip, and maybe even put him on his TV series.

The old man went slack-jawed: he couldn't believe it. Ray *loved* that show, even though he hadn't seen it in a while—what with the Kaos Kousins and domestic folderol. So *that's* the fellow they'd been pushing him to call! This guy Cesar Millan was a real shaman: in 10 minutes he could transform a pet *and* its owner's lives. He was some kind of magician who made good dogs from bad, inevitably attributing whatever trouble was going on to the lazy or ill-advised habits of the masters themselves. The biggest problem stemmed from people treating their dogs too much like human beings. He said dogs got confused when that happened. Millan's mission was to make the owners into pack leaders instead of neurotic, babytalking bleedinghearts. Ray didn't exactly think of himself in that category but hell, maybe he was (or wasn't) doing something that perpetuated or even exacerbated the Friar's current problems. Millan was warm and "calm-assertive," a no-nonsense Mex who'd been raised on a ranch, with a healthy respect for all species—including his wife. They had a couple of boys and sometimes the whole family was on the show. Each episode began with the Whisperer on a skateboard being "towed" by a dozen Red Zone dogs. Red Zone meant the worst of the worst—rottweilers and scary pit bulls that Millan had completely rehabilitated.

Jesus, with Millan's intervention, they might even be able to keep Friar Tuck after the baby was born. He'd have to maneuver Big Gulp into watching a few shows; Ray knew she'd become an instant fan. If anyone could help, it was the soft-spoken *macho* from Distrito Federal. He could "whisper" sweet nothings in the Friar's ear to his heart's content.

Hell, he had to have seen far worse.

✳ ✳ ✳

A few days later, the Dog Whisperer dropped by Mercantile Road without a film crew. Ray made sure the cousins had decamped beforehand. Cesar—he insisted on being called by his 1st name—was a gentle spirit but not anyone to be trifled with. He was polite and direct and looked into Ray's eyes, unblinking.

The old man told him Nip/Tuck had always been good, but since the shooting he'd "gone paranoid." (Cesar, who had a sense of humor, preferred "Nip," possibly having been influenced by the folks at the Center.) Ray was upfront about his pregnant roommate—Ghulpa poked her head in to bobble a mute hello; she was a little starstruck, having watched some of the National Geographics—discreetly adding that the doctors had ordered her confined to bed. If they taped a show, she preferred not to be on camera. Cesar said he didn't want to put the cart before the horse—or the dog, in this case—but if he did decide to film, that wouldn't be a problem.

He spent an hour at the house, half talking to Ray, the other working with Nip. Cesar let himself be sniffed, and deliberately never looked Nip in the eye. He said that because of the trauma— to both dog and owner—"the Rausches" were probably letting the animal get away with bad behaviors. That was understandable, he said, but not helpful to Nip's recovery. Ray and his "roommate" needed to use *dog* psychology, not *human* psychology. Cesar said it was his feeling, from everything he'd been told, that Ray was the "pack leader"—before the shooting. Since Nip had returned from the hospital, their roles had reversed, and the dog was now dominant.

"America does not have a pack animal mentality," he said. "That's why dogs are so neurotic. 3rd World countries don't have that problem—*neuroses.* The neurotic dog and neurotic owner. In America, it's all about 'doing it yourself.' I am trying to change that. That's why I came here, to the States. I thank America every day for teaching me about women. Respecting women. Here, you have laws against hitting women, spanking children—not so in 3rd World countries. In America, when there is a divorce, the woman gets 50/50! In 3rd World countries, men can move on, and the woman gets nothing. In my social class, it was all *mind-body,* no 'Good morning, darling.' 'Good morning, darling' was practiced by the upper classes, and even *then* it wasn't authentic. My grandfather always taught me to go to the *authentic*—that's why I went through a period where I was antisocial. An outsider. I came here 14 years ago but 1st had to learn English: then how to relate to Caucasians, Blacks, Koreans. Everyone needs to be taught differently. Dogs would follow Castro, not Gandhi. Gandhi had stooped shoulders; he was fighting with *submission.* Castro was fighting with *domination.* My wife and I are 'co-packleaders.' I had to learn to give her what she wanted. In 3rd World countries, the women are depressed. They work like mules. Work and exercise is *not* what they need 1st; they need affection, appreciation. That is what America taught me. With dogs, it's a different way. They need discipline, exercise—*then,* affection."

They took out the bowl and put food in it. Nip bared his teeth and tried to attack. Ray flinched, but guessed the Dog Whisperer could handle himself. Cesar grabbed Nip by the neck, firmly, and made short, hissing sounds until Nip lay down. When he tried to eat, he stood between Nip and his vittles, blocking and frustrating the dog's efforts. Cesar said this was a way to establish dominance. Ray couldn't believe it, but after a minute Nip rolled on his back. He hadn't done that since before the shooting. Cesar said he was now in a calm-submissive state, and it would be good to reward him. He encouraged Ray to stroke his belly. A dog, he said, should never be rewarded or even spoken to when he wasn't in a state of calm-submission. Dogs do not listen, learn, or respond when they're in the dominant mode.

They talked about Nip's exercise regimen and the Dog Whisperer stressed its importance. Discipline, exercise, and affection were the holy trinity. "In America," he said, "we treat dogs like people. That helps *us,* it doesn't help *them.* We need to see Nip as an animal 1st. Species: dog. 2nd, we need to see him as a breed: terrier mix." (Ray had taken to calling the Friar "a terrier on 2 wheels.") "3rd: we see *personality.* Then, but *only* then, can we see 'Nip/Tuck.' *That* way, we work toward a calm-submissive, happy dog."

He showed Ray how to use sounds and harmless "bites" with his hand to get Nip's attention, and deter him from disobedience—clucks, shushes, and other nonverbal exhortations. They took him for a jaunt. Because of the Friar's acting out, Ray hadn't walked him in a few weeks; it was just too difficult. Cesar said he understood that Ghulpa (Ray finally told him her name) couldn't take the dog out in her present state, and Ray might not have the energy—he knew he'd recently recovered from a heart attack—but stressed how important exercise was to Nip's recovery, particularly a 45 minute walk. The Center staffers were already incorporating that into his regimen and Cesar thought it might be a good idea to let him stay at the facility a few weeks until Ray was strong enough to take the walks himself. It was important for the old man's recovery as well.

When they got back to the apartment, Cesar smiled broadly.

"So: would you and 'Mr Nip' like to be on the show?"

"Why, sure!" said Ray, beaming. "But you'll have to ask *him*. He has a mind of his own!"

Cesar squatted and rubbed the dog's chin.

"Would you like to be a TV star?"

The Friar seemed not unhappy with the proposition.

"I guess that's a yes," said Cesar, and with flawless timing, Nip licked his hand. "This guy's gonna be a star!"

The men laughed.

"You've seen *Dog Whisperer*?"

"Yes, I have. Religiously."

"There's a woman whose dog has been sick—a King Charles. He's skittish, fearful. This usually has more to do with the human than the animal. She's a very nice lady. Her grandchildren go to school with Will Smith's kids. Do you know Will Smith? I work with his dogs."

"Not so much. But I saw you on *Oprah*."

"Wonderful person, Oprah," he said, with that unbeatable smile. "A pack leader with humans, but not so much with dogs! I thought it might be good to work with Nip a little, and work with the King Charles—then bring them both together. I don't know how long this dog is to live. But it's very important to make him comfortable and wag his tail in the time he has left. And to make his owner happy too! This is a *gift*. We are trying some new things on the show. I think you've met this woman before," he said. "The woman with the 'little King.' Her name is Cora. The dog is Pahrump."

At 1st Ray couldn't place them, but then he remembered.

"Oh yes!"

"She said she met you in the waiting room of the hospital where they did Nip's surgery."

"Yes! Nice, nice lady. He's at the Center now, isn't he? I'm afraid my Friar wasn't so welcoming. Kinda went after him."

"That's one of the reasons we want to get the 2 of them to-gether," said Cesar. "Wouldn't it be nice for them to be friends, without the fears?"

LIX.

CHESTER

H<small>E</small> was in panic seizure.
Something happened to Maurie while he was on the massage table.

911 had been called.

Maurie had been taken away—while Chester and Laxmi were having their Sacred Stone massage and Desert Volcanic Fango Body Mask/Sage Body Polish.

Horror when they 1st found out.

Or, as news anchors liked to say: *Hawhr*.

They emerged from the sanctum sanctorum, unknowing. Exfoliated, kneaded, luminous, renewed—while Maurie was in some desert ER being violated by needless, tubes, and electrodes.

What—?

Chess knew. He must have had a freak reaction to the supposed Viagra! It was just a joke, the FNF payback: Maurie liked to get high and Chess said he had some Oxycontin (80 mg) he got from an online pharmacy. Which was true, but he gave Maurie Viagra instead. He carefully sponged the pill until it was white, not blue, so if Maurie had ever taken it before (Chess was sure that he had), he wouldn't recognize it, and besides, those offshore Rx's always looked different. That would have been his explanation if Maurie had asked, which he didn't. All Chess had to say was that he'd already used some from the same batch. He'd had a general conversation with Maurie about sexual "supplements" only the week before. He mentioned Viagra and "Le Weekender" and Maurie claimed he "didn't need that crap." Chess knew his friend was bullshitting, but said he didn't need it either. Peer pressure and all. Still, you could never tell. Maybe Maurie was one of those horny Jews who wouldn't need help in that area until he was 90 fucking years old. The heebs were notorious horndogs. Upstairs in his room, while Laxmi and Levin had their little "rest," he sponged the pill down

just in case. Didn't want anything to screw up the prank. It was ge-
nius. The thing is, Chess knew Maurie was kind of a homophobe;
that's why he wasn't totally sure he would go for the massage/masseur
switcheroo. But evidently he did. He probably didn't have the energy
to get off the table and make a lame excuse about suddenly not feeling
well or whatever. Or maybe he hung in because he got freaked or shy or
paralyzed, or thought the jig would think he was racist if he walked. Or
maybe he just really needed a rubdown and said fuck it, laughing to
himself. "Just so long as the shvug don't show me his shvanz." Chess
wouldn't really have cared if Maurie had balked and canceled; he was
determined to get back at the cocksucker one way or another—but
funny, not cruel, like the way he'd done Chess. There would be no in-
juries. So he gave him the 'Oxy' about 20 minutes before the massage
with the idea that Maurie would be thinking he was getting high for
the happy ending, but in comes the nigger, and his hopes were that
Maurie would just say fuck it and lie back to enjoy the rub and lo and
behold, about 10 minutes in, the guy would inadvertently brush his
cock, they always did, even if it was one of those towel-adjusts, and that
would be enough of a trigger to give him a massive Viagracized blue-
veiner while Hutu gave him the old deep tissue. Tu-Tu-Tutsi, good-
bye! That Hu-tu what you-do so well . . . that's all Chess was thinking
about during the Sacred Stone thing, he laughed aloud a few times, al-
most explosively, and the woman laying on the stones probably thought
he was nuts, so Chess had to make something up about remembering
an "unrepeatable joke," how funny and dirty it was, he couldn't share
it, blah. But something *must have—Jesus, maybe those fraudulent*
fuckers mailed Chess poison, or buffered it with something Maurie
was allergic to, they couldn't be trusted, they were all shell companies,
gray marketers, you could never even call them back, no way to contact
them, but no—he would probably have heard about something like
that by now, there'd have been a mass occurrence, a 60 Minutes or
Dateline exposé or whatever. Chess knew you could get a headache
with Viagra but even that was rare. They said you could go blind too
but you probably had to take it about a million times before it was sta-
tistically possible and anyhow that was something the lawyers made
them put in the literature just to cover themselves. If Maurie had an

*embolism or some shit like that it'd have been such an insanely rare
thing, maybe even independent of the Viagra. Or whatever it turned
out to be. He wondered for a minute if they would check the Jew's
blood and find out. Do a panel. Still, something must have happened
with that pill, Jesus H, because they said he'd had a stroke and it was
just too coincidental. Why would Maurie suddenly have a stroke?
While getting rubbed by a smoke? He was in pretty good shape, as far
as Chester knew. . . .*

THEY sat in the waiting room, in shock. Laxmi cried and
Chess fantasized about going to jail. *Who should I tell?* He
thought of fessing up. But what if Laxmi turned on him, with a
weird, unpredictable vengeance, destroying whatever pathetic
chances he imagined he had in terms of her love? He was stunned
to be thinking along romantic lines in a situation like this. *What am
I, a sociopath?* What if Laxmi *completely* flipped out, and accused
him not only of performing a sick practical joke but of trying to *kill*
Maurie for his *FNF* trangression? Murder him! What if she said
that Chess must have given him something *else,* on *top* of the "Viagra," like *arsenic,* and it was her *duty* to go to the *police.* Some kind
of malevolence might kick in, for sure, especially if his conspiracy
theories turned out to be true and Laxmi was in cahoots with *Friday Night Frights* (after all, she *was* on the payroll), and seriously in
love with Maurie, whose dick would no longer work even if you
pumped concrete straight into the shaft. Chess sat there, his brain
short-circuiting, wondering if he should blab, then preempt her
potential snitching by spilling his guts to the cops himself. In that
case, why tell Laxmi 1st? Too dangerous: she might unload on a
doc or nurse, or make a beeline for the phone to call whomever.
Maybe he should get in touch with Remar. Attorney/client privi-
lege—he could tell Remar he'd fucked a corpse and the guy was
legally bound to keep quiet about it. Or maybe that wasn't even
true anymore. They used to say shrinks and priests couldn't share
confessions with the authorities but if you paid attention to recent
news events, that bond had been severed with a fucking chainsaw.

There *was* no sanctuary anymore. The trouble was, Chester Herlihy had *motive*. Not only had Maurie Levin caused him physical
and emotional injury—*that* was public record—but there was evidence he was in love with the Vic's girlfriend! Evidence the girl
herself *could*—and *would*—provide. She might be a pot-smoking
Kārma Sūtra–reading black-donkey-paraded cow-dung-covered
child-molested Mansonette but she sure as hell wasn't going to
condone the homicidal actions of a pain-addled pseudo-paramour.

He saw himself in one of those *Forensic Files,* and his stomach
soured. At least he could get medical care in prison. There was a
guy he saw on CNN, 72 years old, doing time for killing someone
who banged his wife. That was 20 years ago. Since being incarcer-
ated, he'd had 3 strokes, 2 heart attacks, a bypass, a knee replacement, and cataract surgery, costing California taxpayers about a
million and counting. *Not too bad* . . . though if he *did* tell Laxmi
the "truth" (it didn't really seem like the right word), she might
play sympathetic while secretly fearing for her *own* life. The cops
would make her wear a wire and tape future meetings. *At least
that way, if it was drawn out a little, maybe we'd still have the chance
to fuck.* He shook himself out of his lunacy, as if trying to awaken
from a hebephrenic nightmare.

A nurse-type came and asked if they were family members.

They said they weren't, and didn't know if Maurie even *had*
family (which the 2 suddenly thought odd: the fact that they
didn't know). Just before the woman went back in, Chess asked
how their friend was doing. He hadn't expected any sort of mean-
ingful response but when she said "OK" his hopes soared—then
crashed, realizing the answer was rote, a devious nicety, because,
of course, nothing *could* be revealed, *doctors* were the only ones to
do any *revealing,* especially not to "friends." "OK" was vague
enough that it could have meant, "Yes, as long as you're going, a
latte would be nice," or "He is now able to sit up," or "Your friend
is dead."

He flipped through an old *People*. An article said that Don
Knotts was "upbeat and getting chemo." Suddenly, Chess had a
giddy, half-stoned moment of optimism—that Maurie *was* sitting

up and talking, they'd given him one of those fast-acting clot-busters that downgraded strokes and maybe tomorrow morning or even tonight he'd be going back to LA—if such caprice turned out to be real, the dilemma of whether to fill his friend in on what Chess had *done* quickly followed. How would Maurie react upon hearing something like that? He might be so embarrassed, he'd say *Just forget it.* They would shake hands, Chester would drop all legal action, join the staff of *FNF,* and that would be that. Or maybe he'd be pissed, and countersue, only his suit against the scout would be far stronger than *Herlihy v FNF* because in *Levin v Herlihy,* a lawyer could prove *malicious intent.* No: he'd wait. They'd stay a few extra days at the Morongo until he was certain Maurie was *plus perfecto.* There was that woman at the spa to deal with; no way anyone in authority would even be interested in talking to her, but if someone did, the most she could divulge would be the "birthday" prank, the switcheroo. It was kid stuff. The cops would probably have a laugh. (In fact, the cops would have a laugh about the whole Viagra thing; just the type of shit they probably pulled on each other all the time.) The prank alone obviously had nothing to do with what happened, whatever it was that *had* happened, medically, which was, clearly, to outside eyes, a flukish mystery. Besides, the spa chick would keep her mouth shut because she wouldn't want her bosses to know she took a bribe, even if it was all in good fun. *Customer satisfaction.* No, Chess had other problems . . . sitting in the ER, he began to pray, the way people are prone to, in extremis. *Please G-d let the Jew live and prosper. Please G-d let none of this be happening. Please G-d let me awaken in my house, never having come to Morongo. I promise never to see Laxmi again nor have impure thoughts of*—then he got the idea to cut a deal (with G-d) and give a large portion of his pending settlement *over,* in confidence of course, Maurie would have to agree to the caveat, to sign something to that effect, be-cause the proposal might not be strictly legal, to fork a chunk over to his friend, if G-d would only please please please reverse the stroke. *I'm talking 80%.*

. . . again, he wished it was all a dream. Escaping into a tiny bubble, Chess took a deep breath and pretended he didn't even *know* Maurie Levin, that he was sitting there waiting to be seen for a cough or waiting for his Mom who'd had a little chest pain— Chess pain!—or to fill out an application to work as an orderly, sitting beside this pretty freckled flowerpower girl, another applicant, whose name he didn't know but with whom he would fatefully wind up sharing a desert apartment when they both were hired. (Like that Palm Springs movie *Three Women,* with Sissy Spacek and the tall, far-out gangly girl who reminded him of Karen Knotts.) At this moment, he gratefully remembered the Xanax in his pocket—*not* ordered online, he would have to throw all that offshore shit away *ASAP,* not only from the fear it was tainted but because the batch could wind up being *evidentiary*— after getting a Diet Pepsi from the vending machine, he took a handful along with 5 Vicodin, he almost offered some Xanax to Laxmi but knew she didn't go for that, she was more into weed, maybe they should do some in the parking lot, probably not a great idea, then a shudder went through him as he fantasized about giving her an offshore benzo or Oxy by mistake instead of the tried-and-true, name-brand antianxiety agent and her collapsing in a weird reaction of her own, suddenly splayed on a gurney right next to Maurie behind ER drapes—then he would surely confess, at least it would all be over, the police would come and he'd be taken away on charges of illegally providing prescription drugs, automatically refiled 72 hours later to reflect a double homicide. He saw a documentary on television about prisons being warehouses for the mentally ill. He knew—had always known—that jail would break him. He'd be one of those men who stop taking their antipsychotics and throw feces at the guards who then ramrod their way in, 8 cops in chemical suits and goggles, fitting him with a spit-guard and a soft helmet so he couldn't head-butt, crushing him with a mattress and causing nerve damage with high-tech handcuffs and low-tech chokeholds. There was no lawyer on earth who would touch a case like that; *Inferno* time. After fishing him from his cell, they'd send him to a psychiatric hospital just like the guy in the doc, 3 months of segregation and relatively decent meals, 3 months of stabilizing meds before reassessment. The prison shrinks would sit and look at his file, like judges from *American Idol,* and say he was much improved, that now it was time for him to go *back,* back to the Big House, he was doing *wonderfully,* that's actually the word a therapist used in the doc, and Chess remembered the prisoner, who was quite smart, saying, "Yes—'wonderful' in *this environment,*" meaning that he was doing well in the context of the *regularity,* the *care,* the rather *humane isolation,* but they wouldn't listen to the simple logic of the man's proclamation, his time was up, there were probably state guidelines for how long a prisoner could remain, they'd send Chess back to whatever original hellhole, maybe Twin Towers Correctional Facility for the cycle to begin again, until 4 or 5 months later he was flinging feces and they were breaking into the cell to smother him with half a ton of bodies wielding blood and shit-encrusted mattresses before shipping him to the psych ward again, more nerve damage, paranoia flowering so completely now that soon even the most powerful of psychotropic weedkillers they had to offer wouldn't do the trick.

All this went through his head as they sat waiting, waning, wondering what their next move should be. Ask for their friend's personal things? Hey! Where were his wallet and cellphone? Still in the locker at the spa? (The paramedics brought him to the ER in a Sage robe.) There might be important numbers they could access from his Treo, not that Chess knew how to use it, maybe Laxmi did, but the cops had probably thought of that, maybe not, maybe it didn't warrant it, they weren't really all that efficient, but still, the Man could be at Sage this very minute, the chick he bribed could be opening up the locker—maybe Chess and Laxmi should just go back to the hotel and see if Maurie had something in the room, maybe there was even weed or other contraband that needed to be flushed or stowed or eaten. When Chess brought that up in a whisper, Laxmi said *he* should go back, she wanted to wait till she could at least see Maurie or talk to a doctor or *something,* and Chester suddenly quietly freaked at the idea of being alone, leaving *her* alone, *being* alone, and panicky, back at the hotel, Laxmi sensed his distress and placed a hand on his, and the cycle of guilt revved up again, the terror and remorse, the worry that his life had ended just when he thought he had a chance to begin again, what with his imminent fortune and budding affair with Maurie's presumptive ex. *Why did I do it? Why why why? Mother-fucker—*

At midnight, they drove to Morongo in relative silence, with Laxmi, her face gone puffy, snorting and snuffling. They sat in the hotel parking structure before leaving the Benz 500 cocoon. She told Chess what she saw.

Maurie's eyes were open but didn't "track." When she leaned over he *seemed* to focus, but couldn't, and didn't try to speak. His eyes welled up but Laxmi said she wasn't sure if that was related to anything. She wiped them with a Kleenex. "The ducts might just have been leaking"—*Chester, he looked so awful!* Then she said she thought for a second that he *may* have been looking at her and asking for help . . . trapped in his body . . . Oh! Oh God! Oh God!—

Chess heard himself say, *No,* involuntarily.

He didn't want to hear any more.

They went to the suite but couldn't find his wallet. Laxmi said she'd go down and get everything from the locker. Chess said the place was closed and they could do it in the morning. She started to cry again. She said that while they were waiting in the ER she read an article about a 35 year old African elephant called Wankie who died after being transferred, over the objections of animal rights people, from the San Diego Zoo to Salt Lake City. The article said she "collapsed in a metal crate somewhere in Nebraska"—the 3rd elephant to die after being moved from the Wild Animal Park. Laxmi sobbed, screaming about how Wankie's last hours were spent surrounded by 20 zoo workers and vets as she rested in a sling and they massaged her legs, warming the helpless animal with water.

"Then they executed her!" she said, almost gleefully, her face crushed and distorted, the grin fractured and perverse.

Chess was stoned—on top of the pills, they smoked a roughly

rolled joint right when they got to the room—and before he knew it, Laxmi stripped off her clothes. He thought she was going to take a shower but instead she began to unbuckle his belt. They shagged on the shag, abrading themselves.

He split the cicada, mounted the tortoise, fluttered the phoenix, and monkey-attacked—

In praising unions of the left hand, the Chandogya Upanishad says that the woman's call is the prelude, lying beside her the invocation, penetrating her sex the offertory, and ejaculation the final hymn.

LX

MARJORIE

RUDDY Marone was a lot like his name. His silver hair and polite, cowboy demeanor reminded her of the movie star Jeff Chandler. She told him so, and Marj thought he'd probably never heard that. There weren't too many people left who remembered Jeff Chandler.

Agent Marone said that the FBI, in cooperation with "LAPD Fraud," had been tracking " 'Mr Weyerhauser' and his gang" for well over 10 months. (Of course Weyerhauser was an AKA.) He told her she hadn't been the 1st victim of the Blind Sisters lottery scam and probably wouldn't be the last, bluntly adding that he wasn't sure how much, if any, of her "funds" could be recovered. He was still confident they "had a pretty good shot" because the "noose was tightening on Mr Weyerhauser and his merry band of thieves."

Bonita Billingsley—another alias—was part of the group, and Marj found herself strangely fascinated. Malone showed her a book of deglamorized mugshots, photos taken from earlier arrests in different states. They looked like common criminals. They had "played this game before," he said, and were good at it. Over the next few days, the agent got a wealth of details from Marjorie about the gang's MO. She showed him the ornate check that had been issued to her, Lucas's business card (she still called him that; couldn't help herself), and the various papers she had signed, papers with personal information the agent said had actually given them open access to her banking accounts. The old woman wanted to know about the original draft she had made, for more than $11,000. It was written to the State of New York— how could they have cashed it? He told her they probably hadn't, and that it was "bait." For them, it bought their trust and at the same time "gave them further insight to your liquidity." Malone assured that he had already been in touch with the folks at Wells Fargo. She was finally able to tell him about the shopping trip with Bonita and the fiasco at Spago. She felt so ashamed, but it was good to be able to talk to someone. He had heard it all before yet retained his sympathy and compassion. He said that his mother was around her age.

The scenario she described was basically the same they employed with other victims. One thing puzzled him, though. Usually, "Mr Weyerhauser, et al" pressed their "marks" for more money—if the well hadn't run dry, they'd find a way to "dip their bucket." In Marjorie's case, it seemed the gang stopped short, which seemed "irregular." They were outrageously bold, almost recklessly so, and in the agent's experience, grew bolder upon sensing the law closing in—almost a way of tweaking their noses at Marone and his men.

"Aside from the *big* check you wrote, did he ask for any more monies?"

"I don't think so."

She was confused. Which check was he talking about?

"The one for $565,000."

That just didn't sound right. Could it have been so much?

She blanched, feeling the fool again. He picked up on that, handing her the glass of water that sat on the table.

"I know this is difficult, Mrs Herlihy. But I think you should consider yourself *lucky*. Most of the time these people prefer wire transfers—the money is then laundered overseas. They have electronic mail-drops where nothing can be traced. This *particular* group of individuals is off the charts in their degree of sophistication. *Very* creative. And they clearly enjoy their work! That's why I'm so anxious to get my hands on them—I enjoy *my* work as well, and they're going to find out just how much, believe me. Now, it's fairly unusual that our 'Mr Weyerhauser' didn't become more aggressive about getting a hold of *the remainder*. (And believe me, they knew exactly what you had, to the penny.) They call that the 'reload.' That's the parlance. And that they *didn't,* I think, shows a fair measure of desperation—which is *good*. But *not* so good in terms of our catching up with them. I'm worried that they've skipped town; maybe even the country. I haven't put all the pieces together, but one of our main concerns is that he may have learned we were getting *extremely close* to an arrest. In that case, our 'Mr Weyerhauser' may have sped things up a bit. Cut his losses, so to speak. But, I want to stress, compared to some of the other marks I've spoken to—and remember, these are well-educated people, just like yourself—you, Mrs Herlihy, are one of the lucky ones."

"I don't *feel* very lucky!" she said, with a gracious smile.

"I didn't mean that to sound the way it did. And I shouldn't have said 'mark.' It's a lousy word."

"Oh, that's all right!"

"Is there anything I can do, to help you out? I mean, aside from finding the sonofabitch, pardon my French."

"Well . . . I haven't told my daughter yet. I've been wanting to call, but I'm just—so—*embarrassed.*"

"What's your daughter's name?"

"Joan. She's an architect."

"Would you like my professional opinion, Mrs Herlihy?"

"Yes!"

"I think you should call her. I think you could use all the help and support that's available, and much of that will come from family. Your daughter is going to have a measure of sophistication and . . . *objectivity*—and believe me she is going to want to help—that's what family is for. You need to know that what happened to you happens to thousands of good people each year. It's pandemic. And you have to remember it's the *other* guys who are bad. You didn't do anything wrong, Mrs Herlihy. All you did was hope, and trust. So: make the call. Don't leave your daughter out of this, you can't afford to—and I *don't* mean financially." He stood. "And not to worry. We'll catch these guys."

Before he left, he told her that a "trap" had been installed on the phone line, just in case "our 'Mr Weyerhauser' " tried contacting her again. (He didn't think that likely.) Agent Marone said she could make and receive calls as she normally did; she wouldn't even know it was there. He also assured her that no one would be listening in on conversations. She was, of course, to alert him immediately should anyone from the gang get in touch.

SHE felt a little better, but couldn't bring herself to think about having lost most of Ham's legacy. He'd have been so upset with her. How stupid! One always expected this sort of disaster to happen to others—but there she was.

She went next door.

The grandkids were trying to play with Pahrump, but he cowered in a corner as if they were strangers. Cora said the veterinary people told her that wasn't uncommon, given what her baby went through. She said that a special psychologist who knew the inner workings of the minds of dogs was going to make a housecall and maybe put Mr P on television. The grandchildren were so excited about the prospect, you would have thought it was Christmas! The world would finally see Pahrump for what he was—King Charles the 1st!

EARLY that evening, Agent Marone called. "Are you sitting down?" he said, warmly. There was a break in the case and they were about to make an arrest. He asked if he could drop by. "I have a little present for you."

He came within the hour, accompanied by a woman in a blue business suit who worked at Wells. She smiled and presented Marj with a check for a hundred-thousand dollars. That was the amount the old woman's money market account was insured for by the FDIC—and because of Agent Marone's efforts, the bank had drastically shortened the reimbursement period, cutting through the red tape with a little-known statute that such funds might possibly be used to aid an ongoing federal investigation.

The agent winked at Marj and said, "We have our methods."

She wiped away a tear and thanked both of them.

"This is marvelous."

"A hundred thousand down, 450,000 to go," he said, patting her arm.

But he'd said they were about to make an arrest . . .

"2 people matching the descriptions of 'Bonita' and our 'Mr Weyerhauser' were in your branch only hours ago, just as it was closing. Guess what they wanted to know: your current balance. Now, *that* was a gross misstep—and a clear indication the gang is getting sloppy."

"My balance?"

She was befuddled.

"They told the clerk that you were ill, and they'd been granted POA—power of attorney."

The woman in the business suit spoke up.

"They even presented documents to my branch manager— very *authentic*-looking documents—a fairly amazing thing to do considering the current climate of fraud directed toward the elderly."

"It's the equivalent of waving a red flag—and they *know* it."

"I've been in this business *many* years and stranger things have happened, but *this* . . . well, it's pretty close to flabbergasting. They were cool as cucumbers."

"And this is *one* cucumber we're going to slice and dice—with your help, Mrs Herlihy."

"It's like a Sherlock Holmes!" said Marj.

"We'll make a Miss Marple out of you yet," said the agent.

LXI.

JOAN

HE asked her to fly with him to Paris for the weekend. They hadn't discussed the pregnancy any further. There were 3 pilots and 3 stewards, 2 master suites, and a full spa. The bathrooms had special black toilet paper from Spain.

She was a little under the weather, but the Ritz didn't make her feel any worse. On both days, Lew had a full slate of meetings, except for when he insisted she come with him to the Marais to look at a 4 foot tall 122-lb Christian Bailly automata, a complex mechanical figure called the Bird Trainer, in the lineage of 18th century creations. It took 6 years to build. 6 years = $6,000,000. Joan thought everyone was kidding.

She liked spending time alone.

The Bentley—which for some reason had a sink in the back— shuttled her to anonymous vintage clothiers, hidden away in unlikely arrondissements. Lew kept the car in its own climate-controlled "condo," and the driver-caretaker lived above. He could view his collection, including a Czech Tantra 87 and a 1933 Maybach Zeppelin, on a Webcam from wherever he was in the world. He told her the Maybach's orange paint had been matched to a Moroccan ex girlfriend's pubes. Joan said, *"TMI, Lew,"* and he laughed.

A boutique in the hotel sold 35-hundred dollar Japanese jeans (woven with platinum strands), a knee-length jacket made out of fetuses cut from ewes' carcasses, and a 32,000 dollar cellphone. He wanted to buy them all, for kicks, but she said no 5 times. (When she returned to LA the jeans and phone were waiting for her at ARK. At least he didn't send the coat.) Though he seemed to relish her spirited refusals, he absolutely would not let Joan turn down his offer of a Guerdon credit card. At that point, she caved.

He is going to be the father of my child. She bought a 12,000€ belted Lagerfeld dress coat at Anouschka on Avenue du Coq (Catherine Deneuve was having lunch in the vestibule with an employee), a Goyard doctor's satchel, an incongruous pythonskin ultra P&G bag, a Spaksmannsspjarir sweater with button-on collar, a tacky Andrew Gn coral print coat, a black Lurex Boudicca shirtdress, and a reworked 20s flapper gown from a husband-and-wife team who called themselves E2.

She walked on the street.

She hated the bustle—people stuffing their faces with food, on the fly. It was the same all over the world. She hated watching daughters or wives or mistresses attentively watching their fathers or husbands or lovers talk on cellphones: the men usually spoke with bizarre, heightened urgency, as if negotiating with abductors. Everything was so intensely grave and poppycockish, and she knew that if she could understand what was being said it'd be the most mundane thing imaginable.

She watched television back at the hotel. Larry King again, always a comfort. All Larry, all the time. This one was a BTK rerun. A cop was talking: "I always thought he had the misfortune, given his aspirations, to live in a small media market. He never got the attention of an LA or New York market because he lived in Wichita." On the BBC, Condi Rice was telling an interviewer that she was a social scientist; Condi was weirdly comforting too. Sexy.

A soap came on. Some kind of Latin couple. The guy said, "I am not going to make love to you." The girl said, "You *are* going to make love to me." The guy said, "How can you prove you made love to me?" The girl said, "Why would you want to make love to me?" Nothing made sense. Maybe she wasn't paying enough attention.

The ads were mostly tourist promos for other countries. She liked the slogans: MADRID ONLY HAPPENS IN MADRID. UGANDA—GIFTED BY NATURE. MALAYSIA TRULY ASIA. DO BUY IN DUBAI. (RWANDA IS FOR LOVERS.) A funny one was aimed at the Arab Emirates; people there were so

parched that India was offering trendy new "monsoon mania hol-
idays," even though recent floods had killed thousands.

GOA—COME FEEL THE RAIN.

DARFUR—FEEL THE JANJAWEED.

Condi's moment dissolved into a feature on Viktor Yu-
shchenko, he of the toxin-ravaged face. One poll taken said the
Ukrainians thought he was shit and things were now worse than
before the revolution. But the poll that closed the news segment
said 2/3s of the populace were "very happy." *Shit Happy Shit
Happy Shit Happy.*

She drowsily focused on another image byte—people in New
York shouting, "Where's my Xbox? They promised Xboxes but
it's a lie!"—before drifting off to sleep.

T HEY were supposed to fly on to the small Swiss town of
Rossinière, where Lew had been asked by the widow of the
painter Balthus to see a dusktime outdoor puppet show, an invitation which, through the intervention of Louis Benech and Trinnie
Trotter (who had codesigned the landscape for one of Samuel's
homes), took months to procure. Setsuko and her daughter,
Harumi, lived in "The Grand Chalet," a converted hotel-castle,
supposedly the largest of its kind in Switzerland. But at the last
minute, the widow became ill and regretfully informed she must
bow out. An intermediary told Lew that Setsuko would still be
delighted if he came, even if it meant they might not meet. Since
Harumi was in Los Angeles, as much as he wanted to visit the legendary place, Lew decided it wouldn't be right.

T HEY gave it to Goldsworthy."

"What do you mean?" said Joan.

"I just talked to Eugenie—at Guerdon. They're flying Andy in
from Scotland next week so he can do his *walkabout.*"

"Barbet, what are you saying? We already *knew* that. We knew
Andy was going to do *something.*"

"And we were correct. But evidently, it's a little more than 'something.' From what I've gathered."

"Like what?"

"No details immediately forthcoming."

"So it's totally over?"

"Let's say we've gone from dark horse to *black hole* horse."

"It isn't funny."

"I'm not laughing, Joan."

"Lew would have *called* me. He's knows I'm going up there with that fucking maquette!"

"You still *are*. And here's to you, Mrs Frei-berg, Jesus loves you more than you will know. *Wo wo wo.* Maybe he's going to make you a different sort of proposal. A *decent* one. You've already won the mother of all commissions, right?"

"Oh bull*shit*. Anything on Rem?"

"Definitely *out*. Outré. Rien. *Rien Koolhaas!* At least we didn't lose to Dutch Schultz. Pointy-head bitch motherfucker."

"I cannot believe this."

"Well, you'll always have Paris."

She was so angry at Lew and herself and the world that she felt on the verge of serenity.

"What about the maquette?"

"Being trucked to Mendocino and delivered in a crate as we speak. *In situ.* What a *situ*-ation. Honey, look: I'm drinking and cannot be disturbed. The guys'll meet you at the property."

"But *why?*"

"For the unveiling."

"Does Lew *know* about this?"

"Of course he knows! I told Frieberg I wanted him to see the thing, in the *chapel*. In twilight time. *Goin to the chapel and we're . . . gonna get mar-ried*—not! Maybe it'll turn him around. Isn't that brilliant?"

"You mean he wants us to go through the motions. *Sadist.*"

"Motions? Um, *no*, not *us*, that would be *you*, *ma chérie*. 'Distant as the Milky Way' . . . *no shit*. Your fucking *motions* made us who we are today! Or who we *aren't*. I meant *fucking* motions. But don't worry, Mrs Robinson. Still plenty o' mems in them thar hills."

That was last night.
       She'd been home for 2 days, and now it was noon. She turned her phone back on. She was hungover from the Ambien CR. The jet was leaving at 3. Her conversation with Barbet seemed like a bad dream. She didn't know whether to give it credence; Lew could be playing mindgames. Who was this Eugenie at Guerdon anyway? Maybe Barbet had a mole. A moll. A Molly. A fuckmole. She felt strangely secure, or at least secure in her own insecurities. It was probably because of the baby. As fanatical as it seemed, Joan still wanted the Napa commission more than anything; maybe even more than the child itself.

She turned on the Impressa and listened to her voicemail while fishing soy milk from the fridge.

A blasé sobered-up message from Barbet wished her luck. He was going to his house in Rancho Mirage, shorthand for having made a new conquest. *The Molly.* He sounded depressed, and she knew what he was up to: fucking his way out of it, per usual. *Call when you get to Mendocino so I can help coordinate.* Completely unnecessary—she'd phone the art guys directly to make sure the model had arrived intact—but it was Barbet's way of doing the team thing. The ARK thing.

Pradeep called from Delhi, saying what a wonderful time he had with her and how sorry he was they hadn't hooked up before he left. Then came 2 rather tentative calls from her mom; she thought about waiting until she returned from up north but decided to check in.

"Mom? How you doing?"

"Joanie? Hello."

"What's wrong." Silence. "Mom, are you all right?"

"Joanie—something happened."

Her heart seized.

"What is it, Mother?"

"A man came to the house and said that I won a great deal of money."

"Oh God."

"Joan, please!"

"But *when?*"

"A few weeks ago."

"Why didn't you—was he a scammer?"

"They think so. Yes. Please don't be mad."

"OK. OK. I won't be mad. I'm not mad."

Joan got the details, best as an agitated Marj could deliver, then made her read the phone numbers of Agent Marone and the bank officer so she could get in touch. She realized she'd been abrupt, and told her mother not to worry. She would ring back after making a few calls.

Shit.

There were 2 for Agent Marone, and she hoped her mom had gotten them right. She tried the 1st: voicemail. The 2nd was the antifraud division of the FBI. A woman asked if she wanted to be forwarded to his inbox but Joan declined, saying she'd already left a message on his cell. She thought twice and had them transfer, leaving word that she was Marjorie Herlihy's daughter.

Then she called the woman at Wells Fargo.

"This is Cynthia Mulcahy."

"Hi, Cynthia. It's Joan Herlihy, Marjorie Herlihy's daughter."

"Hi, Joan," said the woman, as if in condolence.

"Can you tell me what's going on?"

"Have you spoken to Agent Marone?"

"I left a message on his voicemail."

"You talked to your mom."

"She wouldn't tell me how much the guy stole."

"About $550,000."

"Oh my God!"

"I know," she said, with a kind of warm yet steely sympathy. "A hundred thousand of that is insured by the FDIC. I'm not sure if your mother told you, but we got that back to her, and it's resting in a special account. There's no way that anyone—except Marjorie, of course—can get to it."

"But how are you going to *catch* the guy? I mean, I've heard about this stuff and they *never* recover what's . . ."

"That's not entirely true, Joan. Agent Marone is *very* good at chasing money. I've worked with him before, and he's got a *great* group of forensic accountants. And, as I said, the federally insured amount has already been credited to her account, which is unusual. Most of the time that process takes 90 days, but we have Ruddy to thank for that."

"Ruddy?"

"Marone. That's Agent Marone. Have you seen her yet?"

"No—I can't. The timing is *horrendous*. I'm on my way out of town on what is probably the single most important business trip of my life. I'm not sure what to do."

"I understand. If it's any consolation, the banking industry is in the middle of a virtual pandemic in the area of geriatric fraud. And the people who took money from your mom are probably better at it than any group I've ever seen."

"Oh, *great.*"

"What I mean is, your mother is very sharp. From the conversations I've had with Ruddy, she was circumspect; you can't imagine how skillful these men and women are at establishing trust. That's what they *do.* But she is definitely of sound mind, and didn't just give her money away. I know that sounds hard to believe when we're staring at the results, but it's important for you to keep in mind."

"I appreciate what you're trying to say, Mrs—"

"Mulcahy. And it's *Ms*—but Cynthia, please."

"I appreciate it. She's not *senile.* OK. She's alone and vulnerable, and I probably have something to do with that."

"Don't go there, Joan."

"But the money's gone nonetheless. And it's a *lot.*"

"I know. Look: everything that can be done is being done. Are you going to postpone your trip?"

"I don't know. I need to think."

"OK. If you do go, when will you be back?"

"I was just going for a few days, but I'll cut it short. I can actually be back late tonight. It's a presentation," she added needlessly.

"All right. Why don't you give me your email and cellphone number. You left it for Agent Marone?"

"Yes. But not my email."

"I'm sure he'll call within the next few hours. I don't think there's much you can actually do by being here, Joan, aside from hand-holding—which she *definitely* needs. The poor woman hasn't had an easy time. There's a lot of shame attached to this type of thing when it happens. I wish I could say I hadn't been through it with other clients."

"You've seen it before."

"More than I wish! Many, *many* of our customers. And it isn't just widows and widowers: it's married couples, folks in their 50s, we're generally talking about savvy, well-educated people. Babyboomers! They become *mesmerized*—the groups preying on them are like—well, they're just so seductive. Whether or not you postpone your trip is completely up to you, but you *should* take comfort that the agent in charge of your mother's case is *extremely* competent. We're keeping a close watch on Marjorie's account. I am, personally. If you're back tonight or tomorrow morning, I don't see much difference. It's your call. It's an emotional call."

"Do I need to get a lawyer?"

"*Absolutely.* Why don't you come see me the minute you touch down—with or without your mom. I'm here all week. The Pico-Robertson branch. That's Marjorie's home branch. We can discuss all your options and I can give you a list of people—attorneys—you might want to get in touch with."

Joan called her mother and said she'd spoken to the lady at the bank and had also left word with the FBI agent. She was leaving at 3 to give the final presentation of the Memorial, but would be in constant touch. When she broached the possibility of returning on the same night, Marj would hear nothing of it, which only made her feel worse, accentuating the offer's hollow ring. (After speaking to the Wells Fargo woman she had pretty much settled on staying in Napa until the following afternoon, to get closure on whatever the hell was going on.) She patiently waited for her mom to get a pen and write down Joan's cell number, asking her to repeat it back. She told her to keep the Nokia turned on as well (the old woman didn't have the heart to say she'd forgotten her *own* mobile number—thank God Joan didn't ask her to recite it—but didn't think it made any difference, as long as she had it charged and ready), and not to leave the house or answer the door. If anything "seemed 'funny,'" Joan said, "I want you to call 911 *immediately,* and then call the *agent,* and then *Cora,* and then *me*— in that order. OK, Mom?" Her daughter said it sounded like everyone was doing what they could, and not to worry. It wasn't that much money in the scheme of things *(the fuck it wasn't)* . . . you have your health, your children, and your house free and clear. These things happen to people of all ages. *It's a pandemic.* (She hated parroting the woman from the bank and hated herself for wanting to soften things before they hung up. She had years of experience hanging up on her mother.) She tried to end on a cheerful note by bringing up the hundred-thousand dollars that Cynthia said had been deposited back in her account. They spoke another 5 minutes, but Joan was on autopilot, her head already in Napa.

A s the Town Car ferried her to Van Nuys she put on her warpaint, strategizing how to surf the cauldron of india ink that abutted and slapped the great and perilous cliffs of Losers Coast.

She decided not to refer to the baby unless Lew Freiberg brought it up. She would promise an abortion if that was what he required—a stone lie, yet one that might buy her time. All Joan wanted was a fair shake at winning the Mem: if securing the commission, *publicly,* came down to an order to scrape the womb, she would give notarized assurance. (In her heart she felt he would never tell her to do such a thing but she had to prepare for the worst). The prime imperative, as they say, was for ARK's design, *her* design, to be inseminated into every media outlet that mattered, up, down, and sideways. She wanted to win a prestigious foreign prize. She wanted to be profiled, a smoldering headshot in the sidebars of middlebrow magazines that sit in doctors' offices: *Time, Newsweek,* what have you. She wanted the whole international elitist enchilada. She wanted to be *recognized* then move on. Let Lew Freiberg try to pull the Mem plug late-term—but *she* wouldn't, she would have that child. And if Joan Herlihy couldn't have her commission, why then she'd just build a baby, like her brother said, because time was running out, all around.

What could be a more intelligent design?

LXII.

RAY

THE Dog Whisperer came with his camera crew, and went for walks with Nip.

The sorcerer worked his calm-assertive magic: the Friar was easier to live with, and his wounds were healing nicely because he no longer reopened them out of compulsive, neurotic behavior. He didn't cry or throw up anymore when he heard loud noises in the middle of the night. Once in a while he growled during meals but Ray knew what to do. Having established dominance, the old man could now replenish the bowl during a feed without incident.

Ghulpa was another story. He joked to Señor Millan that his girlfriend (he didn't say "roommate" anymore) might need a little training on the side. She'd become a handful, even for the cousins. She was nauseous most of the time, and in general discomfort. It wasn't her fault; being pregnant at that age had to be tough. More than anything, BG hated being confined to bed. The only thing that cheered her was news from the lawyers about the money, the sum of which kept threatening to arrive any day now; Ray knew she'd feel a whole heck of a lot better once she could hold the check in her pretty little hand. He told her that after she dropped the kid (she hated when he used that phrase, and he said it just to get a rise), they'd take a trip somewhere—the Grand Canyon or Yosemite. Big Gulp frowned like an angry god: she would *never* take her baby *camping,* nor waste money on "frivolities." She was a tough nut, and he loved her more each day. She wanted to put money down on a house and leave the rest in the bank, where it could accumulate interest for the baby's education. *All right. Good deal.* BG even wanted to buy insurance so "if something happens," the child's future would be secure. Everything was pragmatic, and well thought out. Very Indian. She even spent hours budgeting

wardrobe, year by year. She was convinced they were going to
have a "boychild."

Yet she was plagued by fears. She didn't want Nip/Tuck around
the baby when it came, she didn't care what that Dog Whisperer
said, and had recurring dreams that she took as bad omens. Her
cousins brought sweets and fussed over her, but Ghulpa's disposition remained fretful, gloomy, intransigent. The doctor said it was
hormonal.

A van came and took Ray, Nip, Cesar and his wife and kids,
and the camera crew over to that lady Cora's. Mrs Millan's
name was "Illusion" and the old man had never heard of something like that. He thought it was beautiful.

As they pulled up to a large, well-manicured home in the modestly upscale neighborhood of Beverlywood, Cora's son and
grandchildren stood on the sidewalk.

Cesar led the Friar to the lawn, making sure he was calm-
submissive before allowing his own kids to pet him—then invited
the grandkids to follow suit. They were eager and affectionate.
The dog was on his back now, tongue out, tail wagging, paws up:
in the pink and generally pleased as punch. Stein ebulliently
wielded a flyweight digicam. He shook the Dog Whisperer's
hand, said he was a "big, big fan," and told him he had "full run of
the house."

When Cesar asked about Pahrump, Cora, who was the shaki-
est of the bunch, said he was hiding in the backyard.

"I think he probably sensed you were coming," she said. "He's a
bit camera-shy."

Cesar said "No worries" and everyone went inside.

Ray felt a little weak, and stayed behind to catch his breath.

A minute later, Cesar appeared in the front door.

"You OK, my man?"

"Oh fine—don't worry about *me*. I'm just an old guy, gettin his
bearings. How's Friar Tuck holding up?"

"Nip? Hasn't sunk his teeth in anyone *yet*," said Cesar, with that winning, savior's smile. "He's doing fine. And take your time, Ray. Come whenever you're ready. But I don't want to start the show without you."

The old man could hear the rollicking voices of the children from the backyard. Nice neighborhood. Maybe when he got his settlement, he'd move Big and Little Gulp to a place like this. Then he shook his head, because the amount probably wouldn't be enough to buy a home. It was too far from the cousins, and besides, Ghulpa would never allow him to squander money on a fancy house. No, the Indians had their way, and were talented when it came to saving and getting deals. He'd follow her lead. She was the Mom, and could wear the pants too. Hell, he'd worn the pants long enough. Maybe he'd have himself fitted for a sari! Indians knew how to make money *from* money, something Ray never seemed to be able to learn. Not that he was proud of it.

A gaunt-looking woman appeared on the porch next door. She looked about 70 and wore a nicely lived-in, floor-length robe. She peeked around for her paper. He walked toward her, and she didn't catch his eye until they were 10 feet apart. She seemed startled.

"It got caught in the bush there," he said, reaching into the bramble. "Your paperboy must have a helluvan arm."

"Oh! Well, thank you. Thank you very much."

He saw that it wasn't a daily, but a neighborhood throwaway, already yellowing.

"Did you want this, or were you looking for your morning paper?"

"Are you an agent?"

He didn't know what she meant.

"Are you with the fraud people? My daughter told me not to leave the house."

"No, I'm visiting next door."

He wondered if she wasn't all there.

"Oh! You're a friend of Cora's!"

"Yes I am, and hope to know her better," he said cordially. "My dog's having the *real* visit. They're making a little TV show."

"Dear Pahrump—been through quite a misery. He had a cancer. I was almost going to say, 'You wouldn't wish it on a dog,' but . . . I thought you were from the bank."

"No, though that wouldn't be so bad."

"I'm waiting for them."

"I'm waiting for those people myself."

"I've had lots of visitors lately. I just spoke to my daughter—she was on her way over but she had to go out of town."

He nodded. "You take care now. I think they might be ready for my close-up. Or the dog's, anyway."

"Thank you again," said the old woman as she went back in.

"You take care."

She didn't take the paper.

R AY was tuckered out when he got home. He went to see Ghulpa, but she clammed up. The cousins said she was crying all day. Back in the living room, he finally extracted the story.

Detective Lake had dropped off "a care package" that included a videotape of *The Jungle Book* with the actor Sabu. (A few weeks ago Staniel and Ray had talked about Rudyard Kipling, and how he was a mutual favorite.) The cousins watched the movie with Ghulpa, which turned out to be a big mistake. In the 1st half hour, a baby boy's father was killed by the man-eating Bengal, the infant lost in the jungle and raised by wolves. 12 years later, the wild child stumbled into the village and was soon cornered. One of the villagers remembered the lost boy and suggested he was the tiger-abducted son of a woman who still lived there—he was—but the woman said no, that simply couldn't be. Still, her heart went out and she invited him to stay with her until his "true mother" was found.

The cousins reported that BG had been quite disturbed by the production, to put it mildly, and had shrieked, even after the tape was ejected. It took Ray another half hour but he managed to get them to confide that Ghulpa had fallen into some kind of trance, interpreting the narrative as a horrible "prefiguration," a foretelling that the old man wouldn't live long enough to see the birth of their son—and that the boy himself was doomed to a peripatetic, troubled life. Ray couldn't help but laugh. The whole thing reminded him of the movie they saw at the Bollyplex.

He went to the bedroom. For the 1st time, she let him rub her feet. He noticed that Ghulpa had taken her L O V E clock off the wall and put it on the nightstand, for comfort. The face of the "Super Time" formed the heart-shaped *O* in L O V E—the clock was actually a novelty invite she'd received for an NRI's wedding (Non-Resident Indian) back in the days when she worked for Pradeep. It was her lucky charm.

"Why would he bring over such a terrible film?" she asked. "I thought he was a nice man."

"Listen, Gulper, I hate to break it to you, but did you know there's hardly any tigers left in India but in the *zoos?* They've all been poached."

"I am not going to speak with you of tigers."

"I went on the Google with Aradhana. Or whatever the hell they call it. There was a long article on how they searched the main park—now, I can't remember where it was, honey, but Aradhana can tell you, it was a *big,* big park—and they searched it for *2 whole weeks* and couldn't find not a *one.* Evidently, the Chinese kill em and sell their body parts."

Unsuccessful at having the effect he desired, Ray asked if she wanted some fruit or ice cream. BG was inconsolable—she wasn't even interested in knowing about the Friar and his television debut. Hoping to distract her, the old man offered that everything had gone extremely well, and with the Dog Whisperer's help (she wrinkled her nose at the appellation) "the 2 mutts" were on their way to becoming fast friends.

"You cannot whisper to Durgā," was all she said, with that eerie, bobbleheaded solemnity.

Ray let that one go. He did say that Cesar Millan's wife was called Illusion, and if they had a girl, it might be a grand name. Ghulpa muttered "Māyā," and Ray wasn't sure if she was using a Bengali word to rebuff him. Seeing his confusion, she repeated it, *Māyā,* informing him that it was a *name,* and while it sounded

South American to Ray's ears, he thought it pretty as can be. He was surprised she even allowed him to entertain the idea of having a daughter.

But maybe she meant "mā," which is what the cousins called each other. Everyone—every girl—was "mā," even babies.

LXIII.

CHESTER

MAURIE was transferred to St John's.

His mother was dead and his father somewhere in Oregon. The sister, Edith, flew in from Milwaukee, but said she couldn't stay very long.

Laxmi bunked at Chester's. The 1st week after Maurie's return from the desert (by ambulance), they lived like people who'd lost everything in a storm or a fire. The apartment was untidy. It was as if they had the same terrible flu. She often dissolved into tears, without warning. Chess was in a world of shock but couldn't share the deeper source of his panic.

During visiting hours, he held his paralyzed friend's hand and prayed, observing his own emotions with a new and special kind of agony, both exquisite and excruciating. A part of him hoped Maurie would die; a part was filled with self-loathing for allowing that thought. A part of him prayed with vehemence that Maurie was at least incognizant of what had befallen him; a part, with the nonhuman stinging energy of a hornet or wasp, dared insist the Jew deserved everything he got, but then the cycle of self-loathing started anew—like being tortured on the wheel or the rack—each and every siege causing Chess more psychic damage. (A damage that felt real-time and intensely chemical.) Again and again he thought of turning himself in but what good would that do, if Maurie wasn't going to recover? What good would it do if Maurie *did* recover? He *willed* his friend to "snap out of it." He willed *himself* to snap out of it: for the onerous trampoline of reality to bend and warp and spit them up, fluttering the pair down in some other place and time. The doctors refused to give out information because they weren't family, so Laxmi and Chester had to rely on the sister, who wasn't the communicative type, and regarded them with thinly veiled scorn and suspicion. None of her reports sounded good. *I am a murderer,* thought Chess. *No: I've consigned*

him—and myself—*to a fate worse than death. A double murderer.*
He wondered if he should make "bedside confession" but immediately rescinded the thought as self-serving and possibly sadistic
because of the very real chance that Maurie Levin could understand everything being said all around him, and was, in fact,
completely sentient—yeah, probably *exactly* the case, because
Chester's karma *(Maurie's too, right?)* was and had always been
so fucked.

This isn't about me.

When not obsessing, he monitored his own neuroskeletal pain,
the scale of which seemed absurd next to anything Maurie was
going through, but still, it was there, it was authentic, and *this* man,
afterall, had caused it. No way around that one. What if he, Chester
Herlihy, needed surgery related to the *FNF* fiasco, what if something went wrong with the anesthesia or scalpels and Chess wound
up in the same condition? He knew it sounded like an elaborate
justification yet what if what had happened to Maurie was a
macabre preamble to the very fate that awaited him? *Maybe Maurie
was a kind of burnt offering.* He would be damned if he'd let someone put him under, slit his flesh open with a *rongeur,* and remove the
soft discs between bony vertebrae before fusing everything together courtesy of a titanium cage. *Fuck that.*

The hippie and the scout slept together like siblings. They
hadn't done it since that time in the desert, probably because now
they were even more shell-shocked and self-conscious. They
never referred to their post-ER Morongo moment; it was clear
they'd copulated as a reptilian reaction to death, a fairly common
occurrence from what Chess had heard. People came back from
war zones or funerals or what have you and their animal instincts
kicked in. In the face of death, the species shouted (or grunted):
breed.

Laxmi was stoned. She sat on the couch tearfully watching
The Jungle Book for about the hundredth time.

The vultures were singing, "We never met an animal we didn't
like." The couple stared at the screen *very* seriously before begin-

ning to laugh, and they didn't stop for 5 whole minutes. Laxmi started playing the McDonald's What's-A-Fruit-Buzz game. "What's a fruit buzz?" she asked piquantly. "It makes me feel better than knowing my ex boyfriend is still single! It's that feeling you get when everything's 60% off!" Chess retorted: "What's a fruit buzz? It's like snorting coke off a choirboy's cock! It's like doing meth and coming on a fat chick's tits in Bakersfield while her army brats watch cartoons in the same room—and her husband's getting triple-amputated in Tikrit! It's like puking in Maya Angelou's mouth! It's like having diarrhea during sex—"

"With Maya Angelou?"

"—*but you keep on truckin!*"

They howled and did bong hits and ate Trader Joe's chicken dumplings and watched more of *The Jungle Book*.

Then Chess had an epiphany.

He went to the bedroom and called Remar DeConcini.

"Remar! It's Chess Herlihy."

"Hullo, Chester!"

"Listen. Um, I know you're not going to like this—but I think I want to settle out."

"Whoa! You're *right*. I *don't* like it. What's goin on, bro?"

"I don't know. I guess, it's just—I've seen what lawsuits do to people, man."

"So have I, bro! I've seen lawsuits make people *extremely rich*. Dude, what *have* y'all been smoking?" Remar sounded a little fruit-buzzed himself. "Are y'all up in the trees?"

"*Listen*. Lawsuits create . . . shitty *karma*. I mean, I'm starting to feel like *it's* controlling *me,* not like I'm controlling *it.*"

"And here I was thinking your life was being controlled by the *pain* you've suffered because of your injuries. You've got to *chill*, Chester. This is the pain talking. Sometimes it's your worst enemy."

"I just don't know if I want to spend the next 3 years of my life on hold."

"1st of all, Chess, it's not gonna be 3 years. OK? There's just no way it's going to go on that long. *No way.* 2nd of all, your life does *not* have to be on hold. Because *that* way, *they win*. Understand what I'm saying, Chess? You go on with your life. Walk on, walk on, with hope in your heart—remember the song? You'll never walk alone? Well you better fucking believe you won't be walking alone, you're gonna be walking *along,* with a satchel full of cash! *3rdly,* this is a *perfect* jury case, we've talked about that. There is *simply no way* you are not going be awarded with something in the 6 figures. Maybe 7. I'm thinking 7. And *4thly,* you don't need to be making a decision like this right now, aw-ite? Look. I know it can *feel* like this, like you're in some twilight zone. And that's normal. Everyone who was *ever* involved in a case, in my experience, no matter the merit, gets a bug up their ass and says, 'I'm *outta* here.' The higher the stakes, the more fucked up people get. Cause there's a part of *everyone* who can see the armored truck coming with them sacks filled with cash and we get all, 'I'm not worthy!' So I totally get where you're coming from. But what you *don't* want to do is throw the baby out with the bathwater—my *fear,* Chester Herlihy, and I've been doing this a long-ass time so you gotta *hear me,* my *fear* is, if we move to *settle,* the bad guys are gonna smell that *bathwater desperation* and they'll either *stonewall* us—now, they won't *succeed,* but they'll *try,* and they'll eat up that precious *time* you were talking about—or *lowball* us. Stonewall or lowball. And believe me, that's the game they like to play. And you deserve more than that."

Chester sighed, thinking things over.

"You still with me?" laughed Remar. "Still on the line?"

"Yeah. And I hear you, Remar, I really do. And I appreciate it. But I've been thinking about this a lot and I'm pretty sure it's the way I want to go."

"This isn't about the girl, is it? Or anyone else? Have you been discussing the case with anyone, Chester?"

"No, man. It's just about me."

"Because that's like poison. People's opinions are like assholes, OK? You heard that one. But right now, *I'm* the only asshole you should be listening to."

"I haven't been talking to anyone."

"Can we discuss this tomorrow?"

"Sure."

"OK, cool. Now get back up in the trees."

Remar laughed again. Chess could hear music and the low sound of voices. A faraway laugh.

"But I really think I want to end this thing."

"*Listen.* You're *not* a young guy. You're not *old,* my friend, but you're not young. This is your *life* we're talking about, your *security.* We're talkin about you never having to *work* again, OK? Remember that? A little thing called getting up every day and working for a living? Well, that's a pretty big deal. People usually don't get this kind of opportunity handed to them on a silver tray. Aw-ite? They offered *$50,000.* A fuckin insult! But we try to settle out *now,* and I'm not so sure we're gonna get much more. And my friend, that would be *tragic.* Aw-ite? And remember, my fee is a 3rd. The doctors will have to be reimbursed. Even if you were covered, the health insurance folks would want to be made whole. So you're cutting your nose to spite your face and why you'd want to cut your nose to spite your face *at this point* when everything is comin up roses and you're about be crowned Miss Fucking America, I don't know. *Miss West Hollywood.* Aw-ite? So think about it. This is your life, Chester Herlihy, not mine. I happen to have a very nice one and this particular case ain't gonna rock my world one way or another. At the end of day, *and* the night, it's your life. So think about it in those terms. Do you want to cash a check that may very well be negligible? Just to line your pockets with a little bit of green? Now when I say 'little bit' I *mean* little bit! Hell, what we're talking about isn't even enough for *pockets,* we're talkin pock-*ette!* So do you want to line your pock-*ette?* Or do you want to play in the major leagues? Here's another thing, Mr Herlihy: what if maybe next month, or next year, or *5 years down the line*—what if you need some medical work to improve your quality of life? What if this *thing*—which is causing you a *fair* amount of pain, from what all you've told me, and has you rattlin those Vicodin bottles like a voodoo doctor—what if this thing, which don't seem to be gettin any better, unless there's something you're not telling me—what if this thing comes back and bites you on the ass, *hard,* and you need surgery? So far (correct me if I'm wrong) so far I haven't heard the doctors saying, '*Oh, you'll be fine! Thing's going to heal* itself.' You know, nerve damage can be funny, Chess. Aw-ite? And I don't mean 'joke' funny. Hard to *test* for. It's important to have the *resources* to *do* something about it if it *flares.* So I want you to *carefully consider.* Or reconsider. I don't want you left holding the bag. Because more than not, the bag *will* have shit in it."

"I hear you, Remar."

"I hope you do. Let's talk tomorrow."

"OK," said the coldfooted plaintiff, worn out. (That's why he was a good attorney.) But Chess knew he'd made the right decision. It was the only decision possible.

"Over and out."

"One more thing," said Chester. "What about taxes? Will they come out of the settlement?"

The voices and music at Remar's grew louder.

"Not really—we're not talking about much income lost here. As you know. There *may* be. But nothing substantial. That's something I'll have to get into."

Before hanging up, the lawyer tried one more tack.

"Chess, if you *need* money, I *told* you. Let me advance you some. Just *don't* be a fool."

"It's not about that."

"Are you sure? Because the firm can help—it wouldn't be the 1st time. But before we do, you'd have to make an agreement to go all the way with this. We are not a lending institution. We consider you to be an investment. A *rock-solid* one. We consider you an asset. And I just wish you'd start thinking of yourself that way. Stead o' goin all hangdog on me. I'm lookin at you as a Wal-Mart superstore, and you're over there thinking you're a *K-town mini-mart.*"

"Thanks, Remar. Thanks. I'm cool."

"I know that to be true."

"And I'm sure this is how I want to go."

There was a longish pause, then a sigh, almost of disgust.

"It's just such an about-face, man. I mean, I thought we were on the same team. But now it's like you've crossed over to the other side. You've crossed over!"

The last was followed by a deep, syrupy laugh, à la Al Green preaching gospel. His tone became jocular.

"Don't go to the dark side, Chess! Come to the light, baby, come to the light!"

LXIV.

MARJORIE

S HE bought a lottery ticket at Riki's then drove to Wells.
She had an appointment with Agent Marone and the
lady. The lady called to remind her, and said she had spoken
to Joanie. Marj already knew that, and thanked her.

When she got to the bank, there was a double door installed—
something new. She came in from the street and it shut behind her
but when she tried the 2nd door, it wouldn't open. A disembodied
voice boomed that Marj needed to hold up her purse. She was
confused and the voice repeated its command. Once she held up
the purse, they buzzed her in. Well, that was the silliest thing. Did
they think she was going to rob the bank? "I'm not Ma Barker,"
she muttered.

She found a chair by the closest desk and sat down to wait, as
she'd been told. She was there almost 20 minutes but no one approached. The old woman began to think the arrest might have
already happened, or that maybe she'd gotten the time wrong. It
was beyond belief but she'd left her cellphone at home again. The
muleheaded stupidity of it made her groan. She waited another 10
minutes before getting in line to check on her money. It was habit,
a way to kill time.

The teller, some sort of Persian who Marj could barely see behind the thick, smudged security glass, told her the balance had
been "zeroed out."

"But what *is* the balance?" asked Marj.

The Persian said there was "none," adding, "You have closed
the account."

There was a time delay because of an inferior sound system.
The voice of the teller dipped in and out.

Marj reached in her bag and got the business card from the
lady. She read the name to the teller, saying she wanted to speak

with "Cynthia Mulcahy, Vice President, Customer Relations."
She slipped the card under the glass for the imbecile to examine.
Marj said she had an important appointment with Miss Mulcahy
and a gentleman from the Federal Bureau of Investigation. The
Persian called someone over, a prim-looking African-American.
The black began to speak but her voice was low and kept fritzing
out as well. She studied the card and asked Marj which branch the
lady she wished to see worked out of. *This is the silliest thing! Can't
you read? This is not Ebonics, Miss! This is Wells Fargo, not McDonald's. Just please read the card! The woman on the card is your boss!*

The black told Marj to wait. Then the teller asked if she'd
step aside but the old woman couldn't hear and the request was
repeated that she step out of line because there were customers
waiting.

The black came out a few minutes later with a tall, thin man. (It
was a relief to see people without that horrid glass barrier.) He
asked Marj to sit at his desk. The black earnestly hovered a moment before she was called away. The thin man adjusted his
glasses and told Marj that he was afraid there was no one by that
name who worked at Wells Fargo Bank. She said she didn't understand, the business card said the lady was Vice President of
Pico-Robertson, she had even been to Marj's home for coffee. The
thin man kept staring at Miss Mulcahy's card, with an ever-so-
slight nod of the head. Then he got the old woman's Social and
punched it in his computer, calling up her accounts. Without
looking at her, he asked Marj how long she had banked there, and
she became furious because that was something they should
know, they should know their business, she was a loyal longtime
customer, she had just given him her Social Security number and
he had her driver's license sitting right there too, and anyway, he
was punching everything in and she couldn't understand why she
had to be asked questions whose answers were probably staring
him in the face from the screen. To show her impatience, Marj
said, "Well, that's moot." (A remark she would have told Hamilton about when he got home from work—how during the day
she'd had the gumption to tell some bureaucratic fool, "That's

moot.") The thin man said their records showed she had closed
out her money market and personal checking accounts that very
morning. She said that was impossible, or if it was true, it surely
had been done in the course of an investigation, because she was in
the midst of helping the FBI—she was helping an agent, Agent—
suddenly she became flustered, and couldn't remember his name.
The thin man told her she might be the victim of fraud and Marj
got a little irate and said of *course* she was the victim of a fraud, she
already *knew* that, and so did the *bank*, Miss Whatshername, and
so did the *FBI* and Agent So-and-So. I cannot remember his
name. The man who looks like Jeff Chandler. I was meeting both
of them here.

   The lady on the card spoke to my daughter—

   The thin man eyed her carefully now and said he was going to
call the police. Marj said she wasn't sure that was a good idea, because the agent—Agent *Marone* (she had finally gotten the *bril-*
liant idea of digging his card from her purse, which she handed
over to the fastidious bureaucrat, who scrutinized it closely. What
an ass he was!)—*Agent Marone* said they were quite near an arrest,
and if the thin man were to call the police it might jeopardize the
work done up till now. I am to be a critical eyewitness, and the
ringleader, AKA Mr Weyerhauser, is supposed to be taken into
custody at this very branch, Pico-Robertson, and *that* is an action
he should be *extremely* wary of jeopardizing. The thin man told
her the business card of the lady appeared to be "falsified." He dialed the number of Agent Ruddy Marone and hung up, telling the
old woman it had been disconnected. Marj asked him to try again,
which he did, but it was still disconnected.

   He said he was going to phone the police right away because of
the "high numbers" involved, that he felt Marj and the bank may
have been defrauded and it was probably a good idea for her to
wait at his desk until certain matters could be further clarified.
She looked pale and he waved at someone to bring a cup of water.
He said she could go home if she wished, that she didn't live so far
away, according to their records—*well, at least they* had *some*
records!—and he would call just as soon as he heard anything. The

black brought the water and the parched old trembling woman raised it to her mouth. Marj shouted, "Of course you have been defrauded!" and mentioned that the lady from Wells had deposited a hundred thousand dollars back into her account, the amount covered by federal insurance, and why didn't *that* show up on his stupid screen? She tearfully apologized for her outburst, then demanded to know why the accounts had been "zeroed out," to use the teller's term. The black trundled off, and instead of answering, the thin man merely confirmed all of Mrs Herlihy's personal information, by rote—they even had her cellphone number on file—and Marjorie told him yes she *would* wait, but then he got called away, apparently to deal with a customer complaint, that's all they seemed to have around here, and she heard the black start to laugh, and Marj thought, *She'd better not be laughing about* me. *Because there is nothing funny about this or the way it is being handled. People can be sued for their behavior and that woman should know it,* but the laughter was grating nonetheless, distant, over by the vault, she was having a mighty laugh with the Persian, Marj didn't think it was at her expense anymore, probably just sharing a dumb joke, the 2 tittering away like the old woman's problems had ceased to exist or were something that wouldn't stop the world for *one iota of a single second.* Marj had the very same feeling when Hamilton was hooked up in the CCU and she heard nurses laughing somewhere while the life drained out of him. She grew lightheaded and decided to go home without even making the effort to announce her intentions.

SHE forgot where the Imperial was parked then had a violent attack of diarrhea. She found it, almost by chance.

There was a vending machine with free papers and she grabbed some to sit on so she wouldn't stain the leather seat. On the way home she was almost struck by another car and winced at the imprecations of the driver as he reentered traffic.

She stripped off her soggy dress, put it in a Glad bag, and ran a hot bath. She got the notepad with the numbers on it and called

Joan's house, thinking it was her cell, but hung up before being connected. She rang again, got a message, then put down the receiver without leaving word. She thought of phoning Lucas—maybe everyone had been wrong about him and the Bonita gal, but who *was* everyone?—and wanted desperately to call Jeff Chandler and the woman from Wells too, kicking herself for having left their cards at the bank. How could she have left their cards with those bloodless people? Though maybe it was best to sit tight: the pair were possibly "scammers," that was the word her daughter used, even though Marj couldn't believe it. They had been so kind! They were *real*. She didn't trust the thin man, the black, *or* their double-doored nonsense as far as she could throw them. She thought of calling Joan again . . . she wished Ham were there, her white knight, always so protective, like her father was, so polite and respectful yet intimidating, *he* would have known how to deal with these people, he wouldn't have allowed anyone into the house in the 1st place, and now she wondered about that bureaucrat who said he was going to call the police—what police? Was it really her bank, or something that *looked* like her bank? It sure seemed different. She didn't recognize anyone there either. (It was as if they were actors.) Hadn't she been there just a few days ago? How would they have put those double doors in so quickly? That was a big job! Maybe she'd ask Cora about it, but Cora did her banking at Fremont, on Wilshire. Maybe Stein would know. Stein probably used a lot of banks. Yes, she would ask Cora to ask Stein if he'd noticed any renovations at Pico-Robertson. He might even have "information," like businessmen sometimes do. Maybe he would know if this particular branch was notorious for defrauding the elderly.

She turned off the faucet.

It simply couldn't be true that she had no money in her accounts! The agent and the Wells lady made her write a series of checks because they said it was absolutely necessary, in order to catch AKA Mr Weyerhauser in the act, that was the way the Bureau did it so the charges would stick. The Bureau insisted it be done like that or else the gang would "strike again." Besides, there was always the chance it was an inside job and they said that if the money was in their hands, there would be no question of its being safe. *Like a good neighbor, State Farm is there.* So she wrote out the checks and they gave her receipts and told her what time to go to the bank because they would need her to identify AKA Mr Weyerhauser—they always called him that, AKA Mr Weyerhauser—they said exactly when to come because she was "critical" to the arrest, the eyewitness who would seal the ringleader's fate. They needed her to ensure this would *never* happen again.

(She remembered the agent had said, "You are my hero.")

Marj climbed in the tub, along with her soiled slip and underwear. *That was dumb,* she thought, she should have washed herself 1st, but what was done was done. They floated around her like flotsam from the *Titanic.* She soaped up her itchy behind. The phone rang and she leapt from the bath, and barely caught herself from falling, thinking it was someone from the bank. Trudy, from the Travel Gals, was on the line. She'd put together a wonderful "mother-daughter package" at a phenomenal rate—a 2 week trip that took in Bombay, Delhi, and Agra. Marj stood there sopping and shivering and said that she couldn't talk just now. She was on her way back to the tub when the phone rang again.

"Mother?"

"Who—Joan?"

"Mommy, it's me! I was in an accident!"

"Joan! Where—where are you? My God—"

"I—it was my fault. Oh God, Mother! The woman—she's hurt! I'm going to miss my plane. I'm going to lose the job! I'm going to lose the entire fucking job and all the work I've done!"

"Where are you? Baby? Baby! Are you all right?"

"Yes!" She took a moment to pull herself together. "I'm—I'm OK." She started to whimper. "The man says it was my fault and he—he wants to talk to you . . ."

"Hullo?"

"Hullo?"

"Hello, who's this?"

"This is Arnold Mathers, who's *this?*"

"*Marjorie Herlihy.* I'm her *mother.* Is she all right—"

"Well, *I'm* the guy whose car your daughter just hit! My wife is having a fuckin miscarriage! Your daughter hit my wife! I think she's drunk, or on drugs!"

"I'm sure she didn't mean—"

"We are *very* badly shaken up. The paramedics are here and my wife is bleeding from between her legs!"

The man started choking back tears.

"We're going to lose the baby!" cried a woman.

"Take deep breaths, darling. It's gonna to be OK."

"What can I—how can I—"

"Hello? Who is this?"

"This is Marjorie Herlihy! May I *please* speak to my daughter?"

"This is Antonio Borgosa. I'm a lawyer—I saw the whole thing. Your daughter was clearly at fault. It's Joan Herlihy, correct?"

"Yes—"

"We're calling from the County of Marin. Did you know your daughter was up north?"

"Yes . . ."

"Well, she's in trouble, *big-time.* The woman she ran into was 6 months pregnant."

A man said over and over, "I have to go with my wife! I need to go with my wife to the hospital!"

"Listen," said the lawyer. "There's something you can do and the gentleman said he won't press charges."

"What is it? Tell me—"

"Hullo?"

"Hello? Who is this?" said Marj.

"The father of the baby your hopped-up daughter just snuffed!"

"Oh God!"

"That's right—*killed.* Now *you* listen to *me*—"

Joan cried out, "Mommy, do what he says, do what he says!"

"Oh Lord Lord Lord Lord."

Marj sat on the floor, the shit pouring out of her. She was cramping and blanching, her eyes watery from pain. She put a fist in her mouth and bit down.

"Just *listen* to me. I don't want to deal with the insurance companies. I *hate* insurance companies."

"Mommy!" Her daughter grabbed the phone. "Mama, I think my insurance *lapsed*. I don't even think I *have* insurance! Oh God, am I going to lose my job? The job up north? And the condo? Mama, if I can't get on the plane I am going to lose everything!"

"But they said you already—that they were calling . . ."

The nasty man got back on the line.

"I want you to get your jewelry and put it in a little suitcase— *everything you have.* That means wedding and engagement rings, necklaces, pins, all the crap that dead prick husband ever gave you, understand? Put it in a bag, get in your car and *bring* it— now!"

"Please! I don't know where—I don't I can't I—"

"Bring it to me *now,* you hundred-year-old monkeycunt, or you will regret the day you were born! My wife is bleeding internally and our baby is dead! Because of your fucked-up daughter! You spawned her! A junkie pig who turns tricks in Porta-Potties!"

"Mister, please! She'll do it! She'll do it! Mommy!"

"Get the jewelry."

"Mama, I'm so scared! There's blood, everywhere!"

"Get the jewelry and don't forget the opal! *You are human garbage, do you understand?* Get the rings and the diamonds and the *everything,* put em in a bag, and sit your skinny terminal gullible ass in the car and *wait.* In the fucking *driveway.* And don't fucking *talk* to anyone or I will dig the eyes from your daughter's head and fuck her skull with doggie-dicks. Am I making myself clear?"

"Mommy!"

"The baby's dead! The baby's dead!"

"I will lock little Joanie in jail with *maggots* and *animals.* Do you hear me, you deaf and dumb geriatrical cunt? I'll be there in 5 minutes, OK, senile shithole? *5 minutes*—or I will kick your daughter in the stomach till she bleeds from her ass and her eyes!" He started to sob. "My baby is dead! Do you understand, Mrs Herlihy? Your daughter killed my little girl!"

"Mommy! Help me! Help me! Help me!"

"Let me talk to my daughter! Let me talk to her!"

"Hi! This is Antonio *Villaraigosa* again! I am a personal injury attorney with many, many years experience. Listen, this gentleman is agitated, he is very emotional, but I think it is best from the legal point of view that you do as he says."

There was a muffle of laughter and sirens and shouting before a breathless Joan got on the line. "Mommy, are you going to help me? Are you going to do as they say?"

"Yes! Of course," she said, already struggling to remove the ring, the ring she hadn't taken off in more than 30 years. Her finger was swollen and she went to get soap. "I will, baby! Hold tight! Hold tight!"

"Hurry!" screamed Joan.

The line went dead.

LXV.

JOAN

SHE deliberately hadn't packed the vintage hippo-hide Velextra suitcase he bought her at auction, the one that belonged to Maria Callas. She said, *You've really got a thing for carry-ons, huh.* Well, it wasn't *actually* hippo but "the skin of Ari O's testes"—typical gross-out-mode Lew.

Her plan was to stay overnight then rush home to Mom. Maybe Pradeep could help with a referral, but the woman at the bank seemed on top of it. She wasn't exactly sure what a lawyer would do other than steal more money.

Everything Barbet had said was beginning to feel like the truth. The trip seemed a ruse, more of a rendezvous to talk about the pregnancy than anything else. She was determined not to play that game, or capitulate to her own insecurities; she'd made a solemn promise to give it her best. Anyway, there was plenty to distract her. Aside from the thermodynamics of manipulating Lew Freiberg into saying yes to the commission, she needed to oversee the final details of *Full Fathom*'s chapel unveiling (Barbet's impotent little PT Barnum extravaganza). She didn't really have the energy. Her mother's ordeal had sapped her; putting the nightmare on hold didn't make it go away. One of the major comforts—that Mom wasn't dependent on her for financial help—had been yanked from under her.

So she got out her voluminous Prada duffel and threw in a favorite Miss Sixty smock, the Bless skirtrousers, the Loro Piano cashmere hoodie and Van Steenbergen shift, the Judith Lieber minaudière, the Narciso Rodriguez devil-red housecoat, the Project Alabama T-shirts, a D&G tulle/lace babydoll pearl and crystal-encrusted dress (Lew got her that), the Marc Jacobs silk organza ruffle skirt (Pradeep) and Marni taffeta slip, along with Louboutin espadrilles, Comme des Garçons ballet flats, Manolo zebra-print pony slingbacks, MJ mary janes, a pair of black-and-white Converse; antioxidants, exfoliants, extracts, amino acids, and wrinkle reducers; L'Eau d'Issey, Dior J'Adore, and Le Couvent des Minimes creams, balms, and gels. She was a sucker for any kind of overpriced unguent purported to be made for hundreds of years by ascetic nuns or monks. The world was such a load of bull. Even the Pope wore Prada. They called it papal product placement. (Papal Bull.)

Onboard, she flipped through the pimp-ride Robb Reports they always have in private planes and limos. There was an article about a travel agency that specialized in arranging vacations for people and their pets—hiking tours through Provence, "tandem massages" at Las Ventanas Al Paraiso, charters that round-tripped from Jersey to Paris for a paltry $70,000. A sidebar detailed a new fad where people danced with dogs "freestyle"—specialty cruises where everyone got dressed up and big bands played "Footloose" while you boogied in white tie with Rover. They called it "K-9 dance sport" and "interpretive dance to music." "Humans and dogs have essentially the same genes," said an event organizer. "Every gene has a gene with the same function in the other genome. Did you know there are dogs who've been trained to sniff bladder cancer in humans?" She laughed and tore it out to show Lew because he was so big on helping the tsunami strays. Joan had perversely tried to swing some of his efforts over to helping 4-legged Katrina orphans, but ever since Lew heard about T Boone Pickens and his wife arranging Marines-assisted canine convoys to the New Orleans airport, 45,000 dollar trips on 737s to LAX replete with decon sponge baths, solicitous "caregivers," quarantines, archival photographs (for the Internet), and microchip implants, he just didn't want to hear about it. *Operation Orphans of the Storm, Pet Rescue Katrina.* That's what they were calling it. The whole menagerie was heading for San Francisco, and Lew finally laughed when she told him that. He was moved to trumpet his favorite slogan: "We all have AIDS! We all have AIDS!"

—more articles on *El Zorro!* Right there, wedged between the usual glossy, photo-accompanied essays on 3,000,000 dollar timepieces and 7,000,000 dollar collection-of-Ralph-Lauren speedsters: ZH was truly the *fortissimo* fatass female genius-darling of the starchitectural cosmos. Team Hadid was putting up the "1st building on its home turf of London." Well, hoop-dee-fucking-doo. Team Hadid was building an entire floor of the Hotel Puerta América in Madrid—with "no furniture per se: the entire igloo-esque space molded from blinding white LG Hi-Macs, with ame-boid walls, sprout shelves, and an iceberglike slab that doubles as a seat." *Her fat ass* needs *a double seat.* The hostelry, built by Jean Nouvel, was going to have an Arata Isozaki floor, a Norman Foster floor, a Ron Arad floor, a John Pawson floor, an Eve Castro and Holger Kehne floor, a Whatever World-Class Whore They Wanted floor. *But they didn't want* me. *L'il ol Napa winemaker, me. Boo hoo hoo.* And, ohmygod, it said Hadid's rooms had her own branded linens! She was already doing linens! Next thing you know *El Zorro* would be redecorating Wormwood Scrubs . . . she was erecting a tower in Marseille for the French shipping firm CMA CGM. "Zaha Hadid's office is on a roll." Thus went the hyperventilated Robber Baron Report text, accompanied by ZH's usual swoopy silverized stochastic cartoonlike computer renderings. *El Zorro* and her new BMW plant in Leipzig . . . *Extra! Extra! Hadid Turns Auto Assembly Line into Catwalk!* Had the world gone mad? Was it really such a slow news day? Was everyone *all* that interested? The critics were *obsessed.* Z was *breaking down hegemonies* and *evoking the silent spacecraft of Stanley Kubrick's* 2001. Z was *transforming assembly plants into choreographed, mechanized ballets.* "Visually, her early work has all the dynamic energy of a Futurist painting by Boccioni or Balla, but its forms also reflect a desire to reverse Modernism's dehu-manizing effects." Excuse me while I suck Pritzker dick. Cunt cunt *cunt.* Iraqi cunt cunt *cunt. FatIraqifatIraqifatIraqi* cunt. Fat Iraqi *cu*—

Joan dipped into her briefcase. If she was going to be persua-sive, she needed to do a little cramming. She'd brought along a monograph with the detailed history and charcoal renderings of a famous mem that was never built. The structure, called the Dan-teum, was supposed to have been a monument to fascism. The project, fervently embraced by Mussolini (one of the Florentine poet's die-hard fans), was meant to reflect the ineffable canticles of

the *Commedia*. The slim volume had an epigraph that gave Joan
comfort, attributed to Le Corbusier: "In a complete and successful
work there are hidden masses of implications, a veritable world
which reveals itself to those whom it may concern—which means:
to those who deserve it." It made her feel better that Il Duce's
labyrinth had remained imaginary. The grimly intimate illustrations were nothing like the grandiose batshit digital Etch-A-
Sketches of contemporary megalostarchifuckers, being sad and
quixotic and almost macabre, with a precursory whiff of the art of
the Outsider. She wanted to show Lew the quote (not the book).
There were clippings on Goldsworthy in her briefcase as well; a
catalog of pen-and-ink studies by the Romantic "sepulcher artist"
Joseph Gandy, including the visionary "Design for a Cast-Iron
Necropolis"; a totemic lucky-rabbit copy of Vitruvius's *The Ten
Books of Architecture* (with its heavily dog-eared Altars section);
a Penguin Classics *The Rig Veda;* plus a few of Rem K's wham-
bang pseudotrenchant overgraphicized overhyped colleague-
condescending essays—all in all, not much in her quiver. *Baby On
Board. That's what I* really *have, let's face it,* and in the end (or the
beginning anyway) it was way more than nothing: *Baby On Board.*
(Say it again.) (*You can say* that *again.*) Baby On Board—by far the
heaviest blueprint in her portfolio these days. Nothin says lovin
like something from the oven. *Praise the Lord and pass the amnio-
centesis . . .*

What had she to prove, beyond that?

She called her partner from the plane. He had whimsically decided to detour from Rancho Mirage to Wim Wenders's favorite
spa-tel, the Miracle Manor, in Desert Hot Springs. (In Barbet's
world, it wasn't true Americana unless it was already staked,
claimed, and fetishized by some defanged international auteur.)
He told her he'd just spoken to "the boys" and *Full Fathom* had
nearly arrived at the Freiberg Love Chapel. *Thanks for the update.*
PT Barbet reiterated that Lew wasn't supposed to see anything till
"magic hour," when it would be poised for maximum effect; she
actually thought that was one of his better ideas. The dusky Napa
light would look seriously beautiful leaking onto the X-Acto'd design through the church's clerestory windows.

Iᴛ was cold when she disembarked. A muddy Range Rover met her. A steward handed her duffel to the driver, who confirmed that the model was on its way "to property."

The chapel, right?

Right.

Right on.

Hᴇ was on the porch of his brother's house, waiting. They embraced then went in.

She was careful not to be too demonstrative, as if reflecting the superfetated sanctity of enceinte status. She sat in the living room; he vanished and returned. Without mentioning the *issue,* he treated her with nearly comic, infanticipatory courtliness.

He filled her in on what was happening with his son. When the boy set a small fire on the Mendocino property, the shrink made the bold diagnosis that Axel was out of control. Lew and his ex checked him into a hospital in Monterey. He was in lockdown, without family visits for at least 10 days—those were the rules.

Fanny, Lew's 9 year old, bounced in, trailed by a nanny. The sweet, unguarded girl instantly seized Joan's hand, wanting to show off the new playhouses. The Memorialist was charmed and so was Lew. The pigtailed child forcefully led them back through many rooms, past a smiling kitchen staff, out the rear entrance. For some reason, the relentlessly quotidian slicing and dicing of food preparation put a scare in Joan.

Around 50 yards off, there they were: 2 "chalets" with slide tubes and colorful rooftops connected by a bridge. "There's elec-*tri*city," said Fanny. Her caretaker chimed in that a local lady put the whole thing up. Lew added that the same woman had built customized "kiddie-pads" for the broods of the Grateful Dead and the "Don't Worry, Be Happy" guy. As Fanny tugged Joan into one of the munchkin-sized entrances (she had to duck), Drea emerged from the other playhouse. The miniature structures had working plumbing, and were insulated so the girls could have overnights, with chaperones pitched in an adjacent tent. Lew said, "The things cost a hundred and 8 fucking thousand dollars."

THEY had a light lunch.
Lew spoke about acquiring art. He said he wanted to be more of a "radical curator," and not just "play musical chairs" with other collectors at auction. He asked for Joan's general opinion on a few things, nothing heavy or loaded. He told her he'd been thinking about building a large space for a piece by a New Yorker whose latest installation was basically composed of 50,000 lbs of Home Depot topsoil blended with compost, the latter of which came from Rikers Island Prison. He also liked the work of an artist who literally ate her way through drywall—he thought that was "ballsy." When she didn't respond, he said that "Andy"—as in Goldsworthy—had turned him onto the photographed work of Ana Mendieta, "the chick who jumped out the window."

"Jesus," said Joan wryly. "Pretty soon you're gonna want to 'collect' that woman who films herself fucking her patrons."

Lew laughed and said, "I haven't heard about her—but now I'm going to find out."

HE smiled and took her hand as they strolled. Her mind felt clunky; she tried to read the meaning of his gesture, but failed. Everything was failing her, even the light.

She got butterflies, thinking of *Full Fathom Five* ensconced in the chapel where they'd held services for Samuel and Esther, a honeyed, harmonious paradox of modernist design infused by the *wabi sabi* aesthetic of George Nakashima, the exterior resembling a concretized origami folly, the interior filled with shoji screens commingling with lustrous walnut, English oak burl, and even the 18th century ball-and-claw mahogany footware of John Townsend. But mostly, it was Nakashima's show. She remembered Pradeep telling her that the legendary sculptor had been the disciple of a guru in India, and helped design an ashram there; he'd built temples and other worshiperies in Japan, and a monastery in New Mexico too. Lew admitted that his sister-in-law was actually the one who'd turned him onto the old master. Having dutifully done his homework (he was really good at homework), the well-tempered dilettante felt comfortable enough regurgitating someone else's description of Nakashima as "part hippie-Buddhist and part Shaker, a tie-dyed Japanese Druid."

It was golden time.

They were getting closer to the church.

"Look," he said, "this is going to be hard, but I want you to know that I've gone in another direction."

She didn't have a clue what he meant. Was he talking about their child? Had he somehow managed to have it aborted without her knowing? He saw she was perplexed, and segued into the crudely inenarrable.

"You're going keep it. You're going to have the baby, right?"

"Yes."

"Then you've already won the competition."

Joan looked at him as if she were lucid dreaming.

They kept walking as he spoke.

"I fired Mr Koolhaas—he's a Royal Dutch pain in the ass. He likes to 'waste space'—that's what he said! He can waste someone else's—and their time too. I do want to look at what you've come up with, hell, I know how hard you've worked, Joan, and maybe we can wind up incorporating some of it. A compromise. That's why I wanted you up here . . . and for selfish reasons as well."

"You haven't even seen what we've done."

"That's not the point, Joan. It never is. And you know it."

She was in the midst of choosing not to hate him—like being in a wind tunnel filled with thousands of delicate, whirring gears, unmoored, pelting her like moths and molecular machines. It all happened with lightning speed, and once she was finished armoring she would have to reenact the same process, so as not to hate herself.

"I'm going to do something different." Pause. "I'm going with Santiago."

"Santiago?"

"Calatrava. I just fell in love with his *spanwork*. I think that's what this thing's going to require. Have you seen the bridge he did up north? And the winery in Spain? The *Bodegas Ysios*—for *Isis,* the Egyptian god. Am I pronouncing it right? I saw him on Charlie Rose and something clicked. I've already bought 2 of those 'Torso' townhouses. Gonna be the 6th tallest building in the city (if it ever gets built), and I got the top 2 cubes."

Not hating him would be harder than she thought.

She struggled to regain her footing—now she was on one of those bridges (not a Calatrava) from old movies, the threadbare sort spanning mile-deep gorges. She knew his "spanwork" but wasn't familiar with the winery; Lew probably saw it in *Dwell,* or the big Phaidon book. Calatrava was all right; at least he wasn't a grandstanding ass like the others. A plainspoken, humble engineer. Gifted. Still, if Lew was going to "do something different," she would have put her money on Herzog & de Meuron.

She broke away, jogging to the site where her calibrated flatbed pond would have lain. *Bullshit amateur hour idea anyway.* He chased after as she cantered toward the meadow through a fledgling allée of young trees, reveling in the light and open space, the windchill that preceded darkness. *He should just leave it like this,* she thought. *Open, without markings. Anything human would ruin it. That's what Goldsworthy would do. Maybe that's what Calatrava had in mind—a big John Cage* nothing. *Maybe the engineer suggested putting his signature batwings someplace you couldn't even see, 2 white little boomerangs high in a tree, maybe Lew* loved *that and was going to pay millions of dollars for tiny trademark))s wedged in a tree . . .*

That would be the perfect memorial—more perfect than a bastard child.

She was crying like some idiot now and Lew offered apologies, but that's not what she wanted. He caught up right around where the ashes were to be buried, and Joan brought him down onto her, in the grove of crepuscular light.

LXVI

RAY

GHULPA started to hemorrhage and had to go to the hospital.

The doctor said she should stay because he wanted to make certain she wouldn't get out of bed. He didn't even want her up to use the bathroom and wasn't sure she would follow his orders, if at home. The cousins came and went, riding bedpan herd, and giving her spongebaths. They put a cot in the room; there was a futon too. The old man was lonely and slept over a few nights but she finally kicked him out. Ghulpa said he was in the nurses' way, and besides it wasn't proper since they were unmarried. He said he could remedy that, though now whenever Ray mentioned "getting hitched" she grew stern, saying it was impossible, if anyone were to ever find out where she was she'd be sent back to "that terrible country," and because of her ingratitude, she couldn't rely on the CG—Pradeep or his wife, the saintly Manonamani (she cried as she mentioned her name)—to help, especially considering her "illegimate" condition.

One night Ghulpa had a fever and spoke of the Bengals. She said (and it was eerie to Ray) "the boy killed the tiger in the water with his tooth, as the serpent watched." She was still talking about *The Jungle Book*—that was how Mowgli killed Shere Kahn, with his long-knifed "tooth." "Bapu, I don't want to be a greedy girl!" she exclaimed, snapping her head toward the old man. He asked what she meant and she said, "They looted the cavern and dressed themselves like kings. They killed the old cobra, who no longer even had any poison left! But they could never leave the forest! *They were cursed because they wanted rubies.* I do not want rubies!" She lifted up from her bed just like a Bollywood actress. "I only wish to take care of the child, Bapu! Our baby! Raj, I am not a thief—*we are not thieves!* I do not steal from the City of Industry!"

After a moment, she said softly, "The city of Calcutta is my mother. Kali is my mother. Durgā is my mother."

He tried to calm her and the delirium soon passed. At the moment, there were no cousins to help him. He put a wet cloth on her forehead and she smiled.

DURING the day, the Artesians pressed Ghulpa's feet, which seemed to settle her nerves. One of the cousins taught the art of "Indian milking"—massaging the feet of infants—to rich, "desperate housewives" in Los Feliz, Brentwood, and the Palisades. Westerners paid a hundred-and-50-dollars an hour to be taught the "water wheel," "rowboat," and "butterfly." They even bought special massage mats for their babies, insisting the "doulas" (a chic, catchall term) use organic extra-virgin olive oil for the rubs. The various techniques were supposed to relieve constipation and colic, improve bonding, and enhance weight gain for preemies. The cousins laughed at an American handbook suggesting parents ask their babies' "permission" before a massage. They turned to one another and began a roundelay—"Would you like a massage, *baby?*"—and there was something musical about it, lovely for the old man to watch, like a scene from an operetta.

THE City of Industry had nervously preempted the lawyers' plans to request the agreed upon amount (500,000) with an offer of 750. All's well that ends well. The money would be available within the week, about half a million after legal fees.

Ray called Detective Staniel Lake. He wanted to tell him personally, and of Ghulpa's (difficult) pregnancy, and how much that had played a part in his decision. He wanted to invite the men who broke into the house that night to dinner as well, at the Pacific Dining Car. He wanted to tell the detective he had no hard feelings, in fact, it was the opposite, he wanted to say how much he appreciated Staniel's kindness and attention, and that he was only doing what he had to, and that he hoped he would understand.

He wanted the detective to run it past the others, to let everyone know he would be deeply honored to blow them to a round of porterhouses and the finest scotch whiskey. He really felt he owed them. In a way, they'd helped him begin a new life, and allowed an old man to right some old wrongs.

H E ran into Cora at the Center.

She was seriously considering putting Pahrump on a plane to a "resort spa" in Pittsburgh called the Cozy Inn. It had a great reputation and a 2,000,000 dollar building called the Mozart wing which the owner, a lady named Carol ("just like Cora, but with an *l*. Well, almost!"), had named after her terrier mutt, who died from the same type of cancer that afflicted Pahrump. All she needed was her son Stein's final word for the go-ahead. She went on to say there were 2 indoor pools, in the shape of a bone and a paw. Apart from "full medical," the Inn offered facial massages, weight-loss programs, leash-free nature walks, and acupuncture. But what moved Cora most was when she heard about Carol spending $85,000 to fly her Irish wolfhound to Colorado for a bone marrow transplant that extended his life for 10 months.

"Carol said it was the best investment she'd ever made."

They visited awhile longer while their pets got rehabbed, talking about the rumors of when the *Dog Whisperer* episode might air. Cora said there'd been *so much* excitement in the neighborhood since they came to film "our little show." And oh yes—the conversation drifted this way and that—her next-door *neighbor,* a *sweet,* sweet widow, had been *attacked,* right in her own driveway, and it was a *"tremendous thing"* because not too long ago, a "very nice Indian man" who owned the liquor store around the corner had been shot and *killed.* Cora said neither murderer nor attacker (the police said they weren't connected) had been found, and people were ordering security systems "en masse." Stein already had one installed and even considered surrounding the house with a tall fence. She was fighting him on that one, though if he agreed to sponsor Pahrump's trip to Pittsburgh, well, she just might have to cave in.

The old man shook his head at the general misfortune, but didn't connect the widow with the gal whose errant paper he'd fetched from the bush. Then one of the staffers walked toward them with Nip on a leash. He had a gleam in his eye, a bounce in his step, and his coat had been brushed. Ray remarked he looked "pretty as hell."

LXVII.

CHESTER

MAURIE Levin was transferred to rehab. His sister went home to Milwaukee. He was in a good place insurance-wise, but hadn't improved much physically. He couldn't talk and only his right hand showed spidery signs of life. The doctors didn't know whether the fingers' lightly spastic movements were involuntary or not; Chess *hoped* they were, because of a typically paranoid, free-floating thought that one day Maurie would be able to pick up a pen and "point the finger." Chess had the persistent feeling he had actually *spoken* to Maurie about what had happened, or that his friend *knew* the details of the prank through some sort of *osmosis*.

No one was sure how much he understood what was said to him either. Maurie occasionally made rubbery movements with his mouth, as if laboring to speak, but no words came. Laxmi stopped visiting because it was "just too sad." Chess went every day, and she respected him for that, not knowing he was driven by guilt. He continued to vacillate in regard to telling her the truth, or what most of the time he imagined the truth to be; whenever Chester courted confession, he fantasized about the consequences—Laxmi having an unexpected, antagonistic reaction, police becoming involved, etc—though lately he comforted himself with the heretical thought that Maurie's "TIA" (*trans ischemic attack,* as the doctors put it) was definitively coincidental to Viagra, and he'd been putting himself through the ringer *por nada.* Hell, medical journals and blogs reported cases of the Woodpecker actually helping to *save* kids with pulmonary hypertension. So how the fuck could it have felled an indestructible, able-bodied, cynical Jew like Maurie? Sometimes Chess thought if he told the cops they'd just shrug and put it in a report where it would gather dust. Besides, how could you even prove something like that? If they'd already run toxicology, no one ever told Chester the results. Maybe they told the sister. It'd probably have been negative, except for traces of weed—and weed never stroked anybody out. So if he *did* tell the cops, they'd either think he was a nut, or be unable to pursue it, because any traces of Viagra would long since have been pissed through a catheter or shat into a bedpan. (And who's to say the guy wasn't using it on his own.) Probably the police wouldn't even bother *taking* a report, that's how negligible and surreal the whole thing had become. *How viaggravating.* When Chess had such epiphanies, it stopped the nonsense in his head and made him feel as if he'd achieved context and clarity; then the moment would pass and he became paranoid again, eating away at himself.

The nurse said Mr Levin was in hydrotherapy but Chess could "go ahead on." The RNs liked it when friends or relatives showed interest (not the norm in cases as far gone as Maurie's). Visitors provided distraction and eased staff burden—unless they were pushy or demanding family members who stopped by just long enough to assess that their loved (more accurately, "liked," or unloved) ones were being treated with appalling indifference: troublemakers who never felt enough was being done. Chester clearly wasn't that way. He was in the "How can I help?" category, and his arrival brought smiles.

He walked down the hall, past rooms of stranded patients. It was strange: while there didn't seem to be any bonafide interaction between so-called caregivers and charges, the place was a blizzard of weirdly concentrated bustle, as if employees were preparing for a presidential visit. Chess felt as invisible as the inmates, which was actually a relief.

He found the hydrotherapy room, a large metal vat attended by a jovial fellow with ⌷ SERVANO–P.T. ⌷ pinned on his shirt.

"Hey, how ya doin?" said Servano.

Chess hovered in the doorway.

"All right."

"You a friend of my man Maurie's?"

"Yeah. How is he?"

"Maurie? He's the *king*. Doin *real* good. We're getting Maurie ready for the Olympics. *Special* Olympics. Ain't that right, Maurie?"

The patient was supported by a wide canvas sling, to prevent him from going under. The water churned and Servano PT's arms dipped beneath, working Maurie's legs.

"See, someone so young? When they're hit *hard?* My feeling is: get em in the water, *ASAP.* Cause he's a *young* man. Some of these docs'll tell you we can do this kind of work when they're in *bed,* but there ain't no *way.* I've seen water work *miracles.* Doctors want to write a lot of these patients off. Now it don't *look* like the King is doin much, but this is all about *retraining.* Retraining muscle groups and electrostatic energy. Ever heard of chakras? What's your name?"

"Chester—Chess."

"Your daddy a chess player?"

"Not that I know of."

"Well, *Chester Chakra,* I'm a big believer. In unlocking energies. I seen it happen too many times! And you don't need a stem cell transplant neither. Sometimes the brain decides to throw a roadblock up and you got to *lift the barrier.* Happens all the time, man, and they call it a miracle, but I just call it perseverity. Without *perseverity,* you're not gonna have no *miracle.* I seen it. Dozens of times. I seen it happen to my *on*tee. This was a few years ago. I went back to visit? In Alabama? She was just *layin* there. Man, the flies were on her and ain't *no*body there to wave em off. See, cause everybody too *busy.* Everybody in the *world* too busy to do what they *supposed* to. What they *paid* to do. And I said, Man, get her in the friggin water! What's the matter with you? You got a tub there just sittin, *put the lady in.* You ever heard of Lourdes, Chester? And I ain't talking Madonna's daughter, neither! She's cute. I seen pictures of her. Looks just like her mama. Eyebrows all bushy. Probably gonna know how to make *money* like her mama too. I stayed in Alabama a *month,* doin it all myself. Puttin Ontee in the water. And they let me do it too, cause they knew I was trained even though I didn't have a license. Not in Alabama, no way. The only license they care about in Alabama is a *driver's* license! Caballero, you better be carrying one when they stop you or they'll lock your brown ass in jail and throw away the key! So I worked with my ontee and I worked some other patients too— I'm an equal-opportunity healer when it comes to water—we lifted a lotta roadblocks, cleaned up *muchos* chakras, those folks practically gave me the key to the city when I left! I can go back and practice PT anytime. Hell, I could have myself a *private* practice. But I like Southern California. I was a little worried about em but the Alabamians turned out to be good people—not too many places would've let me do *half* the stuff I wound up doing. See, people are cool if you give em the chance. There's a few bad apples but mostly the world's full o' good people. And my ontee is *fine.* Now she walks with a cane, with a hand-carved owl on top. Don't even use a walker. And this is someone who was *almost* as bad off as the King here. She's 63 years young. And she's *workin* now, works out of the house, doing telephone surveys. She *good* at it too! *A productive member of society.* If you'd have seen her that 1st time? See, I used to work with a vet, in a vetirary hospital. *Very* fancy one. This vetirary was like the Hilton! The cat's meow! That's what they should have called it—cute, huh? The Cat's Meow. I told my sister that and she *laughed.* She said I should try to sell that name to someone on the Internet. My sister *good* at the Internet, sells shit on eBay all the time. So this vetirary facility was the cat's meow, and the dog's bark, too! And I saw *all* our furry friends getting better in the tubs. Most of em didn't like it at 1st but they chill. See, it's *all* about the water—ain't it, Maurie? Yeah, he doin fine. He doin *real* fine. Gonna be walkin outta here real soon, aren't you, King?"

Suddenly, Servano PT laughed.

He switched off the churning and motioned Chess to come over. He pointed in the water—Maurie had a hard-on.

"Now that's a *good* thing! See it? See how the water'll do ya? Now that's bad*ass.* That's badass *healing* chakra, the roadblocks are *liftin!* That's like the Red Sea parting! See? That means he's feelin better *already,* that's his way of *tellin* us about it! Isn't it,

King? H$_2$O'll *do* that to ya. Get you *excited* about shit again. And when the body starts to feel itself come alive like that, it's *all* good. That's the lower-body *chakras* workin and that leads to the heart and head chakras, *all* that's gonna be flowin. Sorry, Maurie! Ramona don't have no shift today!"

He laughed and winked and flicked on the churner. The visitor leaned against the wall, his mood plummeting. After a few more minutes of bullshitting, the PT asked Chess if he was aware that Medicaid was reimbursing rapists and child molesters for their Viagra prescriptions.

Servano said he thought that was a crime.

Why is he telling me this?

"The state does all *kinds* of crazy shit. See, Maurie, he's one of the *lucky* ones. It don't look like it but it's true. See, most these places are warehouses, but the doctors here are pretty good. We gotta pretty good level of care. Hell, *prisoners* get better treatment than civilians on the street. I mean, the jails are in bad shape, man. They got TB and syphilis and AIDS and now they got drug-resistant staph—everybody walkin around with boils on their faces filled with pus—guards too. Prisons are a natural breeding ground. Worse than kindygarden. But instead of cleaning up their act, they spend millions transporting these rapists. Know where they take em when they get sick? Beverly Hills! I am *serious,* Chester! They get breast implants too! I'm not shittin you, man! Hell, that nurse killer? What was his name, Speck? Speck kills 8 nurses, then goes and gets himself *implants,* on the tax-payer's expense. Now ain't that a bitch? Guess I should've said, Ain't *he* a bitch." He laughed at his joke. "I'm pretty sure he's dead now. Maybe his knockers got all infected or they were too heavy and smothered him in his sleep! Triple Ds! Stupid mother*fucker*—the state probably would've paid for a breast *reduction*. Naw, I think somebody killed him. I remember reading that. Or whatever. That was one fucker who *deserved* to die. I'm sorry to use bad language, Chester, hope you're not offended. But a man who shows no mercy should *be* shown no mercy. They should have thrown a nurse's outfit over those tits and hunted him down like he did those poor young girls. *Candystriped* his sick ass. I'm tellin you there's *hundreds* of these guys in jail, serial killers, baby rapers, cold bitches like the Green River Killer or the BTK, they'll never know how many lives they took and you know what? They get their teeth fixed in Beverly Hills cause if they don't, they can *sue* the whole *system,* they get their little pills for *herpes* and antidepressants when my *sister* can't even afford the *copay* on *Effexor.* Hell, just talkin about it makes me want to go all Prozac! But the BTK? He don't need no copay!"

T HE disgruntled lawyer was still opposed to settling out but Chess was adamant and Remar had no choice other than to concede. He said he'd get word to him soon.

The moment he hung up, Chess's phone rang—someone from an offshore pharmacy. They'd taken to calling at all hours to see if he wanted to renew his Vs: Vicodin, Valium, and Viagra. (They sent emails too: "FEEL BETTER TODAY!!!") Why had he given out his cell number? That was insane. *And why the fuck did I ever order online. They got my credit card now too.* Yesterday, the person from "Support Team 24" sounded like a righteous gangbanger. The cellphone flashed UNKNOWN CALLER and when he picked up, a Mexivoice said, "How ya doin, man?" The salesman/homeboy quickly corrected himself: "I mean, how are we doing today, sir?" There was a big turnover among the refill drones, and people were obviously being recruited from streets and malls. The most loyal Internet customers were the readily identifiable dope fiends; every 2 weeks Chess was alerted that it was discount week, and he was "good to go." What a farce. As a goof, he'd taken to saying, "Mr Herlihy overdosed—he's dead." But they just kept calling. He was in the machine now. Scary.

A piece of mail awaited, from New Horizon Credit Recovery. They were acting "on behalf of the US Department of Education" regarding a student loan Chess took out 25 years ago. He couldn't believe what he was reading. The collection agency was demanding 83 dollar monthly payments in lieu of "garnishing wages." They said it was in their power to seize tax refunds and even Social Security payments if he didn't comply. Chess panicked—the loan came to almost $27,000, including 7% interest. What if they found out about the *FNF* settlement? They were probably onto it already: that was their stock-in-trade. He got paranoid, and popped an Inderal/Vicodin/Xanax combo.

The timing of the letter was strange, to say the least. Maybe he was in a secret database of people who were about to get windfalls. He wondered if that was something he should consult Remar about but the lawyer wasn't too happy with him right now, and might use it as another reason why Chester should hold out for a jury. A fleeting thought occurred that Remar was actually in cahoots with New Horizon, or even that the "recovery center" was a "dummy" entity the law firm resorted to using with hard-head clients. It didn't really make sense—that would be totally illegal, and he doubted if Remar would so actively jeopardize his livelihood. But if New Horizon *were* real, maybe the lawyer *had* been in touch, promising them X amount on the dollar, and was soon to leverage the debt as a tool to *force* Chess to hang in and sue for everything *FNF*'s parent company was worth.

He pushed the weird notion from his head.

He lay down and smoked a joint, drifting back to that 1st time he was alone with Maurie after the "incident." It was at the desert hospital: Chess cried and told his friend he was sorry. At least, that's what he *thought* had happened. He distinctly remembered *something*. Still, much of it was a blur. (Chess figured he probably had a little PTSS goin on.) He couldn't perfectly recall if, in a seizure of guilt, he had actually *said* something to Maurie about having pill-*Punk'd* him. The more stoned he got, and the more he obsessed, both false and real memories became deeply plausible. Why did he have such a big mouth? If Levin *did* get better, and was finally able to write or speak—even if he was still wearing a *diaper*—it would *definitely* be the major thing on his mind to share. with the world, i.e., *hospital staff and police*—every fiber of his being would be marshaled to ask Chess what the fuck he'd meant by his weepy bedside apologia, or even likelier, stealthily bypass the man who had paralyzed him and wheel his drippy ass right to the authorities, or *Servano PT*, or whoever was handy.

Chess was seized by vertigo. He gripped the mattress and waited a few minutes for it to pass. He washed down 3 Compazines with a can of Squirt then idly picked up the letter from New Horizon. At the very bottom was a paragraph that said the debt would be canceled if a physician signed a form stating the borrower was "totally and permanently disabled." Yeah well there's my "out" right there. Maybe I should just change my name to Maurie Levin. It was almost funny.

He left the bed, steadied himself, and sat in the den to do a bit of Googling. There were chatrooms devoted to articulate people victimized by "credit recovery scams" long after falling on hard times. The collection agencies supposedly added 20% to whatever you owed. If the company going after you was legit—and your debt was remotely tied to some defunct government loan program—there was no way to dodge paying it back, not even through bankruptcy.

"These people are like the *Sopranos*," wrote TheLoan-Deranger. "You'd have to enter a witness protection program to get away, and even then it wouldn't help":

> the principal cellist of the Louisiana Philharmonic owed a hundred thousand dollars and the lawyers said he should cut back on expenses like *Internet access* and *gym membership* and his *cat*. They actually told him to get rid of his f-ing cat!!!!!!! This is a *musician* who teaches at *Tulane* but only makes 20K a year!!!!!!!! Because that is what AMERIKA pays its artists!!!!! So a judge threw the case out but it was *overturned* and a fed appellate court said he should go find a job *as a music store clerk*. He can't even visit his sick mother anymore!!!!!!!!!!!!!!!!!!

He got depressed and went back to bed.

He was running low on cash. Remar said that once the settlement was agreed on, it would take "around 2 weeks to cut a check." Before *that* happened, Chess would have to sign a release. Maybe he'd call the firm and ask the secretary if he could come in and take care of that early, to save time. She probably wouldn't know anything about it and would put him through to Remar. He doubted if the guy'd even take his call, unless it was explicitly about reversing engines and going ahead full steam with the suit. He thought about asking for an advance but remembered the lawyer saying he would only do that if his client promised to go all the way. That was out of the question now. Still, Chess was convinced he was doing the right thing.

He decided to go visit his mom again.

LXVIII.

MARJORIE

A T home, Joan tried getting into the bathroom but it was locked.

"Estrella?"

"Si," came the shyly muffled voice.

"Jesus," said Joan audibly. She stripped off her clothes right then and there. *I really need to get in, Estrella.*"

After a minute came a flush. The maid emerged with a tight smile. There was a stench.

"I've *told* you," said Joan. "If you have to use the shitcan—which you always *seem* to—*don't do it in the master bath.* Is that so difficult to comprehend? Is that asking too much? Because you can find another job. I can find you a job where all you do is clean *huge office building lavatories,* so that when nature calls—and nature seems to call a lot!—you can go do your business without disrupting your workday. OK, Estrella? Comprende? Comprende? *Bueno.*"

She was taken aback by her own fury.

She drove to her mother's, on the phone with Barbet most of the way. He was tender and supportive, pissed at Freiberg for stringing them along. Her partner swore (not that she needed reassurance) the Calatrava thing wouldn't happen because Lew was a mercurial Perelmanian headcase. Then he actually said she should "have the kid" (not that she needed his advice), but Joan didn't want to get into any kind of a thing about it, not on that level, and not now. She didn't want this sacred being tainted by his throwaway spite. She knew where Barbet was going next: she'd better have the lawyers put something on paper guaranteeing the child's future, something *exceedingly* in her favor. Joan wasn't worried—she would have the baby, and it never had anything to do with getting or not getting the Mem (Barbet informed her he

was having a tattoo inked on his left shoulder, the traditional
heart-pierced-by-arrow, only with MEM instead of MOM inside),
it had to do with the fact she was almost 40 fucking years old and
this was how God happened to have said *Ha*. Still, she let him rail
on. She knew he was hurt and only masking his disappointment.

They wound up talking about another job coming down the
pike, a Demeulemeester boutique in Belgium. When Barbet said
he'd make sure *Fathom* was on its way back safe and sound, Joan
told him Lew loved the model so much that he wanted it "on permanent exhibition" in the gallery Richard Gluckman was building in Mendocino. Barbet laughed out loud.

"Let him have it! *For a hundred-and-50,000.* It's no longer a maquette, now it's *art,* right? Keep it, baby! But send the check!
We'll invoice Guerdon."

W HEN she got to Marj's, the old Imperial was in front, the
window on the driver's side wavily broken.

It looked like there was blood.

Joan ashened.

Cora approached, holding the King Charles in her arms. It
yapped and she shushed, nuzzling its half-shaved crown. Shocky
and breathless, Joan asked what happened and the neighbor said
Marj was at the hospital.

Which hospital.

"Midway."

When.

"Last night."

Is she—

"I talked to her on the phone this morning."

That was the extent of it.

Joan got back in the Range Rover. Cora ran after to exclaim
through the passenger side that she had been the one to find her
mother, right here in the driveway. *What happened.* She said
Pahrump was "acting funny" and she was going to get Marj's
opinion about whether to call Stein or just take him to the vet but
no one answered the door, and on her way home she saw, or

thought she did, someone sitting in the car like a mannequin—it was Marj. She'd been assaulted. *What do you mean.* Cora said she was careful not to "disturb" anything before running to the house to dial 911. Then she returned with a damp towel, but didn't know what to do with it, and suddenly thought that the people who were responsible for this unspeakable act might still be "lurking."

She jerked the car into the street and headed up Robertson, speeddialing Barbet to tell him what was going on—he didn't answer and she left a message—then started to call Chess, before pressing END. Why bother?

The usual mindlessly galling, passive-aggressive encounters with testily indifferent functionaries and grinning eunuchized volunteers ensued, a tangle of nerves, short circuits, and wrong information, before mother and daughter reunited. Marj looked so awful. She smiled valiantly then collapsed in tears; the women held each other and Mom whispered, "I was so afraid they had hurt you!" Joan, uncomprehending, said she was fine and stroked the old woman's hair as they wept. An RN came to check vitals. She casually said that whoever had done this had broken the jaw and it would need to be "wired." Marj was half-naked. Joan reworked the cheap gown to cover her. She said she wanted to be alone with her mother and when the nurse ignored her, Joan insisted on speaking to a doctor. The Angel of Mercy, suddenly churlish, said she "would have one paged but they're *very* busy." Joan noticed wet bedsheets and the nurse assured her she was aware of it and would have them changed as soon as an orderly was free. Joan said if she would bring linen, or show her the linen closet, she would change them herself. The RN said she would have to wait and Joan said, Do not fuck with me, I want those sheets *changed,* do you understand? At that moment the nurse didn't have what it took to go up against her.

She was trying to digest it all. She sat holding her mother's hand. The orderly came with fresh sheets. He spoke to Marjorie as if she were a child, and it was tender and comforting to behold. Joan helped him put Mom in a chair. She told Marj she was going to make a few phone calls but the helper gently cautioned not to leave her because she might fall. The orderly said he could "loosely" tie her to the chair but Joan said no, she'd wait till the sheets were changed, and they could put her back in bed, with the rails up. At least he was a human being.

When it was done, she caught her breath outside the room. Who to contact 1st? She found the number of the FBI agent but it had been disconnected. (Joan didn't have the chance or even the inclination to check in from Mendocino. She'd been so black-jacked.) That gave her a funny feeling. She was digging in her wallet for that lady Cynthia's Wells Fargo card when a different nurse came in and handed her the name and number of a cop. Joan dialed and got right through—a direct line. Short introductions were made. The detective said he had just been heading to the hospital for a chat with Mrs Herlihy. He asked how her mother was doing (shorthand for *Do you think she's up for an interview?*) and Joan said not too well. He said that was understandable and wanted to know if Joan would be there when he arrived—that would be helpful—she said of course. The detective told her it would be 45 minutes or so depending on traffic. Joan wondered if it'd be OK to go to the house and pick up some things for her mom, and he said that was a great idea. *See you soon.*

She told Mom she was going home for her robe and toiletries and was there anything else she needed. Marj said, with a feeble smile that stabbed Joan's heart, that all the jewelry was gone, even the wedding ring Hamilton designed. Joan said not to worry, not to worry about anything but *getting better,* everything was insured, and that she was *here* now, her daughter was *here,* and wouldn't leave her, all she wanted was that Marj use her energy to get better, that was *the only thing that mattered.* OK, Mom? So is there anything else you need? Anything you can think of? Marj said there were a few books by the bed, one about Jesus and his visit to India, another about Christian missionaries. Also, if she'd keep an eye out for her addressbook because she wanted to phone Cora and check on Pahrump but couldn't for the life of her remember the number. Joan said she had it in her Treo, she had Cora's number, and Stein's too, and anyway she'd just seen Cora and would give her the message when she went back to Beverlywood. But did she want a special blanket or quilt? Something homey? Marj just smiled and shook her cracked, distended head, thanking her. *You are the most wonderful daughter.* Joan knew that she wasn't and it broke her heart all over again. They cried and hugged. Marj said to be careful with the addressbook because tucked inside was a fortune cookie message "with important numbers" that she used whenever she bought a lottery ticket at Riki's. Joan smiled and said, "Your secrets are safe with me, Ms Morningstar."

T HE house was musty. She opened a window. Then, suddenly mindful of the violent, mysterious intruder, slammed it shut; the glass trembled and paint flecked off the old wooden frame. She would get the detective's take on all of it—who was this person, and was he likely to come back? Shouldn't they be dusting the car for prints? That sort of thing.

A dress was on the bathroom floor, crumpled and soiled. There were new bags from Neiman's and Barneys, with extravagant receipts inside. That seemed uncharacteristic. The tub was filled with dirty water. Stockings and underthings floated like ratty, lifeless swamp creatures. Everything smelled of excrement. Joan wrung them out and drained the bath.

She wandered from room to room, each one somehow permeated by her mother, as if she were walking through Marj's body itself, and even though Joan had been there recently, it was such a long time since she'd actually *looked* with her eyes and her heart, so long since she'd stepped outside the castle of Self to consider Marjorie Rausch Herlihy née Donovan as a separate, living being, fading balletomane, frail and mortal, with longings, dreams, and desires, who'd suffered abandonment by one husband and death by another and the abandonment/death of her children too. Shame washed over her; Joan no longer recognized who she was. She may as well have been the thug who had violated the woman who bore her. Here and there were things from India she'd grown up around and still remembered from girlhood. Here and there were photographs, her father, Raymond, carefully excised, the

technique divorced women sometimes favored, memories halved
or quartered, images of Joan and her brother at an early age without either parent, when the proper editorial couldn't be surgically
achieved. There were unopened boxes of incense, and little wood-
and-copper Buddhas that she liked to give away as "friendship"
gifts.

On her mother's nightstand, a tidy stack: *The Life and Works of
Jesus in India, The Da Vinci Code: The Illustrated Edition, The Automatic Millionaire,* and *Die Rich and Tax Free!* Joan smiled when
she saw a picturebook of the Taj Mahal, and decided to bring that
along; maybe they'd make the trip afterall. *Is that her consolation
prize for the beating? You wretched cunt? You are such a cunt. Who
are you who are you who are you—*

It took longer to find the addressbook. The fortune cookie
adage was indeed tucked within. Tiny lottery numbers—the last
digit altered by Mom's quivery cursive—were printed beneath:
LOVE IS AROUND THE CORNER.

WHEN she returned to Midway, the detective was already
talking with Marj—though it was hard to understand her
through the clenched jaw—who was propped on pillows, and
seemed animated, enjoying the company of a gentleman. Joan
shook his hand then kissed her mother on the forehead and
showed off the little suitcase she'd retrieved. (The same one Marj
had packed for New York.) She pulled out the addressbook too,
with a corny magician's flourish, eliciting a broad, pained smile;
then set everything down beside the chair. Joan noticed the IV had
backed up with blood and rang for a nurse. Just then, the old
woman was brought a liquid supper. (The fracture had been
scheduled for repair tomorrow afternoon.) Joan said she was
going to have a talk with her "gentleman caller" and would be
right back. A volunteer, close to Marj's age, helped arrange the
tray on an overhanging bed table.

Detective Whitsell had a folder with a few phony documents
Marj had been given by the people who had drained her savings,

and assaulted her—he was convinced they were one and the same group. He shared everything he'd been able to piece together to date, which, in such a short time, seemed quite a bit: the initial, elaborate "Blind Sister" lottery scam; the "reload," where Mrs Herlihy was asked to virtually empty her accounts; the "recovery room," with an FBI twist, promising justice and restitution—the victim even brazenly asked to participate in capturing those who defrauded her; and finally, the blackmailing that began with the impersonation of Joan herself, the chaotic traffic accident and "miscarriage," the superfluous on-scene personal injury attorney, and so forth, ending with the robbery of precious jewels and aberrantly sadistic beating of the helpless mark. The detective had only meager remnants of the gang's handiwork (he'd worked a case 10 months ago that bore a striking resemblance)—receipts and other effluvia tucked in Marjorie's pocketbook; she'd handed them over when he arrived—and doubted that a search of the house would reveal much more because the team would have wisely erased the paper trail, covering their evidentiary tracks. They were very, very good.

Joan hyperventilated as she listened, unable to suppress her rage and her soul sickness. She told Detective Whitsell that she had spoken with the lady at the "bank" and been completely fooled. He said the gang excelled at "phonework," even using sound effects to make it seem like they worked out of large agencies or offices. He called them "stormchasers," elaborating how they exploited any form of natural disaster or human weakness. For example, he knew that a splinter gang associated with the group that fleeced her mother was still working Katrina, siphoning money from bogus Web sites. "You can't tell their homepages from the Red Cross's. Some are Aryan Brotherhood, believe it or not—*extremely* well done. They've got viral embeds: click on 'Hurricane Rebuild Update' then *Zap!* your personal info is history. Your identity's gone and you'll *never* get it back. One guy set up a site *before* the storm hit Louisiana! (They should have made him head of FEMA.) Other scams are a little 'dirtier,' like the Nigerian stuff we see, the '419s.' Misspellings, boldface pleas for money—is it boldface or baldface?—it's *baldfaced,* right?—'I lost everything including my wife.' That sort of deal. I've even heard of crews going down there to pick through garbage. And I don't mean Mardi Gras 'krewes.' What they're looking for are water-logged bank statements, Social Security cards, driver's licenses, and the like. Hell, a buddy of mine caught one up at Lindy Boggs—the hospital? They go right in the nursing homes and pick through patient records. It's pretty much beyond the pale.

"But we have individuals out *here* who are just as imaginative. You might have read about a fellow in the paper who gave a dona-tion of a hundred-and-12,000,000 to a little college in Northern California. They were so thrilled, they gave him a 1st edition of *The Origin of Species*—and arranged for the guy to be blessed by the Pope! A convicted felon! Of course, the pledges turned out to be completely spurious. The human animal has a primal need *to believe.* It's very important to *believe,* and there are folks out there who take advantage of that. I think it was St Mary's—St Mary's College. So at least your mom's in good company."

S HE stayed overnight at the hospital. Barbet stopped by. They had coffee in the cafeteria and commiserated.

After he left, she watched television while her mother slept. The usual reports of bombings, bird flu, and mass burials; anchors spoke of Death's details—always sketchy and sexily half-baked, like a stairwell dry hump—with a breathy, erotic edge to their voices. She zoned out and tried to read. It was after 10. There was a segment about a former TV journalist who'd recovered from cancer and now devoted his life to helping others who were dis-abled or trying to recover from catastrophic illnesses. The feature ended with a visit to a quadraplegic who spoke with the aid of a synthesizer. When the retired newsman asked the quad how he would now describe his life, the electronic voicebox replied, "I—am—happy—always."

She thought of Mom's fortune cookie *(love is around the corner)* and collapsed in silent tears.

LXIX.

JOAN

SHE punched in the destination—Detective Whitsell was kind enough to get her the exact address—and followed the yellow brick Mercantile Road to the City of Industry.

It was funny to her that a robotic female voice (*I am happy always. Love is around the corner*) guided her from point A to point B, point B to point C, and so on. The Woman was relentless and unwavering, automatically lowering the volume of her CD (a haunting Rachmaninoff chorale) to tell her to hold fast to this or that lane of this or that freeway; the Woman cut into phone conversations like a switchboard gossip, ordering Joan to exit, turn left, go a quarter of a mile to this street or avenue, *keep right*—a warmly disembodied automatrice, shepherding a 4-ton machine over subexurban grids until Joan reached the heart of the heart of the matter, the apartment complex fixed in ever-mutable nonnegotiable space and time where her supposed biological father allegedly resided, reverse paternity, aging mitochondrial DNA/GPS entity, who, like Mom, had recently been assaulted (unwarranted warrants) under true/false colors of authority, all interchangeable now, good cop/bad cop neverending.

The Woman said, "Your destination is ahead on the right. Your route guidance is now complete," and Joan laughed.

Oh, is it really?

She scoped her father's building then turned tail. Found a liquor store and bought Marlboro Lights, a Diet Coke, and a jumbo bag of Lay's chips (she hadn't smoked in 5 years). Sat in the car listening to *Rachi* then shut it down for a reality check. The symphonic backdrop for her own personal opera was overkill.

Drove back to the apartment and sat some more.

Took a cigarette out, didn't light it.

More scoping: a cheerless but well-kept area.

Left her car. Walked upstairs to the 2nd floor.

(Must be a haul for an old guy.)

Saw a brightly painted door, different than the others—replacement for the one they kicked in?

Got closer till she was staring at it.

Some heavy breathing on her side—#203B.

Heard the television: *loud.*

(Probably losing his hearing.)

I better just do this.

Because it was too easy to walk away: because she was effulgently depressed: because she was prone to hair-trigger tears: because her mother and the baby and the hormones had kicked her ass ragged, and broken down the doors of her own house.

Knock. Knock knock. *Knock knock knock knock knock.*

(She had lost, she was lost, *I am lost.*)

He stirred.

Stood.

She saw bearish shadows slowly moving.

Her heart snagged.

Ray greeted her—a dusty, frazzled screen now between them. He looked at her and smiled. She lost it. He was startled. Joan said she was sorry. He laughed with befuddlement while she wiped her eyes and shoved down tears. He opened the door. *You OK?* Asked how he could help. *He's kind.* She said—again, with sobby strangled self-conscious actressy laugh—I think you—I think you are my father. *I think you are my* He took a not unfriendly step back. (Literally taken aback.) *Oh. What is he going to do.* He asked her in, surprising. Pungent smell of Indian leftovers. *Are you . . . Joanie?* She nodded and sobbed and he offered his semifancy easychair. She couldn't take it. She needed something upright so's not to slip into a dream. *My Lord,* he said, not thinking to turn down the TV until he appeared cudgeled by its blare. *My Lord My Lord My Lord*

She told the old man her friend had read about him in the paper, a friend who was aware of her "other name." The Rausch name.

Oh my Lord. *Oh my Lord.*

Neither knew where to start but had already begun, brought together by the fates and the CG and the GPS, matchmade and ready-to-order by adenoidal androidal *I am happy always.*

(Love was just around the corner.)

Joan asked if he was all right, a good neutral question, meaning she heard he'd had a heart attack, or actually read about that, it was in the article. Yes he was, he said, eyes moistening now, hand trembling too, yes, he was all right.

Somewhere a dog squealed, cowering behind a chair.

Why, that's the Friar, he said, that's Friar Tuck. We call him Nip/Tuck, Nip for short. It gets a little complicated around here. She cautiously put her hand out but the dog lowgrowled and hunch-hunkered. He'll get used to you. Best not to pay any attention, that's what Cesar says. Don't lookim in the eye. Doin a helluva lot better, that one. *Did he get shot? I mean they said, I read, he got shot.* The man—her father!—said yes, the cops "put a slug in him" by mistake but he was much better, had a surgery, now he was just about 100%, tough old coot. Outlive us all.

The Friar waddled over and licked her hand and she saw the shaved patches, Raymond Rausch said for some reason the hair wasn't growing back in, and Joan thought of her mom—his ex!— and the awful beating she took, and again: wave of lipquavering tears. The nice thing being that a certain awed politesse had mercifully overtaken and they rested in quiet ancestral reverie not much different from the folksy, civil calmness between strangers who meet in extremis, no hurry, no worries, there was time, unbridgeable time, too much to speak of, no catching up to do in the usual sense, only a kind of tacit, preternatural, subterranean filling in, the homemade soupy soak of skinspirit and lineage, cellular charades, boardgame of the secret society of genomes, conditioning and destiny, of double helix and timespace serendipities. It was understood that for now there'd be no discussion of wife or mother, brother or son. For that, again, there'd be time and opportunity, at least that was the mutual assumption, which was, afterall, part of what was nice, nicely nice and relaxing. He *did* say, "What do you do?" and was pleased and nonplussed by her answer.

Once Joan got most of her tears out and Raymond leaked some

more as well, he offered her tea—she liked that, he could have said how about a beer or pot of coffee, which would have been fine, actually, any of it would be fine, what was she saying, what did it matter, *fuck my endless judging,* still, tea was what he suggested, jasmine, saying that his girlfriend *I hope he doesn't have a young girlfriend, she's probably younger than me oh shut up shut up* hadn't been well, she was "in hospital" (OG Victoriana-sounding phrase) adding with wizened not uncharming sprightly twinkle that his "gal" was "Preg. Nant" *oh God she's probably like 17* that made Joan cry then later laugh at the thought she could or should have blurted out *I'm pregnant too!* and also how surreal that maybe soon she would have a sister she had always wanted a sister, the tears not as heavy now as when she 1st arrived but still in shock. Watching her cry, for a million reasons Raymond Rausch sweetly seemed to feel bad for her, or with her, bad about that, about everything, and wishing/not knowing how he could help. She thought maybe he thought maybe he'd said too much? or the reference to a baby on the way   *Baby On Board* was insulting because of the fact she had been a toddler he'd discarded. But how nice that was, really, at his age, that's what her sunrise smile showed him, all unspoken, how nice though at his age ancient daughter suddenly materialized before him, how nice and mystically twisted the multiplicity of lives, the knot of this life, all life, their life *he was trying to remember what he used to call her, what was the nickname* and said it had taken him by surprise— the pregnancy—and she wasn't a young woman—the girl-friend—*what does he mean by not young*—and that she had to go to hospital and stay put awhile on doctor's orders.

She asked if there was anything he needed. *I guess this is my time. To ask of my parents what is needed. My time to caregive.* No, he said, he was going to have a nap (she could see him in his frailty and that her visit had packed a wallop). He thought he would lie down, she knew he meant the bedroom not the easychair, but Joan was welcome to stay and watch television, he made the invitation to be cordial, and that was lovely, truly, it was genuine, she stanched the tears again, saw he was knocked out, her visit knocked him out, knocked both them out. Her father was an old man.

Your route guidance is now complete.

They embraced when she left and she wept *again* and this time for some reason was embarrassed, Ray sensed it, she took a hard look at him now, all this time not having bothered to age him up in her head the way computers did on *CSI,* adding 70-odd years to the dad she hardly remembered, no, nothing, she saw nothing, she looked for Chess in his bones as a last resort but no, nothing, she would need to visit Beverlywood, maybe there existed a single photo Marjorie hadn't sheared but Joan wasn't sure; she flashed on movies about people who find lost loved ones that turn out to be impostors, arthouse films and even *Vertigo* (one of Pradeep's favorites), and in the same instant she thought, Stanford grad-student mode again, it's the *idea* of it, Myth of Reintegration, *regeneration, that's* what mattered—instinctively Joan thought, *No, this isn't the case, he is no impostor. This is my father,* Raymond Rausch—and there would be time to tell him everything that had happened since he left, though she would ask nothing in return, ever, wouldn't care to hear his explanations (if he had any), both too old for that, the porno cliché that Now was all that mattered was true, if he wanted to *share* it would be at *his* pace, the pace of myth, or maybe at the pace of what *she,* Joan Hennison Herlihy née Rausch could take, *that* was how to go, how they would do it, slowly but surely they'd turn, no urgency, competition/animosities long past, she had given the Memorial her best shot, the commission awarded to someone else, and now she was building something in her womb that needed no plan, committee, or ruling, no client permission, persuasions, consensus. There was nothing to decide. The site was selected and end-date affixed . . .

A burden lifted.

She felt even lighter as she swung onto the freeway, and—this time, aural navigation deactivated—wound her way home unguided by voices.

LXX.

RAY

MAIL had accumulated since Big Gulp was *in hospital.* He anxiously awaited the settlement agreement. Even though the attorneys said it was to be hand-delivered, the old man found himself retrieving mail with a lilt in his gait while the Friar followed, wagging his tail. Monsignor Tuck was in goodly fair shape. *Fare thee well.* Life was grand.

He opened the letter from an insurance company.

Frankly, <u>Raymond</u>, I'm puzzled . . .

Our marketing team is often confused over why more people don't request the facts about long-term care insurance. Knowledge is power!

If you've been putting off getting information, <u>Raymond</u>, <u>it's time to take another look</u> . . .

In 1999, with the enactment of The Health Insurance Portability and Accountability Act, our government provided tax incentives for long-term care insurance plans that meet certain standards. <u>Raymond</u>, <u>you should know about these tax incentives.</u>

The way I look at it, <u>Raymond</u>, you have so much to gain and absolutely nothing to lose. Thank you.

There was another:

Dear Raymond Rausch,

My name is Max Kibblerohden. I write the "Equity Builders" column for *MoneyInvest* magazine and serve as Chief Executive of Kibblerohden Portfolio Investments™. My firm manages over $15 billion for institutions and high-net-worth individuals.

I recognize you may not be considering doing anything differently with your investments right now. Regardless, I'd like to
send you a "care package" of useful insights, free and without
obligation.

A separate letter contained the "Confidential Request Form for
the Kibblerohden Portfolio Care Package™." It asked for appli-
cants to ✓ their "level of interest."

Total Investment Size:

O $0—500,000   O $1,000,000—3,000,000
O $500,000—750,000   O $3,000,000—5,000,000
O $750,000—1,000,000   O$5,000,000—10,000,000
                              O $10,000,000+

Mine'll be "$0–500,000."
(Ray wondered what would happen if someone ✓'d "$0.")
Without the settlement, he'd be in a terrible bind. What would
happen to his Big Gulp? He didn't care about himself, he was a
salty old dog just like the Friar, but he sure as heck didn't have the
kind of money you needed to support a newborn. The ACLU
even worked a deal with the hospital so BG could stay all this time
without financial worries. That was a lot of scratch.

Ray didn't think of himself as political but it seemed like every
day there was something on the TV or radio about how people
were hurting. The article in AARP said that 700,000 families
were driven to the poorhouse each year because of medical emergencies, middleclass folks with houses, college educations, and
good health coverage. Going bust over things like copays and cremation fees. Couples were still paying $800 a month for medica-
tion. 800 a month! How could that be? The article said these
people were *insured*. It made no kinda sense. Folks were alone and
isolated, the highlight of their day being when Meals on Wheels
dropped off supper. It was just like the Depression. Jesus God, he
didn't want to end up that way! He wanted to be a provider, to
provide for his woman and child. He'd screwed up the whole

thing before and wasn't going to let it happen again. (He realized that he hadn't properly apologized to Joanie when she was there—it still seemed like a dream—hadn't apologized at *all*. He'd been so shocked by her visit, it made him cross-eyed. She left her phone number and he would make sure to remedy that in the weeks to come.) He was done with screw-ups. He just read a pitiful story in the paper about a man who was sick the day his fellow employees pooled their money for Mega Millions. The "Lucky 7" worked at Kaiser Permanente and won $315,000,000 for the $3 each they'd put in. The poor bastard was suing. Claimed he should have been included but the "Lucky 7" said there wasn't even a casual agreement, that it was spontaneous, and anyhow the last time he'd gone in was over a year ago. Still, Ray could sympathize. "His day off cost him 39,000,000"—that's how the article began. That would be damn hard to take. No, Ray wasn't going to be left behind. Not like the captain in that *Twilight Zone* whose ship crashed on an asteroid and he became a kind of Mormon-style patriarch, keeping crew and passengers—and the generation to come—together in sound mind and body with tough love brimstone discipline, until one day, 25 years later, they were finally found by an American search-and-rescue team. Everyone couldn't wait to leave but the old man refused to board (his stubborn pride) and just as they were taking off he realized he was stranded. Alone. Changed his mind and chased after the ascending rocket. *Too late.* That hit Ray like a ton of bricks. Stuck with him from the day he 1st saw it.

He read a lot of magazines when he visited Ghulpa—*Time* and *Newsweek* and *Forbes*—they said big companies were dropping healthcare plans altogether and that seemed to Ray a crime. The corporations were gutting pension funds too (especially when they got bought and had their books cooked) and telling people to go invest hardwon earnings their damn selves. The workers could just go to hell. In *his* book, no one was supposed to be able to touch a pension fund, that was a God-given. Had someone changed the law? Social Security was going the same way with the blessings of the White House. Social Security was dryin up and they were putting an end to Amtrak too. The damn country wasn't going to have any more trains! But all those CEOs were rich men and didn't have to worry, they didn't *need* trains unless it was a hobby, in which case they could just go out and hire a private railcar and take a tour on any timetable they pleased. The article in *Time* said these CEO gents—homely looking nabobs in eyeglasses—could make 60 or 70,000,000 just by quitting their jobs! The CEO of Morgan Stanley got a hundred-and-13-point-7,000,000 dollars for *leaving*. The contract said that after he was gone, he was still entitled to full medical plus $250,000 a year plus an office and a secretary *for the rest of his life*. (Why would a man need an office and a secretary if he wasn't working?) That was no golden parachute— hell, there weren't enough elements in the Periodic Table to say what kind of parachute *that* was. He shook his head in disgust and laughed. Then off they'd go and get another job, sign another contract. Being a Chief Executive Quitter got you into a special country club. Somebody figured out that when that Exxon fella retired, he'd been making $144,573 a day *for 13 years*.

He wasn't on their level, but still thought himself a king. Ray had the notion that with the settlement from the City of Industry (he bet that BG would triple it in no time), he could buy private health insurance. If anything ever happened to Ghulpa or the baby, they'd have the finest treatment in the world. The old man wasn't thinking of himself—his shelf life, as he liked to put it, had long since expired. Even so, he made the cousins do a little research, and they used their computers to find a special kind of coverage that would pay for a decent convalescent home; he didn't want to drain money from the main account. The settlement would buy peace of mind and other things too, like the down payment on a house with a nice yard for the Friar.

A yard for their Lionel to crawl around in, and the cousins to throw parties. Maybe they'd even get married there.

G HULPA got ornery and wanted to leave Sisters of Mercy against medical advice. Even the Artesians couldn't influence her; they were having a hell of a time. The doctors finally said she could go home, but made BG sign a release. The family was worried she wouldn't stay in bed. Ray was afraid she'd miscarry. He was scared as hell but there wasn't a thing he could do about it. She was a hardhead.

He wasn't going to mention that his daughter had come to see him. The timing wasn't right. Anyhow, he hadn't wrapped his head around it himself—his Joanie!—not at all. Such a strange, strange deal. So beautiful, so educated. She dressed carefully, fastidiously, fashionably, like her mother. Since the visit, he'd been flooded with memories. He and Marj officially met in 1960 on a dance date. They went to the same church and he'd had an eye on her. Ray was on the rebound, still getting over a stormy shackjob with a redheaded waitress. A trumpeter friend, Bill Peterson— Jesus, the names from 50 years ago were really coming back, isn't that how it was with old age?—said he knew just the gal to cheer him up. Marjorie Donovan was an assistant to a mid-Wilshire bookkeeper. She was younger than him, on the brink of 23, a religious gal, not too stuffy. Ray wasn't even sure she'd say yes, he probably had Bill to thank. They wound up downtown. She was shy but quickly dazzled; he could tell she thought dancing at the Biltmore was the height of sophistication. (It came pretty close. Ray Rausch was a 30 year old man and knew a few tricks. He earned money as a part-time bartender but was a free spender and had to tap the trumpeter for the big night.) They swang and sashayed to the golden oldies, and the silver and brass ones too— "Save the Last Dance for Me." He could hear that in his head, note for note, clear as day. Marj was living with her father, a widower, and had the queer idea she wanted to go to India for missionary work. Ray remembered picking her up in his 52 Ford. Her dad would greet him, pipe in hand, very debonair. He'd been in the clothing business, fabric and knickknacks, a friendly man now retired.

The couple went horseback riding in Griffith Park. Ray couldn't believe he'd actually climbed on a horse—laughing at the memory—he got thrown and there was something about the way

she dusted him off, a sly grin reminiscent of Claudette Colbert
and Myrna Loy wrapped in one, and that's when he knew they
were going to have some kind of life together. That night he proposed and was befuddled to watch a diamond teardrop make a
plumb line to her smile. (Soaked it right up.) Her father wasn't too
thrilled, which surprised Ray at 1st before it didn't, and they
eloped to Bakersfield of all places, couldn't remember why, he
borrowed money from his friend again (Bill was making good in
the studios) and they moved to Culver City and had 2 beautiful
babies. Had wonderful times and a picket fence and then the
times weren't so wonderful and on a sunny nameless day he just
walked, like in a country song. Might even have said he was going
for cigarettes; it was like that. The old man quaked at the thought.
He told himself all these years that's what being married did,
some kind of allergy, never would have guessed it—but that just
didn't wash. Leaving the kids behind nearly killed him. Like the
Twilight Zone and the reluctant rocketeer: by the time he ran toward the ship, everything was finished. The children were aloft.
By then he was almost 40 and hated himself. He hated himself a
long, long while.

Now this old dog was gonna be a new daddy and God in His
merciful omnipotence had orchestrated that his daughter appear
at the door like a ghost in a play. He knew Marjorie had done the
job for which he wasn't man enough; she'd raised those kids
alone. He could never give her enough credit. She had mothered
and fathered them—how could he thank her, or express his pro-
found remorse, his regret? Suddenly, he focused on the boy. *I
should have asked Joanie about him. Why didn't I? I should have asked
about Chester. Joan probably thought: The heartless old coot, he didn't
even ask about his son!* But that wasn't it, and he hoped she understood. He didn't have it in him. It was enough just to look at her.
Almost too much having her there, it sucked the air from his
lungs, from the room. He was glad she had cried so much, not
glad, that wasn't the word, but it had been a good distraction
for Ray to comfort her, easier than falling apart. No, he would
have time, *now* he would, *they* would, all of them, it seemed God

wanted them *all* to have time, that was His plan, time to learn everything they needed to know about one another and just about anything else. Like one of those reunion stories he devoured in *People* or *Reader's Digest*. He would take his grown children to the Dining Car and knit everyone back together.

How amazing! All the while he'd been having funny dreams about Chester, but look who shows up at his door.

STANIEL Lake phoned to congratulate him on the settlement and Ray said, "Well, esteemed sir, you beat me to the punch. I was just going to call *you*." He could tell from the detective's tone that he was all right with it. Ray said to "keep it under your hat" because nothing had been "signed and sealed." Mr Lake laughed and said that might be difficult. Meaning, somehow everyone already knew.

The old man explained about Ghulpa and the pregnancy—Staniel was genuinely surprised and thrilled for them—and how he didn't hold anything against "the boys." He let the lawyers be lawyers because he wanted protection for his new family. The detective said he had absolutely no hard feelings, that no one did. Hell, he said he'd have done the same thing and that meant a lot to Ray. That was big of him.

He extended the Pacific Dining Car invitation and the detective said his colleagues would be honored to break bread. Ray wanted to make sure Staniel invited everyone who'd busted into the house, including the rookies. Staniel laughed and said he would but that Ray might have "quite a bill." The old man said not to worry, and began feeling upbeat for the 1st time in a while. Clean. He wasn't a user, and prided himself on doing the right thing. It particularly gave him pleasure to express gratitude when least expected—something which seemed to have gone out of style. Ray liked to think of it as one of his better traits, his faith in the essential goodness of people, he was an optimist about the human condition, he respected good intentions and longed to do kindnesses in return, except that he'd failed when it came to Marj and the kids, utterly and abysmally, and he knew it, but had to believe it was God's plan to teach him the hard lessons that made him what he was today. Truly, man learns through adversity.

His thoughts drifted back to the Biltmore, and how Marjorie felt in his arms, fevered and new, her glittery eyes reflecting the festively lit runway of life as they taxied toward its mysteries. He recalled his fears that night as well, compulsively checking his wallet to make sure the trumpeter's borrowed bills were still in place.

He'd really had a crush on that girl.

But Ghulpa, save the last dance for me.

LXXI.

CHESTER

His mom had been home a few weeks, her jaw sealed shut. What an intense bummer. It freaked him out to see her like that but he grew accustomed. Wirecutters were kept in the bedroom and kitchen in case she spit up and they needed to clear an airway. That was standard. Otherwise, people in her situation could choke on their own vomit.

Chess saw more of his sister than he had in years. When Joan 1st told him about the scammers he exploded with rage. He wanted to get his hands on them, for real. He didn't think *anyone* was pissed enough, including the cops.

Laxmi volunteered to help take care of Marj but his sister politely declined, having arranged for RNs during the day. Someone came to stay at night if Joan couldn't herself. The feeling he got was that she didn't trust him to sleep over, not alone anyway. That was cool. He'd rather not but the vibe was galling. Whatever. Let her do her princess controlly thing. He just wanted Mom to be comfortable—the woman had been through hell. If Joanie needed a lot of warm, hired bodies around, so be it. As long as they didn't steal anything, *no problemo*. If he caught anyone stealing, heads were definitely gonna roll. There *would* be blood on the tracks. Still, he didn't dig the *posturing*. She'd actually told Chess not to smoke weed "in front of the caregivers" and that was weird. Like that was his big plan. He started thinking Joan didn't want him to spend the night for fear he was going to nod out while Mom aspirated or whatever. The thing that *did* bother him was Joan's attitude toward *Laxmi,* who was nothing but a fucking Good Samaritan. Joan was a bit condescending, not that Laxmi even noticed, but Chester did, and he was ready to mix it up with little sis before realizing the whole thing was probably about age difference. *What a drag it is getting old.*

Laxmi was *hot* and Joan was *not* (so much anymore, anyway)—
so he let it slide.

MARJ made sure someone continued going to Riki's for lottery tickets chosen from the fortune cookie numbers. It was
the highlight of her day. The doctors said that Marjorie was depressed (she was now on Adderall, which Chess cadged when he
was bored: he thought he could make a killing with *Speed Thrills*
T-shirts) and that whatever gave her pleasure was a good thing. If
Joan or Chester couldn't make it to the liquor store, Cora or one of
the helpers went.

Mr P had taken a turn for the worse and was hospitalized
again—if you listened to the neighbor, he was the Lance Arm-
strong of Doggie World. She was down in the dumps herself; running little errands and reading the tabloids aloud to Marj were
pleasing distractions. She was a nice lady and all, and Chess could
see how it cheered her up just to hang with someone who was so
much more fucked. But that was cool. Just human nature. Even
though he didn't feel that way when he hung with Maurie.

The situation with his mom was a distraction for Chester as
well, and he visited Maurie less. He slowly understood that seeing
his friend wasn't such a healthy thing because it emanated not
from compassion but rather to assuage his own conscience and
even monitor the invalid's progress—to see with his own eyes if by
some fluke Maurie was getting closer to being able to articulate
what Chess may or may not have tearfully confessed. (If he *were*
getting better, the consequences could be both wonderful and terrible.) He still dallied with the idea of telling the police what happened but that fantasy was getting tired. Chess had even gone
online a few times, nearly presenting his case (anonymously) à la
"this is what went down with '2 friends I know,' and I was won-
derin what y'all out there think, blah," though he always chick-
ened out and just sat staring at the screen. It wasn't safe, even if
everybody lied about everything, on- and offline, and no one really cared; nowadays keystrokes could be traced with spyware,

and *that* would be Chess's karma—to get busted for testing the waters. There were people monitoring email just to see what your likes or dislikes were, and they didn't even need a subpoena. For all he knew, his buddy Captain PT-109 Servano might already have had his suspicions and be a member of some medical watchdog association, logged on to his keyboard and connecting the dots whenever Chess went surfing. Like that guy Pellicano: the phones he tapped supposedly rang in his own house so he'd be able to eavesdrop from the comfort of his own bed or shitter. Chess remembered the story of the guy who copped to a murder during an AA meeting and everybody thought about the moral dilemma (anonymity, right?) for like 3 seconds before snitching. There was *another* AA guy who wrote a letter to some chick he sorta raped way back when as part of his amends. She snitched on him too and even though he changed his story, it was too late and his overly contrite ass was headed upriver. Still, the confessional scenario did bounce around in his head and he thought that as long as Maurie hadn't died (it bothered him to even *go* there), the authorities wouldn't come down too hard. And as long as he *didn't* die, Chess probably wouldn't cop, but he knew that if Maurie passed, he wouldn't be able to hold his mud. What could they charge him with? "Death by Viagra"? Like fuckin bad Agatha Christie. That would be tough. He could already hear the jokes on Leno and Letterman. Maybe they'd give him probation or, say, a year in the tank, at worst. But what did *he* know—he'd *planned* the thing, right? *Motive* could definitely be proven, revenge and jealousy demonstrated: 2 classics. Lady Justice didn't look too kindly on premeditated crimes, *no* sir. And if Maurie *did* die—because face it, healthcare workers fucked up *aplenty,* it was almost a rule of thumb, a given, people croaked from routine errors every day, patients were fucking *offed,* and Chess was pretty sure that most of the time no one ever found out (aside from the nurses who were serial killers, and most of *them* probably hadn't even been caught), there was so much incompetence at so many levels, he'd just read an article in the paper about a drunk surgeon who went ballistic because he had to wait too long for sterilized instruments and was wrestled to the ground outside the operating room by 5 cops, and for someone like Maurie—look at Chris Reeve—well, quads always got pneumonia or complications or whatever, they wound up circling the drain no matter how much money they had or how famous they were, except maybe Terry Schiavo, she'd have lived to a hundred if they hadn't executed her, so why was he beating himself up?—he couldn't even remember his train of thought. If Maurie *did* crap out, say, as even an *indirect* result of the original incapacitation, Chess was thinking he would *definitely* be charged with homicide. Then he had an epiphany. *How stupid am I?* It *wouldn't* be homicide, it'd be *manslaughter.* He'd watched enough TV to be pretty sure. Maybe he'd suck it up and visit a free online legal clinic to ask a hypothetical, couching it in whatever. He'd have to think of a way that wouldn't sound too suspicious because even online lawyers could smell shit; might be worse than a chatroom. But they could *never* prove intent to kill. Since when was Viagra a weapon? Anyhow, maybe it hadn't even *been* Viagra, *plus* he didn't exactly overdose him; he'd only given him *one.* I mean until the Supreme Court rules stiff dicks to be weapons he was in the clear, there never *was* a weapon, Chess would consent to a thousand lie-detector tests, and happily take the stand. Swear on a stack of Schiavos. Half the jury would probably laugh before letting him off. If Robert *Blake* was innocent, Chester *Herlihy* was a fucking saint. A capital charge would be *insane.* That would be equivalent to saying the *Friday Night Frighters* had premeditated murdering Chess himself. *No way* would homicide stick. Maybe he could attract a celeb attorney, *fuck* Remar, Remar was a bush-league bush baby, he'd be able to get one of the big boys, because the case would be such a media magnet. Might even make a good little movie on Showtime—or something classier, with Ed Norton as Chess and the pudgy guy from *Capote* as Maurie and someone like Lindsay Lohan as Laxmi. He started to breathe easier; he'd gotten all worked up. For nothin. Maybe the charge would be something even *less* than manslaughter, like "reckless mischief" or "marauding" or "annoying" or whatever, there were all kinds of funny little obscure statutes (like the one about "bothering" children). They could probably get him on slipping someone a controlled substance without their knowledge. Yeah, that one was a bitch. That one he couldn't dodge. But if the controlled substance led to the person's *death* . . .

His wheels began to spin again.

When the settlement came, he'd reassess his options. Chess wanted to be a free man and live in modest luxury—free, white, and 41.

Was that so wrong?

U SUALLY, he hung with his mom during the day.
At Cora's prodding, her stuck-up grandson came over to visit. She thought everyone would enjoy that; she was fucking wrong. "The Son of Al FrankenStein" was about 11 and spouted off about all the real estate he'd been buying. He said he had a thousand acres. Chess thought he was a retarded dipshit and began calling him Mister Trump, which the kid didn't like ("Son of Al FrankenStein" would have gotten back to the dad). After a while, mostly because of tortured looks from Marj, Chess played along, asking if he was ever going to build a house on his "property." The kid said he already *had* built houses and was charging people rent to live there. He finally copped that the land wasn't real, or rather it *was* real but not in the normal sense, it was land on the Internet. You couldn't really *live* on it but it still cost money, you did it through PayPal and people all over the world were involved. Pah-Trump spoke with a measure of disdain but the old woman thought him "amusing." (That's the word she used through gritted, wired skeletonmouth. Mom had great tolerance and affection for Cora and her spawn.) Chess surmised that when you got to be Marjorie's age, and been through what she had, any ol tyke who wasn't gluing your ass to a chair fell into the category of *amusing*. His mother didn't understand the concept of "virtual real estate," even when Chess tried to explain. Chess didn't fully get it himself.

✳   ✳   ✳

THE woman on the afternoon shift was leaving but the night person hadn't yet arrived. Chess said it was OK for her to go; he was supposed to call his sister in a situation like this but fuck Joan and her protocol.

For the 1st time in awhile, he and Marj were alone. No biggie. Maybe she wanted him to reheat some soup? She shook her head; Mom was cool. Not hungry. She couldn't really talk much, and didn't have the energy. It was like being with a pet. Chess could tell she liked having him there though. Circumstances beyond anyone's control had forced him to spend time with her and it actually felt kind of far-out. He enjoyed it. As long as he didn't have to use the wirecutters. She patted his arm, affectionately. He kissed her cheek. Fuck Joan. *I slid out of that womb before* she *did*. I can handle this, this is a fucking delight. What does Joan think, I have no feelings? I have *too many* feelings. Does she think I'm incompetent? Well, what has she done with *her* life that's so fucking amazing? Except spread her legs. Where are all the *buildings* she's built? *I'm the 1st born. 1st built*. Fuck *Joan*.

Larry King was on. People were talking about near-death experiences. (He thought of Maurie, naturally.) He asked Marj if she wanted to watch something else but she liked Larry. There was a pretty black reporter who got hit-and-run right in the middle of an on-air news segment. She couldn't move her arms as a result of the accident. Jane Seymour was a guest too and looked really old (Marj loved *Somewhere in Time*). The actress talked about going into shock when antibiotics were mistakenly injected into a vein instead of muscle, and how she'd been "out of body," watching from the ceiling as the medical team scrambled to save her. Gary Busey chimed in—everybody and his uncle was on this fucking show—and riffed on his motorcycle accident. Jesus, like, wasn't that a long time ago? He wasn't there in person, they had him hooked up by satellite. Mustah been a slow news night for Larry. Busey said he saw angels, but they didn't look like everyone thought they did. He said they were bright lights, filled with warmth and love. For some reason, that didn't sound dopey.

Marj asked him to help her to the can.

He held out his arm and she pulled herself up. He walked her in then retreated, standing by the door, which he left partially open. He wished Joan could see how gentle and vigilant he was. He heard a high-pitched laugh, but realized it was just Mom farting. He waited for it to stop before raising his voice.

"Ma? Joanie said those crooks got your savings, but you still have the house, right? Because this house is worth a *lot.* It's totally paid off, huh? Cause something you might think about is *selling* it. You could move to a place where you wouldn't have to *worry,* a place that has *people*—not *riffraff"*—a phrase he'd heard her use through the years—"people with *money,* who don't want to live *alone* anymore. I'm not talking about convalescent homes, Ma, I'm talking about one of those luxury *condos* like they just built in Beverly Hills. In back of Rite Aid, over by the old Taj Mahal. Remember that place?" he said, with a smile. He heard the whinnying again—like air escaping the lip of a balloon—and waited for it to subside. "They tore it down. I couldn't believe it. I drove by the other day and there's just a hole. There's just a big patch of sky—it's *weird.* But those new places all have assisted care, it's like, built-in. They're pricey but that's just Beverly Hills. I think it's 8 grand a month, that's, like, the highest. But there's tons of places, Mom. We can look. It doesn't have to be Beverly Hills. Assisted care residencies are the new thing, the new wave. I've read about 10 articles! I just think it's safer—I'd feel better if you didn't live here by yourself. Too much upkeep. You're too alone. I know there's Cora . . . but you shouldn't have to worry about anything—like that—happening again. People coming to the door. Remember when I was talking to you? About that? Weird, huh. Like a premonition. Or we could get you an apartment, we could *rent* an apartment, you could have *all that money* in the bank again, as the principal. Just live off the principal. We could *invest* it. Joanie's got a good head for that. She's made *investments, believe* me, she doesn't talk about it, but I *know.* Would you think about it, Mom?"

Marj groaned. He heard the "laughing," then her bowels erupting into the water.

"How you doin? How you doin in there?"

He thought she said her stomach was bad from a new pill. It was hard to understand her.

"You gotta cut back on the caviar!" he said. He could smell the stink—it was a doozy. "Anyway, all I'm saying is it's something to mull over. Because this is a *lotta house* for one person, Ma. I just think it'd give you peace of mind to have some money in the bank again. If you could get that monthly statement in the mail, and see you were in the *black,* not the *red*—I think you'd feel a *whole lot better.* Wouldn't you, Mom?"

The doorbell rang. It was the night person.

"Hold on!" shouted Chester. "Ma, you OK?"

He went in. She modestly tried to cover herself, grimacing on the bowl. He could see her hardscrabble snatch.

"All right," he said, averting his eyes. "Ambara's here. You take care of business and I'll let her in. I'll tell her you're making your 'toilette.' She'll help you out in here, and get you something to eat."

"I *can't,*" said Marj, hissing through the wires.

"Through a *straw.* Jesus, Mom, I *know* you can't 'eat.' Ambara'll make some soup, to soothe your gut. She makes that soup you like. And I know you hate it, but you *gotta* try Pepto-Bismol. Works like a charm. Coats the lining. You need to put something in your stomach, Ma, you can't just waste away. You gonna be OK while I let her in? You're not going to fall, right?"

"No, Chester! I am not going to *fall.*"

"OK, Ma, easy. Easy, Tiger."

The doorbell rang again.

"Coming!"

He let the Caribbean girl in and told her where his mother could be found. On the way out, Chess took 2 20s from the petty cash Joan left the nurses for emergencies and sundries. He'd return them tomorrow.

LXXII.

MARJORIE

IT was lovely to spend time with her kids. They took great, good care, even buying her daily lotto. (It brought tears to Marjorie's eyes.) She made them pick the same numbers each day—the fortune cookie numbers. Cora visited too, and sometimes brought her grandchildren. Poor Mr Pahrump.

The old woman worried about the expense of the helpers. There seemed to be someone in uniform at the house, around-the-clock. Joan said Medicare was paying for it but Marj had her doubts. Her daughter was capable of extravagance and she didn't want to put her out of pocket. Besides, all those people simply weren't necessary. She wasn't helpless.

Advil alleviated the pain from her jaw. She didn't like taking anything stronger because it made her queasy. As concerned as she was about the cost, it was actually a comfort to have someone there during the "witching hour." Sometimes she had nightmares and upon awakening thought she saw figures outside the window. Usually, that was during the Santa Anas, and it was only the cypresses buffeting about.

Joan said she'd been poring over the Taj Mahal picturebook, and it would be nice to make the trip to Agra when she got better. Marj couldn't believe what she was hearing; it overjoyed her. Joan had even spoken to Trudy, who said that by the time her mother was ready to travel, the monsoons would have passed. Joan said Trudy was a sweet woman and had been devastated to hear what had happened. She wanted to stop by for a visit but Joan sardonically told the Travel Gal to "put it in idle"—a phrase her adopted father had loved, and whose employment she knew her mom would get a kick out of.

Marjorie's dreams became vivid and strange. She was taking Restoril for sleep and the doctor said sometimes that was a side effect, but the old woman *liked* the dreams; they were so marvelously detailed and wildly colorful, yet cozy and intimate at the same time. She dreamt of Lucas Weyerhauser and Bonita Billingsley, Agent Marone and the woman who accompanied him from the bank. Sometimes the pretty hostess from Spago seemed to be in her room, poised to escort Marj to her table. There wasn't anything frightening about the visitations—in fact, though she would never admit it to her daughter or the detectives, she missed them in her waking life. They had to have been desperate, and don't desperate characters do desperate things? Who could cast a stone and say they had never acted out of desperation? They were all the children of moms and dads, had experienced the slights and heartbreaks that children do, and the slights and heartbreak of being grown-up. They were very *creative* people, no one could say they weren't, albeit their talents had been used for bad. Even Joanie—*and* the detectives—had marveled at the worlds-within-worlds they'd created. In her heart, Marj didn't think that Lucas or Bonita or *any* of "her gang"—that's how the old woman thought of them, "her gang"—she just couldn't imagine a connection to the terrible person who attacked her. That would have had to be a whole different group.

During the day, while reading a book or magazine or taking her lunch through a straw (the caregiver watching TV or listening to the radio), Marj remembered her time with them. Yes of *course* they were criminals and she hoped they'd be caught so that no one else would have to undergo such an ordeal—though part of her hoped they would get away, and realize on their own the harm they had caused, and be better, stronger people for it—but still she remembered what fun she'd had, the excitement of Lucas's visits, their Chinese dinner together, her shopping spree in Beverly Hills . . . all of the beautiful certificates and papers she'd been given, and the planning she'd made for the trip to New York; she could almost feel herself stepping onto the private airline. She put the bad things out of her mind—wasn't that what people did? Forget the bad and remember the good? How else could one survive? What was the point of feeling like a victim?

Dr Phil and Oprah were *loaded* with them. But that wasn't her, that wasn't Marjie Herlihy. Not for a minute! At the strangest times, she could even smell Agent Marone's aftershave—and he *did* look like Jeff Chandler. She smiled when she thought of him. Now she remembered what comforted about that scent: it somehow evoked her 1st husband.

All manner of things flitted through her mind, memories of her parents too: the pungent Jungle Gardenia (there was Mr Kipling again—the lure of the jungle) that her mother wore and ambient recollections of the hospital room where she'd lain the weeks before she died; the flowers her father brought that only the nurses seemed to appreciate, always bright red peonies. She remembered when Dad said she had passed, and Marj wanted to know if they could bring home the peonies and he told her they'd already been given away by the nurses to children in the sickward. That stung afresh. Sitting in the living room with Ambara, half listening to Oprah, she recalled the lesson she'd learned when her father said the flowers were gone—things happen so quickly, one day her mother was well and the next, so it seemed, she was dead, even the flowers in her room handed off with dispatch like batons in a relay race. Life was a whirlwind!

Within the next year, the whirlwind blew her all the way to India. When she saw the beggarchildren and poverty and disease, she told her father she was going to be a missionary and return one day. He was so happy with this declaration that he cried, though in reflecting from her daychair on this windblown Beverlywood afternoon, breathing through her nostrils, metal-braced mouth filled with warm pea soup, the old woman began to remember all the times, or most of the times that her father cried, and saw them connected to her mother and not so much with any charmingly resolute pronouncements his daughter might have made. When he became a widower, she, little Marjorie Morningstar, numinous remnant of the woman he had loved with all his heart and soul, well, she must have lit up his life just like the incandescent peonies left to grace hapless children's rooms. Idly, she wondered if the nurses had actually taken them to sickwards or had brought them home. She pushed the cynical thought from her head—why would it have mattered, if they gave someone pleasure? As long as they weren't thrown away, which she doubted. In those days, people weren't so quick to throw things out.

Suchwise did Marjorie spend her hours, startled to saunter through a decorous, riotous jungle of gardenias and fiery peonies, unhurried perambulation and inventory of her life, and as eventide came, she remembered Raymond and their courtship, a kind of whirlwind (or whirlpool!) too. He was the 1st man she had been with. She wouldn't let him do everything he wanted unless they married, and—another thing she'd never tell her kids—that was why she had finally relented and agreed to the union, knowing Dad was initially opposed. (There was an item in the paper about a starlet who eloped to Bakersfield and that's where Ray got the idea.) She wanted to experience the world of sensual pleasure "full-throttle," blushing even now as the phrase floated up and danced its burlesque like the debauched cypress silhouettes before her bedcurtains. She remembered the delirious pressure between them as they had their public dance, 1st time she felt a man press up against her like that. At the end of the night she pried herself from the backseat, every window wet as a sauna. The physical side—she and Ray never *had* a spiritual side; that was something more with Hamilton, though still a spiritualism shared "half-throttle"—was glorious, even though it didn't last but a year or so. When the children were born, it died on the vine. Maybe that was her fault. There were always things a woman could do. There were things a woman *should* do to keep her man—   *the passing of the flowers, to sickbeds, wards, and private apartments. Perhaps to lovenests long since picked apart and scattered to the 4 winds: Love is just around the corner. The passing of the peonies and the angry thoughtless handing off of batons. She didn't feel she was at all done with flowers and footraces but she had to have those kids and then suddenly it was over then suddenly he was gone*

... she had night-thoughts and day-thoughts, night terrors and daydreams—bright and dark and shiny, she could reach out and grab them like at carnival, manipulating the machine that picked out prizes with a small steel claw. Get whatever she wanted: sights and sighs and sounds and smells overwhelming: secret joys and languid stillness.

Restoril in peace.

She looked forward to the narcotic of bed and pillows, because then came a *different* kind of grab bag, where geegaws surfaced, without needing to pick and choose.

This night, before floating to her sumptuously fractured cornucopia, her grifter's gallery and frangible frangipani, her ganged-up flowery recrudescence, she lifted the book from her nightstand while the helpmeet watched cable in the living room, and read about *the Australian missionaries, a family called the Staines, Christians who'd been burned alive by a mob in a place in India called Orissa, Orissa, where even Jesus had been, and she*

LXXIII.

JOAN

wanted
to go back to visit the old man but there was just too much to take care
of. She and Barbet already agreed that after what her partner was call-
ing "the Freiberg fiasco," Joan would take an immediate "sabbatical." (That's what *she* was calling *that*.) Mercantile Road tugged at
her but there simply wasn't time. She was incubating a baby. (She
did have time to order online, Tummy Rub from Mama Mio—
which supposedly erased stretch marks—plus Resilient Belly Oil,
Cellex-C, and Basq's lavender/pear-scented Sweet Dreams.) She
still hadn't told anyone except Barbet and Pradeep, hadn't even
been to her gynecologist, though she'd come close to telling Marj
because she thought it would make her happy.

She needed to get a few things straight with Lew. Joan didn't
want to bring in a lawyer—yet—but had sought advice from a
honcho, a friend of the former consul's, in the Bay Area. Knowledge was power.

She decided not to inform her brother about Raymond Rausch.
Chess was too volatile right now; she didn't want him racing over
and scaring the old guy. Besides, he was acting weird. She wasn't
sure what was wrong but aside from that he was way stoned, all
the time. He reeked. The nurses were pointing fingers at each
other for taking money from the kitty without leaving receipts,
and Joan soon put it together—Chess was the culprit. She didn't
have the energy to confront. He would never do anything to hurt
their mom but she didn't exactly trust him either. He was fairly
grandiose and continued to speak of a pending "7 figure" settlement related to his back injury. She thought of asking her brother
if he needed a loan but didn't have the energy for *that*. No, bad
idea to throw Father into the mix. Let Chester keep seeing Mom
(who really did enjoy his visits), smoke his ganja in the backyard,

fuck his hippie girlfriend, and swipe his petty cash—more than
that, Joan didn't want to know from. At least this way, she could
keep half an eye out.

A N attorney from Guerdon LLC called to say he wanted to
discuss a "personal matter" between Joan and Mr Freiberg.
She haughtily said that if it was related to the maquette fee, "you
can contact my partner, Barbet Touissant, at ARK, in Venice."
The lawyer told her it was a "separate, personal issue," and she
hated the sound of the words in his mouth. "You *listen,*" said Joan.
"If it's so *separate* and *personal,* have Mr Freiberg call me *himself,*
understand?"

She almost added *motherfucker* but hung up instead.

(Probably a good thing, she thought.)

(*But,* man, *that pisses me off.*)

She was so rattled, she called Lew's private line.

(Every therapist Joan ever worked with told her not to act on
impulse—her Achilles' heel. Even Pradeep compared her to
Sonny, from *The Godfather.* It was her ferocious and unyielding
nature to go off on people, her weakness and her strength. Barbet
once taped a Chinese proverb to her G5: "If you are patient in one
moment of anger, you will escape 100 days of sorrow.")

"Hello?"

"It's Joan."

"Hello sweetheart."

"One of your attorneys just called."

He was in a jovial mood.

"Did he slap you with a maternity suit?

"Look, Lew, I don't want to deal with lawyers, OK?"

"Fine by me."

He sounded like he meant it.

"I don't know exactly how we're going to do that, Joan, but I
like the concept."

"I want to have this baby—you know that."

"It's yours to lose," he said, both wry and cruel.

"I've had 3 abortions and 3 miscarriages in my life and I really don't think I'm going to get another shot. So I'm going to do everything I can to keep it."

"They were just trying to arrange a blood test, or whatever they do. For the paternity thing. You don't object?"

"Of course not. I was already on that, I just got busy with my mom."

"How's she doing?"

"Much better."

Both of them sighed, and could hear each other breathe.

"It's yours, Lew. I know that it's yours."

His tone grew serious but not unfriendly.

"We just need to be sure, Joan. *I* need to be sure. That's the only reason he was calling."

"I'd appreciate it, Lew, if the next time, you'd pick up the phone. Is that too much to ask? Would that be so painful?"

He laughed. "Everything's painful."

She didn't feel like sharing his *whimsy.*

"Just call and tell me who I should see: who, where, and when. I don't want to hear it from an attorney. OK?"

"That's fine, Joanie." He laughed again. "Now may I please, *please* leave the principal's office? Please?"

"I'd prefer it to be someone down here—because of my mom. I don't want to have to get on a plane."

"Got it." Short pause. "Look, darling: I just don't want to be a new daddy. I have 3 already and it's gonna be awhile before I do my Tony Randall/Larry King thing." Short pause. "How does that grab you?"

"I don't need you for this one." Short pause. "I've decided to go in another direction," she said, throwing his own words back at him. "I'm going with Santiago."

When he heard that he roared, and she laughed, and that broke the ice.

"Do you want to have this conversation now?"

"Love to."

"If it's mine, I'll give you 5,000,000, straight up. Which should more than amply cover his or her education, lifestyle, whatever comes down the pike. That offer will come in the form of a contract, so eventually you're going to have to deal with one of my guys. I'll make it as painless as possible. But *I do not wish to be named,* Joan, in any private or public context. A breach of that would negate any and all agreements. I have my reasons, and I expect you to honor them, as I'll honor yours. So: if it turns out to be mine, I will write you a check for $5,000,000 straight up but in turn, you will have to sign a confidentiality agreement stating you *will* not disclose the child's patrimony until he or she is twice the voting age. I will also make you sign—"

"*Ask* me to sign," she interjected, with astringence.

"*Ask* you to sign," he assented, "an ironclad rider stating in explicit terms that this child has no claims, nor do you, in any way, shape, or form, upon my present or future estate, or assets related to Guerdon LLC and myriad holding companies. Another thing. If you've already spoken about this (I don't begrudge you that), if you *have* brought up my potential paternity to, say, a close *friend,* or *Barbet,* I would politely yet firmly request that you inform them, at the right moment, that the blood test came back revealing otherwise. They will believe what they will believe but you will stick to your story, on and off the record. I don't care who you say the father is, we can even provide you with an entity—I just don't want it to be *me.* Does all that sound reasonable?"

" 'Reasonable'? That's a funny word."

"All right, Joan: does that sound *fair.*"

Pause.

"I'm glad you've given this some thought, Lew." She wanted to steady her nerves by sounding neutral before she pounced. "Do you want to know what I think sounds 'fair'? Do you really want to know? I mean, are you *interested.*"

"Yes. I really am." Short pause. Breathing. "I'm all ears."

"If we're going to have this conversation, let's *have* it. I mean, for *real.* It's 2006. Do you know what $5,000,000 is? I'll tell you what it was a few years ago. The judgment against a British tabloid for leaking Catherine Zeta-Jones's wedding photos."

"That was 2,000,000. And it was overturned."

"$5,000,000 is what certain friends of yours spend on bar mitz-vahs. $5,000,000 is a bone you throw your alma mater."

"I didn't do college, hon. Remember? I'm a dropout."

"OK, your *brother's* alma mater. $5,000,000 is the call you get from your curator because she's got a deal on a French *commode*. $5,000,000 isn't even enough for the fund you draw on to pay off the chef who slices a *tendon* while cooking for you and Al Gore, or Billy Joel, or Tiger Woods, or Grand Duke Henri, or *whomever.* Lew, I'm a big girl. I'm gonna go away and I *mean* it. I *want* to go away. I don't have any fatal attractions—I just have *natal* attractions."

He laughed again. All good.

The warmth returned to their negotiations.

"I finally figured out who you remind me of." Short pause. "Maureen Dowd."

"I'm *already* out of your hair, right? I mean, what could possibly have been easier? You've got $11,000,000,000, or whatever it is you have, which will probably *triple* by the time our daughter reaches voting age."

"It's a girl?"

"I don't know. I have a feeling."

"Have you thought of a name?"

"Guerdon."

"Ha! I guess that's better than 'LLC.' So: how much, Joanie. What are we talking?"

"20. Isn't that what Barkin got? *Sans enfant.*"

Long pause, then:

"That was a *marriage,* Joan. Long-term."

Long pause, then:

"I don't *know* what she got."

Long pause, then:

"Done. Sold. Signed, sealed, *undelivered.*"

She began to shake.

"I don't want to sound cold, but if you don't carry to term—"

"Don't even go there."

"They'll call—*I'll* call—when everything's ready to go. With the doctor, then the agreement." (She could tell that his pulse had remained steady throughout; that was the thing about him that turned her on.) "Did Barbet tell you I want to keep the model?"

"*I* told him. You told *me*."

"He wants a hundred-and-50,000 for it. Can you believe the gall? That's a dealbreaker, Joan."

"I'll take care of it." *That's it, then. That was the caveat. Home free.* "What are you going to do with it? You're not seriously going to put it in the Gluckman gallery?"

"I don't know yet. *The Lost Coast.* I love that title."

"It's only a model, Lew. It's inchoate."

"I like looking at it. It reminds me of you."

LXXIV.

RAY

THE men carried her upstairs on a gurney. Big Gulp was happy to be home; the cousins followed like an entourage. Thank God for those girls.

He put roses by the bed along with a dozen DVDs. A man from the computer store fixed her laptop so Ghulpa could use the Internet without a wire. When Ray surprised her with that, she said, "Oh Gawd!" and got happy as hell. She was even nice to the Friar, who, thankfully, was on best behavior. The old man hadn't the energy to take him for walks, relying on the Center instead. Still, Cesar was right—exercise was doing the trick. The little fellow was a champ, and acting the total gentleman. His animal sense probably picked up that BG was carrying.

A gaggle of Artesians prepared food in the kitchen while Ray showed off a copy of the settlement papers. She smiled broadly, resting a swollen hand on her gut. He reiterated that it came to half a million, free and clear. She asked *When?* and he answered, *Any day now.* Ghulpa rubbed her stomach like one of those sleepy, big-bellied buddhas—it was about the best homecoming she could have had. She kissed the old man on the mouth to show her pleasure (at being home again too), nothing fancy, but a cousin who came into the room with soup sniggered and quickly disappeared.

HE got his suit out of mothballs and slapped on the Old Spice. Big Gulp looked him over from the Sealy and bobbled her head, clucking and smiling. He said never mind about *me,* just make sure you stay *put.* He admonished a pair of cousins to make sure she did.

The plan was for Staniel to pick him up but at the last minute the detective phoned with an emergency. If it was all right, he'd meet Ray at the Dining Car. Might be a tad late.

Now the old man thought *he'd* be late, which, as host, would be in poor form. Not that it was anyone's fault. He was too nervous to drive and wound up hailing a cab. He'd been to the bank and drawn out 15 C-notes—he knew the steakhouse wasn't cheap (part of the reason why Ray chose the detectives' atmospheric haunt) and his credit cards were maxed. These boys meant a lot to him. He wanted to do it up right and show them a good time; he'd even extended the invite to wives and girlfriends. Not all of the cops who broke down the door were available, and knowing Ray's fondness for *Cold Case Files,* Detective Lake had petitioned a few "closers." Staniel said he would probably recognize some faces from the TV show.

As it happened, he got there 1st. He told the maître d' he was "with Detective Staniel Lake" and felt a surge of pride on being escorted to a large table in the back room—just like he was LAPD. Slowly, the younger officers began to arrive, and introductions were made. They were a handsome, bashful bunch with big gold rings and a lot of hair. (All wore suits; Ray was glad to be "in uniform" himself.) The seasoned investigators came in a 2nd wave, paunchy and ruddy and not afraid to show their wild side. A few rounds of drinks were consumed before Staniel finally made an entrance, all apologies. That's when things really started loosening up.

Ray didn't remember any of the men, even though some said they were present on the night of "the mishap" on Mercantile Road. True to Staniel's word, there was a fellow from the cold case squad, and a detective from the West Side who Lake went to the Academy with.

No one brought a date—it was stag. They toasted the old man's pending fatherhood (instead of congratulating him on the settlement, which might have been awkward) and pretty much treated him like one of their own. The officers never condescended or made him feel small; they seemed genuinely moved when he raised a glass to them and choked up. There was a nice mix, a good cross-section—a motorcycle cop, 3 of the SWAT guys who broke down the door (one said he was sorry about putting the cuffs on too tight, which triggered a whole, off-color discussion about hookers and handcuffs. Ray could see why they didn't bring any lady friends along), the cold case chap, and a detective or 2, one of whom was retired. They were raunchy and "regular," and didn't censor themselves. They talked about the Aryan Brotherhood, "hot prowls," baby-rapers, panty sniffers, and necrophiliacs—nothing was off-limits. Some of it Ray didn't even catch. He swore to himself he'd never repeat any details to Big Gulp.

LA's finest shot the shit about a breed they called the lowest of the low: those who prey on the elderly. For a moment, the topic's irony was tacitly noted—afterall, this was a group of men Ray had met under circumstances that might, in a stretch, be so classified—with the faintest nod of the collective's bent for black humor. The motorcycle cop spoke of a 90 year old who died in the act of fellating her attacker—which he forced her to do *after* slitting her throat—while he sat on the washing machine eating a sandwich. Before he left the house the guy impaled Granny on some gardening shears and stole the money she'd saved for her own funeral. Another fellow—a WW2 vet—was nearly beaten to death by his dopefiend neighbor. The hospital released him a week later when Medicare ran out; the orderlies literally shoved him in a taxi with a catheter strapped to his leg. The driver half carried him into the house, where an hour later the dopefiend beat him *again*. This time he died from his injuries.

"I don't know," said one of the cops, with mock skepticism. "Sounds like Death-by-Celebrex."

"Oh, we get the *sophisticated* ones on the West Side," said Detective Whitsell, Staniel's friend from the Academy. "None of that meth-lab trailer trash you guys have to deal with. We're chasing a gang now who gotta thing going you wouldn't *believe*. It's essentially a lottery scam—we call em the Blind Sister Crew. They just grabbed a million dollars off the sweetest old lady you'll ever meet. She took a pretty good beating from em too, which was unusual. I mean, these guys are ferocious. Terrorized her just for jollies. But they're *amazing*. Talk about *imaginative,* I'm impressed!"

"You sound like you want to spread for em."

"Yeah, right after you—I got dibs on the washing machine. But before you blow me, make me a sandwich, will you?"

"How about pork?"

There was laughter all around and Whitsell continued.

"They had to wire her jaw."

"She can't open her mouth? *Cancel that sandwich.*"

More laughter.

"They walk *right in the bank* with *seriously* forged papers. They claim to be hooked up with Pataki and Bloomberg, and make sure their marks check out the Town Cars they ride around in—they all have chauffeurs. I mean, these guys could write bestsellers. *Da Vinci Code* shit. Their scams are so convoluted, the department's in fucking *awe*. Have you ever seen any movies by David Mamet? He's pretty good. Kinda unrealistic, but pretty good. He has a show on cable called *The Unit?*"

"I got your unit right here."

"Your dragqueen snitches already told me it's nothin to write home about.

"I seen that show. It's good."

"Entertaining. He writes plays and does movies too. *The Heist?* I think he wrote *Scarface.* Naw—something else. Anyway, he did—what's it called?—I'm blanking—most his movies are about people getting short-conned. Well, these 'Blind Sisters' could give Mamet a run for his money. I'm telling you, if they knocked on my door, *I* might fall for their shit. And the horrible thing is, I just got a call there was a fire over there. At her place— the old lady's."

"No shit," said Staniel.

"Did she burn?"

"Naw, she's all right."

"It was the crew? The people that shook her down?"

"We don't have evidence of that. At this point, I'm not sure I'd be surprised."

"That's *evil.*"

"Nice house too—*nice* little house. She wasn't hurt. Had a nurse staying with her. Everybody woke up."

"Fires tend to do that."

"Or not."

"If you don't have a smoke detector."

"Our African-American friends tend not to."

"Where there's *smokes,* there's fire."

"Racist motherfucker."

"Blow me."

"I told you, 1st make me that Maytag sandwich."

"So they had a little barbecue?"

"House is *torched.* They pulled her from the bedroom. She's OK. Shaken up though."

"*Tell* me about it."

The men slipped into simpatico mode.

"On top of everything, they had to use wirecutters cause she was hyperventilating."

"Jesus."

"At least now Ma Clampett could give you some acton."

"You're evil."

"Diet Coke evil."

"Her *money* stolen, *beat up,* jaw *wired,* house *burned.* Not exactly the Golden Years."

"More like the Golden Shower Years."

"Hey now! We're not talking about what you do with one of your hookers—we're talking about a sweet little old lady."

"Think it's arson?"

"ATF's all over it. We're not even close to ending our fraud investigation."

" 'The Blind Sisters.' Got a nice ring to it."

"Hey meester," said the motorcycle cop. "Wanna fuck my blind seester?"

More laughter.

"Kinda makes you wonder," said Whitsell, "what they'd have been capable of if they applied all that energy to something *positive.*"

"*HIV* positive."

"Yeah. Makes you all wistful."

"Seriously. These guys could have been CEOs."

"Right. Too bad. They could've founded Halliburton."

"They coulda come up with the iPod."

"Or built special washing machines for blowjobs."

"Only thing is, if they *were* CEOs . . . their rapsheets would probably be twice as fucking long!"

They laughed uproariously and tucked into their steaks.

Ray flagged the waiter for another round of drinks.

LXXV.

CHESS

In consideration of the payment to me of the sum of EIGHTY-FIVE THOUSAND NINE HUNDRED AND 00/100 ($85,900), I do hereby release and forever discharge GlobalWorld Productions Inc., a Nevada corporation, and its boards, officers, agents, servants and employees from any and all claims and causes of action which I now have, or may hereafter have, on account of injuries sustained resulting from or arising out of an accident which occured on 04/14/06, at 4891 Glen Oaks Way, as particularly described in Claim File No. D7-49117.

For said consideration and as a further inducement to Global-World Productions Inc. to enter into this compromise settlement, I further agree: that this release shall apply to all unknown and unanticipated injuries and damages resulting from or arising out of said accident as well as to injuries and damages now known, disclosed or anticipated; that I have executed this release upon my judgment and that of my own physician and not in reliance upon any statement or representation by any employee, representative or physician representing or purporting to represent Global-World Productions Inc., concerning the nature and extent of my bodily injury or injuries or the nature and extent of my damages or the legal liability therefore; and that I expressly waive the benefits of the provisions of Section 1542 of the Civil Code, which reads as follows: A general release does not extend to claims which the creditor does not know or suspect to exist in his favor at the time of executing the release, which if known by him must have materially affected his settlement with the debtor.

I further understand and agree; that this release is not to be used as evidence of an admission of liability for the damages alleged and described in said Council File No. D7-49117 filed with the City Clerk of the City of Los Angeles; that said payment by Global-World Productions Inc. or by any of its officers or employees is the sole consideration for this release, and is in full settlement and satisfaction of my said Claim File No. D7-49117 and in full satisfaction of all other claims and causes of action which I may now have against GlobalWorld Productions Inc.; that there are no agreements or promises not expressed herein; that the terms of this release are contractual; and that whenever the singular is used herein it includes the plural.

LXXVI.

MARJORIE

"Mother? Mother, listen. *You have to listen,* OK? Are you with me? Mama, I don't know why all this is happening the way it's happening. But they—the police—don't think the fire had *anything to do* with the people who stole your money. Do you understand? Because I don't want you to feel you aren't safe. You are! Completely. I'll take *care* of you. I *love* you, Mama! Everyone thinks it was just a coincidence, a *horrible, horrible* coincidence. It was *electrical*—they think it was electrical. Do you understand? I am *so sorry.* Sometimes bad things happen in this world and I know you've had your share of terrible things—*worse* than terrible—all in a row. And it's *crazy.* But you're *safe* now . . . we could have *lost* you—I could have lost you in that fire! And the insurance company's been *great.* The house is *completely covered.* (Which was a lie. The fastidious old woman had understandably missed the last, ill-timed premium payment; Joan was planning to fight that fight with her lawyers). Are you taking any of this in, Mom? There are some things I want to tell you. Need to tell you . . . I'm going to have a baby. I'm going to have a baby, Mom! I met a man on a job I was up for in Northern California. Remember? The memorial in Napa? And he's a very wealthy man. Well, I didn't get the job, but I got a baby! Isn't that *crazy?* We didn't plan it. We haven't discussed marriage but he's *extremely* wealthy—one of the richest men in the country and the *world*—and I think he's *really* excited about having this child. *And so am I.* And it's *really* important because of my age that I take care of myself so that everything goes smoothly. I can't wait for you to be a grandmother! You're going to be a grandma! Isn't that the most fantastic thing? Mom? You are going to be *so amazing,* there is going to be *so much you can teach her.* I'm saying 'her' but I don't know what it's going to be yet—it's just a feeling—I told the doctor I don't want to find out. I just want to *have* it. I feel so *incredibly blessed*. I can't wait to feel what it's like to have a baby. You have been *such* a wonderful mother—*you are such a wonderful woman*. Mom? You heard all that, right? That I'm going to have a baby? And I know that *you* aren't feeling so blessed right now and I can't imagine going through *any* of what you've been through. What those people did. But I want you *with* me, you're going to *live* with me, I'm going to buy a house. I have the money now. I'm going to have *a lot* of money. I want us to *stay* together. The man I'm having the child with wants us to live at the Beverly Hills Hotel until we find a place, he's going to pay for everything, 2 big bungalows, we're going to have the time of our lives! I'm taking a sabbatical from work and we're going to spend tons of time together, isn't that fantastic? The Beverly Hills Hotel is in a *really* beautiful area—you know where it is, right? The pink building up on Sunset? They call it 'the Pink Palace' and it has that famous wallpaper?—there's a park across the street and we can go for walks, *every day*. We can have lunch in the coffeeshop downstairs, remember the little coffeeshop? I took you and Hamilton there once and you said it was like a cruise ship. Ham said it reminded him of the QE2—remember, Mama? There was a movie star eating at the counter? Sandra Bullock? Remember Sandra Bullock? Everything is *paid* for, Mom, and the hotel has *tons* of security because it's owned by *the Sultan of Brunei,* so you can *totally* feel safe. And I *might* get married but that's not something we're really thinking about right now, there's been too much excitement already, don't you think? Don't you think we've had a little too much excitement, Mom?"

Joan laughed and her mother smiled.

They had tears in their eyes.

The Pink Palace. The Taj Mahal Palace.

"It's a different world now, and people don't always *get* married. Goldie Hawn and Kurt Russell—you like Goldie, don't you, Mom?—don't you like Goldie?—they never married and they have kids and have been together about a hundred years. Rachel Weisz? She got the Academy Award. And David Letterman, and

Johnny Depp and his girlfriend? You probably don't know him but he's a *big,* big star. And Brad and Angelina! And they're all really happy! But anything's possible . . . so my boyfriend, Lew, Lew Freiberg, the father of my child, is arranging for us to have *2 whole bungalows* at the Beverly Hills Hotel (which was true; a Guerdon "write-off") and we can go for walks when you feel better, walks will be good, for me too, I can do yoga and Pilates at the hotel, there's an amazing spa there, for *you,* saunas would be *great*—the doctor said you don't need the wires back on, isn't that good? Mom? Isn't that great?—and there'll be a nurse with us *at all times,* Lew is paying for it, he *insists,* and Chester can come visit just like before. It's going to be so much fun! And if you're feeling better, we can go to India in a few months, when the monsoons end. OK? I can travel when I'm pregnant, my doctor said it's completely fine. In fact, now's the time to do it! Before I get too big! Trudy's setting *everything* up. I really want to go! There's a train we can take, with an ayurvedic spa, that is *just* like the Orient Express. I am *so excited.* Mom, you're going to have a grandchild! Isn't that so amazing? *You never have to worry about anything again. You will never have to worry about being alone.* You know where we can walk? To that movie theater you took us when we were young. On Beverly and Wilshire. Remember? The 'Taj Mahal'?"

"No," said Marj, tremulously returning to the real world.

"No, what?"

Joan was at least glad that her mother was engaged.

"It is not there."

"Of course it is, Mom! It's not a movie theater anymore but it still has that beautiful roof . . ."

"No."

"It'll be our little way of preparing for the real thing! Walks will be *good.* We need our strength because we're gonna be doing some hiking over there, Mom. *I love you so much.* I am *so sorry* about everything that's happened, I am *so sorry* I haven't been there for you. All I wanted was to show how independent I was but I was *such an asshole.* Forgive me, Mother! Will you forgive me? Please? Please! You're not mad at me, are you? Please forgive me for being so selfish and so fucked up! I'm going to have *so much money* and we'll put back in the bank *every cent those horrible people took from you,* all right? We'll put it back *times 10.* I'll have the ability to do that, Mom. OK? Do you hear me? We have a deal? OK, Mom? You love me? Mama? Do you love me? Are you mad at me? Did you hear when I said you were going to be a grandma? And that I was rich? And that we're going to move into the hotel?"

"Yes," said Marj.

Joan smiled, and wiped away tears. Maybe—just maybe—everything would work out.

"Did you know that's where Howard Hughes used to live? I think we're going to be in the same bungalow. The one he had all his affairs in. Isn't that exciting?"

"Did you get the ticket?"

"The ticket? To India?"

"No—the lottery ticket. Did you buy it today?"

"Not yet."

"Use the same numbers. You don't have to go to Riki's if it's out of the way, but—"

"Of *course* it's not out of the way, silly!"

Joan laughed and cried at once.

"But if you can, that's my lucky spot. And the same numbers, Joanie! The lucky numbers."

"OK, Ma. I'll go—I'll go *right now.* I *love* you."

"Love you too, sweetheart."

She kissed Marj twice then left in a storm.

LXXVII.

JOAN

THEY moved to the hotel.

Tests proved that Lew was the father. Joan cried in relief (she was crying a lot lately) even though she never had reason to doubt. Not long after, she met with attorneys in a nondescript building on 3rd Street—one hers, one a mediator (pointedly having no cross-connection whatsoever with the Northern California behemoth, but rather, a man whose trade was child custody cases and others closer to that ilk), 3 from Guerdon—to sign the papers. She did as she was told, dutifully reporting to the somewhat surprised Barbet and Pradeep that test results, now forever sealed, had shown the dad to be someone other than Mr Mem. Lew thought of everything, providing a respectable "entity" as he said he would, giving Joan a plausible one-night-stand backstory; nevermind it not helping her already sluttish image. But she was among friends. The donor of choice was in fact a real guy, early 30s, one of those aging code-writing kidz (they showed her his picture. Cute). They were careful to find someone who had never worked for Guerdon LLC, and whose background check revealed him to be reliably bricks-and-mortar, also being compensated and sworn to secrecy, and who would, if gossip should surface, affably go on record to having spilled his seed—again, only if and when Joan were ever pressured, for the sake of veracity, to point the finger. Which remained a hypothetical, and that would be where his involvement ended. If, say, an enterprising tabloid PI or dirtblog were to dig deeper, a tactical paper trail of endorsed monthly support checks (about $3,000 each, reflecting his more modest means) waited to be uncovered, a trail that would roughly begin a few months prior to the moment she left the legal offices where the contract was hammered out.

SHE needed to "handle" Chester. She didn't want him hanging around the hotel agitating their mom. (Her brother could agitate the Dalai Lama.) He kept talking about "getting" the people who set fire to the house, that the cops were wrong, it probably *had* been set by the gang who took her money, and wanted to "finish her off" in case anything came to trial. *Not helpful.* When he persisted in asking who was paying for the bungalows and all—she still hadn't brought up the pregnancy—Joan said, Marjorie's insurance. Chess didn't believe it. She went off on him. *"I'm* paying for it, then, OK? I'm paying for the nurses and the bungalows and the whatever. Now, did you want to help contribute, Chester? Cause if you *don't* then *leave it alone."* That shut him up, for now. If Mom said anything about the benefactor and potential husband-to-be "up north," she'd just tell her brother Marj was delusional, or that ARK was taking care of it out of a special account. She hated to even be worrying about this kind of shit. Her nest egg hadn't even fucking hatched.

Joan wasn't sure if that bullshitty story about getting injured on a reality show was even true. It was so lame. She *did* suss the girlfriend, Laxmi, loitering in the lobby outside the Polo Lounge. Her brother said she gave great massages, and it would be "a healing" for Marj to be on the receiving end of those helping hippie hands, "gratis," but Joan said she didn't think that was such a good idea, Mom was too spooked to "meet new people" ("She knows Laxmi!" shouted Chess), and besides, the nurses were taking care of her physical needs. *If anyone was going be giving Mother a massage, it won't be your New Age consort.* At least he wasn't too combative about it. There seemed to be a cloud hanging over him; when he pushed too hard and Joan pushed back, Chess instantly relented, his face contorting in despair. Something was definitely going on, beyond drugs or sexual obsession. It was discomfiting but Joan got it to work in her favor.

SHE was going to rent a house at the beach but didn't have the energy. The hotel was so easy, everything was there, everything done for you, the food brought, rooms cleaned, clothes laundered, the pool and spa, Town Cars when you didn't feel like driving. The sweet, starched nurses in revolving shifts were thrilled to be working in such a luxe environment—one of them, a Jamaican, thought Marjorie Herlihy was a famous old movie star. Another popular rumor was that Joan was a department store heiress. The bottom line was that everything at the hotel was intensely manageable.

She needed things to be manageable.

W HEN Chess said he and Laxmi were going to Joshua Tree "to chill," Joan took the opportunity to see their father again.

She phoned beforehand. Ray said that his partner, Ghulpa, was home from the hospital and if Joan didn't mind, he didn't want to introduce her as his daughter just yet. *No offense offered; none taken.* Ray said "my gal is still a little shaky" and hoped she would understand if he called Joan his niece instead. There was something awkwardly poignant about it. "Oh, I understand very well!" she said, with levity, hinting at the slinky complications of her own life, and Ray was relieved. There was plenty she didn't want to share with her dad yet either, like the details of what had recently befallen his former wife. Joan thought he would be OK with anything she had to say about Chess—wasn't much going on there—but sensed the old man would be hurt if apprised of what happened to Marjorie in the last 6 months. Shit. It was hard enough for a complete stranger to hear.

She concocted a story on the way down (she was getting good at that). She would tell him Mom was traveling—that Marj had finally returned to India, and Joan was planning to join her. The machinatrix interrupted her machinations; she felt stupid using the Woman but had completely blanked on how she'd gotten to her father's house that 1st time. *Keep left, on the 6-0-5.* She eyeballed the mesmeric navigation screen embedded in the dash and shook her head in amusement, recapitulating the "cover story"—

her life a tangled techno-tango'd web—at last (at least), mother and daughter would fulfill the lifelong dream to visit the whipped cream shrine of the virtual Taj Mahal.

When the Woman announced, *Your route guidance is now complete,* Joan did as before, U-turning to the liquorstore *to the lighthouse* for Diet Coke, Marlboro Lights and fluffy Lay's, then drove to the apartment complex and had herself a smoke. She was actually looking forward to seeing him because this time her nerves had settled. Relatively. He was so unaffected, so *unmythic,* and didn't seem to want anything from her. (She wondered what she wanted from him.) Joan thought that today he might ask her simple questions. She was ready. It wasn't about being interrogated, from either end. She was prepared.

She stood at the door, which this time was open

LXXVIII.

RAY

---

and smiled from the other side, old man/twinkle-eyed smile, remarking on her Diet Coke. *I don't know what they put in those things but it can't be good.* She brushed by and he smelled the cigarettes—why did she think she could pull one over? why had she even tried? she was still his little girl and didn't want him to know that she smoked. She thought it so dear: he'd bought Diet Cokes at the store in anticipation of her visit, and had "a cold one" waiting for her.

The dog immediately bit her ankle.

He swatted it and the thing yelped and hid under a chair.

Joan kept saying *No worries* as her dad flushed Nip out and corralled him in the kitchen, swatting his behind, more yelping as they went. Please, no worries! She thought he might have another heart attack. Joan heard voices in the back—the "galfriend." A woman in a colorful sari rushed out (was it *her?* No: too young), smiling diffidently on her way to the kitchen just as Ray and the dog ran past. Joan laughed: kind of a French farce. Water whistled and the sari made tea, wordlessly offering some to the guest. Joan shook her head then teacups were spirited to bedroom, the cousin grinning absurdly and bobbling her head at both as she fled.

"They're helping out my gal," said Ray.

An image was frozen on the living room television.

A cop, lying in the snow.

"My favorite show—*The Twilight Zone.* Ever see it? They play marathons on Thanksgiving Day. They'll put on a whole season's worth. Old ones, the classics. I think I've seen pretty much all of em. They've tried the show a couple times since, I mean a redo job, but they just can't get it right. That fellow Serling was somethin special. They broke the mold. He was a smoker too! *Busted.*

Back in the days when they didn't hide it. Ed Murrow and Jack Paar and all those fellows. It was glamorous. Now they herd people out of buildings to puff up, like dope addicts. *Busted.* You see em on the sidewalks. Anyway, they did a movie—helluva long time ago. The actor got his head chopped off by a helicopter."

"Vic Morrow."

"That's right!" He was pleased his daughter had the factoid at hand. "The director was gonna to go to jail but he got off."

"John Landis."

"Why, yes! I think that *was* his name. That was a *big* trial."

He aimed the remote and said, "You know, Marjorie and I used to watch this together. My my, that was '61, '62."

Joan's gut clenched.

"How is she?" he ventured.

"She's great! She's traveling."

"Married?"

"Her husband died last year."

"Oh. Oh. That's too bad. I'm—I'm sorry to hear that."

Why did I say—that wasn't part of the cover.

"Were you close?"

Joan thought he meant she and Mom, then realized what he was asking.

"Not close, no. But he was a very, very nice man."

She was glad not to have blurted out the fact that Ham adopted her, which definitely would have hurt him.

He pressed PLAY and they watched the DVD.

A police officer had been shot outside an old woman's tenement door—she looked like Marj!—and when he asked for help, she was afraid to let him in. She kept saying he was Mr Death, and that he was just trying to trick her. The cop (a babyfaced Robert Redford, no less) said he was bleeding and asked her to at least call someone for help. Compassion got the best of her and he leaned on the frail, frightened woman as they crossed the threshold of her front door. She put a blanket on him and he slept. Now she seemed happy to have a visitor and when Redford awakened, she fed him hot soup. He realizes she hasn't called the doctor because she has no phone and there aren't any neighbors because they've all moved away; the tenement has been slated for demolition. She finally tells him why she never leaves the house.

"I know he's out there! He's trying to get in. He comes to the door and knocks, *begs* me to let him in. Last week he said he was from the gas company. Oh, he's clever! Then he said he was a contractor, hired by the city . . . I sent him away! He knows I'm onto him. I know it sounds crazy, but it's true."

Redford tells her not to cry, that he's not going to hurt her.

"At 1st," says the old woman, "I couldn't be sure. I was on a bus. There was an old woman sitting in front of me, knitting. Socks, I think. Then this young man got on. There were empty seats but he sat down right beside her. It upset her. He seemed like a nice young man. When she dropped her yarn, he picked it up and gave it to her—I saw their fingers touch. He got out at the next stop. When the bus reached the end of the line, she was dead."

"But you said yourself that the woman was old."

The tenement lady ignored the logic, lost in a dream. "I've seen him since, several times. I've seen him in crowds, watched for him. Once he was a young soldier . . . a salesman . . . a taxi driver. Every time someone I knew died, he was there. I *knew*—because *I* was getting old and *my* time was coming. I saw more clearly than younger people."

She said she hadn't always lived like a recluse. People used to tell her she was pretty. She loved the sun even though she'd been warned it would spoil her complexion.

"I didn't care. I've always hated the dark and the cold. I've lived a long time and I don't want to die! I'd rather live in the dark than not live at all."

Redford said there was nothing to be afraid of. Just then, a burly man interrupted, pounding at the door. When she opened, he pushed in and she swooned. The old woman came to, and the man was relieved she was all right.

"I'm sorry, lady, but I've got my orders! Look, I don't get no pleasure busting in doors. I got a crew and equipment coming in an hour or 2 to pull this tenement down."

"Are you really not Mr Death?"

The intruder didn't seem to hear what she said.

"All I know is I got a contract to demolish this row of buildings. You were notified months ago, right? These buildings were condemned by the city—this building's had it! It's worn out, used up; all these buildings have to come down! I ain't no monster, lady. I've got a heart just like anybody else. I can see how you can get attached to a place, but the building's got to come down and make way for the new. That's life, lady—I just clear the ground so other people can live. A big tree falls and a new one grows from the same ground. Old animals die and young ones take their places. Even people step aside."

"I won't!" she cried, closing the door.

"Now what's the sense of locking a door that won't even be here in an hour? Look, I've been trying to go easy. If you insist on staying here, I'll have to call a cop."

She silently beseeched Robert Redford to help. After the intruder left, the old woman asked why he hadn't come to her aid.

He told her to look in the mirror: his reflection was absent.

"You tricked me!" she shouted. "It was you all the time!"

"Yes," said the handsome cop. "I tricked you."

"But why? Now that I let you inside, you could have taken me anytime . . . but you were nice. You made me trust you."

"I had to make you understand," he said. "Am I really so bad? Am I really so frightening? You talked to me. You *confided* in me. Have I tried to hurt you? It isn't me you're afraid of—you understand me. What you're afraid of is . . . the unknown. Don't be afraid."

"But I *am* afraid!"

"The running is over. It's time to rest. Give me your hand."

"But I don't want to die!"

"Trust me."

"No!" she said.

Arm outstretched, he softly called her *Mother.*

"Give me your hand."

Their fingers, then palms, touched.

"You see? No shock. No engulfment. No 'tearing asunder.' What you feared would come like an explosion, is a whisper. What you thought was the end . . . is the beginning."

"When *will* we begin?" she asked, faintly excited. "When will we go?"

He nodded toward the bed, where the old woman saw her own body lay—lifeless.

"We already have."

Joan felt foolish sitting there bawling at a kinescope. Her father said something about how well-done the shows were but she couldn't hear him for the roaring in her ears. So as not to make a scene for the ladies in the next room, Joan quashed her sobs into snuffles, a grotesque pulmonary collapsing-in upon herself—like demolished rooms. Her father handed her Kleenex and was glad she was moved, it was gratifying and sensible that his "blood" would appreciate the Golden Age craft, the emotions evoked, it never occurring to him she was responding on a multitude of levels, and Joan was grateful for that, for his simplicities. Then he made a dry little laugh *and said the show reminded him of that night when the officers*

LXXIX.

CHESTER

---

prayed to the 4 directions, something she'd been shown by some kind of shaman in Northern California. Chess never took mushrooms before though once did acid as a teenager, by mistake, his friends said it was psilocybin, whatever that was, he still didn't know, supposedly something milder but it turned out to be "Tim Leary's Blue Blasters" and scared the holy shit out of him: 12 hours alone in the basement rec room Cinema-scoping krazy kavalcade of buxom breasts while every fiber in his being fought not to go mad or run upstairs to tell his mom.

Now here they were in the desert, insurance check on its way, "set and setting" a groove, Laxmi an old hand, said she would only take half a dose herself so if he "freaked" she could take care of him, they were going to do some MDMA 1st to chill him out, *so* beautiful she said, but then *goddammit,* he started stressing over what happened to Maurie, his culpability, same ol same old, *shit,* everything had been going so well, he'd been determined to tamp that down and mellow out, he thought he was succeeding yet here it was, OK, that was his demon, that was all part of it, but what if he got stuck on a guilt-trip in the middle of his visionquest and spilled his guts/ran screaming into Joshua trees of red-armied boulder dusk, coyote-mauled and soulcrushed by the Great Cactus-Needled Karmic Wheel? Suddenly worried the vertigo might come back too. *Jesus, I'm a bigger Jew than Maurie Levin.* Why was he even doing this? *Because it's righteous and* she's *righteous and this is my path so fuck you.* Chess shouted at himself and wished he were dead, hated being in his own skin, being Chester Herlihy was such a fucked-up chore. This was supposed to be his *Journey of a Lifetime.* They had watched that show on the Travel Channel, the guy who plays the agent on *Entourage* went over to India, it was corny but cool, the actor visited orphanages and 5-

star spas, did Laughing Yoga, stumbled into elephant processions, met a guru, and generally had a high old time. Still, that was pussytime compared to mushroomville. Finally he became resolute: *Fuck it, this is how it is, this is my fucking path, my* Journey of a Lifetime, *and guilt is all right, vertigo's all right, guilt and vertigo are part of it* anyhow, *this shit probably* cures *guilt and vertigo.*

He told Laxmi his plan (the plan that dropped down on him one day and had motivated him to settle his suit, stoked by bad vibes, the fear that Maurie would wake up and accuse him, or that Chess might weaken and turn himself in to the cops—further aided and abetted by the paranoia that what happened to his mother was karmic retribution, and preamble to his own fate should he remain in the City of Angels): that he wanted *them* to go to India, he would buy their tickets with the monies, that way she could see her dad and Chess could get away from everything *I mean fucking everything* his mom was in good hands with Joan, get away from all the *bad energy* and the *failure* and the *years of bullshit* that clouded his life, find a new road in that epic magisterial dirty consecrated country. Of course he didn't Viagrashare; there was no need. She was so moved by his invitation and stratagem, everything he said sounded so right, not just for Chess, but for her as well; *this* way, he said, she could confront *her* demons, plus see her old man yet not be dependent, the settlement would last them *years,* God knew how many rupees it translated into, and even if it *did* run out (which it wouldn't), by then they'd be off into something else, earning their keep, Western ingenuity, teaching English, founding schools or hospitals or whatever, until that illusive unlikely impossible time when funds dried up *lifetimes* stretched before them, a life in which they would never have to worry about survival, a life in which to heal, to write (her eyes welled up, because Laxmi knew he was referring to her book), a life to do yoga and cleanse, to be of service, *to help others*—Laxmi called that "Karma Yoga," a supposed actual ancient term—Chess said he wanted to stop taking painkillers, India would be the perfect place to detox, he was confident he'd get better there, repair himself physically, spiritually, emotionally, like a sidewalk preacher the more he spoke the more he believed, talking about it was medicine, the *doing* of it would be the cure, and his makeshift girlfriend, fellow traveler, Journeyer (Journaler) of a Lifetime, said she knew he was right, *he was so right about everything, she was so glad God brought them together!* that *everything* was right and had happened for a reason, they had met through Maurie and been "broughten" together through Chess's injuries, that awful thing happened at Morongo *for a reason,* and Chess winced then quickly recovered because he *knew:* no malice behind it, no malice of *Universe* behind *anything,* an *ethereal* rather than satanic plan—what a concept!—for the 1st time Chess became *aware,* She made him aware, *She,* goddess and woman, in the cool stunned fading lucid heat of high desert he let all of it in, erstwhile canned notion of Higher Power—it sounded so pathetic through the years, the AA slogan, but it was *true,* Chester Herlihy was an instant convert, there *was* a Higher Power, how could he have not known or thought that, how could he be so arrogant to believe it was a cliché, to believe or not in *clichés* had nothing to *do* with what Maurie had visited on him or what Chess then visited upon his friend or what Laxmi/Chess/Maurie made of their triangle (pyramid)—it was only what had *happened,* without judgment or reason, the Universe did not *plot,* was not engineered from guilt or shame or pride or desiring, it was gloriously unbuilt of jigsaw *happenings* and *events.* Chess realized he would have to learn a new language: old gates need be abrogated, he'd molt like a snake, be-*come* someone, *was* becoming, some *thing,* different, *that* was the Path because what he still/once is/was had broken down and no longer worked.

They prayed to the 4 directions and to earth, moon, and sun. Laxmi read from a book written by a saint she wanted to visit in Bombay, about having your head "in the mouth of the tiger"—there was no escape if one continued to fight with the Self—true freedom meant not liberation *from* the ego but liberation *for* it. Chess made a bad joke about Siegfried and Roy, how the one who didn't get mangled might have a different opinion, but she attrib-uted his clowning to sheer nerves. Suddenly he remembered a book he loved as a boy (they weren't coming on yet, though Laxmi said they were close to the stage where you wondered if you *were,* or *should* be, even though you still felt sorta normal), he began talking about it 10 minutes after Laxmi diced up "the little ones" (what the cognoscenti called *cubensis,* they'd swallowed them with banana to cut the bitterness), Chess saying that as a kid he hardly read but the book he loved more than any just happened to be called *The Wonderful Flight to the Mushroom Planet.* Laxmi sexily guffawed. When the title came out of his mouth, neither of them could actually believe it. What an omen! she said. He told her that the most beautiful thing about it, the thing he could never forget, and thought of even to this day to calm himself when times were tough, was the rocketship that a tribe of children built in the middle of the night, they rose from their beds and went to the beach to blast off *(Tim Leary's Blue Blasters!)*—"How *amazing,*" she said. "Isn't that amazing?" he countered, their *amazing*s somehow perfectly overlapping—maybe they *were* coming on—rocketship on blackvault oceanshore seemed to embody everything, all wonder of cosmos harmoniously attuned until adolescent cynicism snowed under, "the headlamps of childhood," as some writer put it, headlamps onto motes of orgiastic Mystery then wattage dimmed and lamp cords frayed before one grew callous, hidebound, and rueful over what he could no longer feel, taste, see, or remember, so far from the awesome messages once carried on beachwind of infinity-looped, dead-on summer nights now dead.

They lay quiet awhile—Laxmi said they should be quiet—and Chess thought maybe he hadn't taken enough little ones—then had the thought he *might* be coming on—then *definitely,* even though Laxmi said with a vacant smile that *she* wasn't. Which made sense; she took half. Or maybe she lied and swallowed a full dose and only *said* she'd taken less because she knew how spooked he was. (Maybe *she'd* be the one to lose it.)

(Doubtful) (The *Nancy Nurse* fantasy was bullshit anyway)

He *was* coming on now. Oh. No. Industrial-strength—"ego-leveling dosage"—another favored phrase of the shamanguides—queasy and afraid. Stomach hurting. Body/mind

changes churning vertigo/*hawhr*fear: *why did i do this i shouldn't*
have done this what if i/we need a hospital what if it's the same hospital
they took Maurie. They hadn't left their room at the perfectly
named Miracle Manor, beautiful minimalist hotel with sweet utilitarian kitchen, clinical desert tile whites, he didn't at *all* want to
go outside. He lay on the floor.

    feeling the presence of elephants.

        He could sense the duststorms stirred by
their powerful legs.

    THE DISTANT MUSIC EMANATING FROM THEIR TRUNKS.

    Trumpets.

Chess asked Laxmi if she minded if he spoke, that he was
going to tell her "essential truths."

She said she would like that: excited for him, giddy almost.
And he said, like an anchor in Iraq

    these are Her imperial troops. i am on the outskirts of the army's
gathering. these elephants are the imperial guards. because i have taken
the little ones, the cubenses, *they are allowing me here, but i can only*
be present at a great distance. getting too close would endanger. i feel
like huckleberry. what is his last name. Finn, she said

    these are Her imperial guards—

He sat flummoxed and shocky with the holiness of it and
Laxmi grinned, quietly eager and respectful. He asked for reassurance that she'd help, that Laxmi would help with whatever
came up because *She*—that's how he referred to this energetic entity, misty mythopoeic colossus the elephants were guarding—*She*
could easily crush him and all that is or ever was built or imagined. It would be nothing for Her! Laxmi made gentle oath. His
girlfriend and journeywoman, splinter of She, was generous and
bountiful, just like that whom the elephants guarded. But there
was no danger in Laxmi, the human manifestation . . .

Chess began to cry and said

    She *is learning about me through* you. *She sees that i am*
afraid because i brought you, laxmi, to help. She sees i am a frightened,
frail being, and because of that, She is going to treat me with tender-
ness. He convulsed in tears. *Oh!* (Laxmi cried with him, softly

though, so as not to upstage) *can you imagine? this being*—(Laxmi told him it was Kali-Durgā)—*this being who could crush me—crush the world if She wished—has deigned to treat me with such* compassion *and* tenderness *i am so ashamed! i was so afraid, and among the infinite tasks She has before her, She has taken the time to make certain i am unharmed! for i am a fragile*

Laxmi put her arms around him and said to let everything just wash over, and that she loved him.

How can there be shame? When
She never rests! he shouted, wild-eyed, filled with grace. *because of her compassion she allows the elephants to guard Her, but only because She knows that is what they* wish—She knows they are guarding nothing! (Laxmi was crying again) *can anything be more beautiful than that? oh! so sad! it's so sad! the plant! i feel the* sadness of the plant—*how can we bear up against the sadness of a plant?* he asked rhetorically—quietly, Laxmi changed "plant" to "planet" but he didn't hear—*how can we bear the sadness of a* plant, *how can we* take *that, laxmi? She says that She knows we can't. She knows we are too weak and that our backs would break under the weight of even a single tear of this mushroom, Her favorite pupil, Her most devoted student, can you see? She says the mushroom likes to observe the world through our eyes and that She lets us see things through* Its *eyes, though not for very long because it's too much, we're too frail, so She lets us be human, lets us forget, because it would destroy us if we walked around remembering*

For hours (4 hours), Laxmi tended him, bringing fruit drinks. Still, he had no desire to go outside.

There was no outside.

Once, on her way to the kitchen, Chess said with a laugh: "I don't know if I'll be here when you get back."

He wasn

rode beachrocket from marinesub to subcontinent, Old and New testamentary Worlds, found himself at sea as well, Homeric ship on tsunami wave, crest of voice imploring him to let go, *let go of the mast*—Her again, commanding—*let go, for the mast is already broken.* She whom imperial elephants guarded and for whom mushrooms were merely students and Chess a speck *Chesapeake* of submarined subatomic dust, showed him *cubensis* Cubist crystalline prismpink mosaic of amethyst-emerald alien cityscapes, high-tension tessellated grids, he literally got knocked down by her wedding train—merely one more groveling suitor. He began to shiver/shudder, felt his mother Marjorie, the plant ingeniously wafting him from cosmoec-staticdemonic to interpersonal, now on Freudian couch feeling melancholic pain of that old woman's heart and body—there were so many Mothers, why should Marjorie be any less scared/sacred? He was already in India, thankful soon to be faraway, sadness and anxiety of separation and necessary revolt. Rocked in Laxmi's arms. Those men beating Mom's small white body in the night, robbing her, Mother alone without him, his protectorship, saw himself taking her money, asking for money, *Die Rich,* how could he, how could he make such a joke, he killed with his jokes, 1st Maurie than Marj, and now it must stop, *She,* the Great Mother, would help him, *must* help, he would call on Her imperial army, guarding nothing, do what he had to, he was good for Nothing, he would leave the useless killing part of himself behind, rocking *a rock* in Laxmi's arms, Laxmi, cheap ineffable wondrous sterling knockoff of She, It, Chess now stereoscopically keening and wailing at Her unfathomable horror and Mercy.

I will go to India for I cannot be here for her death. I could not be here for her life.

O Mother Mother Mother I have

LXXX.

MARJORIE

---

discarded the paper at her feet
which she lifted to read the dingy ad blaring out at her

from the floor of the bus that would take her (though she did not know it) to Long Beach.

The LOVE IS AROUND THE CORNER fortune and lucky numbers were tucked in pocket, she had gotten the original scrap back from Joan after her daughter had promised—sworn—to write the string of numbers down once and for all. They were to be used without exception when buying lottery tickets.

Marj left the bungalow while the nurse was dozing. She strolled the gardens awhile—a lovely hotel, she'd been to a reception there once with Hamilton—before going south on Beverly Drive to Wilshire where she sat and looked at the gutted Taj Mahal, the theater she took her babies to when they were young. *A tear of sorrow on the cheek of time.* Wasn't that how a poet had described the palace in Agra?

Joan would be angry with her for sneaking away. Her daughter had been so kind but that hotel was costing too much, *had* to be. Why were they at a hotel in the 1st place? Joan was acting strange and solicitous, as if Marjorie were a child. She spent money like water on nurses and room service. It just wasn't sitting well. Joan kept telling Marj she would soon be a grandmother, but she knew that couldn't be true, Joan was too *old* to have children, and not even married! Marj didn't want to say it but she was truly concerned. She thought Joan was and always had been barren, and worried she'd quit her job as an architect too soon.

She rested on a bench and let the buses pass. Then she walked to another hotel, kitty-corner to the vanished Taj—the Regent Beverly Wilshire—also quite lovely. (She remembered having been there with Ham as well, at a bar called Hernando's Hideaway. There used to be a big bookstore inside, but all that was long gone.) She wandered into a restaurant with black-and-white floors called The Boulevard, they spelled it "The Blvd," but suddenly had to use the restroom—a young woman pointed the way, though it took a while for Marj to find—and as she sat in the opulent marble-floored fully enclosed stall (reminding, as a certain opulence usually did, of Bombay's Taj Mahal Palace Hotel), she thought of Bonita and their excursion to Neiman's. She even imagined retracing their steps yet didn't have the strength, not today.

She wiped herself then looked for the lever but there wasn't one—nothing at all! How could such a splendid hostelry have skimped on a basic fixture, installing a toilet that couldn't be flushed? Perhaps they were on timers; that seemed rather crude. She wondered what to do. She decided she'd go tell someone. Marj stood from the bowl, gathering her skirt around her. She didn't like leaving all that in the water, it was ugly. A moment after she got up, she heard a flush. Something must be wrong and she still thought she should mention it at the reception desk, but shrugged. The old woman washed her hands with the sweet-smelling soap, glad that she wouldn't have to share her travail with the staff, who had so much else to tend to.

Maybe the toilet had fixed itself.

She walked to the grand entrance (where the swimming pool used to be way back when) and asked the doorman in the marvelous costume for a cab. She gave the driver the address of her Beverlywood home. As they turned into the street, Marj felt bad because she hadn't brought anything for Pahrump.

The coachman slowed down, looking for the house. Darkness

was descending. She told him this was it, the charred lot (she didn't say that in so many words), and he made a snorting sound. She said just pull into the drive please and let me out. He was one of those horrid, judgey men from unknowable countries who had an agenda on top of getting their money. Marj gave him a nice tip and he shook his head, ogling her as she stepped to the sidewalk, like she was a crazy person. The old woman was about to investigate the remains of her residence but saw the driver still sitting there gawking, and she looked him straight in the eye until he shrugged and sneered and snorted again or whatever it was he did and put the car in gear and pulled away.

She couldn't get onto the property because of a wire fence.

"Marjorie?"

It was Cora.

"Hello!"

"Marjorie, what—what are you *doing* here? Aren't you at the hotel? Joan said you were at the hotel."

"Oh yes, we're still there, but there's no place like home!"

"But—how did you get here?"

"I cabbed it. Cora, why *is* there this *fence?*"

"For safety. The kids in the neighborhood were climbing all around."

Cora stared at her old friend.

"I am *so sorry* I haven't come to see you, Marj—you're at the Beverly Hills? But, well . . . you see, I had some bad news of my own. My Pahrump passed away."

"No! Not Mr P!"

"Yes. Yes, he did."

The 2 began to cry.

"And there I was for the last few hours wondering what to *bring* him . . . oh darling, how dreadful!"

"The doctors said they did everything humanly possible, but it just got to the point where—I thought it was cruel. I put him on DNR. 'Do Not Resuscitate.' "

"He was *so brave.* Oh, that Mr P! Cora, it was his *time.*"

"Well, yes, I suppose. He lost his testicles at the end. You know,

Steinie said they do prosthetics now, for dogs who get neutered. Just like a breast implant, only *down there*. But the doctors said the surgery would have killed him." She smiled that incongruous cookie-jar smile. "Come! Come inside, Marj, it's cold. Does Joan know you're here?"

"Oh! I imagine."

Cora sensed something was wrong. She wanted to get her friend into the house, maybe get some food in her while she called the hotel and told her daughter what was going on. (She had a sneaking suspicion Mrs Herlihy's whereabouts were unknown.) All she could think was, the poor darling has been through hell.

Cora parked her in the living room. She brought a glass of water and part of a Reuben sandwich from Factor's that her grandson left, and the maid had wrapped up.

"The most wonderful thing was, just before my Drummer Boy passed, these extraordinary people came and put him on film— he's a television star! Now they're going to dedicate the entire episode to Mr P. Oh Marj, let me show you!"

She put on the *Dog Whisperer* DVD that Stein had "burned." Marjorie wasn't sure what the whole thing was about but it *did* give her a chance to see Pahrump again, and that was fine. There was another dog too, who'd been shot by mistake, so awful, but the animals seemed to be busy making friends. She recognized some of her neighbor's grandkids. Cora was on the show too, "in the wings," and Marj thought she comported herself well.

She called the hotel from the kitchen and left a message with guest voicemail saying, "Joan, your mom is here." When Cora hung up, she realized that in her excitement she stupidly hadn't identified herself, and phoned again. This time, it took longer to connect her to the room. "Joan? I'm *so* sorry—that was me!—but I don't think I left my name. It's *Cora,* Cora Ludinsky, Marjorie's neighbor. Well, she's here in my living room. I wasn't sure if you knew, but she's *right here in my living room, right now."* It came to her that she had Joan's cellphone number somewhere; finding it would be another story. Also, that she probably should have said what time it was.

She went back in—Marj was already standing at the front door. Cora begged her to stay, but Marj was adamant and the neighbor said she would give her a ride back to the hotel. Marj told her it wasn't necessary, that "Lucas sent a Town Car," and it was waiting on Robertson because she didn't want to "put on airs" or suffer the embarrassment of the chauffeur seeing her beloved house in its undignified burned-up condition. Cora knew that was nonsense and wild talk. She pleaded with Marj and tried to stall, saying she wanted to show off some of the new garden furniture Stein had bought. Marj left almost hastily. Cora went straight to the phone to reach her son but didn't have any luck. She began to look for Joan's cell number.

The old woman stared through the Cyclone fence at the ruins of her home. It made her think of that ancient city the Travel Gal mentioned, Benares, where Jesus learned the art of healing— where corpses were set on fire and thrown from ghats into the Ganges, the proceedings watched over by Lord Śiva, god of Death. (She looked it up in the old *Encyclopedia Britannica* her father had bought for her Sweet 16th.) The river, between the Varana and Asi rivers, was said to have sprung from Śiva's matted hair. When his girlfriend Parvati died, a jeweled earring fell to earth and landed in the exact place that became the holiest cremation site—"the Manikarnika Ghat." She was amazed to read that it took 100 kilos of wood to render a body to ashes. All day and all night one could hear the chant, *Rama nama satya hai* ("God's name is Truth"). Benares, she read, "is also known as Mahashmashana, the great cremation ground, the final resting place of the corpse of the universe at the end of its vast cycle of life." Trudy said that Benares was nothing but a "wretched ant farm."

She began to walk. Just before turning the corner to Robertson she looked back to see Cora, distressed, standing on the side-walk—*the neighbor called out to her but Marj couldn't hear and besides, quickened her pace.*

Within 5 minutes she was on a bus, heading for Long Beach as she

LXXXI.

JOAN

---

came home from visiting her dad, the caregiver was frantic.

After tearfully admitting to the possibility she had napped during *Oprah,* the RN said that her mother had somehow managed to "slip out." Upon realizing "the client" was gone, she became distraught and went looking for her. Joan asked if she'd bothered to notify security; she hadn't, and was tormented afresh by her own incompetence. Joan picked up the phone. The staff said they would immediately alert the police in case Mrs Herlihy had "wandered off-site," and begin to check ladies' rooms, pool and cabana areas, and the hidden fern-choked nooks that were plentiful on the grounds—everywhere they could think of.

Joan thanked them, then saw the envelope under the door—a message from the hotel operator, saying "Cora Ludinsky" had called.

She retrieved the voicemail informing that Marj was back in Beverlywood. The neighbor hadn't left a number and Joan didn't have it in her Treo afterall (*of course*) but it didn't matter, she jumped in the car and went right over. On the way, she phoned the detective who had helped with the fraud case; he said he'd do what he could. Of course when she got there, her mother was gone, and Cora didn't have much to add, except the disquieting reference to "Lucas." No one was sure if she'd flagged a cab or gotten on a bus or was just meandering—in a follow-up call, the detective thought the latter a more likely scenario, that she was out there confused, and someone had most likely given refuge, and was in the process of contacting authorities—so Joan canvassed the neighborhood until it was pitch dark. She even stopped at Riki's and the young man said yes, she'd been in, not too long ago, to buy a ticket. Cora said that Marj was wearing a stylish green coat, and Joan was positive it was the Jil Sander she bought for her that 1st week she'd come home from the hospital. Mom liked to wear it when they ate at the subterranean hotel coffeeshop. She passed that on to the detective.

Joan and Barbet had plans to go to Locanda Portofino for her birthday—a supershitty day to turn 38. (She hadn't expected her father to remember, and chided herself for even having the sappy, babyish thought that he'd send flowers and a 6pack of Diet Coke.) They wound up meeting at Kate Mantellini's because the restaurant was sort of between the hotel and the old house; that way, Joan could feel halfway in her skin. There was nothing to do for now and at least she had the gut feeling Mom would soon be found. The detective had his "eyes and ears out there" and was waiting for a high-priced PI colleague to return his page. Joan awaited that callback as well—she'd already emailed a picture of Marj and there was no reason the PI couldn't get started right away. She told the detective to give his friend a number—$25,000, as retainer fee—and he said that was way too high but Joan insisted. She knew it guaranteed action. She needed someone who would knock on doors if it came down to that.

She dumped all this on Barbet and he was an enormous comfort. He brought a gift, an iPod with the complete downloaded audioworks of Trollope and Dostoevsky (unabridged). Even her favorite, Bulgakov's *The Master and Margarita,* was on there, bless his soul. A feature allowed you to fast-forward narration without distorting the text, a kind of "speed listening." (She couldn't wait to zip through *The Idiot.*) Barbet managed to get her laughing, and Joan needed that because she was beyond hysteria. She was beyond beyond. He started riffing on Kate Mantellini's, which was actually designed by Thom Mayne.

"I know," said Joan. "Did you see the thing in the *Times* today where Mayne ass-licked *El Zorro?*"

"The Phaeno Science Center, in Wolfsburg."

"Will the shiteating never stop?"

"Not as long as there are anuses. Would you *look* at this restaurant? It's like a house in Vegas, commissioned by one of the boobs who hit it big in Blue Man Group. This waterhole's *so*

fuckin ugly. Are those *boxers* carved out of metal? Is this supposed
to be, like, a postmodern sports bar? I mean, *whuh?* Look, babe,
consider yourself *lucky.* You *could* have fucked Ground Control to
Major Thom, and be about to give birth to some illegitimate Icha-
bod Crane Pritzkerfetus who needs anger management. Some
bitch-slapping toddler with close-cropped hair and a mean streak
who's destined to do yoga with Saul David Raye and eat strawberry salsa *à table,* at *Table.*" He pretended to masturbate then
looked around, shivering with disgust as she cracked up. "Even
the *people* here. *Realtors* and loser *comedians* with *trust funds.* The
feng shui makes your *flesh* crawl—the ambience! The whole experience is . . . it must be like the aftertaste people get when they go
for *chemo.* That *Writers Guild* crowd trickling in from Doheny;
they go see movies for free or listen to Bill Maher 'in conversation'
with Ariadne Huffington"—he was so bombed (he'd had a head
start) that's what he called her—"for the hundred-thousandth
time. *The vibe here is so creepy.* Don't you think? *A nouveau riche
sports bar* with Major Thom's usual warm, fuzzy edges—the poor
waitresses must get *impaled* when they turn the corner into the
kitchen! At least *you* didn't get impaled on a Thom Mayne hard
edge. At least *you* had the sense to be inseminated by a Jew billionaire!"

Her partner knew the paternity issue was conversationally off-
limits, but what the hell. He never believed her one-night-stand
Geek Squad story anyhow. *"Entre rien"* (as Barbet put it), he suddenly asked if she wanted to join him next week at the Airport
Hilton to "experience" an avatar called Amma, Mata Amri-
tananandamayi ("Say *what?*" said Joan. "Amma means mother,"
said Barbet), popularly known as the Hugging Saint. He said that
someone tried to stab her not too long ago in Kollam, where the
Big Wave hit, and Joan riposted, "You're nobody till somebody
stabs you." She was actually surprised to hear Barbet was even interested. He said wryly, "Why not? Everyone can use a hug. Especially after a fucking *memorial* reject. Besides, I have ulterior
motives."

"Don't you always?"

"One of our pretentious potential Buddhist clients said I should go."

"Ah. Is there such a thing as an *unpretentious* potential Buddhist client?"

Barbet smirked, and said it might give ARK the edge in getting "the job."

"*What* job?" she said. "What are you *talking* about?"

"Some temple in Taos."

"Been there, done that. Haven't we had enough faux Buddhists for a while?"

"Well, that ain't *my* faux. Anyway, Lew Freiberg isn't a Buddhist."

"I *hate* fucking Buddhists," said Joan. "I'd rather get raped by a Getty conservator than be invited to another Steve Ehrlich Zen brunch. There are *no American Buddhist people of color.*"

"What are you, the ACLU now?"

"They're *rich* and they're *white* and all they do is spend *thousands of dollars* making *precious little pilgrimages* to Dharamsala or *wherever* so they can write 4th-rate prosepoetry 'essays' about their *cushy, cosmic adventures* for *Tricycle,* or *Travel + Leisure.* They all suck the Dalai Lama's 12 inch dick. Legends in their own *luminous minds.* Oh! And they *love* to talk about 'sitting'—you know, my meditation practice can beat up your meditation practice. 'Just sit'—that's the big famous phony Buddhist motto. *Just sit*—on your Prada meditation pillow. You know what I say? Just *shit.* Take a *big shit.* That's what *I* say."

"You know why I love you, Joan? You're the only person angrier than I am."

Just now, he knew she had every right to be.

"Have you read the *magazines,* Barbet? I've done a lot of research—*as you know*—and I'll tell you! Here's what's on the covers, *every month:* Robert Thurman Robert Thurman Robert Thurman, Pema Chödrön Pema Chödrön Pema Chödrön. Robert Thurman in conversation with Robert Thurman in conversation with Pema Chödrön in conversation with Robert Thurman eating out Pema Chödrön. Sharon Salzberg! Sharon

Salzberg in conversation with Pema Chödrön! Pema Chödrön in conversation with Sharon Salzberg! Jack Kornfeld on a panel with Jack Kornfeld on a panel with Jack Kornfeld sucking his own dick while Pema Chödrön blows Rudolph the red-nosed Rinpoche!"

"*The Aristocrats!*"

"Richard Gere Richard Gere Richard Gere! bell hooks bell hooks bell hooks! Oh! And the big *controversy*—the letters to the editors—are these *pathetic assholes* who try to *distinguish* themselves in the *hierarchic pecking order* by declaring how they think things should be *spelled*. Barbet, I am *serious.*" She began to sing, "You say *nirvana,* I say *nibbana,* you say the *dharma,* I say the *dhamma—nirvana, nibbana,* the *dharma,* the *dhamma*—let's call the whole thing—"

" 'Nothingness,' " Barbet interjected, arching an eyebrow. She ignored the comment; he grew secretly glum when she didn't acknowledge a bonafide witticism.

"They even spell *tao* D-A-O. Like that idiot woman who just *had* to recycle *Swann's Way: The Way by Swann's.* Dumbshit!"

"You mean 'The Shit by Dumb.' "

"And what is *up* with the Dalai *Lama?* Did you hear he said Katrina happened because of people's *karma?*"

"Their *khamma*—"

"Now he's Pat Robertson! Then I read something about how ol HHDL sat—*just sit!*—"

"Is that like DHL? UPS? FedEx?"

"—His *Highness* the Dalai *Lama sat* with this guy who set himself on fire because of the way the Chinese treat Tibetans. The guy sets himself on fire and goes into prayer position, OK?"

"I do that after sex."

"But he *lived.* So Lord Lama comes a-callin! The guy has 4th degree burns and His Holiness gives him a lecture on why he shouldn't hate the Chinese! The piece of toast tries to sit up—just sit!—out of respect, but keels over! At least His Holiness got his shot in! His parting fucking shot!"

Barbet was howling.

"You know," said Joan, with a minxy smile. "You're a pretty good straight man. *And* you're straight. *We* should have had a baby."

"We tried."

"Yeah, we did."

"Besides, I'd be too raged out."

"I still think you should help me raise it."

"Help you *rage* it."

"Fine, help me rage it. But just help me."

"That's a given."

They gave their 2 miscarriages a moment of silence.

"There *is* something far out that I saw in the *Times,*" said Barbet. "You could send it to Freiberg. It's *really* interesting. They found 2 fossils fused together, *fucking.* 65,000,000 years old. In some state in India. Insect lovers or whatever. Now it's just microscopic fungus, but you can *actually see them in the act.* Died in the Paleolithic saddle. How's *that* for limbic dissonance? Not too bad. I think you should send it to Jew—I mean Lew. You know, the whole Sam and Esther shticky: the Way We Were."

Another quiet moment.

"So: will you come to the Amma thing?"

She threw back her head and laughed as the waitress brought a pile of calamari.

"Sure."

"You have to take a number for a hug—seriously, Joan. We need a 'token.' Sometimes this woman hugs, like, 9,000 people."

"Sign me up. But can't you reserve? You know: 'Dial 777-HUGS'?"

The Treo rang.

It was the PI.

Joan mentioned her price and he said he would find her mother within 24 hours.

LXXXII.

RAY

H<small>E</small> showed BG the deposit slip from the account, with both their names: Raymond Rausch *or* Ghulpa Kṣemaṅkari. After attorney fees and sundry expenses, the balance was $488,383.51. Ray joked that "it would buy a lot of Pampers."

Ghulpa was glad, but having bad dreams again.

A tiger was killing her Raj, her Bapu bled in fields of thousand-foot mangroves, searching for honey in forests of Sundarbans, from his blood and plasma sprang ordinary demons whom Durgā and black Kali (jumping from their puja *pandal* as Little Gulp's schoolfriends led them to the Hooghly River) lapped up like thirsty whores, then shook as did palm fronds in a storm, quivering with delight while they decapitated and quartered the old man, stuffing him down their gullets. The honey, redolent of oak and lavender, poured like ice wine; amber at dusk but saffron-colored in the day, and so very sweet—yet human flesh was sweeter! A single drop on a newborn's tongue would keep it healthy for years. BG wanted that drop for *her* child, even if the price (how it wrenched her heart!) was to be paid with the death of her husband—she'd finally acceded to his proposal though they hadn't set a date; there was talk of a consecration of conch shells, knotted scarves and ghee, of how the darker the hand-henna wedding day designs grew (and the longer they remained), the better the augury—but the raucous cats from Bangladesh showed no mercy, and would not let her near the nectar.

The cousins selflessly, cheerfully, efficiently, assiduously, comically rushed to and fro, as their Ghulpa became engorged with a sleepwalker's dread. She called out *Bapu!* it seemed every few minutes or so, asking him to enter the room so she could see him in the flesh. The human flesh!

The old man couldn't ride the shuttle with the Friar anymore (the dog was down to twice-a-week visits to the Center), couldn't even leave the house because BG was afraid that something terrible would happen and he wouldn't return.

The tigers.

That is what her dreams kept telling her.

She stopped watching television because the news frightened her, nor did she watch the DVDs that Ray and the others procured. Tech-savvy cousins brought a thin black Nano jukebox but she only listened to radio. One night, Ghulpa closed the door and lowered her voice in great secrecy to ask Ray if he'd pick up a "golden oldie" that mesmerized her (weirdly, a song he had wooed his ex with) and her enjoyment of it sorely perplexed; his mind stammered. Might Joan have told her about it? No—Joan and Ghulpa hadn't actually met. Where had she heard it? The *radio,* of course . . . but still, so strange.

—*don't fear, my darling, the lion sleeps tonight.*

A FTER BG fell asleep, he called his daughter's cellphone. She sounded a little frantic.

"Did I catch you in the middle, Joanie?"

"No—it's fine. It's just—I have—there is *so much stuff going on* right now."

It sounded like she was outside, and out of breath.

She had a busy life. And wasn't used to getting calls from her daddy.

"Hi, Ray!" she said, as if starting over. "It's really nice to hear from you."

"I'm sorry if I got you at a bad time."

"No, no! It's cool—it's *fine*—go ahead."

"Well, it's been a little rough but I think we might have seen the worst of it. The City of Industry came through, and I wanted to ask"—*could he need money? no no no could he be asking*—"and I wanted to know if there was anything that you or your brother Chester . . . may I inquire how you're 'fixed'?"

"Oh! I'm—no, I'm fine!"

"Because I'd like to give you—both—a little gift."

"You don't *have* to. It's *so* not necessary."

She saw him in her head, envelope ready, like a wedding guest in The Godfather.

"I know that. I know that. But I figure there's a lot of gift-giving opportunities I missed along the years, and I didn't want to miss one again." He heard her softly crying. "So let's say this is an opportunity for an old guy to feel good, and for a young gal and her brother to *make* an old guy feel good." He cut her some slack. "You don't have to tell me just now, Joanie, but think about it. Won't you? And won't you tell your brother Chester about my offer, and y'all can put your heads together? Now, as long as it isn't a private plane," he said, with country-club bonhomie, "then I'm pretty sure I can swing it. Tie it up with a red ribbon."

"That's—that is . . . *very* sweet, Dad"—both realized it was the 1st time she had called him that—"but I'm fine. We *both* are. But it's—I can't believe how *thoughtful* that is."

"You sure?"

"Pretty sure, yeah."

"Like I said, you don't have to tell me now." Pause. "Joanie—Joan—do you think that Chester . . . when you've discussed—did he say—do you think he might want to see me?"

"Yes," she lied.

She lied because she hadn't mentioned Ray's existence, and now she never would. She didn't want her brother touching a cent of the old man's hard-earned settlement, and was unconflicted about her decision.

"What does he do, Joan?"

"He's . . . in the movie business. He finds the places directors need—the *locations*—for their films. You know, if they're looking for an interesting-looking *building,* or a big house with a *pool*—or *bowling lanes* . . ."

She spoke to him as she would to a child, without knowing why. It was the way she talked to Marj.

"Important job," he said, like his daughter had just told him

Chess was a virologist at the CDC. "I was thinking it would be nice for the 3 of us to have dinner. There's a helluva place downtown, near MacArthur Park—the Pacific Dining Car."

"Yes, it's a wonderful restaurant."

"You been there?"

"With clients. It's still open 24 hours a day, isn't it?"

"That's what they say. I don't know how they do it—must be a wealthy family owns it."

"It looks amazing. It's really 'old Los Angeles.' "

"Just like me!"

"It's been in lots of movies."

"I blew some detectives to steak and lobster there the other night, and I thought it might be quite a thing for us to have a meal—just the 3 of us. You, me, and Chesterfield. My treat! You could even tell your mother; I'd love to have her—if she's back from India and all, and feeling up to it. Probably unlikely. Did you say you were joining up with her? I wouldn't tell *Ghulpa,* hell, that's one I'd mark 'Top Secret'! Have you told your mother we've been in touch, Joanie? Have you told Marjorie you've seen me?"

"You know, I haven't had the chance," she said, smiling thinly through the phone. "The only reason is, she's been away. It's kind of a heavy thing to drop on her while she's traveling. She's a fairly independent woman, Ray—"

"Oh yes, I do remember!"

"And when she goes to India, she's not so easy to reach. She's got a cellphone but I'm not so sure she knows how to use it! She stays at the Taj Mahal Palace, in Bombay, kind of her homebase. But it would take a search-and-rescue team to track her down."

Joan started at her own words, the pathos of it—tears streaming down her face again.

"She goes there a lot?"

"Couple times a year."

Where was she where was her mother why haven't they—

"Well, I'm glad she finally realized her dream. She was gung ho on that place ever since I knew her. Went there with her dad, but you already know that. Ghulpa's from Calcutta, did I tell you? Mother Teresa country. I've always wanted to go—not necessarily to Calcutta—but India itself. *Marj* would find that a surprise, but people change. Ghulpa isn't very keen on the place just now! That's how it is sometimes with 'natives.' They've had enough. But maybe things'll be different once the baby comes. Boy, she's been on a tear talking about 'man-eaters'—the Bengal tigers. The doctor says it's more to do with hormones, but that should go away soon enough. Sure would be nice to travel. I'm a little tired of this scenery. I think LA does that to you. *Any* city with a hundred freeways and a concrete river is gonna do it to you. Now the Ganges—*there's* a river! Do you have any children, Joan?"

Why is he doing this? Why is he doing this now—

"I—no. Not yet."

She wanted to get off.

She needed to get back to Barbet.

She needed to get an update from the PI.

She wanted to call Pradeep—

"I don't mean to get personal, but there's just so much to ask, to catch up on—*my* fault, not yours. Guess I'm feeling chatty tonight; the pills they give me for my heart put my jaw on overdrive. Either make me dopey or make me into a 'talkaholic.' I suppose it's easier for me over the phone. I don't mean this in the wrong way, Joanie, but it's a little hard to look at you. But that'll pass. That'll pass. In time. We can talk at a later date, darling daughter."

She surely thought he was going to sign off.

"It's just—I don't really know anything about you! Would you . . . would you *like* to have children?"

"I—well, sure! Yes. Yes, I think I would."

"You're 34?"

"I'm 38."

Today, Dad. Today's my birthday.

"Does Chester have any?"

"No. Um no, he doesn't."

"Did your mom have any more?"

"No. He—her husband—had 2 from another marriage, but they were somewhat estranged."

"Everybody's 'estranged.' Why does everybody have to be estranged, Joanie? I have no business talking. I guess I was pretty much the worst example. Worst of the worst. I could understand if you decided not to have any kids. I was a pisspoor role model."

"No—"

"I meant, I could *understand.* I'm nervous about having this one myself, let me tell you! But I'd like to do it differently this time. And I don't mean—I don't mean it to sound any other way than it sounds."

"I understand, Dad."

"It makes me so happy and so sad to hear you call me that! Mostly happy though. I—I would truly like to get to know you, Joanie—you *and* your brother—just a little more, if that'd be all right. Life isn't short—what I mean is, life *is* short! You really feel that—when you're my age, and you find yourself in the hospital like I was. But I think the Lord might have blessed us with a period of grace to get to know each other a little better. That we know each other at all is some kind of miracle! Big Gulp (that's what I call her, cause in the summer that's all she drinks) has this wonderful saying: 'When you're born, you cry, and everyone around you is laughing; when you die, you laugh, and everyone around you cries.'"

Joan held a hand over the phone so he wouldn't hear her weep; Raymond did the same. The crying game.

"Marjorie and I had a song—'Save the Last Dance for Me.' She ever tell you that? We used to go dancing at the Biltmore. 'Darling, Save the Last Dance for Me' was our song. But we loved the one about the lion—

"Do you know what? She's—Ghulpa's singing it right now! Now isn't that funny. And you know *I just can't get her to*

LXXXIII.

CHESTER

---

tell any-
one where they were going, not that their itinerary was firm. That was
the last thing he needed; to be tracked by Interpol should Maurie
of a sudden awaken and recall the bedside confession that Chester
to this day was unsure of having made, though as the event of
his friend's catastrophe grew dimmer (which it did, surpris-
ingly, gratefully, mercifully), so too did the murkiness of his
own memory, swaddled in the Chronic leafiness of what both
Remar *and* his smalltime dealer called "the trees," camouflaged
by the extra-pyramidal exuberantly potentiated depressive fog
of pain/insomnia war: Neurontin, Ambien CR, Vicodin, Well-
butrin, Lyrica, Motrin, Sonata, Haldol, Seroquel, fentanyl, et alia.

He picked up the check during law office lunch hour, happy
not to run into the chrome-domed, congenial killer fag who left
word with his secretary that Chess should hang until he got back,
so they could at least say hellos and goodbyes. But Chester Herlihy
was a man in a hurry, all up in the trees, and waited for no one.
Naw—Remar was OK. Good people. Just doin his job; in this
case, the client had made it *hard.* Fact was, if not for the "complications," Counselor DeConcini mighta got 15 times the settled
amount. Probably thought Chess was a pussy. And dumb on top
of it.

But karma and expedience had dictated otherwise.

There were factors beyond factors . . .

He grudgingly put the money in the bank, having attempted to
make a futile arrangement to circumvent the notorious 10 day
hold. It was the Era of the 10 Day Hold: *10 Days That Would Not*
Shake Your World. You couldn't move your bowels without someone holding onto your shit for *10 business days* before flushing. It
was a Friday—he'd have to wait 2 full Fridays for the check to
clear. (Chess sensed that Remar knew he was skipping town. The

lawyer probably thought he was going to Vegas; no doubt he had witnessed everything that anyone in throwing distance of white trash could possibly do with a windfall, and it wasn't pretty.) The motherfuckering banks were *all* robbers, he still felt Wells must have had *something* to do with the draining of his mom's account. Also—he had to visit Marj before he split and *that* wasn't going to be fun. Kind of an official unofficial goodbye. He would need a story to tell Joan too. No biggie. He'd say he was gonna go see Laxmi's family in Vancouver or whatever. She looked like someone with family in Vancouver.

E VERY time he thought of Marj he entered that mushroomy space again—he was entering that space a *lot* lately, tripping on elephants and India and the Great Mother that was Time and Space. He thought of the mushroom's tears and how She had warned him that a single drop could break his back. The experience was so heavy and unexpected and indecipherable that Chess felt somehow transformed, like a soldier who made it through his 1st firefight, but it was beautiful too, *warfare* could be beautiful (from what he had read), awesome and terrible and beautiful, and he realized that as long as he paid proper obeisance, as long as he never became arrogant toward She, the 5-and-infinity-starred general who had informed and saturated his presence on ecstatic battlegrounds, as long as he remained steady and humble, then he would be forever welcome in Her army, a rider on the storm, grateful conscript to the anagogic anagalactic weddingtrained outskirts of the legion of tusky gods who helped protect that which needed no protecting.

C HESS had to get rid of the stuff in his apartment. Donate to Goodwill or just throw it away. Buncha crap anyhow. Still, he needed to be fairly meticulous, not lazy about it, so as not to raise any flags. He would just rent a pickup—he'd done it a thousand times before.

He went to see Don Knotts's daughter. He said his mom was

sick and he was going to move in and help out till she got better. Karen was so sweetly empathetic, such a wonderful woman, she could have used the moment to talk about her father's death, her *own* experience, the way people do, but graciously let Chess have his time. He felt like a cad, or whatever. She told him she would return his last month's rent and security deposit (another 24-hundred or so. In India, that would take a year to spend). She even asked after Laxmi. Chess said they were still "going out" but Laxmi was back in school at Northridge and might have to go see her father back east. And oh, he'd be scouting in Colorado for a few weeks. As he heard himself talk, Chess thought he should have had a better story, maybe keep the Vancouver thing congruent so he wouldn't get caught in a lie but it didn't matter, it wasn't like anything sounded suspicious or like his soon never-to-be-seen-again landlord was going to sit around trying to put the non-pieces of a nonpuzzle together. He saw his paranoid days fading, and the need to make up stories as well.

He only had a few lies left in him.

H E went online to check out one-way tickets to Bombay. The cheapest way seemed to be through Frankfurt.

While Chess was doing his thing, the mailman shoved a rubberbanded sheaf through the slot—a couple of local Thai restaurant flyers. Another student-loan dunning notice. *Oh, fuck you.* A brochure about 2 old guys "coming soon to Anaheim & San Bernardino!!!!!" One of the dynamic duo wrote a book, *The Millionaire Next Door,* and his buddy penned a "bestseller" called *$elf-Made Millionaire$.* Call NOW and you get in free—the events were guaranteed to sell out. *Yeah right. Sold out but they'll let you in free cause it's like U2 picking you out of a fuckin mob.*

The phone rang. No one on the line. Chess's heart jumped; he flashed that it was Maurie. *Stop being crazy.*

It rang again.

"Hello?"

"Mr Herlihy? Hello? This is World Pharm calling about a refill on your recent order for—um, Oxycodone?"

He was going to hang up but decided to place a final script and have it FedEx'd. One for my baby and one more for the road. His plan was to detox once they got to India but it never hurt to have a transatlantic stash. Might come in handy during that skinhead rally in Frankfurt.

The idea was to hit Bombay and visit this old guru Laxmi was into. Some of his philosophical writings were in the Bodhi Tree stash she'd given him—the screed about having your head in the tiger's mouth—and Chess struggled through a few random chapters without hooking onto anything. (He was way more into the *Kārma Sūtra*.) "Ramesh" was almost 90 years old, a rich guy with his own apartment building, a former bank president who gave talks from his living room each morning. Laxmi called it *satsang* or some such sanskrity shit. Then they'd take the A-train to Nashik and Trimbakeshwar, swing on over to Aurangabad, shuffle down to Ratnagiri and Goa (which from all accounts was this fucking amazing half-Portuguese beachtown where you could live on the cheap, raving on hasheesh and Ecstasy at night and getting your liver drycleaned by day. The Goans were renowned for their healing colonics, which would be great for his detox.) Thus far Chess had resisted doing any Lonely Planet–type research; that stuff put him to sleep. Much groovier to just get on a plane, no preconceptions, and learn as you went. You didn't really have a choice, any way you cut it. It was sink or swim.

HE rode over to the Beverly Hills Hotel.
Parked on a sidestreet and knocked on both bungalows' doors. No answer. Joan never gave him a key and for some reason that suddenly pissed him off. *Now don't get all rattled. Just chill.* He took 5 vikes and 3 Klonopin. Thought of approaching the front desk and announcing who he was, asking for entry, but didn't feel like undergoing the embarrassment of getting shot down.

So he sat in the lobby and waited, mulling shit over. He decided to tell his sister he was leaving—on a scout somewhere in Mexico, for David Fincher or Doug Liman or one of the Scotts. Probably be away awhile. A big production, a hundred-and-50,000,000 dollar movie. Or maybe he'd say he was doing an indie, something under Ang Lee or Soderbergh's banner, something small and intimate, whatever, funding came through and he was finally producing a long-gestated pet project—not Maurie's, he didn't want to drag Maurie into it—he was going to Costa Rica or maybe even Vancouver. That way he'd kill 2 birds because he could still use the visiting-Laxmi's-people story. Yeah, maybe that was a better way to go. Vancouver, plus a film of his own: something with a little pizzazz and prosperity. He was sick of everyone thinking he was a loser.

He passed the Polo Lounge and took the long, wending path to the bungalows. Hotel staff stepped aside and bowed heads, as if he were royalty. Maybe Joan and his mother had returned from chores or wherever, or he'd bump into them in the midst of Marj's daily constitutional with one of her 7 fucking caregivers. He still couldn't figure out where the money was coming from. Maybe Ham left her more bread than he thought. Or maybe the fire insurance had come in and his sister was drawing on that, with plans to downscale Mom into a care home.

The more he thought about it the *better the idea of his having stumbled into a prestigious, paying gig seemed in terms of something to tell Joan and his*

LXXXIV.

MARJORIE

---

nattily dressed woman who after 2 hours asked where they were and the kind fat black female driver said, "Long Beach. End of the line," asking if she needed any help but the old lady smiled and said she'd be fine, and God Bless.

Marj felt buoyant and alive.

Unencumbered.

She intuited the presence of Hamilton—as if somehow guided by him, her actions sanctioned.

It was dark and as she walked she caught her reflection in the windows of closed shops. Long Beach was such an empty, pretty place. Occasionally the quiet cool of the night was interrupted by stinging sounds or shouts. Someone in a passing car yelled, "Raggedyass bitch!" and threw empty cans out the car. Probably just kids. Marjorie smiled—there was nothing anyone could do to dampen her spirits. She was in upbeat missionary mode, and it was about time!—back to the girlish days when she dreamed of spiritual repatriation, an Indian pilgrimage to give succor (and red peonies) to the destitute and dying (and be succored by them as well), to be lifted up and ennobled, oh she *had* loved Mother Teresa so, heart filled with respect and admiration for this frail giant of incalculable courage and resolve who sought out the poorest of the poor, to love their very diseases and rotting limbs, a saint who wished only to feed them and touch them and wash their wounds. In other words, *a true Christian. Was* there such a thing as a true Christian anymore? In these, the last years of her life, she was finally ready. She would work from the Taj Mahal Palace, in nurse's whites, rent an entire floor for homebase, she would use the monies from the fire sale of her land, the Travel Gals could arrange it, Joanie too, she said she would come if her pregnancy didn't interfere but Marj *still* wasn't certain she was pregnant, maybe it was a ruse, another excuse to back out, but no, she didn't think so, her daughter really *did* want to come this time, it didn't *matter* if she did, Marj was doing this for *herself,* and in a strange way for *Ham* and her *father,* she wanted to be a true Christian, *this* was the time of life such plans came to fruition—just like that socialite from Beverly Hills who went to live in a jail in Tijuana, Marj Herlihy could make a *difference,* but without fanfare, no books written about her, this was *her* time to give, and give *back,* so many moribund beggars and stunted needy children all within a stone's throw of the Gate of India—she'd seen them again in that marvelous Judy Davis movie—*that* was where she was needed, not some fancy Sunset Boulevard hotel. Had not the burning of her beloved home been a sign? In the middle of the night, she'd been pulled from the flames by a mother of mercy, angel in white, the flames hadn't frightened but instead filled her with longing for the great Indian festival of lights, Diwali, the one she'd been so privileged to see with her father, millions of lanterns and butterlamps, was it not the good Lord's way of showing that her time as missionary had arrived? The Beverlywood conflagration was like that which surrounded Kali in her picturebooks and the articles in the *Britannica* as well. There was nothing left, her children were grown, they were independent people leading independent lives. They didn't share much with her and that was all right, they were basically damn good kids, even if Marj didn't approve of everything she knew (and didn't know) about them, that's how it was supposed to be, they'd left the nest long ago and now stood on their own 2 feet. Her parents and husband and children were gone and it was time. Even poor Riki's death—wasn't he from Calcutta, like dear Mother Teresa? no, maybe Mumbai— even his brutal murder had illumined her path.

Suddenly came a stabbing pain and she had to use a powderroom. The streets looked desolate. The old woman grimaced as she looked in all directions. She saw something distant, a brightly lit intersection, and made her way. Her angular, half-dancing gait was comical and she knew it and tried to laugh at herself—how I must look!—the only way she could walk to hold it in. Marj realized she'd been riding around all that time without "going," unusual for her, she'd been lost in thought, she distracted herself with images of the journey, as she got closer to the bright Conoco lights she conjured the Taj Mahal Palace and Towers, how soon she would be going, with *Joan,* it seemed like her daughter talked about it every day! they even sat in the hotel watching the DVD Nigel gave her (Marj felt bad for not having yet returned it) and she wondered again if Joanie was telling the truth about that baby (if she wasn't, why on earth had she lied?), the insistent story of impregnation by a rich man, she had watched her belly with discreet diligence but it never seemed to get any rounder, when Joan pulled up her blouse to show, sometimes it *was* distended but that was probably just the food she was packing away, every time you turned around hordes of room service brought pancakes, club sandwiches, Waldorf salads, banana split sundaes, and what have you, Marj winced again at what it must be costing, still, she didn't think her little girl would actually *invent* something like that, so drastic, just to cover up a weight gain, not unless she was planning on going to hell in a handbasket and putting on 50 pounds, no, that wasn't her, Joan wasn't crazy (not like her brother), she was a *professional* woman, with a respectable *architectural practice,* she was vain, and didn't tell lies all the time like Chesapeake did, not that a falsely claimed *pregnancy* was a badge of honor, but if Joan was going to gain a few pounds it was more in her character to let it all hang out, that's how she was, not one to conceal such a thing, especially some extra padding, she was almost 40 years old, common enough for a gal her age, you start to thicken up at 40 and there isn't much you can do about it, those silly diet books don't work, you could run on a treadmill to your heart's content just like Mr Pahrump did before he died but at that age no matter what they say it doesn't help *one iota,* anything you do only works a few months then you bounce right back to whatever weight you were struggling not to be. (Even those surgeries didn't help, where they stapled your tummy, and besides, before you went that route you had to be truly obese, even afterward the people who had it done still looked fat.) But maybe her daughter *was* pregnant and that'd be *divine*—wouldn't it?—in which case the trip to India would have to be postponed, at least on *Joanie*'s end (if they didn't leave right away), but Marjorie dug in her heels, she *would not be derailed,* she'd take steps if Joan tried to prevent her—the way everyone had been treating her like a child lately anything was possible—get a lawyer involved if need be, she *would* have her freedom, she'd call Ham's old friend, the one who had helped with the term life policy, but was certain that wouldn't be necessary, no no, *closer now to the Conocolights* the old woman would just go straight ahead without Joan, Joanie couldn't stop her, she wouldn't dare, like it or not, Marj Herlihy was going straight ahead with her missionary work *full-steam* and Joan could catch up when the baby was old enough to travel, the work was too important, yes of course she wanted a grandchild, but the *work* was the thing, at this stage of her life, and she would use the Taj Mahal Palace as homebase. Once her "offices" were set up she'd send for them—Joan and the baby—not that India was the best place for an infant, that would be up to Mommy, but *plenty* had done it, plenty of wealthy, intrepid folks had raised their kids in all *kinds* of places, my God, Africa or even remote parts of America, if Joan didn't like the idea than Marj would tell her to just stay put—*in Beverly Hills*—but Joanie was headstrong . . . like someone else she knew! Once her daughter set her mind to something she was hard to sway. So if she wanted to come, that would be that. Plenty of room for everyone. The Taj Mahal Palace and Towers could handle just about anything! You could see that from the DVD, if they could handle President Clinton after heart surgery they could certainly handle Joan Hennison Herlihy (who'd informed in an aside that she was keeping the Herlihy name, married or not) with a newborn. The hospitals *were* marvelous—she'd watched the *60 Minutes* rerun with Mike Wallace and oh! that young man Nigel had been *so right,* even *Cora* saw the segment about the woman who went to Delhi for a hip replacement and stayed at a special post-op spa. It was *paradise.* In fact, she wouldn't be surprised if the Taj was included in one of those surgical packages . . . you had your operation, then recuperated by the pool. And *not* at "pink bungalow" prices!

Marj broke into a lurching run.

When she got to the 76, the man in the glass booth (just like the one at Wells)—he wore a turban and looked Indian—told her the bathroom was broken. She said it was an emergency and he saw how crestfallen she was. He said she could use the mensroom, and slid a key attached to a wirehanger into the metal tray. She stood there until he waved his arm showing which way to go.

She went around back. A door was open. She ran into the darkness. She couldn't find the switch but as her eyes adjusted she saw a wood board over the bowl, and a sanitary napkin dispenser. She was in the ladiesroom. She hobbled to the men's, jiggling the key in the lock but it was broken and she tried again, about to run to the Indian, when the door gave way. It wouldn't shut but she was in trouble, again no light, this room darker, she managed to find the toilet by the indirect hard fluorescence the banks above the gas pumps cast through unclosable metal door and high tiny window over the bowl, nature calling, no time left to even check if there was paper, hiked up her dress, sitting on the cracked, sticky bowl, and everything splattered out. The room so filthy and malodorous but she was grateful, she thought of Mother Teresa then almost with shame at how much wealth and ease she, Marj Herlihy, had experienced in this life, what was this but a minor discomfort, and how soon she would be home, at the Taj Mahal, the Taj Mahal Palace and Towers, the simple comfort of a clean cot was all she would ask for, all that she needed, there she could reach out to the poorest of the poor, their world so much worse than this ruined powderroom, gut now settling, relieved, panting from the effort, she would reach out from the Taj as Jesus did from Orissa, *yes, not many people knew it but Jesus had been mentored in India and spread the gospel there,* he had even been to Benares where bodies are burned and thrown in the river except for children who are wrapped. So this dank little lavatory would not trouble her, she would not let the debacle of outhouse smells intrude, she would spin them into perfume, they were afterall nothing and would soon be a memory. She hadn't even thought about where she would go—when she finished her business. She would ask the Indian man. They were a friendly culture, like an enormous family, why, it might turn out the man behind the glass knew Riki (whom she'd be sure to mention), and if he didn't, perhaps he'd have heard of him because of his martyred, somewhat notorious death. They might establish a bond that way.

She heard someone at the door and thought it was the turban'd gentleman. "I'm in here!" she shouted. "Someone is in here!"— because she wasn't yet done, cramping again and splattering, at the same time groping with her eyes because they had failed to adjust enough to find tissue paper—on that front she had not had much luck. There was a big box stuck to the wall that was supposed to have seat covers but it was empty.

He burst in, not the Indian but someone else, she knew it wasn't the Indian because he stank, and scuttled like a bony spider before she might even gasp, there was no turban and he tore her off the seat, she was on the cold floor, numb, face slammed hard and cold where the jaw had been injured, pain seared through, she tried to speak but he slapped and the corrosive pain jabbed at the still-healing fracture, he ripped off the blouse and stuffed it in her mouth and she was thinking how can he why would he I haven't even cleaned myself *I am so old*—she felt pain down there and splattered and peed and that made him angry but she couldn't hear the words he was saying, he was trying to mute himself, mindful, she thought, that the door could not close and perhaps someone, the Indian, or passersby, might come, and while he kept on she distracted herself by thinking again of the work she would do once she got home to the palace in Bombay, the work she would do with men like him, spidery men who'd known nothing but sorrow and horror and disease, bereft men who descended like locusts on children and missionaries like herself and burned them or mauled them like sick wounded tigers, empty dank men who knew not what they did, and she was not there, she was no longer there for the longest time, she smelled his breath and his vomit, an alcoholic man, a drunken drug-addicted man, then somehow she was on her feet with the green Jil Sander wrapped around her, spiderman gone, of a sudden she was outside, a person pumping gas into their car stared, the turban glimpsed her through the glass, gesticulating, she realized he wanted the key back but she kept going and was not really there, kept walking until she came to a group of homeless smoking and laughing and she wondered if they were the ones who threw the empty cans but she wasn't there and 2 of them were women and they made jokes at 1st like the girls that night at Rite Aid then grew warm and concerned and saw she'd been hurt, called her Mother, Moms, Poor Mama, one of them was hurt as well and they took Marj along, pied piperwalking it seemed forever but telling her all the insufferable way they would soon be there *she knew that her journey had begun* and when they reached the tiny building with wire fence and neatened closecropped lawn—more like a cottage, same size as the Beverly Hills bungalow—they were met by a kind lady in a white coat, nurse's coat, caregiver's coat, a clean, middleaged gal in whites, ethnicity undetermined, and the kennel-like barking of dogs, they barked and barked, a stern, confident, friendly chorus, the clean white-coated lady seemed to know all of the people Marj traveled with, the ones who had come to her aid like missionaries themselves, and the white-coated lady didn't really see Marj at 1st, she looked at the other sick one and said, That arm is infected, it is abscessed, she would give something for the infection, the dogs kept barking and then the white-coated lady suddenly saw Marj and was taken aback (as if only used to seeing this street tribe *without* her, solving their troubles best she could, kindly middleaged gal a true Christian, what Marj aspired toward), when she saw the old woman with hammered swollen face and bloody shitsmeared legs trying to cover her modesty she gasped and said, My God, what *happened* to her, Mercy, and the others said they didn't know but found Old Moms near the 76 and she was in a bad way, looked like a *rich* lady, and White Coat spoke in such sweet delicate overtures, did someone abduct you, but Marj was beyond words, she couldn't understand, did someone *assault* you, she was so tired, still silently distracted with thoughts of the Taj Mahal Palace, she wasn't really there, she was in Bombay, not there with the tribe, and the dogs kept barking and the lady said she would call 911, Marj needed real attention, "hospital attention," and the police, they would have to be—it was a police matter, at the very mention of the word some of the gaggle peeled off and vanished, but the one with infected arm helped put a blanket on Moms, who the middleaged woman said was in shock and *she went to call while the others gathered round and the dogs barked and barked and barked and barked*

LXXXV.

JOAN

---

until the call finally came. The PI recommended by the de-tective had learned about Mrs Marjorie Herlihy's whereabouts from LBPD.

She was in the ER at St Mary's.

Oh God. Oh God. Oh Oh Oh

God.

Oh! *Oh*   Oh   *oh* God!

Barbet—

He met her at the bungalow and they took a Town Car. She cried in his arms most of the way down. Her mother had been assaulted in the mensroom of a Long Beach gas station. How! Why! That's what she kept saying—shout-ing—to Barbet. Of course he had no answer; had more sense than to even attempt. They were in the realm of No Answers, where her mom had been living for months upon months. All he could say, and Barbet thought it OK (because it was true) was that what had happened to Marjorie was like something out of the *Inferno.* What happened to Marj Herlihy in the last ½ year was literally Hell. Joan clutched at him and sobbed, he felt the heat of breath and body, even the heat from her eyes. He said he would be with her through all of it, he knew how hard—no, he amended that he *didn't,* he *couldn't,* couldn't *imagine*—but wanted her to remem-ber she had another life to think of now, the one "growing inside" (everything sounded like a horror film!)—and that she had to be careful, about her own *health*—not to suggest she could or should be doing anything other than what they *were* doing this very *mo-ment,* and not to suggest she could or should be doing anything other than *exactly* this—urging her to take deep breaths and know that she had his love and support, along with that of so many others. Joan tried to smile. She tried to smile at *him.* The driver stole glimpses in the mirror. She solemnly nodded because she knew Barbet was right and the baby would—*have* to—keep her centered, it was just that she wasn't *used* to thinking of anyone else (especially something *growing inside*), now there was this un-formed Nautilus shell, this hairless membranous wingless be-winged being already nudging her toward a selflessness that might even help her to stay sane through ordeals neverending. (Maybe that was a selfish thought; miscarriages and dried-up mil-lions danced through her head like sugary caffeinated demons. She couldn't withstand another Lost Coast.) No, she would keep it simple: she needed to stay *intact* so the child would at least be born healthy. She wouldn't be able to bear a *Medical Incredible,* a kid with major organs born outside his body. A kid with a face like a rotten cantaloupe. That would surely make her world come tumbling down.

When they got to St Mary's, the PI was waiting and why not, muttered Joan to her friend, *He should be fucking offering hors d'oeuvres for what I'm paying.* She was moody and distraught and unraveled until Barbet gave a gentle dis/course correction: "He's on our side, Joanie. He helped find her." At this, she wept, and Barbet said darling why don't you go to the bathroom and wash your face? Get it together before seeing Mom.

A really good idea.

She thanked him, then thanked the PI as well.

Joan did as she was told, and stared in the mirror. The thought of that bathroom where her mother was attacked made her shud-der. How could someone do that? What kind of monsterworld was this? Who decided that Marj Herlihy, a kind, gracious, intel-ligent lady in the autumn of her life, would be courted, cheated, robbed, beaten, and burned from her home? And *this*—it was too much! She threw more water on her face, drying herself with rough paper toweling. She started to leave but got dizzy and went to sit in a stall.

All was water. She rubbed the belly where her baby floated. Remembered the story of the 6 year old boy in New Orleans who led younger children to safety through the parish floods. To sanctuary:

Darynael, Degahney, Tyreek, Zoria . . . why did the names stick in her head and what the fuck was up with black people and their baptisms? It was like something out of a Dave Chappelle sketch. Deamonte was separated from his mother but shepherded them to high ground. (The bastardization of diamond. Wasn't there a Diamond Sutra? She thought she'd seen a copy of it among Esther's books, in Napa. Buddhists always spoke of "diamond-pointed" this and "diamond-pointed" that.) His last name was Love. They finally reunited Diamond-Pointed Love with his mother, and her name turned out to be . . . Katrina. The world was an ecstatic poisoned mystery. All was Katrina and Kali, all was Durgā, the Great Mother and Great Destroyer, all was Love and Money and Diamonds and Rust.

She breathed, like Barbet suggested, for the baby's sake. *Inspired.* She didn't want its tiny spirit toxified by this night's madness but how on Earth would that not be possible? How could Joan stop her body from strafing the womb, mutating her baby's blood cells, altering rhythm of soul and heart?

She rejoined Barbet and the PI in the waiting room. An officer who'd responded to the call was chatting with them—he knew the PI, at least by name, duly impressed by the reputation, as is said, that preceded him.

Joan was introduced.

Then, just like a TV show, the handsome doctor walked in, asking if she was Mrs Herlihy's daughter.

HE took them to a room just beyond the examination areas. "Your mom's going to be all right. But I want to tell you, straight out: she was raped."

Joan crumpled.

Barbet grabbed her under the armpits.

He told her to breathe.

The doctor asked if she was OK.

She said yes.

The doctor paused until Joan gave the go-ahead.

"There was some damage. Some anal and vaginal tearing—I

really think minimal, in that we're dealing with a woman of her age and the violence of the assault."

"Don't. Don't say that," said Joan.

There was quiet, and then she told him to go on.

"She'll have to be tested down the line for HIV whether they find the assailant or not. She's in shock but she's comfortable. There's no question she needs to be admitted—of course, that can be to a hospital of your choice. Whether someplace closer to home—Cedars or UCLA or St John's"—implicit in the remark was a winking knowledge of Joan's rarefied economic strata, which she assumed the canny MD had grokked by her dress, Barbet's pedigree (she was certain he thought her partner was queer), the well-heeled presence of the PI, etc—"for observation, fluid intake, all the goodies. Again, because of her age. How are Mom's cognitive functions? Is she generally lucid? Does she hold up her end of a conversation?" Joan stared at him blankly. "Because she's a little *out* there—not making a whole lot of sense right now, part of that's the morphine and part of that's—it may be trauma, it may be a host of things. That would be another reason to do a more extensive work-up. You'd be surprised, but people can be remarkably resilient. They bounce back. Before you see her—and she doesn't look too bad, considering what she went through—I want to tell you that she was helped *enormously* by a group of homeless folks she encountered sometime not too long after the incident. In particular, she was ministered to by a lady who's with her now, kind of a legend around here. Dottie Ford. She's a vet."

"From the war?" said Joan, smiling surreally.

"A veterinarian. Dottie has an animal hospital not far from where your mother was attacked. We have a fairly large street population in Long Beach (we're not proud of that), most of whom don't have ready access to medical care for a multitude of reasons, not excluding budget cuts stemming directly from the wisdom of our *current administration*. To our chagrin"—he actually used the word—"many rely on Dottie for 'outpatient' care. She has a big heart and of course refers anything to us she doesn't think she can handle."

"My mother . . . my mother saw a vet?" said Joan, in disbelief.

Barbet let a smile creep to his lips as he and Joan locked eyes. Another ring of Hell, but what could you do?

"She wasn't *treated,* but Dottie made sure she was warm and comfortable until the paramedics came. She gave her a compress to stop some of the bleeding, which again, was minimal. Probably prevented her from going further into shock. So the world does have good people in it."

"The world is good," said Joan. She meant to sound sarcastic but hadn't the energy to give it that spin. "Well, *cool.* I mean, so long as Mom doesn't say 'Woof' when I see her."

The men grinned, glad to see that Joan was all right.

"Shall we go in?" asked the doctor.

S HE phoned to tell him what happened.

Chess sounded flat. He asked *When* and she said, *A few days ago.* (Joan didn't think he'd get huffy about the time delay, and she was right on. He was probably relieved not to have been involved, and sounded too loaded to put on a show.) Her brother kept saying, *I can't fucking believe it,* which, after the 1st few times, *really* got on her nerves. What was there not to fucking believe, *dickwad?* She found herself thinking less and less of him as a human being; each time Joan thought she might be motivated to share something *real*—her baby, their father, whatever—Chess revealed himself to be a narcissistic stoner she wanted nothing to do with.

He asked where Mom was *now* (Chesapeake Herlihy: Location Scout! Man of Action! The Decider!), and Joan said she'd been transferred to St John's but was on her way to a "premier" care center called Golden Grove. Marj's insurance had "really stepped up to the plate" and he needn't worry—*not that he would*—Joan and Barbet (she threw her partner in just to make her brother feel his own useless appendagehood) had already checked out the "assisted living village," which was far beyond anyone's expectations, more like the Four Seasons than a rest home. She knew he would respond to that kind of shit; assisted living at the Four Seasons was Chester's ultimate retirement fantasy.

He said he might not get a chance to see Mom before leaving. He was about to go "on a Vancouver scout." He wasn't actually finding the locations himself, but "overseeing the process, as producer." *God, you creep me out.* She resisted the impulse to make a crack about his bogus lawsuit and trumped-up pain. His bogus *life.* Her good deed for the day.

It would be better if he didn't see Marj *anyway. Probably just make her nervous. Besides, she knew*

LXXXVI.

CHESTER

---

he wasn't anxious to visit Mom after what had happened. Especially when he found out where they were putting her. He couldn't believe it. Golden Grove: of all fucking places. That old devil karma, working against him.

Everything was conspiring to make Chess want to leave the country in a hurry. Some psychogroid had beat and violated his mother in a 76 station shitter. What the *fuck*. That's what America was about: a horrorfilm rapeathon pileup. Listen to CNN: Wolf Blitzer talking about a commuter plane that went down and even though it was obvious he knew full well it was too early to get answers, the Wolfman was all necro'd out, breathy and methy and cockstiff for Death, husky-throated fratboy Peeper, a misery pimp hemming and hawing as he circle-jerked his pack of Nielsen jackals while they metaphorically peered through the submerged windows of a broken aircraft; he engaged on-retainer Talking Headless ghouls in redundant inane pointless dialogue, timekiller sexperts at dragging nonevents out for hours like Chess used to do when he snorted speed and flipped through porn rags. Jim Lehrer would probably have given it a minute's worth but the Wolfman dragged Death and Time like a nigga tied to a bumper, police pursuit and arousal (speed-bumps relished for more pain), especially when it came to body recovery. They *always* got *way hard* whenever the moment came to say (coal miners/earthquakes/terrorist acts), *The search and rescue has now become a recovery operation.*

This morning, the headline shouted: LARGEST STUDY OF PRAYER TO DATE FINDS IT HAS NO POWER TO HEAL.

The Pentagon was blaming an antiquated computer system for the fact that it had hired collection agencies to go after stumpy, braindamaged, paralyzed soldiers for reimbursement of damaged "equipment" left on Iraqi battlefields.

Marj was probably going to get a bill for her reaming; he was afraid the search and rescue had now segued to recovery.

Wolf would be happy to hear it.

Fast food slow death nation.

Laxmi read about a zoo in Illinois that had a wake for the chief gorilla. All the apes filed by, sniffing and stroking the carcass, paying general respects. More dignity and nonbullshit nobility present than any human funeral he'd ever heard of.

The more majorly free-floating pissed off he became, the more Laxmi tried to soothe. "It's all about nonattachment!"—if you're so *nonattached,* why still such fucked up *emo* re Suicide Mom and Molesting Dad? *What am I doing. Why jump on Laxmi. Pull back, dude, pull back. You've been through too much. That stuff with your mom's some sick, heavy shit. Pull back. The craziness with Marj, and Maurie . . . be glad your sis is handling it. Be* very *glad.*

He did manage to find mystic comfort in letting the memory, if you could even call it that, of *cubensis* wash over him—compassionate teachings of the sacred shroom and Her imperial army. Tainted by more words from Laxmi and her avatars: one mustn't get attached to *anything,* not taste, feel, touch. *That's gonna be tough.* In India, the heat grew so strong that elephants sometimes drowned in the very ponds they jumped in to cool off. The great beasts, usually so careful about assessing water's depth, got reckless because of their attachment to coolness and comfort, which proved fatal. So said Avatar of Unpronounceable Name.

You know what? The fuckin gurus ought to give elephants a goddam break. The gurus ought to check their own *attachments. Tell me what my hoary, gerontic* mother *was attached to, to get herself raped in the Conoco head. Oh,* right: *she was attached to taking a shit then*

the rape-o attached some homeless lesioned pud to her fossilized
mouth/cunt/anus. Jesus, who would want to fuck that? She looks like
Mark Felt! And don't tell me it was karma—there is no karma.
Karma's just some Catholic trip, Eastern-style. What's karma got to do
got to do with it what's karma but a secondhand

                                        devotion.

CHESS got the stones to visit "the Grove." New carpets and
lighting fixtures in the atrium. Lithographs he hadn't seen
during prior visits. Everpresent whiff of turds and urine and
Lysol—you could throw money and pile on the designer touches
but certain things you just couldn't polish. As they say.

He was going to drop in on both of them: kill 2 birds, stoned.

Maurie was the same: some kinda tetraplegic, with only inci-
dental blink of crusted eyes belying cognizance. Chess thought it a
miracle his friend could breathe on his own, which he did, smooth
and unlabored, without apparatus. That's what felt eerie, dream-
like. It didn't seem like he should be in such a state—waxy taut
shinyskin, Schiavosmile, dandruffscalp, longish-nailed fingers
beginning atrophied inward curl. Funny thing being that as Maurie "settled in," so did Chess in his fashion; the tissue of guilt,
warm diaphanous tube between he and bedridden friend, organic
living bloodsausage umbilicus, began to dissolve. Maybe it was all
part of a natural process, Time shifting and Space softening tired
old concepts of accountability that maybe weren't so solid (the
gurus would say) to begin with. *Shit happens* never rang so true. In
the words of the elegant old tribesman in that tsunami documentary: *We remembered what our ancestors said, that land and sea always fight over boundaries. Things keep changing. Nothing is safe and
intact. The earth rests on a gigantic tree that can be shaken by spirits
blah blah* but the dude had a point. Right? Nothing is real and
nothing to get hungabout. Strawberry fields forever.

Chess began to let things go. An audiotape Laxmi got him had
some "tulku" (reincarnated being) saying that it was best to for-

give, and if you couldn't forgive then it was best to forget, forgetting was the next best thing. "Too much thinking about past or future created suffering." Now, *that* was right on. He leaned over Maurie to beg forgiveness then ask *him* to forget. Forgive and forget, live and let love. Chess said he was going away for awhile. He told Maurie his mom died and he was moving to Hawaii or maybe Vancouver but would be back to visit in a few months, reflexively covering his bet against the astronomical odds that Maurie should wake up and start running his mouth. (If Levin was listening, and was in the know, he would definitely be confused that the Perp was announcing his plans to return to the scene of the crime.) He thought about the recent case of a fireman who was in a coma for like 20 years then suddenly talked a bluestreak for 16 hours before dropping dead a few months later. Anything could happen.

Soon they'd be leaving for Mumbai. He wasn't sure *what* to call it—*Moom-bye* sounded weird. Peking/Beijing, whatever. Certainly was a strange turn of events. If you'd laid it out a year ago, the Jew and the Location Scout would have had a laugh (about everything but the coma part). Life was *too* fuckin strange and *The Wonderful Flight to the Mushroom Planet* only confirmed it; you'd never *begin* to be able to comprehend. That's what Maurie was teaching him. That was our downfall—we thought we could *understand.* His own personal guru was *staring right at him,* or kind of, from the hospital bed, probably taking a crap at the very moment Chess was saying goodbye.

How beautiful and fucked up was that?

He changed his mind about seeing Mom.

He didn't want to have that image in his head when he got on the plane.

CHESS was mostly looking forward to Varanasi—Benares?— the holy city where Indians went to die. That's where Siddhartha hung; the Bodhi Tree was just a few hundred miles away. There were these places called the Deer Park and the Forest of

Bliss that he wanted to check out. Laxmi said that after Shakya-
muni Buddha became enlightened, he met up with some ol com-
padres, just like Jesus did with his dissipes. The Deer Park is
where the Buddha did his satsang and told everyone to chill, and
not be so extreme. Laxmi said the Brits built an opium factory
nearby, back in the 1800s. It was supposedly still in operation.
Fuck it. He'd do without.

*He would wear a Muslim skullcap and coat his body in pow-
dered vermilion like the guy from* Entourage. *He hoped there would
be temple bombings. None of it concerned him. He'd recite verses from
Kabir and the Koran, and bow down in the Kashi Viswanath, the
Gyanvapi. He would offer Vicodin (750 mg) to the armed guards.
Something inside began to shift and he envisioned himself outside the
perverse damaged country of his birth, country of warmongers no
longer his own, country of the armies of the night that raped dementi-
a'd old ladies in oilhiked steelcage lavatories. Just being there—
Mother India—would be to matriculate with* cubenses. *So vast! Sure
there'd be troubles, he wasn't so naive to think otherwise, he'd probably get hep or typhus but trouble in Paradise was different than trouble
in Hell. India would be the matrix of his new birth, his rebirth and
death. Being there would be like going with Her, ruler of plants and
imperial troops, his betrothed. He would ride on Her wedding train
and soon they*

LXXXVII.

JOAN

visited every day at Golden Grove Assisted Living (a bit of a misnomer because it was sprawling and there was a wing, a separate building actually, for those who needed far more than that—*Night of the Assisted Living Dead.* Some were in vegetative states, but the 2 communities did not intersect), the place where Marj had been transferred after a 3 day stint at St John's.

GG had a warm swimming pool and Wellness Community Village where clients practiced yoga and handicrafts. Doctors and nurses 24/7. Bright commissary ("Rick's Café") with waiters and tablecloth coverings and often a pianist. You could be served in your room if you weren't feeling up to it but that was discouraged. The staff felt it important you socialize. Socialization was the amulet to ward off depression.

Joan didn't want her mother to be there. She'd gone house-hunting in Santa Monica (a Craftsman on Marguerite) and high in the Malibu Hills—and even thought of buying a lot off Sawtelle that ARK could build upon from her own design—old-money folks did that, Ann Janss had lived over there for years—because everything was so costly and she didn't want to shoot her wad. (There were a thousand places for $12,000,000.) Anyway, she couldn't make her move until the baby was born and the money came; they would have to find a rental. She just didn't want her in Golden Grove; Mom deserved so much more. She would not leave her there in this time of life, in this time of *Joan's* life.

Occasionally Marj asked to see her son but she asked to see Ham and Ray and Lucas and Bonita and Jeffrey Chandler as well.

THEN something happened that was beyond comprehension. Barbet had her mom's Jil Sander coat, he brought it to the dry cleaners, emptying the pockets beforehand, and that was when he found the LOVE IS AROUND THE CORNER fortune with 03 15 25 36 38 18, and the lottery ticket Marj got at Riki's on the day of her assault, the ticket with those very numbers. She must have bought it right before she took the bus to Long Beach, and Barbet checked, for the hell of it—she'd won. No one had come forward in 3 weeks and for the hell of it he checked and they were the numbers that won. He told Joan and she thought he was kidding. They drove down to Riki's and doublechecked, and it was true, no one could believe it, there was the widow and son, they checked the numbers in the machine while Joan reminded them who she was (of course they remembered)—Marjorie Herlihy was her *mom.* They knew that something bad had happened to the wonderful old lady, they knew about the beating and the fire but not the recent calamity, and Joan just said Mom had been ill, and staying with her, and would be *so happy* about this, the widow and son were happy too, they were waiting for the person to come with the ticket and now here it was—their friend, their neighbor—now here was the daughter of the woman who had treated them so well. They loved her mother, and were going to get lots of money for having sold the winning ticket, a 173,000,000 dollar Super Lotto with an immediate cash payout, if you so chose, of about half, something in that area, all too much to take in.

On the way back to the hotel, they were giddy yet still somehow doubtful so Joan called the PI who by now had become a kind of friend-on-retainer, and he said Jesus, he would do some checking, then phoned right back, Jesus, oh Jesus yes! it was true, *absolutely,* and they called Joan's lawyer and everyone examined the development like wide-eyed kids finding buried backyard treasure, it *was* true, a lump 93,000,000 after taxes or something like 10,000,000 a year for 20 years if they so chose (they didn't) and still no one could really believe it. *No one.* They soon gathered in Century City and got the lottery folks on speakerphone, told them the situation because the attorneys were mindful of what had happened and didn't want Joan to dissemble, no reason, it could definitively be proven, regardless of Mrs Herlihy's current mental state, that she

was the daughter and rightful heir. Plus, she had POA. The
widow and son confirmed that Marj had been a fixture there
(lately supplanted by emissaries, added Joan), choosing numbers
from a ragged fortune cookie paper strip (the one she got at the
end of her dinner with AKA Lucas Weyerhauser, though not
quite the same since she had altered the very last digit, a detail that
no one would ever trace as a commemorative of the year Marj
went to Bombay with her father; otherwise *many* would have
won, having selected that particular computer-generated se-
quence, which had been dispersed to Chinese restaurants state-
and nationwide, that explained the solo win, the changing of the
last digit, because the lottery people said otherwise they would
have seen a pattern, there had been mass fortune cookie–selected
winners before) and the lawyers wanted to confirm there would
be no problems linked to Mrs Herlihy's current physical or mental
health, and the State said, with what seemed to Joan, some
whimsy or State Fair abandon, that Marj was "a winner," but they
might want or need a photograph of the "lucky girl" for publicity
purposes—of course respecting her current delicate situation—
Joan's lawyers didn't assent to anything right away, though their
client said it might be fun to bring in "hair and makeup" to
Golden Grove and make a big to-do, her mom might like that, the
lawyers didn't immediately assent, trained not to do or say anything with undue speed, yet also trained not to be heavyhanded,
especially when clients expressed warm or playfully harmless desires, all very friendly, in the outrageous spirit of what had happened the lawyers wanted everything kept amenable, which it
was, and would remain, courtesy of AKA Lucas Weyerhauser,
whereabouts unknown—Det Whitsell especially got a kick out of
the development—AKA Lucas Weyerhauser, whose trail was
being eagerly followed by all manner of high- and low-priced
dicks. Nobody was ever to learn that the numbers from the cookie
he gave her that very special night (she hadn't been out to dinner
with a man in God knew how long) were the very same Marj had
fixated on; everyone thought the sweet treat came from local delivery. Marj was known to order in. No one would ever uncover

the source of her insanely macabre windfall: a final, maddening, karmic reversal of fortune.

(Chester was already gone and would never know any of it.)

S HE went with the lawyer to Golden Grove.
Marj was in high spirits.

She'd just been given a shower—Joan was paying for private nurses, night and day—and Cora came to visit too. The former neighbor brought over a special pillow her "Steinie" was marketing called the Hug, shaped like a cushioned torso.

She left behind a brochure. The Hug was covered in velour, embedded with thermal fibers and tiny motors. It could be programmed like a cellphone so if you happened to be out of town, you could "dial" the pillow and it would hug whoever was on the other end. It even generated heat. The pillow could store "hug messages" that could be picked up later if the recipient missed a call.

Joan tried it out—the Hug trembled against her, and she said, "Sign me up!"

I have to tell Barbet about this. If Amma the Hugging Saint ever goes on disability . . .

Her mother was more together than Joan had seen her be in a while, which was heartening. Marj said that Cora got a new dog, another King Charles, she couldn't remember what she had named it but Cora promised to bring him next time. (Golden Grove was pet-friendly.) Joan said, *Hopefully we'll be in a house by then.* She was really starting to show and drew Marj's hand over her belly. Mom slowly began to accept the pregnancy. She shared that for the longest time, she thought Joan was making it up and they had a laugh. It gratified her that such a good thing, a lovely thing, a positive and a plus, was finally sinking in, something that might give her mother fresh hopes and dreams—and joy.

They didn't speak of the trip to India anymore.

Marjorie had her portrait taken by the "Super Lotto," after being primped and fussed over by a squad of Hollywood stylists.

Joan supervised the session and had a ball. But the winner didn't seem fully aware of what it meant. Joan knew there was brutal irony in even telling her mother that she was suddenly worth nearly a hundred million dollars—those professional criminals had said nearly the same thing. She began to wonder if it was a mistake to have told her. Every time Joan brought it up—hoping Mom would grow used to it, as she had the advancing pregnancy—Marj smiled a rictus of puzzled agonized frivolity, fascia taut, clamping Cora's Hug machine *to her bony breast and asked Joan what was she planning to wear to*

LXXXVIII.

CHESTER

---

arrive at 10 PM, hair-raising cab ride hilariously perilous, zillions of lamps and lanterns, and it wasn't until they reached the hostel, which took 2 whole hours from the airport (Laxmi's dad, Mr Reliable, said it would take only 30 minutes), in that entire time never abeyance or cessation of the hundreds and hundreds of thousands of thousands of lights and people, Chester realized this *was* India, its heart and spirit and energy, India multitudinous and hydraheaded, he would never have the luxury of space again, or at least not the kinky bad faith luxury of *American* space, space one could *buy,* all space had its price, even the air above Manhattan buildings was for sale, not that space was something he'd had his fill of, but rather he'd had his fill of everything *American,* all things *America,* the trademarked quality of such space was no longer necessary for his well-being—it wasn't until they reached the hostel that they learned about Diwali, how the lights were a celebratory manifestation of Rama's return, and her namesake the goddess Laxmi! a delirious festival of lights and firefly phosphorescence. The pair thought that of great portent.

Laxmi consulted a slew of printed out Web pages. Their boardinghouse was in a district called Breach Candy—*how cool was that?*—near a famous temple called Mahalaxmi. A fancy hospital and private "swim club" were within view. Tomorrow they would travel to Cumballa Hill, where, at his apartments, Ramesh Balsekar gave *darshan* or *satsang* (Chess didn't have the lexicon down), they would sit at the feet of the retired bank president and one-time student/translator of Maharaj Nisargadatta in the morning, if they managed to awaken. Chess was determined. Laxmi was certain they would, but it didn't matter, how could it, nothing mattered now. Don't sweat the big or small stuff. Because what they had was uncorrupted time, sheer time, to become nonattached adherents, students of Father/Mother/Mentor Time, scholars and undergrads of Time and its birthchild Space, they could wash and soak and worship then wring their rags and follow its banks, wormholes, and bends; merge with tributaries, coalescing ghats and Godspeed, time would be their luxury, an even greater luxury than space, Time *was* Space, time was She the Great Mother, and space, Her imperial guards. The "little ones" had shown him that when Time was mastered, timespace could be entered as bride/groom would a hushed cathedral.

American Time and Space!

(Fell away like dead cells.)

His old life was already a dream.

He wanted a new name.

Maybe Ramesh would give him one.

The instant expats were delusional with fatigue but made comic, cosmic sex from their discomfiture, dislocation, and psychedelic discombobulation. It was a suffocating night and Chess had an apprehension of Indian heat, unlike that of the desert but full, watery, gravid; not the heat of a scavenger's sandbox but of a banquet hall strung with incense and the incest of wilting roses. Still he fell asleep with a preternatural, childish excitement *the headlamps of childhood knowing that tomorrow he would awaken in Mumbai morning light, in*

LXXXIX.

JOAN

---

the final signing of executorship. She would man-age her mother's estate and "affairs." (Legal word.)

She told Barbet she wouldn't be coming back to ARK but would stay on as consultant. (Which was understood, but they formalized it. Her life had become all about formalizing and wit-nessing. Joan Hennison Herlihy was *formalizing,* princess in a prefecture, she was sealing and waxing, embossing and imprima-turing, and felt like a mature woman for the 1st time in her earthy, earthly life.) She was now in charge of some $93,000,000—exclud-ing the 20 soon to be given her by Lew for the care and feeding of the bastard out of (North) California. There were foundations to be tilled, hedges and charities to be pruned and seeded, tax havens to be harvested, analysts and planners to be planted and yanked like weeds. More than anything, she wanted to buy land, thou-sands of acres of open space, with rivers running through. She would build little, fabulous sepulchral follies, her own fucking Marfa loop, and name it Barfa (Barbet laughed at what he thought was an homage to himself) yet make it a serious venture. Spicey Zorritos, Rimjob K, and Thom Pain would all sit up and take notice—even Lew.

Especially Lew.

SHE phoned her brother, knowing it was time to tell him every-thing. Joan was at once melancholy yet winsome because of the baby, that almost abstract unwhisperable wildflower tendril of hope which only visited itself upon the unexpectedly expectant, those blessed and trashed and terrified mothers-to-be, the ones who were older or damaged in whatever way the leaves of the world had rustled *No* to their numb, unmeaning or sometimes su-

perdeliberate bid to create, the Year of the Horse she was, now
having the ride of her life, Joan felt an obscene bounty of san-
guineous spirit—she would *make the call,* to the brother she'd so
ruthlessly judged since they were kids, her little (that's how she
thought of him) Chess, Mama's Chesapeake, Daddy's Chesterfield, fucked-up 1st born who afterall did the best he could, as
had everyone—St Joan the Exemplar! She wanted to give him
2,000,000, just like that, drop it right down, to snap him out of
whatever place he was in or drive him further into darkness, that
wasn't up to her, only the impulse was, the urge was the only thing
she could rightfully own, she would see what it would do, if it
could dislodge him from what she knew hadn't been the best of
places, he was worn out, injured, and embarrassed, it was a motherfucker being a man in America, Joan imagined the look on his
face when she told him, he'd be able to take care of shit he'd never
dared even mention, he would probably throw away the 1st million, what did she expect, none of her business, maybe for that reason she'd give it in 2 hunks of a mil each, *let* him throw it away, if
that's what it took, she'd put governors on the 2nd installment,
contractually lay it out like that, up front and open, she could even
invest the 2nd part, buy Chess a ranch in Thousand Oaks or
Agoura, there were a hundred ways she and her advisers could go,
but all good, fucking *supreme,* she had no control over the results
and could only hope he didn't nut out and get paranoid and chase
after her for the rest of the money, challenging her right to man-
age the estate, but maybe it'd go the best way, and he could settle
down and have a kid or kids of his own. From the legal end, she'd
pretty much covered the *this-is-Mother's-money-not-ours-and-I'm-
the-caretaker* angle, and made it ironclad. But you never knew.
She didn't want her brother going ballistic and eating up a bunch
of the trust by challenging her theodicy, she did what she'd had to,
using Lew's very expensive lawyers to make certain: she wouldn't
tell Chess about that until it was necessary, wouldn't bring out the
big guns about his drug abuse and doctor shopping and priors
having to do with stealing from their mom—in the last 6 months,
he'd forged Marj's name to checks totaling 35-hundred dollars.

No big thing. She wouldn't go there unless he forced her. There was always the chance he'd use whatever money she gave him to somehow find out about her and Lew, to pester the surrogate paperworked geekdad decoy, maybe causing major/minor problems, but that was unlikely. She caught herself being paranoid and didn't like the feeling.

Maybe she wouldn't give him shit.

No, I will . . .

Joan had been nothing if not thorough, that was her nature—attorneys had made stipulations in case of death, *hers, Joan's,* because she knew Chess could get wayward and she never fully trusted him or his buddies, like that Maurie Levin character, or the Squeaky Fromme masseuse, not because her brother was malicious, only because he was weak and exorbitant and pettily grandiose, disorganized and on the dumb side, but that wasn't a crime, it was just *him,* nothing to be judged or punished for, they were old now, or older anyway, how many decades did they have left between them? She had of course designed a simple airtight proviso in the event of her mother's but mostly Joan's demise that would seed the Freiberg monies to Trust so her baby would be taken care of *in perpetua,* not that Chess could ever even remotely get his hands on that, and Joan had her own ideas of what to do with Mom's fortune, how it could best be used to benefit others (excluding her bro), how Marjorie Herlihy's name would live on in the form of the Herlihy Giving Foundation. Still, she wanted to find Chess, Chesapeake, Chesterfield, wanted to tell him everything and present the no-strings cash award, she would say that was part of a gift allowed legally, for tax purposes, from the estate, a gift in equal parts to both of them that stemmed from the lotto windfall, she wanted to find him and sit with him and tell him everything, the wanting with almost urgent maternal longing. Joan tugged toward Family now, the little one growing inside her an advanced scout, a runner's torch that spurred her into the arms of her imperfect flesh and blood. She felt a sea change, literal and spiritual, in the family fortune.

His home and cellphones were disconnected and that worried

her (she would get the PI on it if she had to) so she stopped by his WeHo rental. She'd never even been there, and that fact alone made her feel derelict as a sibling, the desire to help him redoubling. The landlord, a warm and welcoming girl who Joan suddenly remembered was the daughter of Don Knotts, told her Chester had moved out, her tenant said his mother had been sick—"Is she OK?" Karen asked dolefully, with big brown empathic eyes—*Yes,* said Joan, *doing much, much better*—and that Chester said he was moving back to the family place to take care of her.

Joan thanked her and fibbed: *Yes, her brother was coming home,* and Karen said something about him going on a scout, a 2 week scout in the Rockies. *How stupid of me,* said Joan. *Now I remember. It's just—we've been so overwhelmed. I know you understand.* She touched Joan's arm, inviting her in for coffee. Joan politely declined. *What a sweet, sweet woman.*

She probably did more for Chess than I ever did.

Joan called the PI and told him what was happening—her brother was gone. He said he would find him. This is the guy they shoulda sicced on Osama.

S HE drove to the City of Industry. This time she didn't need the Woman to lead her. This time she didn't go to the liquor store for Diet Coke, cigarettes, and chips. This time she didn't wait outside but went straight upstairs to knock at the door but no one answered. Then her heart seized as the dog jumped from nowhere and barked, he leapt on the couch and butted against the window *its snot and wild eyes, the television was on but*

XC.

RAY

the cousins made a terrible scene.

Ray sat insensate.

All the dreams she had were true, but true for her and the baby—not for her Bapu, not for her Raj.

The night his daughter had come visiting, the night Joan came and went (he knew because she'd left a note), Big Gulp felt what she thought to be pangs of labor: towels of blood and clotted cousinpanic ensued and the paramedics took her away. An hour later the doctor said the baby was dead but she would have to wait for it to come, they would give her drugs to break it apart but could not open her up without endangering her life, none of it made sense to the old man but he was no doctor, he even tried to call Detective Lake to see if it sounded sensible but couldn't find him, the medics said Big Gulp might even have contractions—in an hour, in a day, a week or a month—a month!—forcing lumpen drowned nacreous soul into the hands of surgical-gowned death-maidens and the fresh mocking air, failed goddess who could not sculpt life from Her offal.

His Ghulpa could not fathom stillbirth, it wasn't easy for Raymond either to think of such a beautifully wrapped package, the gift they'd been waiting an eternity for, already dead, on top of it now they wanted her to hang fire! Was this Purgatory? He had always heard that Purgatory was a waiting room, yes, why not, they wanted them to wait for the delivery of something dead and broke apart by drugs. God knows what it would look like when it was delivered.

Ghulpa said Durgā killed her baby. This is what she said over and over and over again, that Durgā was astride her now and would take her soon as well. Ghulpa said she was the buffalo and the drops of blood in the field, she could smell the monsoon sharp in her nostrils and she told Raymond (it seemed with some relief) that never, ever would she leave this hospital, Raj, I am returning to Calcutta for the rains, he was surprised to hear her entertain that, even in febrile delirium, wet rag upon broiling head, cooing and softly urging her not to talk, useless, his Ghulpa said she was going to the Hooghly on a flatbed and could smell the ruthless ovarian force of monsoon, *hush my darling, don't fear my darling,* but the beast hadn't yet snatched their baby! it was the waters, tiny lungs had aspirated sacred waters—his Lionel! already drowned and fallen into the City of God's treacherous manhole, tradition bade them keep the lids off to help drain the floods, BG told him that, when they 1st met at the pier, of the place she was born where the lids came off during monsoon but the waters rose and crossing the street you couldn't see the holes that concealed deadly currents beneath and people fell in while wading across the shambolic, fecal-billeted roads of West Bengal, electrocuted in shantytowns, 50 inches of rain in 2 hours' time, down down down they disappeared, 30,000 goats and sheep and buffalo too, all their poor child—Chesterfield!—had ever known was water, life-sustaining purveyor of death (and Ray with his excess fluids congestive arrhythmias and pulmonary edemas), here now his Ghulpa taking in water, death-sustaining eddies, manholes and womanholes too. *You're cruel,* she Tagore-sang—remedial Calcuttan memory keen now, Kṛṣṇa disguised as a ferryman (while the cousins wept)—*Lord of the lonely dark, so far away in Mathurā. In whose bed do you sleep? Who slakes your thirst upon waking?*—the cousins grew inconsolable—*Where are your sun-colored clothes—lost among the trees? And your crooked smile? Whose necklace gleams on your neck? Where have you thrown my wildflower chain?*—cousins hysterical wailing—*my golden love for whom I bloom unseen, you rule my emptiness, my endless nights. For shame, black-hearted one—you're coming with me.*

That girl is suffering.

The cousins yowled and tore their hair—

Raymond backs away as she calls him to

XCI.

CHESTER

---

morning and they go outside, alarmcocked rousing in Time to smells and chaotic embracing stunned-light of Mumbai but the mellow people gathered at the coffeeshop near Mahalaxmi Temple—seekers and pilgrims from Australia and Brazil and England and Italy and Finland and Russia—most call it "Bombay" so that's what Chess starts saying too. (Easier than *moom-bye—Bye, Mom!*) Some of the old hands tell the American couple the most important thing: look both ways before crossing the street because the cars *will* kill you. And make sure bottled water caps are not subtly broken cause they fill em for resale and you'll get sick. (He decides to stick with Coke in a can.) The Breach Candy Swim Club has a pool in the shape of India and that you must see. It's private but if you want to have lunch there we can get you in.

They sat with their tea and Chester felt new-specie'd gladness sauntering past Mahalaxmi, hundreds in line at the temple, women so beautiful, spectacular saris, even the homeliest of the homely, cops and colonial buildings saturated with a bliss he could not fully absorb or recognize, no syntax, everything degraded and dustily decayed/wedding cake layered edible, if you looked hard enough you could find—thrust against skyline—as mathematically complex as anything *cubenses* had shown him— structures of enormous imagination and wealth, private homes like found objects, puzzlepiece jewels within holy impoverishment grid, the entire city like that, a living archaeological dig concealing walk-in walk-out tombs of prosperity, don't be fooled by cliché and nonsense, that obsessive, corny, corrupt Western dream of destitution, yes there was disease/disfigurement, though this too: the ancient sacerdotal sussultorial seat of the imperial armies who guard Her, *She,* and those lucky enough to see they are Her students.

Soon the sweetly bedraggled troop trudged excitedly up a hill (looking both ways before they crossed), then loitered outside a tall apartment house with benevolent guard standing sentry. After 15 minutes, he smilingly gave a sign and the procession began, congregants racing up spiral staircase, shoppers at a spiritual fire sale, *seeking enlightenment is like crying fire in an empty theater,* Chess Herlihy shed his old self with each step, became enraptured on the ascent, the floors—2nd, 3rd, 4th, 5th, 6th—old and beautiful and wood-oiled, woodclean well-kept, each more ornate than that which preceded, at the same time simpler too *this is what the ascent to heaven must be like* doors and moldings of residences on each level, made of teak—whoa! the guru owned the whole *well why not, why always emphasis on poverty-enlightenment, why not a wealthy guru, without Western-style cynicism attached. Any idiot knew an enlightened man need not walk in rags. Why must it always be cartoonish, stupidly familiar? Why must our gurus live in caves? Why could we not*—Chess was now a student of Time— there was so much *noise* outside, like an orchestra, chanting and hornblowing and shouting everpresent (another thing that for some reason comforted). *He was now a student of Time and Her daughter, Space.* At penthouse floor the couple removed sandals, placing them in trafficked rack of sole searchers before entering humble spacious suite, someone gently ushered them to a small but airy room inside rooms where they plunked down on cushions, 30 or so guests, shiny distraught obsequious eccentric crazy-vain grateful beings from all over the merciful Lonely blue Planet who had somehow converged on this coordinate, this very Space and this Time, and after a while the old silver-haired man, handsome and fit, came and sat down.

Chess shivered with delight.

Almost unbelievably, Ramesh looked straight at him and said, "Are you a seeker?"

Laxmi smiled and Chester smiled and said yes, he thought so. "A jetlagged seeker." People laughed and the guru did too.

He asked for Chester's name.

Then: "And what is it you are seeking?"

"What is it I am seeking?"

"Yes—Chester. What is it you are seeking?"

The visitor smiled, but was silent.

He didn't want to fail the test.

"You see?" said Ramesh. "No one is ever able to tell me! Some say 'love,' but to me *love* is merely the other side of *hate.* Yesterday someone asked why the Source manifested itself in the forms that it did: trees, people, objects. Well, I cannot answer that, all I can say is it is *energy,* the Source contains no creations, nor can it contain dissolution. Without the movement of energy, you are left with 'dead matter.' Similarly, without the assertion of the ego in daily life, there can be no world as we know it! We believe that we have *free will.* Some have the sense their 'free will' is *counterfeit.* In other words, *it has been proven* that once one makes a decision, or takes action—which one must, each day! try *not* to, and see what happens!—one has no control over the results. Only 3 things can happen after one chooses an action: you get what you want, you *don't* get what you want, or you get something that was *completely unexpected*—whether that be terrible or wonderful. *That's exactly what happened with Maurie. What I wanted was for him to get hard, then embarrassed; what I didn't want was for him to walk out of the room the minute he saw the black guy; the completely unexpected thing was the fucking stroke.* Hence, *free will* isn't free, it's nonexistent. But if one wishes to believe one *has* free will, *without* the awareness of a counterfeit quality, then by all means that is one's destiny! (To believe that.) If one is to be *frustrated,* not recognizing that the nature of life contains opposites, beginning with male and female, and extending to good health and disease—if this *frustrates* one and one falls into self-pity, then *that* is one's destiny according to the Cosmic Law! One may understand all of this intellectually, but to have the *total understanding,* that is a 'happening,' just like the monsoon, or the tsunami, or Katrina. Like drought or the Holocaust. *There is no meaning to those events,* they are merely 'happenings.' When one feels sorry for how much one

suffers, all one has to do is think of the millions upon millions who would gladly change places with you: then you will thank God for the suffering He has allotted you! All is energy, manifesting itself: without such a manifestation, it would be *dead matter*—eventually that energy burns out and the cycle begins again. *What we are seeking is harmoniousness with our fellow man: with the Other. We have been conditioned to be 'god-fearing.' I choose to be 'god-loving.'*
                    "So tell me, Chester: What is it that
                              her father choked and said that his roommate and baby would not be—coming home—Joan quashed and muted her own horror and said she wanted to come see him but Ray said best not to, not just now, better to speak over the phone (Oh! she would honor that) and yes, he still wanted their Dining Car dinner—*even now, he was thinking of it!*—so pleased when she told him—*one more lie, forgive me, Lord, just one more*—that his son would *love* to come and *so looking forward* to meeting him. *To meeting his*

"Dad," she said, voice clenched from unending desolation visited upon her family, cruciation and glory as well, now the money didn't seem such a laurel, it was dirty, a dirty balm, neck and neck with wretchedness, instead of slingshotting everyone far ahead, but her mood was foul and soon she would again feel soothed by it, enveloped, enwrapped and ensorcelled by and through Money. "Dad, *listen:* I am a rich woman! I am a *very rich woman* and I am asking you to please come live with me. There is so much time to make up. I am going to buy a house in Malibu, by the water. You always loved the water. *Please* come live with me. With *us*"—she didn't care if she sounded like an abject little girl, didn't care a witless whit—"I need my family! I'm going to have a baby—*you are*—going to—you and mom are going to be grandparents! *Please.* You can help me raise this child as you would have raised the one you lost"—should she have said it, that word, *lost,* both now choking because they *were* lost, now and always, all of them children, no matter their age, everyone was and had been lost, but they'd been *found,* just like the gospel song, they'd been *found* as well—"*Daddy, please come.* I'll help close up your apartment and we'll move everything to the new house. We'll have a compound, a family compound, like the Kennedys! Remember the Kennedy compound?" (She knew that was a touchstone.) "I have *lots of money,* Father, *millions and millions of dollars.* Will you please come? Will you *promise* to—will you please say that you'll come? I am asking you for *myself* not just because of what happened, but I think you shouldn't be alone now—*I* don't want to be alone, I don't *believe* in it, *not anymore.* I used to think that being alone was *everything.* But not anymore . . ."

He agreed.

She didn't know if he meant it, or his compliance was just to get her off him.

She didn't care—the weight of the world was lifting.

She would do anything for this man.

He asked if Chesterfield would live with them too and she said Yes, *forgive me my lies, but who knew, maybe he would,* he was traveling now, location scouting, but *Yes*—the important thing being they would make a home together, she had no husband, she did not want to raise this baby alone—quickly adding that Marjorie would of course be there. *Do you mean you told your mother and she agreed? That she*—Yes. *Forgive me Lord the bewilderness of lies but I cannot care anymore*—yet it *was* true, Marjorie *would* live in the compound with nurses, gardeners, and upkeepers, the professional hunters and gatherers, there'd be the loveliest symmetry to it, their marriage come full circle, maypole circle of life and death, what did a little senescence matter, sense and insensibility, Joan not yet wanting to spring it on Ray that his ex was an invalid, traveler in the land of nod and derangement, not wishing to dispense more bad news than she had to, not *now,* whether right or wrong *There* is *no right or wrong* not even wanting to fudge the truth, but rather, to lie by omission. Is your mother still in India, he wanted to know. *Yes,* there it came, the quick efficient lie again, she was nothing but fabric woven from strands of lying DNA, so be it, that is who I am, I do my best, so be it that the carpet upon which we raise our tent is one of untruths, truth is sandy, truth is nomadic, like Freiberg's temporary sultany digs, truth is a memorial, what is so wrong about a permanent nomadic structure for her (un)broken family. Joan said that Marjorie was still in Agra, at the Taj Mahal, and Ray said, Isn't that wonderful, I always told Ghulpa I wanted to see the place then he choked again and she choked on her lies and his dreams, the lies of truth, then Ray asked his daughter if she knew the legend of it, the legend (he read in *Reader's Digest* waiting rooms) of the Taj Mahal, and Joan said no, even though she did, fudging again because maybe he had something new to add and besides she had no strength in her head or her body and that it was good for him to talk. Ray said it was built by a king *she could still see the childhood book and typeface: exalted Majesty, dweller of Paradise, the 2nd lord of constellations, the King Shah Jahan* whose wife died giving birth, she was young, only 39, *Reader's Digest* (or some other waiting room) said ½ a million women a year die that way, 10,000,000 more get some kind of injury during delivery, hard to believe anyone makes it through, old man choking and tragichuckling, adding he didn't know if the king's baby survived, he only knew the wife had died, he choked up again and Joan did too, she thought he was going to go on, about the black marble version of the Taj the king planned for his own crypt, the one that remained unbuilt across the river, dark dream of reflected eternal love, but her father said he had a favor to ask.

"You're—an architect?"

"Yes."

"I would like you to help with the stone, for my dearest, and the baby. There is a Forest Lawn on a hill that Ghulpa always thought was so pretty. I bought a little plot. They got there before me! Would you help with the stone? Would you help, Joanie? I don't know much about that. All of her cousins, I don't think they—I haven't really talked to them . . . I don't know what they . . . I would—would—"

He was choking again and she said of course (her passion rubbing out all the lies she had told) and the old man said he would call her back, he had to get off the phone, yes, I would be honored, Joan said, we'll do something simple and beautiful, I'll start work on it *right now,* you just let me know when you—I'll call tomorrow and check in. How about if I call tomorrow?

She almost said please Dad let me come now.

Then he said:

"The shah was arrested by one of his sons. Can't remember why. Your mother Marj would probably know. Poor fellow spent his last days in prison. But they say he could see his wife's crypt— the Taj Mahal that we know today—from his cell. *He sounded like a disembodied docent.* I think that's why they call it 'a tear of sorrow on the face of time.' You see, it was *his* tear. But I'm just an old man and maybe everyone knows that."

HE said he had to hang up. He felt nauseous, a searing pain in his arm and chest, he collapsed, just missing the table *I am glad I missed the table on that one* though nausea and pain didn't abet. He grabbed the phone to call back his daughter but couldn't read the numbers on the piece of paper with her name so dialed 911 and said he was having some kind of heart attack and they asked a few questions, why would they ask anything, why not just come, maybe they were already on their way while the woman was asking whatever she was, if he remembered correctly they knew where you were calling from even if you didn't give your address, she finally did say they were sending someone out but kept talking and after a while Ray just listened thinking about what Joan had said, how she'd take care of everything, not such a bad deal, he wondered how she'd gotten so rich, maybe she was exaggerating to impress her old man, that kinda ran in the family, he was thinking he was rich too but didn't have millions, didn't have so much but was happy to have a daughter back in his life who could help with the place on the hill for his Gulper and Lionel, he hadn't mentioned "Lionel" to Joan yet, that wasn't so respectful, not telling her the child's name, even a dead child should have a name and be referred to by it, he just couldn't bring himself to say it out loud, Ray was thinking they should engrave Lionel with maybe a lion on the top and a little train on the bottom even though BG hadn't exactly agreed to it, to Lionel, but he thought she was well on her way, she had never said *no,* he definitely didn't want the child unnamed on the stone, you know, "Baby Rausch" or something like that, and as he waited for help he thought about the beach—did she say Malibu? how nice it would be to sit in the sand, the feel of it through your toes, been a long time, he always loved to plant himself in the sand, he particularly enjoyed those hidden covelike beaches north of Pepperdine though couldn't help but wonder about Joan and the "millions," she probably said it to please him in his hour of need so to speak, he knew enough to know that architects don't get that rich or maybe they did but those were the ones with big companies and lots of people working for them and as far as he knew his Joanie wasn't in that category, Ray thought maybe she had told him that because she pitied him, he could understand that, still, all that talk of a compound, she didn't seem like the kind to lie so brazenly, she seemed sincere, genuine—he hadn't the chance to tell her he was a modestly wealthy man himself, he had planned to, at the Dining Car, but wasn't sure when that would even happen (they still needed to co-ordinate with Chesterfield), maybe that wasn't really necessary, not now, just his pride talking, but he wanted her to know that her Daddy made good, had almost $500,000 in the bank and could pay his own way, *wanted* to, didn't need his son or his daughter taking care of him, it was time for their father to take care of *them,* and he could, now that Ghulpa and the little one were gone, they were his own, his blood, it was his fault he had lost them, but now they were found, they were retrievable, maybe Big Gulp and the baby boy were still retrievable, he saw that report on television about the coast of India, now *those* were poor people, a 3rd of the folks in India survived on less than a dollar a day, that meant the whole population of the US surviving on less than a dollar a day, the government sterilized them, once a woman had a few kids, especially if she'd had a son, the government came along and offered to sterilize them for free and after the tsunami a lot of parents lost their kids, *all* their kids, and the government was doing sterilization reversals, reconnecting fallopian tubes, recanalizing so the poor women could conceive again, but it only worked 50% of the time, maybe it would work with Ghulpa, maybe they hadn't fallen through the manholes of Hell into the flood and could still be found, Joanie and Chesterfield had been found, had not drowned, hell there would always be secrets, he could never tell those kids why he left, that was something he didn't fully comprehend himself, how a grown man could leave his kids like that, he could understand leaving the wife but not the kids, what would it be like to see Marjorie again, he was happy that she agreed to the family being reunited, still what would that be like, maybe he wouldn't be able to do it, didn't have the courage, he didn't need to think about it so much now, leave it alone *pain crackling through his arm ohhh* it was good enough she agreed, then the thought came that he had no will, left no provisions other than the monies would go to Ghulpa and their Lionel, now he wanted the estate to revert to his son and daughter but would need to hold on long enough to make those changes, though maybe not, maybe Joan could just go to whomever and say they had reunited, and the courts would be able to prove kinship by reverse patrimonial DNA, just like in the *Cold Case Files, don't think about that, just listen for the sirens, hold on* he threw up, not too much, then tried to cover it with newspaper, like a dog would, the Friar squealing and licking his face, he tried to tell him not to worry but Ray couldn't speak, so many secrets, how could he have left them he didn't know *himself,* something that would remain sub-rosa, a mystery more than a secret, there were *other* secrets, things he could never reveal: he never wanted Joanie to know how only a few hours earlier he found something Ghulpa printed out from the Internet months before: *How to Plan an 800 dollar Funeral,* he knew it was meant for him, for Ray, nothing malicious, merely the Indian in her pragmatically researching the inevitable—the next heart attack that one day would floor him, with or without SWAT-flattened doors:

> *Plan Ahead, Know your rights, Shop around, Avoid a big-ticket urn and columbarium, Create your own memorial, Donate to Science, Saying goodbye*

God bless! The 800 dollar funeral, why not?—she was saving everything for the kid, the Lionelhearted boy, and knew he would want the very same—

now he was at the door, he'd crawled to it, a blond man on the other side said, "Sir? Sir? Are you there? Are you in there?" Through thin curtains, Ray saw the group in uniform, huddling amongst themselves with fish and tackle boxes, peering in. He vomited. "He's there! On the floor!" the door broke and they rushed him with all kinds of gear and IV wetbags and needles and thread: he thought of that day when he first met Ghulpa at pier's end: water stretching out, infinitesimal expanse, fishing rods buckets and smell of bait.

They put a spike in him, so kind and methodical, the blond bent over and said

No engulfment. No tearing asunder. What you feared would come like an explosion is a whisper. Have you seen that episode too? Ray asked.

relax. Relax oldtimer. You're gonna be fine. Clean him up. Clean his chin. Can you breathe? Got a good airway. Nothing in there. OK oldtimer Clean him up All around there were holes in the ceiling of the *tenement with light pouring in*

because there is no sin. The guru said we suffer needlessly from shame and guilt that stem from bad actions but we also suffer pride and arrogance from good actions. Likewise, what happens *to* us is not personal, but the result of Cosmic Law. We are as sandcastles, elaborately carved yet destroyed by children at the end of a summer's day—swallowed up whence we came.

The root of guru was Sanskrit: Gu meant darkness, Ru meant light. *Pain being from the Latin* poena: *punishment.*

The more he listened, the more Chess felt at ease. Ramesh said events happen, deeds are done, but there is no individual doer of the deed. These are the words of the Buddha. Enlightenment is nothing but the removal of suffering, not of pain—we live in a world of pain and pleasure. We live in a world of duality but must not rest in dualism. To be enlightened is like climbing a ladder or racing up the spiral staircase to get to these rooms: until one reached the final step, one was not there, one did not know how much longer it would take, or what the rooms would look like once one arrived. The strange thing is that enlightenment looks much the same; the only change is perception.

They ended *satsang* with a prayer.

> Give me only one boon, my Lord: May I never forget that Your will alone prevails. I will joyfully sing of Your glorious deeds. Give me the association of people who have total trust in You. I don't care for Liberation, fame, or fortune. Tukaram says: If you don't want Enlightenment to happen in this body, let it not happen, my Lord—I don't care.

THEY stayed with Ramesh for 10 days.

They ate boondi laddoos and coconut burfi to celebrate Lord Ganesha and his sister Laxmi, washing down pumpkin-colored jalebi with cups of chai.

Laxmi (the mortal one) wanted to remain in Bombay, she didn't know for how long, and Chess was fine with that but said he was going to move on. He gave her some money. 90% of the settlement was in a bank in the States. When he had a little more energy, he was determined to remove the entire sum and open an account here in India, if legally possible; he hadn't looked into it yet. He should have done that before they left but it was too much of a megillah. Maybe he would open an account in Canada or the UK or Frankfurt or Switzerland. *Anywhere but the States.* (Plus, he didn't like the idea of being traced through financial records.) America was dead to him. America was a country where people went on eBay to buy vintage Hot Wheels for a hundred-thousand dollars, and performed cunnilingus on 7 month old babies in private, peer-to-peer file-sharing chatrooms. America was a place that spent $35,000,000,000 a year to lock up one out of every 138 citizens. The guru's concepts and words made him less paranoid but there still existed a part of him that worried his friend might awaken and snitch him off. He would then be sought after by authorities, and the IRS would garnish his accounts, whether related to the student loan, Maurie Levin, or some other specious investigation/prosecution. Maybe he'd renounce his citizenship, but Chess needed to make certain such an act wouldn't send up any flags. He would have to get his money out of there first. (Renouncing was probably a little dramatic.) For now, he considered himself retired. Gone fishin. The Scout is *out!*

Laxmi wasn't ready to visit her father in Pune yet anyhow, and Chess wasn't surprised. All good, he said. Truth being, he wanted to be alone, travel alone, the guru had bestowed the gift of propulsion and velocity, he wanted to set out by himself—like a proper man. The man he'd never had the chance to become. As had the itinerant mystic-poets, he would visit Ramana Maharshi's 7-storied mountain (itself said to be a great guru), and go to Benares, 35-hundred year old nexus of death and rebirth. Hadn't he come as a pilgrim? He even thought of acquiring a begging bowl. Chess knew he might not have come up with the idea if it weren't for the security his settlement provided (plus he still had a hundred Oxy and 200 1-mg Klonopin; he was still too kulturshocked to feel the *FNF*-induced pain full-bore. He heard you could get morphine tabs in Calcutta, which meant probably anywhere, and that Indian smack was rad. Opium was legal but supposedly hard to get your hands on, whatever with that, but the farmers were fucking licensed. *Opium was the opium of the masses. Ha ha, who said that*) but chose not to judge himself or his real/imagined cowardice, he had made a career out of that, he was casting off, on a new journey, look at him, look where he was, look where he'd been a few months ago, *weeks* ago, money probably wasn't required, not in the end, wouldn't be in the end, maybe the settlement would be abandoned, dormant in his account until turned over to some State Comptroller, maybe he *would* become a beggar, and that was what his teacher Time and Her daughter Space had wished for him all along.

Laxmi wanted to take the motorboat Elephanta Island (not far from her guru's) but Chess thought it too touristy, he didn't say as much, who was he to judge or throw cold water—let her go see the cave temples dedicated to Śiva, he didn't need to, hadn't he already been privileged to serve as waterboy to the imperial army? Mascot to the gods! He had run with them like that boy in the Kipling story his father used to read to him at bedtime—clung in terrified ecstasy to hairy leathered backs while charging dark wet jungle Mysterium ...

No, he'd hit the ashram of Sri Aurobindo at Pondicherry on the Coromandel Coast instead, where lay the grave of a woman called the Mother. A caffeine-swilling seeker mentioned having recently been, it came up in conversation during morning tea shared before *satsang,* a Down Under girl said something about "the Mother," and Chester thought of his own. He wanted to honor Marj, she who brought him into this world, she to whom he'd never said a real goodbye, she whose sand was now being roughed up and returned to the Source—he wanted to honor Marjorie that way—a kind and right thing, an auspicious way to begin his real travels. *She gave him a birthday card last year that said, "You don't remember, but I'll never forget the 1st time I saw you."* Though the ashram was in Tamil Nadu, the Tsunami hadn't affected the city; an old seawall spared it. The Australian said that water buffalo roamed the streets. You could eat cheap and stay in an amazing 19th century sanitorium for $6 a night, rooms overlooking the Bay of Bengal, snakebirds and drongos circling overhead, and at temple the trilingual elephants (responding to English, Hindi, and Malayalam commands) blessed you with their trunks. *I have already been blessed. Though I must take care to be unprideful—I must not suffer from that sin of sins. Still, it is true I have heard their sacred song, their supernatural call to battle. I have already been dusted by the earth that shakes from the stomping of columnar legs. I have had* satsang *and* sadhana *with All Who Matters: She Who Is So Righteously Guarded whispered to me there is No-Thing to guard. And yet, because, because She shared this, I must not swell with pride. For I am no sadhu ...*

They made love then he gathered his things.

She cried as he left but Chester said he would see her soon, on the wigged-out beaches of Goa, the *ash*-rammed shit- and blood-strewn alleys of Benares, the cubensic deserts of Rajasthan, in the dreammachines of Agra. (She said, "Why Agra?"—he thought she'd said something else.) He wanted to scope out Bodh Gaya and Calcutta then join the reunion with Laxmi's Father in Pune. He knew none of this would happen. Best for her to press on alone, there was something to be said about the gravitas of aloneness, the aloneness *America* knew was brummagem, it was *loneliness,* aloneness of comfort and convenience, prideful, convenience store pride, and prejudice, no, now they would seek True Aloneness, not that of hedonists or ascetics, but Aloneness before the eyes of God. Best for her soul to be without him on this journey, he got her this far, she'd gotten Chess further, in her own way, both had done as much as they could for one another.

They would do for themselves, now—in solitaire.

That was how it should be.

He laughed out loud: "My Favorite Weekend"! I should dash something off and fax it to the Times . . . *"I like having satsang with an avatar, after devotions to Durgā. Then my girlfriend and I crap in a hole and*

He was done with little mindgoofs. His goofs had ended with Maur

He walked until dusk

On a vast boulevard of whores where women stood before flimsy curtains and he thought of his camera, what an incredible location, *I am a location scout still* (Ramesh said that on their deathbeds, even holymen responded to their birthnames), but now I am scouting for Her, and for Time and Space. I am one of Her soldiers and mascots, waterboy in Her imperial army. He asked a passerby, a tourist, for money, and they smiled like they didn't understand or pretended not to, maybe he wasn't making sense, maybe he had only imagined he was talking but was really just thinking. He swallowed 3 Oxys. The sky darkened and the inkiness of the bay became like an unruly crowd and he began to beg in front of the Taj Mahal Palace and Towers Hotel but was shooed away and as he strolled toward the Gate of India he asked everyone he encountered, man, woman, or beggarchild for money, asked the beggars themselves! some of whom laughed and some got angry, that is what the guru said to expect, not from begging, but from the world and its dualism: laughter and anger, horror and joy, deformity and pulchritude, barrenness and fertility, poverty and wealth. Chester made certain to ask the poorest of the poor, the most diseased of the diseased, the most indecently scarified, made sure to ask each BardoBeing for cash because what difference did it make, all he had was Time, everything an ocean of time and space, all Hers, did not the beggars share those same radiant choppy waters? were they not created by his teacher? and if they had forgotten and washed ashore would they not return? If only everyone, both prosperous and needy, could *see*—from the dumb pisspoor park of the Gate of India, *Chess* saw—Elephanta Island and flickery boats in the harbor, and thought *i will ask for money with my begging bowl, on the way to see the Mother. i have no shame nor have i pride. i am grateful. and if it is not Your plan to let Enlightenment happen to this body, let it not happen, O Lord! i am but a pilgrim* He thought again of the mushrooms and remembered being brought to his knees, inadvertent posture of prayer in that small desert motel, watching intricate woof of carpet when there was none, head down, as if in a great basilica (which he was), this happened near the end of his *cubensis* journey, end of time with plant and planet, of voluntary conscription in Her army, divine enraptured bugle boy, end of time with Her as overseer, now he was drafted, a careering soldier, and in careening desert recalled these very words: *if at least i find myself in the cathedral, i shall be honored. if in the end i am beggar or pilgrim on my knees and that is all, then i shall be honored. honored and grateful and moved. if at the end i am beggar among beggars in this cathedral, then that will surely be enough. how can i ask for more? how moved i will be. for She has said there is nothing to join nor is there anything to guard or protect, there is No-Thing* to take a number at the Hilton. *Thousands of people: Barbet and Joan were #'s 2,178 and 2,179.* But the feeling was all flowers and love, that old hippie feeling, rose oil and canyon good vibes run amok, and besides, it would take a shitload to bring her down, she was so fucking rich. Barbet held her close and she didn't feel alone. You really need a hug, huh, he said. You need a hug from God. *And you're gonna get one.*

He was funny, her Barbet.

A man in front of them reminded her (physically) of the Nicobar Islander on the Tsunami anniversary show who said the earth balanced on a colossal tree that could be jolted by spirits and that bad spirits were at the tree trunk trying to hurt people and good spirits were trying to save them. She thought of Lew and the branch-hanged Esther, and Samuel's lost skeleton, and kept wondering if Andy Goldsworthy was going to do something like the piece he did in Tatton Park, a sheet of ice stuck between the bole of a Haw-thorn bisected by lightning. Ol AG had a lot of tricks up his sleeve.

She wondered what Calatrava was—

Barbet said they should have brought the pillow that Cora gave her mom. That way, they could've charged money for people who wanted hugs but didn't feel like waiting on line. Then he said, "Oh, by the way, Calatrava's out, Ando is in." "Ando?" *"Tadao Ando.* What can I say. What'd I fucking tell you? The Birdman of Alcalatrava has flown. It's like Russian roulette. Russian River roulette! Seems our friend Freiberg—isn't that like *My Friend Flicka?*—ran into Tom Ford and Richard Buckley. Went to see the pied-à-soleil in New Mexico, with the indoor underground swimming pool? Got all hot and bothered. *Ah so.* So solly for Mr Ando. Tadao now have to deal with body of Jew woman hanging in bonsai tree! Maybe Tadao shrink bones. That way Jew Lady fit in bonsai tree. Tadao then stick Jew Lady and bonsai tree in stone alaah to honor Brentwood Country Mart Buddhism. Andy Goldsworthy make stone snake leading to dhau tree. Mr Goldsworthy make *ness* of dhau thorns, antlers and ice. Mr Goldsworthy make look like Spiral Jetty. Mr Goldsworthy make Eliot *Ness.*"

Joan said Ando would probably do something origami-like, in homage to Esther's Eastern flirtations—like that black steel shop he did in Tokyo, hhstyle.com/casa.

Then she said that standing in line—*and since when do you say "on line," Barbet? What are you, suddenly from New York?*—was like waiting to go on the Matterhorn.

"The Matterhorn's been closed for, like 10 years!"

"OK, then Magic Mountain."

"Also closed."

She swayed gently into him, like a docking buoy against a pier. She emptied her mind then let it go where it would. Joan had looked at a house in Zuma that was gorgeous, 3½ acres smack on the coast. She wondered if it might be too cold for her mother. Plenty of room to build, which was nice. She could design something *fun*. Everything had been set in motion to create the Marjorie Herlihy Giving Foundation. Joan wasn't sure exactly what charitable function it would perform but knew she wanted to do something major in India. For as long as she could recall, Marj had this thing to alleviate misery—it was never too late, as Barbet aptly reminded. Joan was in touch with Pradeep, in Delhi; he was brimming with ideas. She would travel there, maybe a year or so after having the baby, see that part of the world for herself. Who knew? Maybe Mom would be in better shape by then and be able to go along. One day, Joan would pour her mother's cremains into the Ganges at Varanasi. It was the one wish that Marjorie had actually handwritten, in the margin of a travel book, before things went south.

2 in the morning, and they finally closed in on Amma. She was hugging people one after another, the stage garlanded with flowers, and all the time they'd been there—around 5 hours—Amma hadn't left *once,* not to use the bathroom, not for *anything,* at least not that Joan was aware of, she hadn't even seen the woman drink a glass of water. Maybe she *was* a saint. Barbet said Amma was in a trance, her bodily needs "in suspension." The nearer they got, the more serious he became, as if to make up for earlier, sinister tomfoolery.

Why was she thinking of Sheryl Crow. She saw the ad, the got milk? *ad. Please be all right. Please be in remission. She sent a prayer to Sheryl Crow please be all right. The ad said* Milk Your Diet/Lose

Weight! *oh God. To keep the crowd on their feet, I keep my body in tune . . . rock hard.* Oh

Attendants stood by. They told Barbet to remove his glasses for the imminent hug, handing both of them baby-wipes. The couple was asked to wash the sides of their faces that would touch Amma's cheek. Joan was surprised to note that her heart was speeding up. The attendants helped them onstage; Barbet preceded her. Joan saw him kneel and then the holy woman embraced him. Amma whispered something in his ear. Then it was Joan's turn. Her eyes filled with water. As they hugged, the saint whispered, "My daughter, my daughter, my daughter. Yes. Yes yes yes yes yes yes yes yes yes. *Yes.* Yes," *and then someone led Joan off as if in a dream as*

Marj *held the pillow close while it vibrated. She had a yeast infection and was catheterized but felt no pain. Cora had been* to see her and thought, At least there isn't that smell. The neighbor spoke of the pending trip with her daughter to the Taj Mahal but all Marjorie could think of was the Blind Sisters traveling together, holding hands in a row, linked like holy mendicants, all she could see was the Shadow Taj, the black one meant to be Hamilton's crypt but abandoned when the Raja was imprisoned by his own son.

They called it the shadow monument—

Monument to the shadow drawings of the Blind Sisters . . .

S HE was looking for the elephant's ballroom. The man in a turban and beautiful coat said, "Young lady, I've worked at this hotel for nearly 40 years and *never* seen that place myself!"

He stroked his bushy *meesha,* working his teeth with an ivory toothpick.

"But it *is* here," she said, "my father will tell you!"

—so delighted to see Dad again. He looked ruddy and fit and wore tortoiseshell spectacles. She grinned at the familiar tiny beads of perspiration on his upper lip; she'd forgotten about those.

He said *my little one, the monsoon is coming,* and how lucky they

were to be in the Presidential Suite, on an upper floor. But she
wanted to know what would happen to all the poor people.
She was *quite* concerned. Won't they have peonies? Don't you
worry, he said dotingly, we'll make certain none of them drown—
to be sure!—and are fed proper meals, with dessert too. Marjorie
asked about the ballroom and he said it was most likely under-
water by now because it was somewhere beneath ground floor,
no one really knew (she suppressed tears and he touched her
cheek reassuringly), not to worry! the elephants could fend for
themselves—and besides, the whole herd would be rescuing people, that was their job, plucking those who fell through manholes
and such, sucked into the ballroom, why they'd snatch them like
fish from a net, each and every one. He saw that her mood wasn't
exactly brightening so he added that *ballroom* water was *special* so
that people could breathe until "our *very* long-nosed friends"
came to their aid. But what about the dance? she asked. He
laughed, lifting her in his arms. Little one, little *mahout,* don't you
worry. The elephants *love* to dance! They won't let a thing like a
silly monsoon spoil their fun. *Now I said don't you worry, Marjorie
Morningstar*

He dried her eyes till they shone again.

As they climbed the stairs—black marble—sumptuously cos-
tumed guests and impeccably mannered staff passed by, the latter
bearing luggage and parasols and giftboxes and elaborate trays of
spices and foodstuff. The water submerged the lobby and she realized her father's words about the ballroom already being under-
water were probably true. That made her sad but she tried to
remember you could breathe in it and that the elephants were
busy on their rescue missions. Still, she looked down from his
arms at the rising tide and he saw she was afraid and said,
"Joanie!"

Why is he calling me that?

"We'll be safe, little one—safe and dry!"

Marj said she was worried about the elephants and he said
don't you *dare.* They *protect,* that is their *job,* that is their role in
this world. That is Ganesha! They know how to take care of us.

So stop your crying Miss Morningstar. You don't want those tears to add to all the water around here, do you? Now that will make things harder for our long-nosed friends.

She nodded, closing her eyes as they ascended: up and up the spiral staircase through the inordinate, comforting bustle, she could hear the excitement of guests from the warm perch of her father's arms, hear the rushing of water too but knew that he was right, the magnificent Taj Mahal Palace and its brigade of tur-ban'd Ganeshas could never, *ever* let anything happen to them . . . a *lifetime* of climbing until they reached the capacious suite where food was laid out on silver platters. Perfumed lodgers from other rooms, some of whom were countesses draped in pearls, *kundan* and *ariya,* joined Maharajahs in breastplates and tunics bearing insignias of their various kingdoms, the royalty mingling while servants came and went, aristocratic children underfoot as well, stunning-looking well-mannered boys and girls her age; the girls with noses pierced by 22 karat gold. A Nizam and his retinue rose to greet her father who afterall was an *extremely* popular man, Marjorie's mother was there too, she struggled from Papa's arms to get to her, he set his wriggling daughter down but before she could make any headway the moppets ferried her aside to inform in hoarse whispers: *The elephants are dancing tonight!* After they rescue the last of the drowning people, they are going to dance! This is what the children told her. There was *another* ballroom, *here, not in the basement as her father had said, but* here, *on higher ground! And off they went to*

*   the headstone. Ray's girlfriend was to be buried in Calcutta, come hell or high water—that was what Joan gathered from the industrious diligently* sweethearted women he al-ways called "the cousins," one of whom it turned out was actually the dead woman's sister.

Joan told them her father said Ghulpa wished to be buried here in the States, at Forest Lawn, in a plot already purchased, and that was when the Artesian brood confided there were "difficul-ties"—that the "spousal relation" was not "sanctified," that the deceased was in fact not a legal resident. Joan understood.

She asked nothing more.

T HERE were a host of stones to choose from.
      "Do I have to pick it now?"
   "No, no! This is just a selection."
   "Could something—can something be built? I mean, a design
of some sort?"
   "Do you mean a mausoleum?"
   "Maybe. I'm not sure. I'm an architect . . ."
   The woman smelled money.
   "That depends on the amount of space you purchase. I can
check in the particular area your father—"
   "No, it's all right."
   "In terms of 'design,' did you mean a photo?"
   Joan was uncomprehending.
   "There is a wonderful technology that allows us to etch a pho-
tographed image of the loved one into the surface of the stone."
   "I see. OK. Let me think about all that."
   "Take your time! And, of course, we'll eventually need to
know what you'd like to put on the stone."
   "On the stone?"
   "In memoriam. Usually the simplest is best. 'Less is more.' You
know, we actually had that epitaph. The man's name was Les and
the family wrote, 'Les Is More.' Quite clever. But you can do, well,
anything that space allows. It could be a poem. Or a *thought.*"
   "Oh—right! When do you need to know by?"
   "*Absolutely no hurry.* The stone can be put down without a legend and engraved at a future time. Heavens, we have people think
about it for *years.*"
   On her way out, the words slowly surfaced—

   Full fathom five thy father lies; of his bones are coral made; those
   are pearls that were his eyes. But doth suffer a sea change into
   something rich and strange.

—so beautiful but seemingly too fancified for the man she'd only
begun to know.
   Then, opening the car door, it came: the most perfect memorial
she could imagine.

Joan rushed back to the office so she wouldn't lose the courage. She wrote it for the caretaker:

RAYMOND RAUSCH
1930–2006
Father

∾

There are some things Joan would never know, just as there is much in and of the world that can never be known, but the things that would remain unrevealed, were, in the scheme of mysterious gifts which had been tardily gathered, rather small.

As an example, she would never learn that the woman who abandoned this earth with Ray's dead child—Joan's sibling—had once worked as Pradeep's nanny, and had fled, not through un- happiness, not entirely, but because it had been her fate, unlikely as most fates are, to meet a kind old man at the end of a pier one blustery Santa Monica day, an old man who would love and be li- onized by her, who would live to see her death before he himself departed for other realms.

Joan had Friar Tuck in the car while driving to Cora's to give the faithful woman a small keepsake of her mom's. (A copper Buddha.) She thought it a tidy plan to adopt Raymond's pet but had been bitten and was having 2nd thoughts; he cowered and low-growled, soaking the backseat towel in urine. When she arrived, Nip jumped from the open window and rushed to the neighbor's new King Charles, given to her by Stein, her thoughtful Steinie, and the pair sniffed and shimmied and licked each other as if lifelong friends. Cora gave a hug then squinted downward, asking how far along Joan was. She stood back and blinked, but not at Joan's tummy: it was something in the off-kilter gait of her 4-footed friend . . . Wasn't this the terrier who costarred with Mr P on the *Whisperer* show?

The 2 had a moment of dissonance.

Cora explained how she *knew* this creature, she had *met* the Friar—hadn't she? Didn't they call him "Nip"?—Yes! said Joan—who'd been shot—hadn't he been shot by the police?—Yes—well she had *met* Nip and his lovely owner, *many times,* a gemütlich old gentleman with an Indian companion who rarely left his side. They realized (not fully, though, not yet, and would never really be able to compass it) the astonishing coincidence of it all.

Joan asked if she could come in.

They went to the living room, where, over coffeecake and lattes, she told Cora everything. The dogs sat obediently, as if listening to a bedtime story.

"What a strange life this is!" said Cora, in one of the few genuine instances she would ever have such a complexly simple thought. "My, my, that *is* a different dog, that Friar! I remember him when he was *freshly wounded*—I was in the waiting room with Mr P, right on Sepulveda, your dad was there with his ladyfriend. A *very* pretty woman, in one of those colorful—what do they call them?—*saris.* But oh, he's quite a different dog now!"

On cue, Friar Tuck trotted over to lick her hands and face with abandon. The Princess wasn't far behind (Cora said she had to maintain the tradition of the *P*s)—then did the exact same to Joan, as if in goodbye. Again the women laughed, to keep from crying.

"Would you mind if I kept him?" said Cora. "He is a *delight.* And look how they get along! See how protective he is of my Princess? Besides, my grandkids think Mr Friar Tuck is *cool* (they call him '50 Cents,' I'm not sure where *that* started). I know it sounds *awful,* but they see him as a 'gangster'!"

Joan said that would be quite wonderful, suddenly feeling a mild yet fleeting horror over her secret fantasy of having Nip euthanized. She'd gotten the idea from an article in *People* called "The Angel of 'Doggy Deathrow.' "

"But Cora—if you change your mind, *any time,* that's just fine. If he gets out of hand *in any way,* or for *any reason . . .*"

"Don't you worry, he'll be *perfect.* We're old friends! Aren't we, Friar? Aren't we, Mr 50 Cents? My little Princess needs a companion—she's been chasing her tail something *fierce,* and I had the feeling it's from being *lonesome.* I've been thinking, Oh! I don't want to have to call that Dog Whisperer again! He's got far more troubled creatures to deal with!"

Joan gave her the figurine and invited her to the beach house, where they were still settling in. It was important Marj see her old friend.

"You better come visit," she said, wagging a finger. "I don't want Mom 'chasing *her* tail.' "

"I *love* the beach—my grandkids too."

"They're more than welcome, any time."

"You might regret saying that—you're going to beat us away with a stick! I'll bring the sunblock!" she said cheerily.

Joan was glad.

"What will you call her?"

She was nonplussed.

"The little one?" said Cora, nodding at Joan's belly.

"Well, I don't know if it's going to be a girl."

"Of course it will! Marj would *love* another girl. What will you call her?"

"I've been thinking about Aurora."

"Rory!" said her hostess, with sparkling amiability.

It was odd, but Joan knew right away it was true—she *would* have a girl—and she'd always loved that name. Something about those magical Northern Lights (Pradeep once promised to fly them to Alaska for "front row seats"), the evanescent curtain, the rollicking name *itself,* which spoke inexplicably to her of the Old West and the Midwest too, of Rory Calhoun and Annie Oakley, whoever they were, her dream of who they were, but the lights, it was the lights she remembered, in *National Geographic* photos, drawings, or children's book paintings, wonderful fireworked love-letters to our fleeting time on this beautiful world.

THERE was one detail that Cora always thought to reveal during subsequent visits to sandy Point Dume, but always, in the excitement and fussing over Marj, managed to forget.

Friar Tuck had tunneled under the fence that separated her home from Marj's. Joan was going to sell the property but it wasn't a priority; only the concrete foundation remained, barely visible, the earth around it wild and weedsprung. At night, the dog would pass through the hole—Stein kept filling it up, to no avail—and fall asleep where Marj's bedroom used to be. It was the queerest thing. But he wasn't doing any harm, and as long as her little Princess didn't follow (she didn't seem to have the inclination), well, after a while, Cora just thought to let the Friar be. He always came home, early in the morning, sweet-tempered as ever, but not before making a somehow poignant effort to kick clods of dirt to close the gap, as if shutting the phantom domicile's door for at least another day. Sometimes, in fits of insomnia, and when it was warm enough, Cora looked over from her backyard—there he'd be, bathed in moonlight, in the exact same part of that now invisible house, as if at the foot of the old woman's bed, sound asleep, like a clerk at a country inn.

The Friar repeated his routine until the lot was finally sold. From then on he no longer roamed, becoming closer to Cora in many ways than even her Princess, whom she still delighted in telling everyone that she loved "more than life."

E N D

Bombay/Mexico City/Los Angeles, 2006

The Waters of Life

Waters, you are the ones who bring us the life force. Help us to
find nourishment so that we may look upon great joy.

Let us share in the most delicious sap that you have, as if you were
loving mothers.

Let us go straight to the house of the one for whom you waters
give us life and give us birth.

For our well-being let the goddesses be an aid to us, the waters be
for us to drink. Let them cause well-being and health to flow
over us.

Mistresses of all the things that are chosen, rulers over all peoples,
the waters are the ones I beg for a cure.

Soma has told me that within the waters are all cures and Agni
who is salutary to all.

Waters, yield your cure as an armor for my body, so that I may see
the sun for a long time.

Waters, carry far away all of this that has gone bad in me, either
what I have done in malicious deceit or whatever lie I have
sworn to.

I have sought the waters today; we have joined with their sap. O
Agni full of moisture, come and flood me with splendor.

—The Rig Veda

*I was curious. I went for the first time and got addicted. I told my mom
I wanted to work the sea and not the fields. And she let me go. She said,
"It's up to you now. If you want to go, go. I'll be home praying that you
have a prosperous future."*

And then I went to sea.

—A young boy, after the Christmas Tsunami

About the Author

Bruce Wagner is the author of *Force Majeure; I'm Losing You; I'll Let You Go,* which was a PEN USA fiction award finalist; *Still Holding;* and *The Chrysanthemum Palace,* which was a PEN Faulkner Award finalist. Two movies (*I'm Losing You* and *Women in Film*) adapted from his books have been shown at the Telluride, Toronto, Venice, and Sundance film festivals.